A LOSS

ROBERT McCRUM was bor̶ ̶ ̶ ̶ ̶ ̶ ̶ ̶ ̶ ̶ ̶ ̶ ̶
at universities in Englan̶ ̶ ̶ ̶ ̶ ̶ ̶ ̶ ̶ ̶ States. He
has travelled widely in Europe, Australia and the Far
East, and now lives in London, with his wife. He is also
the author of *In The Secret State* and of a story for
children, *The Magic Mouse and the Millionaire*.
Robert McCrum is currently at work on a new novel.

   A Loss of Heart, subtle, thought-provoking and
dramatic, is a remarkable successor to *In The Secret
State* which was hailed by the critics as 'a notable
book' (*Observer*), and 'a cracking tale' (*Guardian*). 'Mr
McCrum is a find' said the *Sunday Express*.

ROBERT McCRUM

A LOSS
OF HEART

'For God's sake, look to the state of England.'
The Troublesome Reign of King John, Anon.

FONTANA/Collins

First published in Great Britain by
Hamish Hamilton Ltd 1982
First issued in Fontana Paperbacks 1982

Made and printed in Great Britain by
William Collins Sons & Co. Ltd, Glasgow

For my Mother and Father

Book One

I

It fell out of the sky and lay quite dead on the pavement of the
Charing Cross Road. Philip Taylor, who was hurrying through
the cold, buttoned up to the chin, but still shivering, stopped
short and, like someone who stumbles and then, by looking for
the obstacle, unconsciously exaggerates his clumsiness, searched
up into the sky with awkward concentration. But nothing was
answered; and the cold blinded him with tears. The frame of
things disjoint, he thought, with his teacher's penchant for
familiar quotation, and he bent over, peering short-sightedly like
a botanist, and saw that the rat was dead, no mark on the body,
only a suspicion of blood in one nostril. Half aware of the early
lunchtime shoppers struggling past up the slope, he stood where
he had stopped, dumbly transfixed by the still beady eyes. It was
strange: he was usually so unmanned by nature, threatened even
by a dog leaping against a fence, yet here he was staring at this
dead thing. Soon it would be trampled underfoot by the Christmas crowds. Then his in-built anxiety to avoid drawing attention
in any way reasserted itself. He straightened up, casually toeing
the limp scrap of fur into the gutter, and as the blood flowed back
from his temples there were stars in the grey winter midday sky.
He walked on, a slight twinge in his back, and not for the first
time recently it occurred to him that he should take some exercise, overcome his shyness and join a squash club perhaps. But
with his usual damaging self-criticism he decided that he was no
partner for anyone, scrawny, myopic and pathetically low in
stamina. He was just thirty and completely attuned to the possibility of failure.

   With an unexpected release of memory, his mind swung back to
childhood; when they were younger he and his brother had kept
rats and mice, reared them in smelly wire cages and sold the litters
to local pet shops. And there was a girl with a glass eye who
bought their animals for the reptile house in the nearby zoo.
Daniel, of course, was always the successful entrepreneur, an

aggressive twelve-year-old who exploited his younger brother's desire to please.

Philip did not care to think about the complications of that relationship; his attention switched with a jerk to a rusty blue Humber estate parked against the kerb on a double yellow line. Car-bomb, he thought. Everything about the vehicle charged his nerves. He was not being fanciful, he told himself. The fear of death was everywhere in the streets. He struggled unsuccessfully to recall the tell-tale letter in an Irish number-plate. As he drew nearer he sized-up the car with apprehension. People had been killed by these things. To run past it would make him ridiculous. With rare self-assertiveness he changed course, inwardly ashamed at his cowardice and superstition, and turned into Soho, looking studiously at his watch. In the old days, he remembered, mentally changing the subject, he and Daniel used to bury some of their pets, cats and guinea pigs and a tortoise called Morgan, in the garden, with crossed twigs. Looking back, that was an unconscious parody of the family faith. It was ten past twelve. With a bit of time before the rendezvous he could at least find a quiet bookshop.

All the boredom and loneliness he was putting up with recently had exacerbated, he noticed, this habit of talking to himself. He had always observed it with mild irritation in his mother, during her painful last years, conducting that hoarse monologue with her cats as they scratched the mahogany in the heart of the old house. But now his own home was empty and he found that he could talk to anything (even, like a widow, to plants), and would strike up banal, one-sided conversations with the postman, the visiting salvationists, even the tall Dutch Moonie girl with the broken horsey smile whose enthusiasm was unabashed by Philip's stammering. Most mornings he would wake up in the darkness of the dead of winter, and listen to the radio like a zombie. (Daniel, he recalled, would always talk back at the radio, would argue with it, shout at it with cries of 'Rubbish' and 'Bullshit'). He would lie in bed, cocooned selfishly in warmth, perfecting the art of not getting up. If Jan had been there she would have told him to pull himself together; she, he reflected bitterly, who had done so much to pull him apart. When boredom and conscience finally won through and when the day had brightened enough for the electric light not to hurt his swimming eyes, pink and weak like rainwater, he would shuffle into the bathroom

4

and start to go through his morning routine like a man with a hangover. Often, in fact, that was the case, and he was now no longer ashamed to see the bottle of Teachers and his solitary tumbler by the bedside. Then, when he had inserted his contact lenses, he would face the mirror and Christ, he would say, half-aloud, you look terrible.

His face had never given him much confidence, though when he married Jan she was quite keen on his left profile which, she said, made him look 'a little bit evil', especially when he allowed his moustache to grow. But that was never his style: in contrast to his brother, Philip was cautious and fastidious about his appearance, never trusting any naturalness of expression to take over. It was odd perhaps, but he felt more secure when his dun-coloured moustache was clipped and trim. His taste in clothes, too, was indifferent and rather conservative (that also made him feel more at ease within himself), but he always took trouble with creases or stains and felt the loss of a button like a personal slight. These days when he looked at his reflection in the bright light of the bathroom, the idea that he might have once seemed 'a little bit evil' was almost laughable. He appeared tired and defeated; his thinning hair straggled badly and, painfully alert to any tremor of emotion, his eyes darted anxiously. Every morning he would go through his usual drill with soap and toothpaste, aftershave and talcum powder, but the disinterested observer, he felt, would say the effort was wasted, like dressing for dinner in a fall-out shelter.

Sympathy, he confessed to his reflection, all I need is a bit of sympathy; but the puritan side reminded him of all his advantages and exacted an English penance, a stiffer upper lip.

Sometimes he wondered what Jan would say to all this – the keeping up of appearances – she who had once been so set on the conventions herself. Taking stock of his position now, he could not deny that, at first, before the intrusions of family and lineage, theirs had been a copybook relationship, though when he tried to laugh with her at its predictability (for him almost a virtue), she, romantic, was offended. It was his first year of teaching at the College, her first term of the course in Librarianship. He had just finished his doctorate in the hagiography of twelfth-century Northumbria, and come to terms with the fact that the job at the Polytechnic was the best he could hope for in the circumstances; she, who had studied English and Comparative Literature at the University of Kent, and was now thoroughly acquainted with

Pride and Prejudice, *Moby Dick* and *Thérèse Desqueyroux*, had just broken off her engagement to the son of her father's best friend and was intent on proving herself. Looking back on it now, Philip supposed he was an easy but promising conquest. He was pleasant, vulnerable, well-qualified and, as Jan soon discovered when she went to the first student union meeting of the academic year, a member of a prosperous Midlands family.

'The Taylor Case' was, in fact, quite a *cause célèbre* for that first term, though, as everyone on both sides admitted afterwards, the issue was more symbolic than real. No one among the students really expected that Philip Taylor would have to resign; his indifference to the accusations made against his family's company and its activities in the Third World was infuriating but unintentionally effective. In time the attacks from the Left began to look more and more like victimisation and quite a substantial and vociferous minority, Jan among them, began to campaign on Philip's behalf. They had already met by then – at a fiercely-picketed seminar on Old English manuscripts, where she mistook his flush of embarrassment at the politics outside for something more personal – and soon in his unassuming way he was beginning to yield to her persistent attention. By the time Philip's complicity in the 'crimes' of Mayhew & Taylor Ltd had almost been forgotten, and his post confirmed by a slightly flustered Principal, they were, as she told her friends at home, going out together.

Philip remembered her in those days as naïve but strong-willed. Her determination to do well meant that, although she depended on him for most of the things (like money and status) which mattered to her, she bossed him completely. He, surprisingly glad to be taken over, was at first half irritated and half flattered; in the end her want for him proved decisive for them both. After his mother died he had failed to find, in any of his affairs with women, the security and warmth that Jan, whatever her other deficiencies, offered with such generosity. Her presence – as bright and varnished as a perfectly lipsticked mouth – seemed to break a depressing cycle of unfulfilled expectations. When she said she wanted to get married, he did not hesitate for long. After the vague gauche ambitions of his student years – a visiting lectureship at Heidelberg, consuming liaisons with tantalising *mittelEuropean* bluestockings – he was now resigned to limited objectives. Marriage to Jan was one of these. It was better than the alternative: isolation and emptiness in the lonely city.

With the news confirmed she became triumphant, her family rapacious. Her fiancé, to recall a term that seemed to give both Jan and her parents peculiar satisfaction, was summoned to cocktail parties and dinners to be exhibited like a trophy, a role for which he was in almost every detail ill-prepared. Despite the candour and fascination of the Grant family scrutiny, Philip, to his present amazement, remained undismayed. He was bemused but happy; his father characteristically suspicious. 'She is after your money, you know that, don't you?' was his warning. 'I can't say any of us here are very delighted,' he concluded, playing the head-of-the-family role he liked best. Philip had anticipated that response. He was glad that, compared with Daniel, he was still on speaking terms with his father.

The wedding – held at the Meeting House in a futile attempt to appease the rest of the family – was not a success. Daniel wouldn't come if his father was there and, as Philip expected, the old man's grudging recognition of the happy event was conditional on his other son's absence. So the inevitable outcome was Daniel's exclusion from yet another Taylor family event and, although – out of deference to the old man's feelings – no one was supposed to talk openly about Daniel, rumours of his latest activities and murmured recollections of his scandalous behaviour in the past completely upstaged the happy pair, at least on the Taylor side. Philip, who had been only too sensitive to the ghost at the feast, retained a strong memory of his surprise to find in the Silence (which he had loathed as a boy) a temporary relief from gossip and controversy. He sat on the plain hard bench and stared at the whitewashed walls, secure in the observation of piety, ostensibly oblivious to the flow of time. A Daniel come to judgement, he thought, quite inappropriately, and stayed still, avoiding the eye of the Elder. It was Jan, finally, who, after minutes of fidgeting, had to break the stalemate and start the vows. Philip heard the words, 'through Divine assistance, to be unto him a loving and faithful wife, so long as we both on earth shall live,' in a trance of wicked joy. Then all at once everyone was shaking hands and out of the corner of his eye he could see someone he knew talking about his brother again.

For the bride's family, the celebration of the alliance at a pricey hotel in Knightsbridge, was a moment of unique pride. Even now he cringed to recall how they had arrived in gaudy carloads, relaxing from the unfamiliar austerities of the Meeting House – cousins, godparents and hatchet-faced aunts all bursting with the achievement of the whole thing – and, insensitive to Quaker modesty, had quite overpowered both Philip's family and his own few friends with boisterous and prodigal hospitality. Their praise for the originality of Jan's wedding gown surpassed, if possible, their admiration of her radiance. She of course was swept away by the excitement, and whenever Philip turned to look seemed to be laughing or kissing, her small thin mouth parted in social rapture, or occasionally lowering her eyes to risk a surreptitious look at her hair which today was all silken brilliance and purged, for the occasion, of its greatest enemy, split-ends.

Someone – he forgot who – had spoken of the 'wonderful adventure of a new life together' and everyone drank too much sparkling cider. When it was all over and Philip was lying in the shell-pink splendour of the bridal suite listening to Jan sobbing her heart out in the lavatory, he was in a strange way grateful for her insistence on all the conventions: the sequence of ritual had saved the occasion from disaster.

Tears he associated strongly with Jan: tears of frustration, pain, rage, helplessness and sometimes laughter. The years of their short marriage seemed punctuated by stormy crises, and each time Jan, who had once made a list in her mind of all the things that Philip offered, emerged less dependent, and more and more determined to avoid the usual self-sacrifices of married women. When her course was finished, she applied for and got an assistant librarianship at the University. Her life became full of post-graduate happenings – seminars, meetings and parties – from which Philip felt increasingly excluded. To Jan's friends he was something of a mystery, and in their company he was always conscious of being a fish out of water, despite his own modest academic background. It hurt him to be at the wrong end of class-consciousness and, as a married man, also an easy target for feminists, much to Jan's amusement. Philip was amazed at the speed at which his wife (a phrase she herself began to scorn) found this new self-confidence. He had never seen it in her before and, when he was particularly low, it made him fearful for their future. His own work at the College became a dispiriting routine, a losing battle against teenage indifference, and his expectations there were now irredeemably locked into the salary-scale. With the end of university expansion, his hopes for a transfer dwindled and when his dog-eared thesis, already turned down by all the well-known academic publishers, was finally rejected by the University of Pittsburgh Press, it was like the slamming of a door. As his sense of frustration and failure grew, so did the tensions with Jan, and, as much as he tried to disguise his feelings, he knew he was draining her emotional reserves. In this way each inhibited the other and together they found that the strengths of their relationship became their greatest weaknesses for which they hated themselves almost as much as they now began to hate each other. So it was Jan, who had once favoured domestic stability above all, who walked out and left him.

In a way he was glad that she had been so decisive finally. Their marriage was suffocating them like an allergy. Every gesture and every sentence had become the source of conflict and bitterness. He resented the freedom she had discovered at his expense. She, sensitive by upbringing to the accusation, found herself challenging him with her suspicions as much to test her new-found confidence as in self-justification. Yet he would never have had the courage to make the break on his own; her move cleared the air.

Looking back on it now, he saw that once the child had died there was no hope for them. The present was bearable when there was hope in the future, but when the future turned and hit them both in the face, everything fell apart and their life together, launched amid so much expectation in the year of the Silver Jubilee, petered out in recrimination and a frantic search for new partners in which Philip, with his pilot-light sexuality, had failed. Jan moved in temporarily with another woman, one who was sympathetic to her predicament and with whom, Philip imagined, she could dissect the crisis of her pregnancy.

He had dreamed of the boy again last night in a grotesque parody of childbirth. The yellow dwarf with the fat cigar, bald as an egg and chattering like a madman, had burst from Jan's legs, unbloodied, absurdly dressed in a double-breasted suit like a gangster. It was almost funny until you dreamed it, and it was your own dead son who had barely breathed five minutes. He still could not bring himself to think about the death, though he believed that Jan, now completely alienated, had exploited the ironies of it to hasten the split between them. She was always very good at blame. He screwed up his thin frame under his coat to fight the shudders that always came with the memory of the recurrent nightmare, stared down at the pavement and thrust his hands deeper into his pockets.

Loneliness made the dreams worse. He found himself taking them seriously, and wondered whether he should go and see a specialist. True to his upbringing and his own tentative, pragmatic personality, he had stuck it out alone. It was now nearly two months since Jan had gone, halfway through the term. It seemed both longer and shorter. In the past they had always taken a short break then, usually with friends in Wales. Last year, when her pregnancy had been confirmed, they had splashed out on a long weekend in a moorland hotel in the West Country. For a few weeks after that, before the baby made Jan ill and wretched, they achieved a transient communion, in which their child, its heartbeat already monitored by the hospital, its first movements stirring beneath Philip's fingers in bed, was beginning to take a part. Looking back, it was an idyll. By the springtime, when the sun was getting warmer and their little garden, Philip's pride, was vain with colour, all that had dissipated. Jan was gross and miserable. They hardly spoke, and at the blackest times Philip wondered whether she was secretly regretting that she had missed the opportunity for an abortion.

After it was all over, the summer stretched out endlessly, wet and cold, a mirror to their mood. Jan was away often, 'at mother's,' she said, turning away. There was nothing new to celebrate when the autumn came, but Philip had tried in a half-hearted way to get her interested in a package trip to Paris. As usual, there was a glorious Indian summer, and he painted quite a convincing picture of the fashionable pleasures of the Champs-Elysées. He was keener to go than he realised. He did not like to admit it, even to himself, but Jan's infidelity and his own fear of rejection and betrayal was making him worry about impotence. He needed the confidence of a holiday. Perhaps that was why she had scorned what she derisively termed 'a second honeymoon' as 'a waste of time'. So nothing was fixed, the new session started up again and when, on the evening of that Friday in late October, she had failed to appear, he was not completely surprised. He sat at home wondering where she was, what had happened, who she was with, who he could turn to. The telephone call from Jessica's had come very late, long after midnight. Jan sounded slightly drunk.

'Phil, is that . . . ?'

'Jan. Jan darling. Jan . . . Where are you? I've been . . .

'Don't worry, Phil. I'm with Jessica now. Quite all right. I'm very happy here. I can't explain now. I hope you understand.'

There was nothing to say. Of course he understood. Later, alone in the empty bed, he broke down. The realisation of his own humiliation was nothing to the pain of knowing that Daniel, wherever he was, would have laughed at him. He had woken in the morning and stared red-eyed at the mirror, wanting nothing so much as to drive home to the silence of the old house in the country where meals were served at the sound of a gong and there were always flowers on the bedside table. But that would be another kind of defeat, so he stayed on in the home Jan and he had made for themselves, surrounded by the secure, permanent things of married life, cut glass and carriage clocks, too paralysed even to throw away the clutter of her abandoned pills and make-up in the deserted bedroom.

On his own, of course, refusing to admit the catastrophe to his father (at least until the end of term), he had got wrecked. The house, on which he had once lavished so much attention, became dirty and chaotic, and littered with old meals. He confined his efforts at normality to himself, to the face with which he faced the outside world, and even that turned out to be a losing battle in which, under pressure, unsuspected flaws betrayed him completely. His slight stammer got worse. Each morning there was the inescapable evidence of balding on his comb. His work at the college lost all meaning and he found that he lectured and taught in an aspirin daze, while a voice at the back of his mind said, you're thirty, you'll be doing this for the rest of your life. Despite his attempts to keep up appearances he was well aware that his colleagues and students knew all about Jan. In his more bitter moments he wondered how many were secretly still inviting her to their parties.

Philip had no doubt that Jessica, a notorious gossip, would claim the break-up of her friend's marriage as a triumph for Liberation. He was a good enough historian to know that there is nothing like ideology to cannibalise emotion. Jan, on the other hand, wouldn't care about the politics but (and this was far worse) would now talk openly about his failure as a husband. Again, he could watch the late autumn raindrops chase each other down his study window and reflect that guilt had strange consequences. It did not stop the pain of knowing that for his few friends and acquaintances he was a failure. Worse, he found that there was something horribly self-fulfilling about his predicament. Isolation made him all the more anxious to please and to match other people's expectations of him; increasingly he caught himself adopting the behaviour and attitudes of the part, to his own inner shame. His efforts to compensate were typically disastrous. He tried to go to bed with one of his class, chose deliberately, not setting his sights too high, took her out to dinner and a smoke-filled disco, filled her up with as much as he could afford and had drawn a blank. 'I'm having my period,' said the girl, sourly rejecting his tipsy suggestions.

It was lucky that the vacation arrived before he lost control of his job and abandoned his self-respect completely. Night after night he had nursed himself to sleep with whisky while waiting for the 'phone to ring, for Jan to say that it had all been a terrible mistake, that she wanted to come back, etc., etc. He had his responses all worked out: he would be forgiving, sympathetic, magnanimous. He would pretend nothing had happened and just hope to pick up the threads where they had left off. . . . Yesterday, when the 'phone rang in the night, long after the hours his students used, these scraps of rehearsed dialogue lurched to the front of his mind.

Philip was at home at the weekend, reading and marking essays and listening to Erik Satie. It was late and he was trying to exhaust himself before going to bed. He could not yet bring himself to take one of Mayhew & Taylor's famous sleeping pills. The telephone rang. He hadn't had a call for days. Pip, pip, pip. A 'phone box.

'Jan?' he said, involuntarily, his voice barking with tension.

There was a click. The line went dead. He put the 'phone down, steadying himself against the receiver; his hand was shaking slightly. He sat down next to the table. He had frightened her of course; he would be more relaxed if she called back. Or perhaps she was just taunting him; or Jessica was; or one of his students. Then the 'phone rang again like an alarm in his thoughts. He let it peal five times first. No hurry. Then: pip, pip, pip.

'Hello,' he said, almost not breathing.

'Who's that?' said a voice, rather low. It was a woman.

'This is Philip Taylor speaking,' he went on, disappointed but curious. 'Can I help?'

'Is Daniel there?'

'Daniel? My brother? No. I think you must be —'

'I have to speak with you,' the voice cut in. There was no menace or rudeness, but an urgency and a strength of feeling that was authoritative and almost tangible.

'I beg your pardon,' he said cautiously, his old self beginning to assert itself, 'are you sure you have the right number?' Then he panicked a bit: 'Who are you? What do you want?'

'Daniel gave me this number,' said the voice, making no effort to identify herself. 'If you're his brother I need to talk to you. It's very important.'

'Can you tell me what it's about?' he queried. 'I very much doubt if I can be of any assistance to you. I haven't seen Daniel for years.' He could feel himself being drawn irresistibly into conversation with this disembodied mind.

'I know.' It was an educated voice, determined but not bullying. 'I need your help. Meet me . . .' There was a quaver of hesitation. 'No, I'll rephrase that — Can you meet me tomorrow, twelve-thirty?'

'I — I — ' Philip's stammer asserted itself.

'You know the Leicester Square tube station,' the voice went on, hardly pausing. 'Down the Charing Cross Road and about a hundred yards on the right is a sandwich bar called Harry's. I'll be there at twelve-thirty, tomorrow. Okay?'

Philip Taylor had never taken a risk worth speaking of in his life. He was only too anxious to justify the good hand dealt him by his upbringing and background, and to be a good citizen and a good tutor. He paid his taxes, voted, attended the regular meetings of his local Ratepayers Association, collected the cheaper kind of antiques, and subscribed to the journals in his field, noticing with mild regret the initials of old acquaintances at the foot of review articles. His colleagues — the ones who did not despise him out of hand on ideological grounds — found him, under the surface, thoughtful and well-meaning, someone standing slightly apart from the usual rush. Privately, Philip had his share of disappointments, grievances and apprehensions. His attitude to his brother particularly was ambiguous. At times he blamed him for everything, but often he wished that the clock could be put back and the estrangement forgotten. He worried terribly about things over which he had no control, wars and injustices, and recently had become afraid of dying. He could never do anything without second thoughts, and every course of action seemed to him to have an equally attractive alternative. But when he heard the anonymous voice on the telephone say 'No, I'll rephrase that . . .' he took heart for the first time in months and became unusually decisive.

'Harry's. Tomorrow. Twelve-thirty,' he repeated, putting the 'phone down with an elated clatter. No one had ever rephrased anything out of consideration for his finer feelings.

2

Now Philip was late. Considering that he had located his rendez-vous with plenty of time to spare, it was ridiculous. He shouldn't have allowed himself to get side-tracked in the bookshop. But then it was pure chance to have spotted that book. His old super-visor from Cambridge days, described in the blurb as Professor of Medieval History at the University of Newcastle upon Tyne, seemed to be getting on pretty well. Perhaps it would be a good time, now that Jan had gone, to pick up the threads of research again, bring his thesis up to date and have another stab at a Fellowship. A friend in high places might have some influence. He had made a mental note to start by ordering the book from the library when, halfway out of the shop, he realised that few lib-raries nowadays would stock such a scholarly volume, however important. After a moment of indecision, he hurried back in again to buy it. In for a penny, in for a pound, he said to himself, thinking that it would be a good investment if it led to a new job. The punk behind the counter was incredibly slow and everyone in the queue seemed to be doing their Christmas shopping with credit cards. As he came to the front, Philip looked at his watch. It was just after twelve-thirty. Out in the street, he turned back down the Charing Cross Road. The rusty blue Humber estate was still parked against the kerb, and though there was no rational explanation why his fears should single out this particular vehicle as threatening a short route to oblivion, he still went by way of side streets towards Trafalgar Square, and emerged just south of the Leicester Square tube station even later than he expected. As someone who was always hours early for trains and also tem-peramentally obsessed by punctuality, he was doubly annoyed with himself. Besides, he was afraid that he might already have missed the girl.

His thoughts went to that strange, disembodied voice. He had to admit he was apprehensive, nervous. What did she have to say? What did she want? Was she attractive? He wondered how he would recognise her. She had not given any description. That worried him. He couldn't accost every woman in the place. Perhaps it was all a joke laid on by his students. 'No,' she had said, 'I'll rephrase that . . .' She sounded intelligent, her voice was firm. Though he didn't even have a name to go on – how easily cowed he was by the unexpected – he decided, as he half ran, half walked, that she would be plain, rather earnest and inquisitive. If she wasn't a hoax, then she was one of Daniel's friends who'd been put up to get more money out of the family. It wouldn't be the first time (as a student, his brother had often treated him as a soft touch when his allowance ran out). There was no denying that if he hadn't been so desperate himself he would never have submitted to this rendezvous business. It was bound to be an awkward meeting, inconclusive and embarrassing. He'd have to hope he could steer the conversation away from Daniel and talk about neutral things, make his apologies and leave. It wasn't as though he was made of money anyway, despite the family. He'd had enough of Daniel's appeals to conscience in the past, and he could find sufficient resentment towards Daniel in his heart to think that after all they had started with the same advantages.

A few yards up from Harry's, his vanity got the better of him and he paused in a darkened shop window to adjust his tie, comb his hair, and catch his breath a fraction. He was sweating despite the cold and dabbed at his dewy temples and forehead with a clean handkerchief freshly ironed for the occasion. The ghostly face in the glass looked better than in his morning mirror, more handsome and purposeful than he expected. The grey tiredness did not show here and even the skin that sagged so badly below his eyes gave his self-absorbed stare a solitary intensity that Philip – appraising himself hastily – found quite attractive, fascinating even, he thought, surreptitiously lifting an eyebrow. Daniel, cruel, had once said that he had the bright desperate expression he associated with tropical diseases. Philip, adopting the idea as his own, but softening it to tease Jan, once told her that he thought he looked like a white settler abandoned in a harsh climate among hostile natives by an indifferent colonial administration. Jan called it his 'long face'. Philip knew it only too well these days; he tried a quick self-conscious smile. But his cheeks were numb with cold and his lips, chapped by the wind, cracked. He hoped they wouldn't start to bleed.

As he hurried forward again, the smell of Harry's, its mingled disinfectant, smoke and frying onions, reached him on the wind. Raising his head briefly from its habitual slump, Philip checked and pushed through the door, stepping like a foreigner into the crowded warmth of the place. It was as he had imagined: people in lumpy coats, raw faces slopping tea, and moisture dripping down the steamed-up mirror that ran along the two inside walls. There was an atmosphere of welcome from the hiss and clatter of Harry's tea counter. He looked about; the electric clock on the wall said twenty to one. He was so preoccupied with finding the girl that he nearly knocked over a dwarf in a grubby scullery jacket shoving dirty glass cups into an old red bucket. He started to apologise, but the dwarf silenced him with an obscenity. There was a girl sitting alone in the corner with her back to him, a large straw basket bulging on the seat beside her. He worked his way up behind and bent across the table.

'Excuse me; I'm Philip Taylor. Are you –?'

He hadn't missed her after all. The girl – she was in her twenties, he guessed – started and gave a quick nervous smile though she did not seem pleased to see him. 'Oh, hi,' she said. He eased himself into the narrow bench-seat facing her. He was aware that she was staring at him intently. 'Hi,' she said again, echoing her first greeting. But she said nothing more, just looked at him with an expression more familiar than curious, as though she knew him already.

'I'm sorry I'm late. I got held up,' he said, with an open-handed gesture that suggested it was not his fault. He found her silence a bit unnerving. After all, it was her meeting. He saw she had been reading a paperback on the damp formica tabletop. Out of habit he twisted his head to see what it was; a battered copy of *Heart of Darkness*.

'Good?' He nodded at it in a friendly way.

'Crap,' she replied, stuffing it into her basket. She said nothing more and he felt too embarrassed to ask what she meant.

'Would you like some coffee?' he asked, to fill the space.

'Yes, thanks.'

He got up awkwardly, squeezing his long legs past the table, conscious that he had only just sat down and must be making an odd impression. The dwarf was now standing on a box behind the counter, rinsing cups in a sink of greasy water.

'Two coffees, please.'

'Milk?'

In a place like this he realised he should have asked her first, but he couldn't face going back. There was something about the girl that was already making him nervous. 'No – I mean, one with, one without,' he said quickly, hedging his bets. Jan never took milk, said she hated the taste of it, but one thing was certain already, this girl was not like Jan. He took the cups back to the table. The girl looked up suspiciously; she seemed on edge. Philip tossed up in his mind and kept the black coffee for himself.

'You've put milk in this,' she said.

Philip was shocked at her anger. 'I'm sorry – I didn't think – I mean I did – here, I haven't touched it, have mine . . .' he swapped the cups, slopping coffee as he did so.

'Are you as dumb and clumsy as your brother says?' she demanded.

He was confused by her unexpected rudeness. 'I don't know –' he began, feebly trying to avoid further offence. 'I mean, what do you mean?'

She did not reply, but studied him as though deciding whether to trust him. Disconcerted by her scrutiny, he floundered to interpret her remarks.

'I know you were sent,' he gabbled. 'You can't have any money, you realise.'

The girl put her cup down. His expectations had been proved wrong. He was finding her oddly attractive, even though she flustered him. There was a pointed, inquisitive expression about her, slightly freckled, that was also tough and boyish, an impression reinforced by a ragged fringe and her working clothes – faded jeans, two or three heavy sweaters and an old parka covered with badges. She looked at him evenly. 'All you Taylors seem to do things the wrong way round. You come here to meet someone you've never seen before. You arrive late. You don't check who you're talking to. You can't even order a cup of coffee without fucking it up.' She spoke in a low, slightly breathless monotone and the speed of her remarks betrayed the edge of her feeling. It was as if she had made up her mind about him in advance. Yet Philip found himself wanting her to go on talking. 'And now,' she concluded, 'for some reason you're talking about money. What's the matter with you?' She smiled thinly with contempt. 'If you don't mind my asking.'

Philip looked at her with embarrassment. She had coloured slightly with the fierceness of her attack, and her mouth was half-open, her breathing slightly asthmatic. Her head was cocked in a scornful challenge. The steady grey eyes he was finding so disconcerting were as sharp as her tongue. He glanced down quickly.

He began to stammer. 'I'm s – s – sorry. I know I'm not at my best. My wife left me recently . . .' When she did not seem interested in this disclosure he ran out of things to say and made a fuss of his coffee.

'I'm Stevie, okay,' she said, out of the blue, with a sudden change of mood and tone that Philip came to recognise as characteristic.

'Thank – thank you,' he said, slightly baffled. 'I'm – I'm –'

'I know. Philip Taylor.'

This was not what he had anticipated at all. The conversation got stuck again.

'Did you have far to come?' he asked, breaking the impasse.

She focussed on him sharply. 'That's none of your business.' Looking over his shoulder towards the door, crowded now with a queue for sandwiches, she said, still very low, 'Why did you ask me that?' as though apologising for her brusqueness.

'No reason.' He shrugged, nonplussed by the coming and going of her irritation. 'I was trying to make conversation.'

She relaxed again. 'You know why I rang you?'

'Not really. You didn't say exactly.' He hesitated. 'It's to do with my brother, isn't it?'

'Yes,' she said, measuring out her words. 'It's to do with Daniel.'

The rendezvous, he reflected, was turning out, despite her unconventional attitude, to be much as he had feared. Daniel. Did this strange girl know the nerve of pain she had touched so casually? As much as he always tried to bury his brother in his thoughts, Philip could not stop himself seeing again the strong, wide brow, the mesmerising chestnut-brown eyes and the adventurous set of nose and lips: a face in bold and arresting harmony. He admitted to himself that he'd like to know where his brother was, too. That extraordinary party was years ago now. He was aware that Stevie was questioning again.

'Sorry?' He exaggerated his renewed attention. 'I was miles away.'

'Don't you know where he is?' she repeated, almost in accusation.

He was not offended. It was not in his nature. He replied without impatience: 'The last time I saw Daniel was before I was married. About seven years ago. He won this prize for young journalists and I went to the celebration party.' He stopped, finding the memory painful, and changed direction. 'The wedding happened quite soon after that. Father wouldn't have Daniel there, of course, and from then on my life took a different course, so to speak,' he shrugged, half embarrassed by this surge of candour, but anxious also to make an appeal. 'It's funny. Now that Jan – that's my wife – has gone it's as though those years never existed.'

'They did for Daniel,' she commented, almost bitter; again her breath came in deep-drawn sighs.

Philip felt his own curiosity quickened by Stevie's moody responses. 'Obviously you know my brother better than I do,' he said with a smile. 'I suppose you know about the family background and all that.' It would help if she shared his code, he thought. It would give him a better chance to soften her animosity, perhaps even win her sympathy. He could do with a bit of that – at the very least, he told himself.

The girl leant forward in an oblique gesture of affirmation. Her eyes, he noticed, never seemed to relax but glinted watchfully, as though searching for an involuntary weakness in his expression, a giveaway in his own eyes that would open a chink on to hidden facts. Her nails, pressed white on the table, were bitten to the quick, and her voice was as urgent as when he had first sat down. She certainly managed to sustain her intensity, he thought, he who always was so exhausted by the prospect of serious commitment.

'We have this house. Don't ask me where; it doesn't matter. We only moved recently. Daniel's not been well. I'd hoped the change would help; you know, lift his spirits, but it's only made him worse. He's been away from the house now for days. It's happened before, when we had the flat, but this time I'm afraid. I can't explain why.'

He listened to her in some perplexity, unable to decide whether she was deliberately mystifying. Had she excluded the possibility, he thought to himself, that Daniel was being unfaithful? . . . and then, realising that it was only his own predicament selfishly intruding on someone else's problem, he pushed the consideration aside in his head. 'Perhaps he's with friends,' he suggested and laughed self-consciously. 'He certainly wouldn't come to me, that's for sure.'

But his words found no echo of agreement in her face. She seemed distracted by his reply. 'You don't understand. There is no one else now.' Her face was crumpled slightly as though she had a migraine. 'He gave me your number once – just in case. Yesterday . . .' When she rubbed her eyes he could see the red rims of exhaustion more clearly. 'Yesterday, I had to call you. I didn't want to, but I'm – I'm desperate, can't you see?' she admitted in a rush, as though something inside her had been suddenly undammed.

'I'm surprised Daniel had my 'phone number,' he said, unnerved by the emotion in her voice. 'We'd lost touch completely.' Then he saw that she was aghast at his indifference and, fearing that she would hate him for it, went on quickly. 'What can I do? I've no idea how to help you. Jan didn't want to antagonise her father-in-law by opening the house to Daniel. It's a terrible thing to have to admit,' he went on with feeling, 'but as far as we were concerned – and as far as I am concerned now – he doesn't exist.'

He realised as soon as he had finished that she felt he was trying to tell her not to trespass, and he was suddenly ashamed of the self-absorption that allowed him treat a complete stranger, Daniel's lover, so insensitively. To keep the conversation moving forward, he began stammering something sympathetic about how he was sure she would understand what he meant. 'It was imp- imp- impossible to keep in contact. You could never plan from one day to the next with Daniel. You know what he's like. I mean, you can't pin him down, can you? No one in our family ever managed that. Besides, a journalist's life is very . . .' He made a distracted gesture, '. . . you know . . .'

Stevie seemed to sense his embarrassment. 'Describe Daniel to me,' she said gently. 'Your brother as you knew him. Go on,' she prodded.

He concentrated on his memories. 'When I knew him well he was a tall, imposing chap in his late teens. He was fit. Played games. Plenty of friends. Loved to argue, to talk. He could be very amusing when he was the centre of attention – which he liked. Very ambitious, of course. He badly wanted to succeed. As the eldest son he was under a lot of family pressure of course. But he was up to that – the challenge, I mean. He was animated, always very animated. And I'd say he has done well since – in his own way – as far as I know . . .' He broke off, conscious that she was looking at him as though scanning a dead face for signs of life. There were dark shadows arching below her eyes and her face was clear of make-up and pale, though slightly yellow, as with a faded suntan. 'Don't you recognise the picture?'

'Oh – no – no,' she denied. He had the sense that she could have said more. 'It sounds as though you admired him,' she added, changing the subject.

'I – I – I – yes, I suppose I did. Looked up to him. He was older of course and very brilliant, we all thought.'

'He's changed quite a bit, I think you'd find,' she said. 'Sadder and wiser.'

'He must be,' Philip made a calculation, 'nearly thirty-five. The middle way of life,' he added, misquoting.

'That's funny,' she said involuntarily, almost warm. 'Daniel said that only the other day. He always seems to be aware of something – perhaps it's the brilliance you're talking about – slipping through his fingers.'

Apart from what he took to be the customary burden of family expectations, Philip, whose resentment at the way in which Daniel was always in the limelight, had coloured most of his adolescence, had never felt anything in common with his brother before. Now he said, 'Until Jan left, that's how I felt too. Suddenly, everything seems to have taken a turn for the better.'

Stevie ignored the frankness of his interest. She said: 'But you never had to fight your family the way he did. You don't know how that ate him up, even though he tried to disguise it.'

'That's father,' said Philip. 'It's been a f – f – feud. He couldn't forgive Daniel's betrayal, as he saw it.'

'Your father sounds like a vicious old bastard,' she said with feeling. Philip was too surprised to be offended. He realised then how big a gulf there was between himself and his brother still.

'I would expect Daniel to think like that,' he said, very reasonable.

'That's not just Daniel's opinion,' she said, irritated. 'That's what I think, if you want to know. A mean, vicious old bastard,' she elaborated with vehemence.

'Well, there are two sides to most stories,' he said, with mildness.

'Oh,' she said, very cold.

'You know the Taylors are Qu – Qu – Quakers,' he said. 'Dissenters. Outsiders. But if you're a group of rejects you have to stick together to survive. That's one explanation for the Meeting House.'

'The Society of Friends,' she murmured to herself.

'That's why we always did so well in business,' he went on. 'The England that nobody would recognise prospered outside the pale and made it great. Quaker always supported Quaker. Daniel has broken that rule completely. Right from the start he refused to conform. When you know our family history you'll see why father saw it as a betrayal. A hundred years ago my great-grandfather was an industrial pioneer, one of the most enlightened men of his time . . .'

As he enlarged on the past glories of Mayhew & Taylor Ltd., and his pioneering ancestors, Philip, excited by the history, launched into a minor paean, part fact, part legend, to his family's achievements.

He talked with pride of the obscure yet heroic beginnings of Luke Mayhew and his friend, the Rugby apothecary, Daniel Taylor, whose first pharmacy to bear the company name, in the City of London, was destroyed by bombing in the last war. By then, of course, it had become chiefly a museum, a polished mahogany showcase for the phials, bottles and crude surgical instruments of Mayhew & Taylor's eighteenth-century beginnings. Little had been rescued from the rubble after the terrible night of February 8, 1941 – 'A present disaster but perhaps a future blessing,' as Philip's grandfather had described it in the company newsletter. But, miraculously, the plaque that commemorated and marked the site of another, earlier miracle – the source of the company's prosperity at the start – had been found and was now set in marble in the foyer of the new company headquarters near Birmingham.

And then he moved back to the origins of it all, to the story of Luke Mayhew's buried treasure, discovered in a hollow of a wall in the new premises into which he had moved when he set up in partnership with Daniel Taylor nearly two centuries before. This unexpected cache of silver, forgotten by some earlier tenant, had, according to family tradition, greatly exercised the conscience of the partners, especially Daniel Taylor, for he had stayed up all night after the discovery, praying for guidance. However, towards dawn, as Philip and his brother had often been told, it was resolved for him by the Almighty that if the money was put to the service of humanity in the form of his ointments, creams, powders, and syrups, then the authorities need not be told. And indeed they never were, to the great financial advantage of the new company.

Looking back, Philip always averred, it was more something to chuckle at than to censure. Besides, Messrs. Mayhew & Taylor ('By Royal Appointment to His Majesty the King'), thus enriched by the benign workings of Providence, proved good stewards of their talents and, thanks to wise investment, the company went from strength to strength. Philip knew all the main pharmaceutical achievements only too well: the early successes with chloroform; the breakthrough in the mass production of pills and pastilles; the pioneering of surgical dressings and equipment, the profits from which blossomed into the great philanthropic adventures at the turn of the century: the new factory and its model housing, illuminated throughout with electricity. More recently there had been the benefits for medicine of two world wars and the great advances in anaesthetics and antibiotics. The story, towards the end, became less heroic and more technological, concerned with the development of the business from natural products towards chemical medicines. At their zenith in the inter-war years, Mayhew & Taylor's research and development laboratories were one of the wonders of the industry and, for the Empire, a quarter of the globe, the company's insignia was synonymous with good health and treatment at any age, a fact rammed home by the advertising slogan on all its products: 'Mayhew & Taylor, The Family People'.

'I like the story about the hidden silver,' she said, interrupting at last. There was a childish enthusiasm in her eyes that suggested she was not dissimulating.

Philip was pleased with the success of his narrative, but also a bit surprised to have talked her round so easily. 'Doesn't Daniel ever refer to any of this?'

She tilted her head on one side – the whiteness of her neck was very strong against the synthetic fur on the collar of her parka. Her expression was almost coquettish. 'Daniel has – how shall I put it? – a rather different perspective on the achievements of Mayhew & Taylor.'

'Every family has its skeletons: fortunately ours are long forgotten.'

'Really.' Something about the way she said it made him feel incredibly naïve.

The conversation faltered. After exposing so much of himself, Philip found his own thoughts flowing like a cold private undercurrent, tugging him back into clannish reticence. He wanted to break the silence that had filled his life recently, but there were scenes in his mind's eye that he could never bring himself to put into words. It was not that he was untruthful; there was a complexity to this family tradition that had a darker side he could never articulate.

'So Daniel let the side down,' she said ironically.

'It's complicated,' he admitted. 'For father there was always an element of self-criticism. You see, after the war we lost our edge. There was something symbolic about the destruction of the Old City Pharmacy. We missed too many chances with the National Health. I suppose we had become corrupted by our own success. So the family got slowly squeezed out of the business. Father lost interest – or said he did. He's an old man in his seventies now; he sits at home listening to the news on the radio in the small hours, watching his investments being whittled away by inflation.'

'And he transferred all his hopes for the future to his elder son, Daniel said.'

'Yes. Daniel was supposed to be the new breed of Taylor, the one who would reassert himself and stop the rot. It was bad enough when he turned his back on the trade to study English at University, but when he gave up his career as a scholar . . .'

As he talked himself out of loneliness and grew easy with the conversation again he surprised himself at the openness of his own words. Stevie seemed quite absorbed in what he had to say; as though this retrospect was an acceptable substitute for up-to-date news about Daniel.

He told her that he thought it was only out of a sense of dynastic loyalty that his parents had never divorced.

'Hannah, your mother, always sounds quite a saint when Daniel talks about her,' she murmured, encouraging his mood.

It jolted him to hear a stranger identify his mother by her

Christian name; somehow it intensified the poignance of the memory. 'They should never have married,' said Philip. 'It was pure infatuation on her part. And anyway she was mostly in love with father's ideals, I think. In the end it became nothing but self-sacrifice.'

His parents had married at the end of the war. His mother was nearly thirty then and feared perhaps that John Taylor, the heroic Red Cross driver from the Normandy landings, offered her the last and only chance of motherhood and a good marriage.

Daniel had been born two years later, when Labour Britain was at its bleakest. His mother had nearly died, but nevertheless, despite the risks, five years on, in the year of the Queen's Accession, Philip had been born. After that, whatever her private hopes, she had to accept the doctors' advice and be content with her two sons, and in fact, as her relationship with her older husband cooled into neutral tolerance, it was the two boys, Daniel especially, who absorbed her attention.

John Taylor had by then become completely submerged in the battle to keep the company in business, resorting to more and more desperate measures to disguise the fact that in almost all departments, commercial and pharmaceutical, Mayhew & Taylor Ltd, outgunned by the European and American giants, was making a loss. Philip described how the most risky boardroom manoeuvre, the buying-out of the Mayhew family shares, had cost his father several friendships in the industry and had, from many points of view, heralded the beginning of the final decline. And when he thought of his father he could see him as an industrial master, a heavy fifty-year-old with the confidence of a general, parading his two sons on unwilling visits to the labs where, out of deference or fear, middle-aged men in white coats checked their natural irritation at Daniel's precocious questions. Later, after one such occasion, when Daniel was still in his early teens, his father in a rage had beaten him, leaving the boy more than ever resentful towards his inheritance.

Stevie said, 'He used to run away, he told me.'

'Yes, he did. Pure bravado, looking back. I was impressed at the time though.'

He told her how he had, as a child, involuntarily looked up to Daniel, always accepted his lead as natural even though his own life had been blighted by the greater success and then the more wounding controversies of his brother's career. From the beginning, he said, he was always in Daniel's shadow, urged at every turn to emulate him, and when Daniel became alienated from his responsibilities, the family's rejection of the older son left him neutered by divided loyalties.

As Stevie peeled away his shyness, Philip found himself able to look more and more freely at her as he talked. Her original hostility had become transformed into deft but pointed questioning, drawing him out by degrees; and her features, at first so hard and suspicious, had opened and relaxed. It was like moving from half-light to sunshine, the way those clear grey eyes had softened from steel to silver. She must know so much already of what he had to say, he thought, and yet she encouraged him to talk on. In the end he found himself grateful for her sympathy; strongly attracted to her independence of mind and her self-possession.

'And so,' he concluded, 'you see why we don't speak of him at home. It's worse now. Mother was always more understanding. After she died . . .' he shrugged.

'He often talks of your mother. Did you know that?'

'I think we both miss her more and more as time passes. When we were kids our relationship was with father. When that went bad we needed her, but she was sick and helpless by then.'

'Cancer, he told me.'

'Of the womb. I don't think Daniel ever got over her death.'

'He blames your father for that, you know.'

'He's got a point there,' Philip admitted. 'Father was incredibly casual towards her illness, as though it was her fault, if you know what I mean.' He frowned. 'It was not until afterwards that he too realised what he'd lost. That was another thing he could take out on Daniel. For some reason, grief did not lead to reconciliation. In fact, it only made things worse.'

The dwarf with the red bucket came to the table. 'Finished?'

Philip was getting absorbed in the scrutiny of his family. 'Would you like some more coffee?'

'Thanks.'

'Two coffees please. No milk.'

'Get them yourself, mate,' piped the dwarf.

Philip was about to get up when he realised that Stevie had already moved to the counter. He admired her neat, decisive movements and secretly acknowledged that he could talk to her indefinitely. Of course that was partly to do with his half-admitted fascination with Daniel which, if he was honest with himself, was in turn partly stirred by sexual curiosity. Stevie sat down again and, his confidence growing, he said: 'I don't remember you at that party . . .'

'Which party?' She sounded defensive.

'Oh – you know – the one for his prize.'

'I wasn't invited.' She paused to sip her coffee. 'We got together later,' she added, rather laconic.

'I see.'

'You're right though – our paths had crossed already. In Africa.' And she gave the Black Power salute in an ironical gesture.

Philip, self-conscious as usual, noticed that one or two people nearby seemed a bit startled by this. 'Oh. Yes. On V.S.O.' His eye strayed to the badges on her lapels; the slogan demands for Peace and Liberation in the Third World began to fit into the pattern of the past.

'In Africa,' she repeated, enigmatically correcting the emphasis.

'I see,' he said, not seeing.

'When we met again in London it was after his time in New-castle. He was in Fleet Street by then.' She frowned. 'He came to interview me.' For a moment he thought she was going to blush and began to smile with embarrassment himself. 'Oh, I know what you're thinking,' she muttered with characteristic candour, looking up at him from under her lashes.

'No, please, I – I – don't –' He could not think how to go on.

'Well, as it happens, you're right.' And she threw back her head and laughed out loud, intensely, as if at a huge private joke. It was rather disturbing. Philip, who had decided that Stevie would never even smile seriously, was silenced, rather wishing she would not draw so much attention to herself.

'He realised I could be of use to him,' she explained. 'And politically, of course, I very much wanted to help him.'

'It sounds as though you had a lot to offer him.' He amazed himself: his words sounded neither patronising nor insulting.

'He needed help terribly. He was all wound up about his story for one thing.'

'The one that got him the prize?' Philip queried.

'No – no. This was bigger. Potentially the one that would put him on the map for good. But he needed someone to talk to, someone to understand what he was saying. He'd come across too much indifference. These are very dead years politically. I don't think you know how lonely he's been.'

'No,' he agreed. 'It's my fault. I should have kept in touch.' He smiled at her. 'In future it'll be different. You must both come round.'

But her eyes had gone cold again, glinting with tears. 'But where is he?' she said, her voice rising.

She seemed to be aware that she was attracting attention and leant towards him to keep the conversation private. The sallow dwarf was hovering about with his cloth, whistling as he wiped the tables. The lunchtime rush was easing fast; the cellophane heap of sandwiches had gone.

He began to equivocate again; half of him wanted to be home.

'Look,' she went on urgently. She had the little finger of her left hand in her mouth and was biting with a grimace as she spoke. Philip noticed that she was wearing a man's watch with a worn leather strap and wondered, searching his memory, if it was Daniel's. 'I don't think you understand what I'm saying. I had a reason for using that call-box last night.'

'Your 'phone is broken?'

She seemed astonished at his reaction. 'Think what you like,' she said with guarded menace. 'I just want you to take what I'm saying seriously.'

'Well, are you going to tell me more?' he queried playfully, as though asking for the next episode in a diverting fantasy.

'Why should I?' She sounded bitter and angry. 'You obviously don't care about what I'm saying.'

He made a feeble disclaimer. 'You can't blame me,' he went on, 'you're being very mysterious.'

'I have a right to be. There's a lot at stake,' she defended. 'How can I trust you?'

She deftly checked his wounded protest, laying a hand on his arm and stressing her words with the pressure of her fingers. Now she was treating him like his brother, or even, he felt, entering briefly her own psychological landscape, like a fellow conspirator in some strange unstated plot. She was still not giving much away, though she did seem excited by the turn the conversation had taken. 'Listen,' she was saying, 'I'm scared when Daniel doesn't come home. I imagine things. Please, Philip. Believe me.'

She had not called him by his Christian name before and she did it with such natural warmth that it seemed to offer the prospect of a better rapport.

He nodded seriously, encouraging her as best he could. The more she talked, this nervous, anaemic woman, keyed-up with doubts and anxieties that he could only half understand, the more he found himself falling under the spell of her imagination.

'You think I'm paranoid, but I'm telling you I think I know what can happen these days.' She seemed to want to invest her words with cryptic significance. 'You have to face it,' she went on fiercely, 'they know they're fucked.'

He was confused by the new direction her mind was taking. 'I'm sorry. I don't understand.'

She spoke as though schooling a backward child. 'You know as well as I do it's only a matter of time before all the contradictions in this bloody country tear it apart.' Philip registered inward disappointment at Stevie's identikit Marxist dogma and wondered if this was all Daniel's influence. 'Yes,' he said weakly.

Stevie seemed encouraged temporarily by his response. 'It's a losing battle of course, but the Establishment will do all it can to hold the line — by force if necessary.'

'I don't see the generals taking over just yet.'

His flippancy angered her. 'But don't you see how old-fashioned that is? State fascism is far more subtle these days. Tanks are outmoded. You don't have to call in the Army to oppress the people.'

The dwarf came slowly past with a bowl of grey minestrone for a late luncher and Philip had the impression that the wrinkled baby ears were straining to share their conversation. Stevie obviously felt this too; she huddled closer across the table. 'Look at Northern Ireland,' she said. 'It's a civil war, but who admits it? They'll manipulate the Army as so-called peace-keepers, introduce so-called Emergency Powers; they'll increase the powers of the Special Branch if they have to. Did you know that everyone coming into the country is vetted against a computer?' He shook his head. 'When you've lost control of something you get desperate.' She stopped, her breath slightly hurried.

Philip, who was becoming stirred by Stevie's vigour and freshness, regretted more than ever the store of polemical stereotypes in her mind. He moved his arm off the table-top, shyly drawing back from her insistent harangue. All this confirmed his opinion that first impressions often turn out to be true. As one who liked to define the world in which he lived very carefully, and who was always afraid of its ambushes, such accuracy of assessment was important to him. Daniel, he imagined, his thoughts turned in that direction by Stevie's inquiries, was much more casual about such things. For Daniel, the world was best when it was uncharted, when it could be explored without fear or caution, a place in which constant readjustments of perception were, like the exploration itself, just another way to stave off boredom. He remembered Daniel's teenage reiteration. 'Isn't this all so boring.' He knew his brother always looked for ways to escape the threat of monotony; but, whatever the risks, he always seemed to survive.

'I can't imagine that Daniel is in any real trouble,' he said, with bland reassurance. 'He'll be back.'

'How do you know?' she challenged. 'There's no reason to say that. Anything's possible. He's been away for over a week now. That's unusual – he's not been well either. He could easily need treatment.' She looked at him deeply. 'The thing I can't stand is the silence. I sit in the house every night waiting for the 'phone to ring or the door to open and nothing happens. It's weird. I can't tell you what it's like.'

'I understand,' he said.

'Yesterday – I hope I didn't wake you –'

'No – no –'

'My nerve cracked. I was afraid suddenly. I can't explain it. I had to talk to someone. I thought you might know. Besides, I didn't want to admit my weakness to the others – my friends, I mean,' she said quickly, as if covering up an admission. 'Daniel had tracked you down in the 'phone book some months ago. You probably didn't realise it but he used to take quite an interest in you. Sometimes he'd go and sit for hours in his car outside your house.'

'I n – n – never saw him,' said Philip, stuttering with surprise.

'You wouldn't have. It was always at night. He was very discreet. But he was fond of you, strangely. He was quite protective and wanted to know that you were all right.'

'But he despised me,' said Philip.

'No – not really. You know that, don't you,' she answered, detecting his defensive lie. 'He was sorry it had all got so out of hand. In a funny way a part of him wanted to get back into the mainstream of the life he had lost. I think that's why he gave me your number. He would never call, but I think he hoped that I would.'

'Not in these circumstances,' he said, rather grim, touched by what she had told him. It was hard to imagine Daniel as curious about his brother's life as he was himself.

Stevie returned to her preoccupation. 'You'll probably laugh,' she admitted, 'but I'm afraid that he's been picked up.' She spoke very low, as though she was giving away a secret.

Philip was confused. 'Picked up by – ?' He was ashamed to sound so dim.

'Oh, by them, of course.' She emphasised the threat of the law with a movement of her head.

'What for?' Philip could not hide his disbelief.

'I don't want to go into that. He's a journalist. He has to take risks. It's not as crazy as it sounds,' she argued with a defensive smile.

Philip was easily disarmed by these rare, unguarded moments. He found himself advising her to look on the bright side. 'I find it hard to imagine that he could be in serious trouble like this.'

'But that's the point. It doesn't have to be serious. Not now. It happens all the time these days.' She sighed, as though she regretted having to convince him of an inescapable truth. 'Besides, Daniel's interests are not always just journalistic. You can't overlook his . . . commitment.' Philip found himself baffled by the hints and stresses of her words. Suddenly she became more down to earth. 'Well, it will only be questioning, I suppose.' She was, he could tell, picturing it all in her head. She seemed turned on by the idea, as if it answered a need for something dramatic in her life.

'I'm afraid I've never cared enough about anything,' he confessed, 'to run that sort of risk. I wish I did. I'm just not made that way.' He gave a weak laugh. 'I even had doubts about coming here today.'

But Stevie was staring into nothing, scarcely listening. 'I hope he's okay. They probably won't let him get in touch with anyone. They break all the rules these days.'

'What rules?'

'The right to call a solicitor.'

Philip inquired, with some interest, whether she had had any experience of the authorities in this way.

'Sure,' she said boastfully.

He asked what that was.

For the first time, she seemed slightly embarrassed. 'Oh – the usual,' she said, offhand. 'I've been on demos. I write for the alternative press. I've got something pretty big going at the moment –' she stopped herself dramatically, 'but I can't talk about that. They keep an eye on us all, I'm sure. It's probably dangerous to talk openly even in a place like this.' It didn't sound very impressive and she seemed to be aware of the fact. She perched up on her seat, and announced with pride: 'You're talking to one of the so-called undesirables of the Far Left.'

He didn't know what to make of this. Stevie seemed to be living in more of a dream-world than he had first realised. 'Daniel was always radical-minded,' he said.

'If you saw him now,' there was a faraway gleam in her eye, 'you'd know what I'm talking about. These last few months he's been totally alienated.' She looked at him significantly. 'It's all going to happen for him now – you see, we've moved into this house.' Assuming she rejected bourgeois conventions, he considered, her pride in property was remarkable.

Philip turned round to look at the clock and noticed, as perhaps he would not have noticed before this conversation, that the dwarf's boss behind the counter, an overweight, choleric stevedore of a man with a comb of black hair, was watching them intently from behind the tea urns. He saw this because the man was ignoring two late customers. The dwarf himself was nowhere to be seen. Facing forward again, Philip was not surprised to find that Stevie had become apprehensive too.

'Why did you choose this place?' he asked.

'What do you mean?' she replied. 'You didn't tell anyone about it, did you?'

'No. Why should I?'

'I told you I don't trust you.' She was tense. 'Do you know the man behind the counter?'

'No. Why?' He shifted in his seat.

'Don't turn round – he's been looking at us for about five minutes.'

'Perhaps he wants us to go.' He tried to defuse her obsession. 'We've been here throughout lunch and only bought four cups of coffee. Do you want some more?'

'No thanks.' She was staring past him towards the counter, preoccupied with her anxieties.

'Well,' he said casually, 'I suppose I must be off soon.'

The mood of the conversation plunged again. 'But look,' she persisted. 'You must help me. You're my last hope. Can't you see?'

'What can I do? I wish I could but . . .' He shrugged. 'I imagine you don't want to go to the police just yet.'

'Well done,' she said, sour as a penny.

Should he invite her home? Now she knew about Jan, she might misunderstand him. Despite his acceptance of blame he knew he didn't really want Daniel invading his life all over again. A siren sounded in the distance outside. Half-consciously he absorbed it as a warning and said, to keep the ball rolling, 'I could get in touch with father. I suppose it's just possible he might know what to do.'

He hadn't meant to annoy her; he found it difficult to follow her shifts of mood.

'Okay —' she was losing her temper finally, speaking in snatches, '— forget it — I'm sorry I wasted your time.' There were tears of rage in her eyes. 'Daniel's got friends who can help. Don't worry. After all he told me I might have known.'

Dumb with shame, Philip feared a scene. He looked down at the table and saw the greasy pattern he had traced with his distracted fingers. There was a cold draught as the door opened and shut again. A lot of things seemed to be happening. Stevie was standing up, fighting her way past the table. It was two-thirty. Harry's was nearly empty. He wanted to shout after her but he couldn't. The man behind the counter was talking to a middle-aged man in a grey raincoat who looked as though he coached rugby at weekends. They were looking round behind him but there was no one there, only his own reflection in the mirror. The Jubilee Queen on the wall faced out at him without comment. The siren in the street seemed to have stopped outside. Philip wondered if there had been an accident. Then he saw that Stevie was talking to the man in the raincoat. Philip knew that he had to help her even if she did misinterpret it. But there was a young man in jeans and a cloth cap, a cross between a hippy and a country squire, he thought, standing in his way. 'Excuse me,' said Philip, but as he spoke the fragments began to make a picture. He stared at the casual young man who said quite softly, 'Police,' and touched him by the elbow. It was almost, Philip imagined, like a gay pick-up. 'Would you come outside, please.'

3

In the city street the winter light was already ebbing and there was snow in the air: the white police Rover was parked outside, one wheel raked on the pavement. Philip glanced at Stevie. Her face had gone hard with concentration. She might, he thought, have been playing a part. She seemed to be bunching herself together, to have turned inward, seeing and hearing nothing as they were escorted into the back seat. He didn't resist either. He didn't even worry about who might be watching. There was a remoteness between himself and the things happening that was only broken when the door slammed and the young man in jeans crowded in beside them, tossing his cap against the back window.

'Okay – let's have some identification.' His manner was matter-of-fact, only menacing because, in the context of ordinary life, the demand was so unexpected. Like a mugger's victim, Philip began to fumble for his wallet in the folds of his coat.

'Is this a formal arrest?' Stevie asked.

'No – you're helping with enquiries.'

'This is all I have, I'm afraid,' said Philip apologetically. He was still adjusting to the fact that the person on the seat next to him, who looked like one of his ex-public school students, was a police officer.

The young man took Philip's credit card. 'P. R. Taylor,' he read, flicking it idly with his forefinger. 'And you?' he said, casually, leaning across Philip towards Stevie; his open hand was raw and blunt like a games player's. Expressionlessly, she rummaged in her basket and dragged out her purse. She passed it over without a word. Philip sensed that her unco-operative attitude contrasted rather favourably with his own craven line of least resistance. The young man was rifling through the doggy scraps of paper. 'Miss Beck?' he queried. He sounded flirtatious, Philip thought, like someone making a blind date. He was beginning to recognise that brutal flippancy was one of the hallmarks of those who exercise unaccountable power.

Stevie nodded, facing away from the man with hatred in her eyes. Philip saw that she too was frightened, but, unlike him, frightened even to show it. She seemed anxious to live up to a role, even if it was only cast in her head. But, despite her taste for melodrama, he recognised that their recent conversation was not as wild as he had believed. He would have to revise his assessment of her; it disturbed him that the world into which he had taken such a reluctant step should prove unpredictable so swiftly.

Someone gave the cue to the driver and the car began to move. As the engine revved and they pulled out into the Christmas traffic, the sirens began to wail. 'Any person who . . .' the older man in the grey raincoat, sitting in the front, was speaking for the first time. '. . . in a public place wears any item of dress or wears, carries or displays any article in such a way or in such circumstances as to arouse reasonable apprehension . . .' It didn't make sense. Then Philip realised that the man was talking about something he referred to as the Prevention of Terrorism Act, quoting monotonously. He found it hard to focus on the words. They were travelling fast; shoppers scuttled to the kerb, cars and taxis pulled over with brake lights glaring. Philip looked at Stevie. She had her basket on her knees and was saying nothing. In the swerving and braking he tried to keep his distance and pressed himself against the young detective. Suddenly, they were shooting through a grubby archway and the blue light sent the shadows dancing round an inner car park. Minutes later, in another hustle, they were swinging through double doors into a long neon-white corridor that made them blink.

Almost before he realised what was happening, Philip found himself giving his name and address to a man behind a desk and obeying the instruction to empty his pockets. With the opportunity to prove his innocence his confidence rose and he began cheerfully to go through his things. There was his new book, still in its bag. His pockets blossomed absurdly. The loose change that he kept in his trousers he slammed on the desk together with an old tube ticket, the freshly-ironed handkerchief, a safety pin, his contact lens case, a scrap of exercise-paper with two students' numbers, a single ticket for the local Odeon, his keys, his wallet and finally half a packet of Polos. It was an absurd collection and at first he felt like a guilty schoolboy, but then the sombre deliberate movements of the man in front of him began to take effect. All his anxieties returned. It was surprising how even the most trivial things seemed to have some significance when a police officer was itemising them and dropping each object into a plastic bag.

Then Stevie was asked to do the same. She said something indistinct about 'rights', but did not refuse. 'Beck,' she repeated.

'B as in Boy. E as in . . .' Philip noticed that her thin white fingers were shaking. He felt threatened by the bottled-up emotion and looked away. The room had an air of hard and constant use. Every surface and corner was scuffed or broken. The atmosphere was functional and dreary. In the middle of a weekday afternoon it was almost deserted; sound carried. A door flapped and an old man carrying a shopping bag came in, escorted by a sandy-haired policeman in a shiny suit.

Philip heard him say, 'You can go home now.'

The old man seemed too defeated to look grateful. After a moment's incomprehension, he nodded vaguely but rambled on about a supermarket.

'Off you go, grand-dad.' The words were careless but cruel. The policeman smiled knowingly at the man behind the desk who winked in agreement. The old man moved slowly away towards the exit. Philip watched his faltering progress and wondered if he should offer help.

'He doesn't look like a bomber,' said the man behind the desk to no one in particular, 'but who knows these days,' he added, staring meaningfully at Philip.

The bent figure pushed his way laboriously through the exit. Philip was momentarily reminded that he owed his old father a seasonal visit. But there was an exchange of voices close at hand that he was missing. He turned back and saw the young man in jeans leading Stevie away down the corridor. He was about to say something, but the duty officer behind the desk distracted his attention.

'Is that all, Mr. Taylor?'

'Oh – yes, yes,' he said, buttoning his coat round him. He found that the older policeman in the grey raincoat was standing next to him.

'Would you come with me, Mr. Taylor,' he said, very quiet and serious. 'There are one or two questions I have to ask you.' He was slightly bronzed with cropped receding grey hair, and the firm line of his mouth and jaw was emphasised by a sporting cavalry moustache. Philip followed him into a small bare room adjoining the main lobby.

There was an empty schoolroom desk and three plain wooden chairs. Philip sat down as directed, and when he looked up from straightening his position in front of the table (hoping that he might thus denote a certain security of mind) he was surprised to discover that another man, with a clipboard, had joined them.

The interviewer, however, paid no attention to his assistant who was already bent over his notes like the clerk of a court. This tactic, Philip recognised afterwards, was sustained throughout the conversation so that he never saw more than the top of a well-polished head, taking its shine, distractingly, from the single overhead light.

The senior officer had removed his raincoat. He was wearing a navy-blue blazer with gold anchor buttons and Philip decided that if he didn't coach rugby, he went sailing on the South Coast at weekends. Perhaps he was an ex-naval commander. He had the weather-eye of a sailor. Now he was pulling bits and pieces out of the plastic bag on the desk. There was a passport photo of Jan.

'Are you married?'

'Yes. But we're separated.'

'Ever been inside?'

'In prison? Good lord no.' He was quite surprised at the suggestion.

'Sure?' The man narrowed his eyes in warning. Philip felt nervous but managed to say, 'Yes. I'm telling the truth, I promise you.'

'I see.' He looked at the telephone numbers carefully. 'You live alone.' It was a statement, but Philip felt compelled to keep answering.

'Yes,' he said.

'These numbers. What are they?'

'My students. I'm a teacher.'

'Where?'

He gave the name of his college and of his Principal as well. The officer was not impressed. 'A polytechnic lecturer,' he said slowly, evaluating his reply. 'What do you teach?'

'History.'

'History,' he repeated with scepticism. 'You mean contemporary politics.'

'Well, I do teach some politics. Hobbes and Locke – that sort of thing.'

'Are they Communists?' The man leant forward attentively. Philip didn't know what to say. Everything, even harmless 'phone numbers and snapshots, suddenly seemed so loaded. The man must be fooling now, but with a purpose, he was sure. He was trying to trap him. Or perhaps he wasn't fooling, and when you drank pints of bitter, standing in your gumboots on the hard at Bosham on a Sunday morning with your mates, then perhaps Locke *was* a Communist. A philosopher certainly. Marx was a philosopher and Marx was a Communist. So all philosophers were Communists . . . He was going crazy. I'm okay, he said to himself, I've nothing to hide. 'I think you've made a mistake,' he replied out loud. 'I've nothing to hide. Everything I've said is true.'

Disconcertingly, the officer did not react. He looked at the scrap of paper again as though it was the vital clue in a murder hunt. He said, 'These students. Why do you need their telephone numbers?'

'I've got their essays. Some of them want my comments before Christmas.'

'I don't believe you. They can call you at home, can't they?' Philip looked at his interviewer from a pit of apprehensions. He didn't know where to go now. He was confused. There seemed to be no truths. He resolved to try some false candour.

'My wife left me recently. I was lonely. I needed company.'

He expected to elicit sympathy but the gambit failed. The officer looked at him in silence with an unwavering stare; his assistant was making laborious notes, apparently oblivious to the nuances of feeling. Philip found himself blinking nervously; his pink-rimmed eyes were full of water.

'Excuse me,' he said, bending over, 'my lenses are hurting. I think I'll take them out.' He felt in his pocket, then realised he had handed everything over. He looked at the items on the desk. 'Could I . . . ?'

'Certainly not,' said the officer.

Philip flinched and, despite his fears of losing them, dropped his contact lenses into an empty pocket. It occurred to him that there was always the insurance; it was a relief to have the faces blurred. Swings and roundabouts, he thought. A piece of paper was being waved in front of him; the familiar voice was speaking again.

'We shall have to verify these telephone numbers of course.' The interviewer had stood up. 'You realise you have been detained on a very serious suspicion?'

'What suspicion?' Philip broke in, emboldened by fear.

'You were overheard plotting against the Army –'

'But that's ridiculous,' he protested, but he was cut off by the relentless voice of the interviewer.

'Our informant has testified that your friend was seen to give a clenched-fist salute.'

'She's not my friend.'

'Oh?'

'I met her for the first time today.'

'You don't expect me to believe that this woman is merely a call-girl?' The thin smile of disbelief was underlined by the contemptuous tone of his words. 'I didn't know that common prostitutes were in the habit of making clenched-fist salutes, at least not in public.' He spoke, as he had throughout, with a steady, slightly ironic, enunciation.

'I wasn't asking you to draw that conclusion,' Philip replied. 'But it is true that I'd never seen her before lunchtime today.' He decided not to elaborate; he didn't want to bring Daniel into this if he could help it.

The officer weighed up his defence. 'I see,' he said at last. 'All right.' He sighed as though it was all very predictable and boring. 'We'll just have to come back to that later.' Philip was aware, despite his myopia, that he was being scrutinised more sternly than before. 'You realise, I suppose, Mr. Taylor, that my men and I are effectively at war.' He sounded almost proud.

'I know,' said Philip, hoping to strike a note of deferential approval.

'Oh, but of course,' the officer went on, mock-theatrical, 'I didn't have to remind you about that. You know it all already. You're pretty far from the front line of the action from the look of you, but you still know what it's like to be hunted by the Bomb Squad.'

'W – w – what are you saying?' Philip was bewildered; whatever he said seemed only to trap him deeper in guilt. He thought he was going to be sick. He tilted forward in his chair, resting his head on his knees with shock and exhaustion. The voice continued, soft but implacable.

'I'm telling you what you know to be true, Mr. Taylor. Perhaps I could persuade you to concentrate your attention for a few moments on your fellow countrymen, the ones that get torn apart in the prime of their lives in violent and unexpected deaths. That's the side I imagine your friends don't let you see. They keep you in the back room, don't they, and let you do what you're good at – research.' Philip started; the unfocussed head in front of him supported a mind that was perhaps not as mad as it seemed. There was a note of triumph in the voice now. 'That way you never have to worry about the consequences, do you?'

Philip was aware that, trapped and immobilised as he was, he was sweating badly. 'I – I – I –' he stammered.

'If you like, I could show you our local mortuary after a bad incident. It's not a pretty sight as they say. People have such a lot of blood in them, you know.'

Philip recalled his own absurd fear of the blue Humber estate. All that seemed a long time ago. He moved uneasily in his seat. The nausea had passed. He was breathing without panic again; he was more collected.

'I'd like to call my solicitor,' he said. 'It's my right,' he added rather lamely. The world of rights and natural justice seemed to be incredibly distant.

The officer did not react.

'I'm innocent, don't you understand. You've made a mistake. I've got a right to discuss it with a solicitor.' He could not suppress the frantic note in his voice.

'It's not a right,' said the voice across the table with satisfaction. 'It's discretionary.'

'But – but –' He floundered for harmless corroboration. 'On – on the television . . .' he began.

'What about television?'

Philip was aware that even the man with the clipboard, bent over his notes, was enjoying this. 'Oh – nothing really – it's just that on television I've seen people ask for their solicitors, d'you know what I mean?'

'Mr. Taylor,' the officer was intrigued. 'Perhaps I should make one thing plain. We're not on television now, whatever you may think. In the real world . . .' he paused, momentarily confused. 'In the real world,' he went on more politely, 'I have to refuse you that particular request at this stage.'

'But – when . . . ?'

The interviewer impatiently waved a neat navy cuff. 'Later,' he said. 'There are bombings. Terrorists at large. We can't take chances. The security of the state is threatened. You say you are innocent. I'm telling you that innocent people buying Christmas presents for their loved ones are getting blown to pieces. It's our job to track down these mindless killers. I will not release you

40

until I am satisfied that you have no connections with international terror.' He was standing behind Philip's chair. 'I am, however, inclined to think,' he said, 'that your story is accurate.' He sounded disappointed. 'Unless you're cleverer than we realise. Some more questions.'

Philip blinked and the man took a small gun-metal tin out of his pocket. 'Humbug?'

Philip jumped. 'Excuse me,' he faltered.

'Have one,' said the man indistinctly, popping one into his own mouth.

'Thank you – thank you.' He took one optimistically and then wondered if this was a trick. All he knew was that he wanted to be free. As the questioning unfolded, more friendly now but still searching, he worked hard to be helpful, volunteering details of his private life with collaborative eagerness. He began to talk freely, hoping that it was what they wanted. He tried to express what he thought was a suitable loyalty, modest but undivided, to Crown, Church and State. At one point Philip grew bolder and countered with his own question: 'Is this taped?'

The man looked at him. 'No – my colleague's record is enough.' The bald head next to him continued to shine like a beacon and the biro moved with practice across the pages of the regulation notepad.

He felt a small glow of triumph: an open response to an open question. He was making headway; perhaps they would let him go soon. The questions moved on to Stevie.

'You want to stick to your claim that you have never met this woman before?'

'Yes.' He described the telephone call in the night.

'And you went to the coffee bar where this woman, Stephanie Beck, was waiting for you?'

'Yes.'

'What does she do?'

'I don't know. She's not a prostitute.'

'Why do you say that?'

'Because – because you did.'

'You must have some idea what she does.'

'She told me she writes articles.'

'Who for?'

'I don't know.'

'For someone who has just spent some time with this woman

you seem to be surprisingly ignorant.' The voice betrayed exasperation. 'Try a bit harder, Mr. Taylor, and tell us where she lives.'

'I can't.'

'Why not?'

'Because I don't know.'

'How did she introduce herself?'

'As a friend of –' He checked: he did not want to stray across the border into Daniel's life.

'Of?'

He gave in. 'My brother Daniel,' he said quickly. 'She was looking for him.'

'Why?'

'She told me he was missing.'

'Missing?' The man looked puzzled, as though the news surprised him. 'Had she informed the police?'

'No.'

'What was her interest in your brother's . . . welfare?'

'She told me that they had been living together.'

The investigating officer remained impassive. He made another note. 'So they were lovers?'

'I've only her word to go on. She said she had lost touch with him and was worried. He had given her my number. It was the first I'd heard of Daniel in months.'

'You're not close to your brother?'

'No – I last saw him about seven years ago. I hear about him occasionally from friends or relations.'

'You don't get on?'

'It's not that so much. It's an old family row. We're really victims of something we can't control. I'd rather not talk about it. It doesn't concern you.' Exasperation crept into his voice. 'Can't you see that I'm quite innocent?'

'But you seem to be implying that Miss Beck is not. Are you trying to incriminate her?'

'I'm doing nothing of the sort. I'd never met her before.'

'And did you offer to help her in her search?'

'I'm afraid not. There was nothing I could help her with. In fact,' he said, yielding up another confidence, 'she was walking away in a fury when you arrived.'

'Then why, if you don't mind my asking, did you even agree to talk to Miss Beck? I don't see the point. Surely you could have told her over the telephone that you couldn't help. Why did you make the rendezvous, Mr. Taylor? Did you only talk about your brother?'

'Yes.'

The investigating officer slammed his hand flat on the table. Philip assumed that his taciturn assistant, who did not flinch, and merely lifted his biro from the paper, was used to all this. 'That's a lie,' he said fiercely. 'Don't lie to me Mr. Taylor. You've already admitted that you were plotting against the Army.'

'To be accurate,' said Philip, resolving to be truthful, 'it was Stevie – I mean Miss Beck, who talked about the Army. And there was no plot.'

'So you do want to incriminate her!' The officer was triumphant.

Philip ran his hands through his hair in a panic. 'Look, I'm only telling you what happened. Isn't that what you want me to do? I'm sorry: I'd forgotten about the Army.'

The officer's silvery moustache lengthened with his smile. 'That,' he said nastily, 'is why I am here. To remind you what you said – and what the consequences are.' He got up and stood over the table. 'Now. Tell me. Did you or did you not talk about the troop situation in Northern Ireland?'

Philip, confused by the unreality of the accusation, hesitated and began to stammer.

'Speak!' shouted the officer, again banging the flat of his hand on the table. 'Don't try lying to me, Mr Taylor. This is a war I'm fighting.'

Philip looked at him, the bloodshot eyes, the flushed, pulsating temples, in genuine amazement and fear. 'W – w – w we didn't talk much about the Army for long. I don't think she mentioned Northern Ireland.'

The man sat down, suddenly relaxed. 'Good,' he said, 'I accept that.' He gave a hideous locker-room wink. 'You don't look Irish.'.

Philip felt encouraged to say, 'You certainly have an efficient eavesdropping system.'

'We've had lots of telephone calls. Co-operation with the public is very good at the moment.'

'You must be very busy if you investigate every 'phone call this way,' Philip commented, almost angry.

'We're only doing our job, Mr Taylor. In present circumstances I think ordinary citizens have a right to be jumpy, don't you?'

For an instant Philip saw the burly stevedore staring at him from behind the counter, the little dwarf fussing round their table, and then the questioning brought him back to the present. The investigating officer was asking him about his brother's employment.

'He's a journalist.'

'Whom you have not seen in years. Why did you arrange to meet Miss Beck, Mr. Taylor?'

He sighed. 'I was bored,' he said in desperation. 'Look, if your wife had walked out on you and a strange woman rang you up and proposed a meeting the next day, what would you do?'

'So you do fancy Miss Beck – like your brother.' The coarse sarcasm and the officer's evident pleasure at it was finally too much and Philip straightened angrily. 'That has nothing to do with it. We met because I was lonely and bored. I must say I did not expect to end up under interrogation in a police cell. You haven't even told me what this is all about.'

But there was no answer. The officer ignored the outburst with an amused private smile and began to gather his bits and pieces together. 'Well,' he said lightly. 'Thank you for your patience. Your frankness has been most commendable. I am sorry we had to detain you. I'm sure you understand. I shall recommend that you are released at once.'

So the end was as sudden and irrational as the beginning. Philip bent forward in his chair and ran both his hands through his scalp with a yawn. He had sweated during the session and he smelt his own fear in his clothes. He flexed his toes fiercely to reassert the sensation of voluntary action and gripped the back of his head hard with his fingertips till it hurt. He straightened up, slightly flushed but confident and ready to leave.

'Can I – ?' he began, but the figures behind the desk had vanished and with them all evidence of the interview. The table was bare. It was almost like a dream. In the silence Philip heard the door click behind him and turned sharply. The room was empty. He sat on the hard chair and waited. He listened to his regular heart beat and heard his breath coming evenly again, and although he had a mild sense of claustrophobia he felt calm and relaxed. As he sat and waited, the noises of the outside world came back to him. He could hear heavy footsteps shuffling outside. The electric light was humming slightly. Far away, a door banged. Suddenly there was a scream. It rose, chilling, to a panic-stricken crescendo and exploded into obscenity and another scream, more obscenity and another scream, more obscenity and then hysterical crying.

Philip ran to the door, but it wouldn't open and he hammered until his fists hurt. The scream came back again and as he leant, exhausted, against the door, he realised with guilty excitement that he was aroused. The man had said, So you do fancy Miss Beck, and he, confused, had evaded an answer, but now as his blood pounded within him, he knew that he wanted her, which was not quite the same thing. He listened to the cry of pain and saw again his wife Jan at the moment of childbirth. He remembered the cry that welled up from inside her when she realised the boy was not living, that there was no baby noise, that it was dead. They had never made love successfully after that day, though he had tried to comfort and arouse her in other, more desperate ways. And now the tears and the scream and the pain that came to him, pressed rigid against the door, stirred in him emotions and desires that made him want to hold the girl Stevie, and feel her tears running over his fingers. There was another scream, physical and erotic, and he wondered if she screamed in love. Feebly, he banged his bruised knuckle on the door again; almost at once it broke inwards and he stumbled backwards as a police constable arrived, loud with anger.

'What's going on in here then? You won't get out any quicker, you know.'

'It's not that – it's the girl. What are they doing to her? She's screaming. I can hear it. It's outrageous.'

The constable was dismissive. 'Pure routine I assure you, sir. The usual search. These people, they put it on mostly. It's not as though it's the first time anyone's been up there, is it, sir?' He gave a vulgar chuckle.

Philip flinched with indignation but, when he found himself being escorted down the corridor to the hallway, he did not react. The screams had stopped as suddenly and as mysteriously as they had begun. He wondered if the interrogation had already started. He imagined they would be more thorough with Stevie. Her attitude invited their kind of investigation. And then, quite ignominiously, all his plans to wait quietly in the lobby for her release, to see her home and perhaps to talk over this dreadful experience together, all these good resolutions left him. He had an overwhelming desire to get away and forget the whole thing as

45

soon as possible. He was amazed at his own selfishness and admitted to himself that it came from his basic cowardice: he would be nervous to see Stevie after this. He knew he wouldn't be able to trust his reactions and his emotions. He had acknowledged his desire for her, but it left him wanting only to run away. When the constable said, 'Are you ready to leave now, Mr. Taylor?' he replied with shameful eagerness.

'Yes,' he answered. 'Have you got my things? I really ought to be on my way. If I hurry,' he lied, looking at his watch, 'I'll maybe keep an important appointment.' And he clicked his heels briskly together in a false intimation of this good intention.

They gave him back his belongings, item by item, out of the plastic bag, as though they might contaminate, and he signed for them, tracing his signature with a jaunty flourish.

He hesitated. There was no sign of Stevie. The police station had begun to fill up as the evening drew on. Now was the time to leave while the going was good; there was nothing to be gained by acts of chivalry, especially with someone like her. The embarrassment of it all. But still he dithered, craning round, just in case.

'Is that all, sir?' The man behind the desk was watching him.

He laughed nervously. 'Just making sure I had everything.'

'Have you lost something, sir?' The query was kindly, but puzzled.

'Oh no. That's all, thank you. Well,' one more glance round, 'time I was off, I suppose.' He tucked his new book under his arm and turned and walked as fast and as unobtrusively as he could towards the door. When he reached the street he checked the time again. It was nearly five o'clock.

The city was as cold as ever and darkness had come down, yellow and hazy, imperfect like a restless sleep. Philip put his shoulders back and took in the air of freedom. But something was wrong. This was the middle of London and he was disorientated. Even when he found his bearings and began to walk it was in the wrong direction. He was uneasy. He tried to analyse his anxiety. The noises of the night, the shadows and sudden beams of light were now more threatening, but that was not all. Directionless and indecisive, he realised that he did not know where to turn. He was no longer a free man. After his rendezvous with Stevie Beck and its extraordinary aftermath, into which, by his own cowardice, he had injected a note of betrayal, he was aware that he was vulnerable in ways he did not yet understand. He had lost the

46

modest anonymity that, without his recognising it fully, had always been a source of security. Although it had turned out to be a ghastly mistake, he felt exposed and insecure; he was frightened. For the first time in his life he was afraid to go home. They had his details; he could always be traced. After all those accusations, he could never feel unambiguously sure of his innocence in the eyes of the law. He wanted to escape but there was nowhere to go. Philip Taylor put his head into a dark corner of a Victorian façade and was sick until his body ached and the tears were hot on his face.

Book Two

I

He came home to the terraced house in North London that he and Jan had bought and decorated together feeling empty and alone. It seemed a long time since he had got up. The house smelt cold and unloved. After he had washed away the rime of sick from his lips and chin and fixed himself a Scotch, he sat looking into the darkness, turning over in his mind what had happened. It occurred to him that he could ring up a Sunday newspaper and sell his story to an investigative reporter. The civil liberties people would have something to say. Or perhaps not; it was probably routine now, no longer worth protesting about. Daniel would know what to do, and would have all the right journalistic contacts; and he felt sure he could rely on Stevie Beck to make the most of the story.

Already he found it painful to think about her and about what he had done, running away from responsibility. Stevie, he said out loud. In his experience, she was extraordinary. In one afternoon this strange restless woman had worked her way into the heart of his imagination. The expressiveness of her hands in conversation, the colour and focus of her eyes, the slightly breathless way she talked and the subtle vigilance of her mind, all this composed an image in his head that he could not wipe out. He supposed that if nothing had happened they would have parted on that note of recrimination and, after a few days, he would have thought no more of the incident, just marked it down as a rare signal from that other world in which Daniel lived. But when Stevie's fears, what she called her paranoia, materialised as they had done, pat upon the hour like the ghost of Hamlet, he thought, she became at once an even more substantial figure. Perhaps everything she had said about Daniel was true after all.

He went to the window and, tugging back the corner of the curtain, looked out into the street, wondering if Daniel was there now, freezing behind the wheel of his car. Philip had only found one of his contact lenses in the pocket of his coat, so he could not see clearly. Stevie's story had left him moved and disturbed. What was Daniel going through that made sense of such behaviour? The night was bleak and cold, voices carried, and the amber darkness of the city softened the wintry shadows of the street; in the distance, a night-shift was drilling the hard earth with a farting sound.

At first he had been ashamed of his cowardice; now he was unnerved by his own weakness. Worse than both was his fear of what Stevie might do. She had heard him give his address to the police. She knew where he lived. He could not escape the accusation that he had abandoned her; equally, he could not cope with the idea that he would not see her again. He was conscious of losing both ways. When the telephone rang he started with hope and anxiety. But he could not answer. It rang and rang and rang and he sat, unable to decide. Finally, he half-lifted the receiver, determined to listen in silence, but when he heard the urgent pip, pip, pip, he slammed it down in a panic.

Lying in bed later he realised that, for the first time since Jan had left him, the sound of the telephone no longer triggered a longing for her in his mind. Even though he now had other anxieties, the discovery that he no longer needed her was mildly exhilarating. After his encounter with Stevie Beck, and the puzzle she had introduced of Daniel's disappearance, the years of his marriage seemed oddly remote, like unhappy terms at a bad school. It was typical of his experience that just when he sensed a new freedom he should be so oppressed by this apprehension of the world outside.

Still, he did what he could to celebrate the mood. At first light, exhausted by his wakefulness, he was up and about, clearing away the ephemeral signs of Jan's presence: shampoo, make-up, scent, powder, cotton wool, baby lotion, soap, postcards, hairpins, and all the usual debris of the bedroom. The house was littered with rubbish, newspapers and half-empty bottles which he bundled into three large black plastic dustbin bags. Only a few bits and pieces escaped his zealous clear-out: one or two favourite souvenirs, an African mug from a forgotten uncle and the controversial ebony statuette Daniel had given them as a wedding present. Then, feeling better, he went round the house and removed all the photographs that reminded him of her and stacked them in a heap in the hall. Finally, with much exertion, he got a trunk out of the attic, dragged it on to the landing and piled into it all the clothes, shoes, handbags and hats she had left behind.

After all this effort, there was his bath to enjoy and then another laborious search through his pockets for the missing lens. Now, with everything fresh and clear again, he was telephoning. His old tutor in Newcastle was away in Houston until next term, according to the faculty secretary, but he was welcome to come any time and use the department's specialist library to get up to date on the literature.

'There've been some amazing new finds,' he was told.

He rang off and dialled Directory Enquiries. But there was no record of Stephanie Beck or J. D. Taylor.

'They've only just moved,' he said, hoping for advice.

The girl was very brisk. 'Then they won't be on the 'phone, will they?'

'No, I suppose they won't,' he said and then realised that the line had gone dead. Defeated, he dialled again, a familiar number.

'It's Philip speaking,' he said. 'I expect to be home in time for dinner.'

The road back to the family home in the countryside was so familiar. He drove fast through folds of the Chiltern Hills peeled white in the winter sunlight. He broke the journey, lunching in a country pub; he sat by an open blaze enjoying the beer and watching the heart of the fire send out shadows of heat. After the decay and tiredness of London, he savoured it all with contentment. Local people and commercial travellers began to crowd in and the snug parlour became noisy with Christmas greetings. He paid up and pressed on, down narrowing lanes, into the misty afternoon twilight. Nearing home, he stopped again, this time in the market town near the family home. In the last few days before Christmas the country people were there in Range Rovers and muddy Volvos. There was a lot of money about; Philip found familiar security in the substantial unhurried assurance of the rural gentry. The world of bomb-scares and street terror seemed very remote. He began to feel less isolated and lonely. He bought some seasonal delicacies, not forgetting Gentleman's Relish as a favourite treat for his father. Then, like a homing creature, he took the last few well-known miles north-east until he was turning down the drive to the Taylor family's small estate.

His father's housekeeper-cum-nurse met him as he carried his suitcases into the hallway. She was very short, which perhaps explained her combative approach to outsiders; her greying hair was always tightly glued in a bun, and the habitual turquoise overall did not disguise her large bottom. She was not from the neighbourhood but from Kent and had a harsh, angular manner of speech and behaviour that some people mistook for bad temper. Philip, who always felt youthful and disobedient in her presence, respected her for the tenacious way she cared for his father after his widowing.

'Will you put the motor car round the back as I always ask you,' she began in her usual critical way, 'you know your father won't have vehicles standing in front of the house.' And she wished him a crisp seasonal greeting before vanishing into the shadowy recesses at the back of the hall.

Miss Groom deputised for his mother, providing his father with housekeeping and companionship. Although she had died quite young, Mrs. Taylor herself had become estranged from her husband long before the cancer, that in the end proved fatal, began to sap her quiet, maternal spirit. Philip, passing her bridal portrait in the hall, remembered her as a refined, gentle woman who indulged her two sons, in particular the irrepressible Daniel, with faint protests of dismay, inspired, Philip had always believed, by his father's more censorious attitude. Daniel, of course, was always the favourite, and he found it difficult, even now, to curb a lingering resentment. It was Daniel who did things so well, so effortlessly and with such pride and zest. Daniel had idolised his mother and, after her death, finally lost all sense of family obligation.

Philip was always diminished by the strength of that relationship, and sought out his mother's warmth and garrulous affection with a pathetic, rather jealous devotion. She, though never disguising her thwarted passion for a daughter, drew out the tentative, divided side of Philip's nature. When the boys were children, visitors to the home always commented on the contrast in their personalities. Daniel was so certain, so buoyant. 'Little Pip', as he was known throughout his childhood, was the quiet one who played silently in a corner, unobtrusive and slightly neglected. Mrs. Taylor found in her two sons, and their complementary temperaments, complete family satisfaction. Before the crises of Daniel's adolescence, they were nourished by her subtlety and compassion. He could not remember his mother without thinking of Jan and making, as always, the unfavourable

54

comparison with which she, in their worst rows, had always confronted him.

'I'm not your fucking mother,' she had screamed, 'and I don't want to be.'

Inside, the old house was as he remembered, profoundly English in its austere Quaker way. There was an expression of sobriety, thrift and philanthropy in every aspect of the building: the white-oak plainness of the furniture, the boxes for Oxfam and the Blind in the window by the front door, the latest edition of *The Friend* on the library table and the family portraits ranged up the staircase, faces from the past coloured in the black and grey and parchment white of their preference. There was no elegance, just unadorned humility in every line and wrinkle. To outsiders they must have seemed bloodless and a bit awkward, peculiar people with ascetic tastes and disturbing religious practices, at once fervent and spontaneous, qualities that threatened the secular arrogance of the society from which they were excluded. Most of that had been lost now; all that was left were the outward signs, empty collecting boxes and unread periodicals.

It was a landscape cluttered with childish memories. Here he had been born, brought up and launched into the world; he had known nothing else; for him it had been complete and fully-integrated, a way of life and a point of perspective, assured, stable and well-off. Those days, it seemed, were always green and summery, and the cool house, friendly with household noises, an escape from the heat and violence of the countryside in which he and Daniel had grown up. Now, in winter, the place was cold and dreary and the past a painful memory. There was a smell of damp; and the lights were low.

He found his father sitting by a single lamp in the shadowy drawing-room. He was reading *Three Men In A Boat*, a book he knew almost by heart.

'Hello, father,' he said, crossing the threshold like a schoolboy.

The old man started and looked up. 'Oh, hullo, Pip. Term over?' It was his repeated joke that Philip's college worked short terms, short hours and short time and that its bias towards the Arts was contributing to the ruin of the country.

Mr. Taylor senior had been a brute of a man, with a face furrowed and raw as if rubbed with sandpaper. His coarse hair was cropped close to a square discoloured skull. His barking conversational manner spoke of time spent in the butts and of giving orders to the tenants. He was commanding and decisive in a way that Philip partly envied. He was an old man now, forgetful, slower, but made more intransigent by his infirmities, more irresponsible and impervious by his age. Philip was always touched, saddened and infuriated by his father. Their conversations were distant and awkward.

'Yes,' he replied rather sharply. 'Don't you know it's nearly Christmas? I called this morning. Didn't Miss Groom tell you?'

The old man looked at him half vacant, half contemptuous. 'Did she? I expect she did. I don't know, old boy. I can't be expected to remember every trivial damn detail at my age.' He became more searching. 'Well, what are you doing here? Where's—where's whatshername?' He flicked her fingers in the way that Philip recognised so well, and turned back to his book.

'I – I – I've come here for the break,' he stuttered evasively. 'To get away. I need a rest.' He heard himself with a premonitory foreboding falling into his usual relationship with his father. It was a bond long ago worn ragged by the old man's bitter disappointment at his sons' rejection of the family business. It was ridiculous standing there in the middle of the parquet like a naughty boy, but the sofas were shrouded and the chilly room unwelcoming.

'Oh,' said his father without looking up, and went on reading.

'What are you reading, father?'

'What's that?'

'Nothing, father. I asked what you were reading. It doesn't matter.'

The old man twitched crossly and settled back in his chair. 'The same silly damn nonsense. *Three Men In A Boat*. I don't know, it makes me laugh . . .' He gave an almost inaudible grunt and turned the page. The floor creaked as Philip moved away to his room. Nothing ever changed though he always returned home hoping. He was glad he hadn't been interrogated about Jan.

Before dinner, over a single glass of Bristol Cream in honour of the season, his father became almost benign. He was wearing his threadbare smoking jacket, a family heirloom, and his cheeks glowed ruddy in the firelight.

'A good journey up, I hope?'

Philip, to distract the conversation, plunged into a long account of his drive and his visit to the local town, mentioning whom he'd seen and what he'd noticed with a desperate cheerfulness. But after a few minutes Philip's garrulous talk dried up and an uneasy lull intervened.

'Is—is your wife coming down?' the old man asked in his stiff, formal way. 'I take it she's still putting on her party frock upstairs. If she doesn't hurry, she'll miss the soup.'

Philip drained his glass. 'Father,' he said, 'Jan's left me.' He stood up. It gave him courage to be able to look down on the bulky figure propped in the club chair.

The old man seemed not to have taken in the news. 'It looks like you've left her, Philip,' he said cruelly. 'What are you doing here? I'm all washed up with a housekeeper and a heap of pills and no wife to look after me any more. You don't want to be coming here. What's happened to you?'

'I've told you. I'm all alone. She's gone. I don't know what to do.'

'She'll come back. They always do.'

He realised that his father couldn't know about the source of his indecision, the strange meeting with Stevie Beck, and could only misattribute his son's vacillation to Jan's departure. He turned away to the fire, unable to go on. There was always so much unsaid. Old Daniel Taylor's famous will and testament was as ever hanging in its plain wooden frame. Philip's eye traced the sloping letters and he remembered his father, younger and more vigorous, pointing at the words in a fury while Daniel, the reprobate, stood and looked out of the window. 'It is my will and mind, that in case my son, Daniel Taylor, when he cometh to years of discretion, incline to betake himself to ye study and practice of physic, that he bee putt betimmes to a good apothecary, in a country town, with one of our profession of religion, if possible, where they have a deal of business for making up of doctor's bills, and for visiting of patients, for three or four years, after which time I would have him frequent some good hospital, where hee may see and learne surgery and the difficult operations belonging to it.' The seal was like a scab; the signature a firm black ligature. Next to the fireplace Daniel Taylor's apothecary's library, Keil's *Anatomy*, Munro on Bones, Douglas on Muscles, Winslow's *Anatomy*, Shaw's *Practice of Physic*, stood in dusty leather columns as they always had.

The old man was speaking again. He could see Philip fingering the battered spines. 'Are you ashamed then?' he demanded. 'You ought to be.'

'You know nothing about it, father,' he replied, vehement and suppressed. 'Nothing.'

The gong sounded for dinner and the old man began to heave himself with a huge effort to his feet. Philip half moved to help and then drew back; the blood-tie had been flouted too often by sarcasm and indifference. He kept his reserve. His father began to totter across the bare oak floor.

'You understand that I won't have a divorce in the family. You realise that, I hope. The Taylor family has still some reputation to keep up.' The tapping of his stick emphasised his words.

There was no point in arguing. 'Yes, father,' he said. He was in no hurry to re-marry.

Grace was said and they ate in silence. After a few minutes his father began, with a rather wooden attempt to lay aside this outburst. 'Tell me, Philip. What went wrong?' He gave a peremptory shake to a small silver handbell.

It was bad timing. The housekeeper came in to remove their plates, bring in cheese and pour more water from the cracked green jug; when the conversation could resume in privacy the right moment had passed. Philip could no longer bring himself to say what was in his mind. To almost anyone else he would have talked about his plans to sell the house – his house, he thought with pride. He was going to get a flat and live near the West End, Ladbroke Grove perhaps or the South Bank. He would look up old friends, take a ski-ing holiday, have a good time for a change, go and see some plays, exhibitions – that sort of thing. He hadn't had a meal in a restaurant for over a year. He was out of touch, he knew. After Stevie he realised how restricted he'd become. But, surrounded by the simplicity and frugality of his father's house, he could find no candour in himself. Philip's was not a world the old man would know anything about. He would have to carry on with his customary deceptions. It was better that way. So instead he said: 'I shall make the best of it. I miss her of course. It's a peculiarly devastating kind of failure. But I'm beginning to come out of the worst now.'

The old man became frank momentarily. 'Your mother and I – we had our ups and downs. I don't pretend otherwise.'

'It's not like that,' Philip countered. He saw now that his father as usual wanted to give him advice, drawn from his own experience. He didn't want advice: he was doing fine on his own. 'I'm getting over it,' he said quite cheerfully. 'I'll have a good time and forget. I'm only thirty. I'll put the past behind me and start again.'

His father looked at him. 'So what are you doing here?'

Philip felt hurt to have his dreams betrayed so swiftly. He regretted his lies, but he could never tell of the events that had driven him away from London.

'I'm taking a break first. A short holiday – it's Christmas. There are one or two things . . .'

'You're hiding, Philip.' The old man was as stern and peremptory as ever. 'I've seen you do it before. You're afraid of London. You can't face your friends. You're running away from your responsibilities.' Although his words were slow and uncertain, his father spoke with typical bluntness. Philip recognised that there was some truth in the accusation, though not in the sense intended, and was crushed into silence by it. The old man was taunting him. 'You've never faced things, Philip. Ever since I can remember, you've run away from your duty.' It was a familiar accusation. He felt slightly reassured to be on known ground.

'Father – I don't think what happened to our company has got much to do with Jan leaving me.' He saw at once that his reply had drawn blood.

'Why did she go? What was it?' There was a quaver in his voice that hinted at sarcasm. 'Did you beat her?' His father was curious, Philip saw, inquisitive about the way their relationship had broken down, as though he was looking at a picture of himself thirty years ago. He resolved not to give him the satisfaction of vicarious self-examination or to gratify his sexual curiosity.

'It didn't work out. Especially after we lost the baby. It was mutual. It happens all the time. All my friends are divorced or splitting up. It's quite natural. I'm okay, father, I'm okay.'

'But you're cowed; you're running away. Have some guts.' He was slumped powerfully in his chair, a domestic tyrant with a taste for family bullying. There was an arrogant set to his chin and his words were slugged out with throaty emphasis.

Philip put down his knife with a shaking hand. 'Like Daniel, you mean?' he challenged with a falter in his voice. He had not uttered that name to his father in so many years and he waited for a violent response. But the wounded look that came back across the table told him that he too had touched a hidden injury. Shocked at his own daring but slightly exhilarated, he went on: 'When was

Daniel here last? Does Daniel ever come home? Are those the kind of guts you want?' His reckless words were cut off by a violent ringing of the little silver bell.

'Miss Groom,' shouted his father, 'Miss Groom, I'm going into the study. I'll have my coffee alone, thank you.' The heavy square jaw was turned away from the candlelight in a fixed statuesque gesture as though he could not bear to look at his younger son. The silence seemed to fill the whole room. The housekeeper was trying to ignore the situation but Philip caught her look of pity and contempt as she helped her patient to his feet. When he stood up his father was as dry and fragile as an old stamp hinge. The slippered feet shuffled through the darkness towards the privacy and stillness of the study. Philip sat staring into the water in his glass.

All his life his father had lived by the simplicity of a codified morality and, at the approach of death, his taste for absolutes was as sharp as ever. For Philip there was no shelter from the old man's caste integrity, the system of thought and behaviour that would make a shoddy private compromise to keep up a healthy public image. So there would be no divorce, and no admission of Daniel's rejection. Now, as on many previous occasions, Philip reflected that it made life both easier and more complicated. Later, in his old room and fresh from the modest luxuries of his London home, he was struck again by the bareness of this non-comformist household, as functional and puritan as its owner.

A gilded spine, stuck in the bookshelf by his bedside, caught his attention. Opening the Bible, he stared at the long-forgotten inscription. 'Philip Taylor, From his very affectionate Father, I Chronicles xxviii, 9.' When he scanned the words of the Old Testament now it was like reading a foreign language in which he had lost his fluency. He squeezed the Bible back next to the other books of his childhood, Stanley Weyman, Seton Merriman, Captain Marryat, Dickens, one or two Scots, the *Child's Garden of Verse*, the hell-fire classic *Fairchild Family*, Bret Harte and an instructional handbook for Quaker school-children with acquatint illustrations of 'The First Sabbath', 'After the Fall', and 'The Naming of the Animals'. One plate he remembered in particular, leafing through the pages for the first time in years, was 'The Temptation of Eve', a surprisingly sexy illustration of which his father, he recalled, strongly disapproved. The pages turned in his hands; he realised he was day-dreaming. Stevie was on his mind again. He shut the book with a thump and crammed it back into the shelf.

But it was hard to resist browsing among the familiar covers, remembering his mother's voice reading aloud. On impulse, he picked out *The Water Babies*; it astonished him now to think that this had been a childhood favourite. 'Below him, far below, was Harthover, and the dark woods, and the shining salmon river; and on his left, far below, was the town, and the smoking chimneys of the collieries; and far, far away, the river widened to the shining sea . . . A deep, deep green and rocky valley, very narrow, and filled with trees; but through the wood, hundreds of feet below him, he could see a clear stream glance . . .' The England of the mind, he thought, turning the edition over in his hands like an antiquarian bookseller.

Next to this juvenile library were back numbers of *Look and Learn* and a familiar album bound in mottled wallpaper, inscribed with his initials, P.R.T. He opened it on the bed. The first page read 'My Scrapbook' in childish royal blue handwriting. He turned the leaf and stared. The first picture was a studio portrait of Daniel aged about fifteen. He studied the flat grey print, remembering Daniel on the last occasion they had been together – at that party in Fleet Street six, almost seven, years ago. As people grow older, he reflected, they become more like themselves, and his mind became preoccupied for a while with his own recent dilemma – how to break out of the predictability of his own future. The photograph was full of fascination for Philip who had followed ingloriously in the wake of his brother's career, disappointing a succession of teachers and coaches.

Daniel was wearing the embroidered blazer of his school colours. He seemed proud and upright, but his eyes, his expression, were slightly insolent as though conscious of playing a part. There was a trace of adolescent acne on his high forehead and a scratch on his chin that reminded Philip that his brother, to the envy of his peers, had been the first to shave regularly. Daniel, of course, had exploited his advantage to the full, and boastfully grown a cadet moustache in the summer holidays, despite his father's fury. In the photograph his arms were snugly folded and, as he looked, Philip could see a signet ring glinting on one half-hidden finger. Rings were the subject of much controversy at the school and were of course forbidden. It was typical that Daniel should defy convention in a formal photograph taken for posterity and the archives.

All that was almost twenty years ago now. He had been only ten at the time and oblivious to the forces that were already shaping his future. This was the time his father had finally ousted the Mayhew family from the board, in retrospect the beginning of the company's troubles and the distant prelude to its eventual take-over. It was a long time ago, almost another age it seemed, when the Prime Minister was an Old Etonian, and there was someone called the Secretary of State for the Colonies and someone else called Secretary of State for War. Looking back, it was an innocent playground where the children sang 'I wanna hold your hand' and the grown-ups discovered that all the time the rich and famous were like them after all.

He turned the page and there was a photograph of himself; a Brownie snapshot, slightly out of focus and badly printed, of a little boy in shorts standing by a school trunk in the drive. Studying it then he remembered with shame that as a boy he always cried bitterly when his mother took him to the school train. He snapped the pages shut. The past was dangerous. He had come to the country to escape and forget. Yet memory was beginning to nag like a migraine. He did not go to sleep easily that night and, while he was still awake, he revolved the events of the last few days exhaustively in his mind. He worried about the meaning of it all, then told himself that it was only an unlucky chance. His life had been so sheltered that he couldn't expect to know about the random workings of the real world. Then there was Stevie. Everything she had talked about left him uneasy, like the outcome of the rendezvous itself. Outside, winter gripped the land.

Much later, when he was asleep, the telephone rang and he heard himself answer. The voice was familiar. But when he called out Stevie's name there was no reply. Then he woke up, or thought he did, and he was standing naked in the middle of the room, goosepimpled with cold and fear.

The solstice dawn was a slow, disturbed lessening of blackness punctuated by the shriek of the cock crow. Philip, unrested, heard the milk arrive glassily and the postman's bicycle grinding over the gravel.

'Did the telephone ring last night?' he asked the housekeeper at breakfast. 'A girl? Very late. Did she ring?'

'A girl?' she snapped, as though he had made an indecent suggestion. She appraised him keenly across the table, breaking dry toast in her fingers. Her sharp eye and starched expression insisted that he continue.

'I thought – I – I – thought I heard the 'phone ring, that's all.'

She looked at him queerly. 'You're right,' she said. 'It did. After midnight. For your father. I had to take it of course. I will not have your father disturbed, as you know.' It was like the enunciation of a rule; she paused, and Philip thought she was about to say more when they both heard a car outside, throwing up splinters of ice as it came up fast to the house.

Miss Groom seemed to be expecting the visitor. 'Excuse me,' she said.

A single peal on the bell was followed by voices, questions, a snatch of conversation and the sound of footsteps thudding in the hall. The housekeeper returned.

'There's a constable from the local station to see your father, but I've told him he's not available now.' She spoke as though she blamed Philip for the intrusion. 'I've told him he must talk to you instead.'

'W – w – what's it all about?' Philip stammered.

'I'm afraid I can't say – I must leave that to the officer,' she said. Philip felt she was concealing some unspecified anxiety with her irritation. He himself, following her stumpy walk down the corridor, was dumb with apprehension.

A man in a dark suit, restless with the cold, was pacing hollow steps in front of the grandfather clock. He had grave classical features and natural brown ringlets that, even in his regulation suit, gave him a rather dandy elegance. Philip was struck by the suavity of his bearing and found it indefinably classy. The man's expression was nonetheless subdued, grey with early rising, and when Philip shook hands he saw there was blood on his collar where he had shaved hurriedly. Philip was often defensive about evidence of affluence in front of strangers but this man seemed incurious, at ease, as though at home himself, an impression confirmed by the quiet refined manner of his speaking.

'I do apologise, Mr. Taylor.' He gave his name and rank; Philip paid no attention. 'I have to see you on a serious matter. It's rather urgent . . .' Miss Groom was hovering behind them. 'Is there somewhere . . .' he looked about.

Philip ushered him into the drawing-room. His anxiety, soothed by the unexpected politeness, yielded to curiosity. He apologised for the dust covers and they perched, like old friends, in the window seat looking out across the lawn. Mist trailed in long scarves round the empty beeches and oaks of the skeleton English countryside. The holly tree by the window was barren as usual. Philip could not remember when it had last produced berries.

'Am I right in thinking that you have a brother, Mr. Taylor?' There was a note of hesitancy in his question.

'Yes, yes,' said Philip, with the astounded sense that his pre-occupations were being anticipated. 'So he's turned up after all. Did you contact Stevie – you know, Miss Beck?' he corrected himself. 'Of course I imagine you don't need to, really. He's quite capable of looking after her himself.'

'I beg your pardon,' said the officer, taken aback.

'Oh, I see – it's his girlfriend I'm talking about. She was look-ing for him. Rather distraught. He was supposed to be missing. Daniel, I mean. My brother.' He paused. 'You don't seem to know what I'm talking about.' A thought occurred to him. 'You are the police?'

'West Midlands division, sir.' The man pulled out his card again. 'Detective Sergeant Mountjoy.'

'Nothing to do with London?'

'In this instance I have my orders from London, yes, sir.'

Philip looked at him carefully. They were almost the same age, he guessed. 'Would it surprise you to know that two days ago I was stopped by the Bomb Squad on suspicion of being a terrorist? It was all a mistake of course, but I do think they might have apologised, don't you?' He realised he was talking too much, but he found it surprisingly encouraging to have an expert to discuss his worries with.

'The Met., sir, have quite a reputation. It's a tough job down there.'

'Yes, I suppose it is. Still, I do think they might have said they were sorry . . .' He laughed. 'Well, one mustn't be too hard, the Christmas spirit and all that. So now they've found Daniel. Well, well. Stevie – that's his girl – will be pleased.'

'Yes, sir.' His visitor levelled his gaze out across the fields, squinting like a marksman. Then he turned back to Philip and said with the same hesitant deliberation. 'I'm afraid I'm here to tell you that we have reason to believe your brother may be dead, Mr. Taylor.' He paused and Philip looked at him in astonishment.

'You – Daniel – I –' he managed to speak, 'What do you mean?' he said. 'What are you saying?'

Before he had time to organise his response more thoroughly, the civilised voice of Detective Sergeant Mountjoy picked up again relentlessly, like a B.B.C. bulletin. '. . . man we believe may be your brother died in hospital late last night . . . was brought in off the street by an ambulance . . . member of the public found him in a severe state . . . cardiac arrest . . .' The phrases, bureaucratic formulae, were a heartless, impersonal refuge for Mountjoy who seemed to be relishing the contrast between the circumstances of his report and his surroundings. Philip heard the words rising and falling, but could only half-concentrate. Wild thoughts about the past, his brother and the girl Stevie raced in his mind. '. . . no positive identification was possible though the deceased was carrying an out-of-date press card at the time . . .'

Philip turned away to hide his emotion and focussed blindly on the empty winter scene outside. He was hearing everything from a great distance. '. . . the press card was issued in Newcastle apparently. We have traced your brother's family after inquiries with our friends on Tyneside . . .' There was something covert and ingratiating about this smooth delivery, as though it might at any moment offer you some cocaine on the black market. '. . . my instructions, however, come from London. I have to request that a member of your family comes to make a formal identification.'

The words had stopped. Philip looked uncertainly at his good-looking visitor. He was disorientated and only half-believing. 'In London?'

'That is where the body is, Mr. Taylor.' The voice was slow and emphatic.

'Have you – have you seen it yourself?'

'That's not my job in this particular case.' He sounded as though he was sorry to have missed the opportunity. 'I'm running errands for headquarters today. We like to keep up the personal touch in this sort of situation.' The public relations voice purred on. 'After your recent experiences you may not believe this, but we do have our human side, Mr. Taylor.'

Philip became irrational. 'I won't do it,' he said. 'I won't go. I've been pushed around by you people enough recently. It can wait until after Christmas, surely.'

'I beg your pardon, Mr. Taylor, but our standing orders are to file a preliminary report immediately with the coroner's court. The matter cannot wait until after Christmas.' Mountjoy paused briefly to let his words sink in, and said: 'I understand your father is here, Mr. Taylor. In view of your reluctance, I must request an interview –'

Philip became defensive. 'You can't see him. He's old. Not well. Until the . . . the facts are established I do not want him . . . to . . . If necessary I shall break the news myself.'

'Do I take it,' Mountjoy murmured, 'that you have decided to go after all?'

Philip gestured helplessly in capitulation. 'I'll just finish my breakfast if you don't mind. Would you like some coffee?'

Mountjoy, who seemed glad to have the co-operation, bowed slightly in assent. Philip escorted him into the dining-room, puzzling at his stately manner.

'Do you live at home, Mr. Taylor?'

Philip, without looking at him, said that he did not. Then, embarrassed at his rudeness, he added, 'I only came back last night. For Christmas.'

'I used to live in London,' said Mountjoy.

The note of regret was rather appealing and Philip took the opportunity to work off some curiosity. 'If you don't mind my saying so, you're not much like my idea of a local bobby.'

Mountjoy smiled self-consciously. 'I suppose I'm not. I'm part of what they call the graduate intake. This is just a temporary posting.'

Philip was intrigued. 'Why the police? I mean – if you have a university degree . . .' He faltered, betrayed by intellectual snobbery.

Mountjoy didn't seem to mind. 'It's a job, isn't it? I'm a bit of a fraud actually. I went to university because I could shoot. My tutor was keen on guns. When it was over and I'd got my third, it was either the army or the police. I couldn't face the idea of the military. The cops are okay. They let me do a lot of shooting.'

'For sport?' Philip sounded alarmed.

Mountjoy laughed. 'Oh yes. Only for sport. We're training for the Olympics at the moment. Occasionally there's some real excitement in the force. I do sieges if I'm around. Like last year there was that siege in the City. They used me for that. Remember? The bank.'

'You mean you . . . ?'

'Yes. I took that one out,' he said proudly. 'It was a hell of a risk of course, but we knew he was all alone, and once he'd started shooting hostages we had to do something. The guy was as mad as hell.'

'At least you didn't use the army that time.'

Mountjoy was contemptuous. 'The military are so messy. And you get all kinds of flak from bleeding heart liberals about the role of the army in civil affairs. You know what I mean.' He stood up. 'We prefer to do things ourselves if we can.' With a businesslike shift of mood, the animation in his voice died away and he began to give directions about the mortuary in London, reading from the notes in his pocket-book. The reality of the visit intruded on Philip's mind again; when the housekeeper reappeared, he motioned to Mountjoy not to say anything.

'I have to go to London,' he told her enigmatically. 'It won't take long. Will you tell father, please.' He was concerned not to alarm the old man. 'It's to do with Jan.' The lie was not difficult and somewhat calculating; he knew that Miss Groom disapproved of his marriage and this scrap of gossip would feed her curiosity for days. When she had gone, he asked Mountjoy, 'Does she know?'

He shook his head.

'You saw I have to lie,' said Philip nervously. 'I don't want to worry father. Jan's my ex-wife.' He seemed to have a compulsion always to mention her somehow.

They stepped out into the bleak morning. Then he was shaking hands with Mountjoy, wishing him well for the Olympics, slamming his own car door and revving the engine to life. The wheels skidded and gripped. Soon the fence posts along the drive were clipping past as he gathered speed. In the driving mirror, the gaunt façade of the Taylor family home receded into the mist.

Approaching London, he followed his instructions. The hospital mortuary was not far from the river. The tide was out and the muddy black heart of the great waterway lay exposed under the flat midday light, choked, unmoving, ageless. As he parked the car, a man with a briefcase came over and said, 'Mr. Taylor, sir?'

'How do you do?' Philip shook hands unquestioningly. He was concentrating on keeping his nerve.

They passed on foot behind the hospital, dwarfed by the walls on both sides. The place seemed stagnant and unhygienic. A tramp, a woman with a blackened face and no shoes, was urinating in a corner of the building. She grinned at them wildly and said something incomprehensible. The man with the briefcase pushed a door open into looming shadows, and Philip followed him through a building that reminded him of school changing-rooms. There were more doors; their footsteps reverberated. Philip had a fantasy they were walking down the stone arteries of a fallen statue. They passed very few hospital staff.

Suddenly his escort said, 'Mr. Taylor for you, sir,' and Philip realised that he was speaking to a senior officer who was standing in the shadows outside a small blank door. They shook hands. Somebody said, 'Good morning.' Philip felt his temples pounding. Everything was happening at once.

'Okay?' The new man was laconic and professional.

He nodded, mute.

They went in. The shock was sudden. Philip, who had expected to approach the body through green shadows, found himself standing in a neon-lit room walled with brilliant white tiles. Immediately in front of him were two slabs. One was vacant. On the other was a body sheeted from head to foot. Faint pink stains showed through the cotton.

Someone said, 'All the usual organs have been removed for examination of course,' and the blood began thudding in his head. There was an astringent chemical smell. It was very white. He felt dizzy. He wondered if he was going to faint. He held his breath while the room capsized; there was a hand on his shoulder.

'I'm fine,' he said. 'Fine, thank you.' The man took the top corner of the sheet. Philip thought, if one ignored the long black hair, streaked with grey and swept back from the forehead and temples, it was the face of an elderly man, with sunken closed eyes, a stubbly uneven beard and cheeks pitted with exhaustion

68

and poverty. It was hard to recall the charm of Daniel's youthful enthusiasm. Ask for me tomorrow, and you shall find me a grave man. Death had forced a cruel repose on the face. It was like a waxwork. He looked and looked, searching for evidence that this was all a mistake. It was so long since he had seen Daniel that he stared involuntarily, fixedly, as lovers do after a long separation. But his memory froze. The face said nothing to him. The past was a blank. All that was left was a disembodied curiosity. He was shocked at his own composure. This is my brother, he said in his head, for years we've treated each other like strangers, and now I have to identify him like a stranger. He became aware that some-one was speaking again.

'Yes,' he said. 'Yes.'

It was what they wanted. The sheet was drawn over again, and, hushed and dazed, he followed the two dark figures out of the porcelain whiteness into the mahogany shade of the corridor.

Everything that happened then was incoherent and fractured. The man with the briefcase was trying to thank him for his co-operation, while his colleague was running through a routine statement of regulations and procedures, trying to establish that Philip realised his obligations towards the coroner's court. Anxious to please and anxious to get away, he tried to answer both at once, and their voices boomed discordantly in and out of the cool darkness. Nothing appeared to be taking place in any order and the rationalising preoccupations of the law seemed pointless. Then the corridor stopped and the last in a succession of dirty cream frosted doors opened. It was a small, military-looking office with wooden chairs and a cluttered bulletin board.

He couldn't remember if it was like this with the baby. Grief had blotted out everything. He had the impression that the doc-tors had coped then. This time there were a lot of documents to sign; his biro didn't work. He waited for them to rattle through the desk for another one and caught the senior officer surrep-titiously looking at his watch.

'I'm sorry,' he said, 'I'm holding you up.'

'Oh – not at all, sir.' The officer straightened up briskly with damaged pride. 'It's best to get things settled, don't you find?' He became confidential. 'You're lucky, sir. The pathologist's verbal finding is very straightforward. An open-and-shut case. No com-plications. If you sign here,' he passed Philip another document, 'you can go straight ahead with the funeral.'

'In hugger-mugger to inter him,' Philip said, spontaneously.

The senior officer was solicitous. 'The pathologist said he'd himself go terribly, sir. He was probably better out of it in the end.' It was as though he were talking about a war; Philip was reminded of the Bomb Squad officer's words.

'You haven't told me where you found him,' he said.

'It wasn't anything to do with us, sir,' the officer replied, confusingly. 'A member of the public made the call. The hospital had to send an ambulance. He died within minutes of admission.' The policeman was still attempting comfort. 'It's better that way in the long run, sir.'

'He was only five years older than me,' said Philip, more bitterly. 'He looked so old,' he added, thinking aloud.

'I see,' said the policeman, feigning sympathy. He was holding out a brown paper parcel. 'This is for you,' he explained and passed it over before Philip could refuse. 'Would you sign here, please, Mr. Taylor?'

'W – w – what's this?' Philip was struggling with his words again, unnerved by this dominant manner.

'His clothes.'

He shuddered. 'You take them.' He held the parcel out with an angry rustle. 'I've no use for them. Here.'

But the two men affected not to notice the panic-stricken gesture and started instead a farewell round of handshakes.

'Goodbye, sir.'

'Have a good trip back.'

'Thank you for your help, sir.'

'You know your way from here.'

'Goodbye, Mr. Taylor.'

His replies jammed in his mind; he nodded and murmured like a zombie. The door banged and, after a false start or two, Philip found himself outside the back of the hospital as before, with the parcel wedged under his arm. It was raining hard; he had not even remembered to bring a mackintosh. The tramp woman was sitting in the shelter of a ventilation shaft, grinning and talking to herself.

He began to walk, flayed raw by the wind and icy rain. When he reached the old river he was becoming almost grateful for the purging cold and wetness of the elements. The water was now running strongly up-river and a skinny rower in a single scull was pulling against the tide in the early afternoon half-light. The

70

bridge shook and reverberated with traffic; overhead, lost in the swirling cloud, a heavy aircraft decelerated whiningly towards Heathrow. He turned his face up to the falling rain, craving its purity.

This was not just the madness of grief. Philip was uneasy, conscious of something wrong within himself. Impulsively, he took the parcel and threw it with both hands into the waves slapping against the columns below him. The splash was indistinguishable in the grey torrent, the brown lump settled slightly in the water and slid swiftly out of sight under the bridge. Philip had a childish urge to run across and see it emerge on the other side. It reminded him of the games of pooh-sticks he and Daniel used to play together. In those days he did not mind that Daniel seemed to win at everything. Now, the later years of resentment seemed trivial. There was only this loss to think about and, worse, his part in it. His eye followed the direction of the current, downstream towards the bend before the city, and he hoped the parcel would sink. Then he began to walk again, dissatisfied and sick inside.

It was only when he was actually standing in the church, astonished at his instinct (it was a Church of England church, almost as foreign and strange to him as a mosque), that he finally recognised his unease for what it was, the sense of a relationship lost beyond recall. At first he took in the Anglican scene, so ceremonious, wordly and indifferent: there was lilies for Christmas, white and fragrant; some elderly ladies in camel hair coats were talking in stage whispers about the Christmas bonus, and a down-and-out was having a nightmare in one of the pews at the back. The Meeting House was not like this, he remembered, a plain, informal pinewood sanctuary. But, though this was no gateway to the Apocalypse, he was still disturbed: there was always the inescapable consciousness of sin. He had wronged Daniel with his silence and now Daniel was beyond reconciliation, dead. Philip experienced guilt, raw and insistent, like a wound. The Victorian stained glass was fever-yellow and framed with a gothic liturgy: O Thou who takest away the sins of the world, receive our prayer. But for Philip there was no comfort: he had no prayer, nor any way of atonement.

3

There is nothing like the loneliness of being alone at a cremation. After it was all over Philip could only remember moments in isolation, absurd details – the minister getting Daniel's name wrong; the muzak jingling of 'Let It Be' – none of which composed a whole picture. He was grateful for the amnesia; it was a remission from pain. A question still buzzed in his head, 'Are you the 3.20 or the 3.40?'

'My name is Philip Taylor,' he answered simply. 'I'm alone.'

The voice – nothing remained of the reverent head bending towards his ear but the hint of expensive aftershave – said: 'Oh goody. You're the 3.20, I think. If you come this way we can make up some lost time.'

Thick carpet he remembered walking over. And the exhausting static warmth of too much central-heating. A tiny shock of electricity sparked when he shook hands with the officiating minister. The welcoming palm was plump, white and damp.

Philip, sweating inside his shirt, knew he was flushed as well. It embarrassed him. He was afraid of smelling. Jan had always complained about his feet. Or perhaps they would think he'd been drinking.

Another distraction: the face he thought he recognised.

'Oh, hello,' he said graciously, heartened all at once by company. 'I'm so glad you –'

'I'm sorry,' said the woman with a quavering exaggerate of her heavily powdered jowls (her hat was brimming over her eyes). 'There must be some mistake. I think I'm the next one.'

'Oh. The 3.40,' he replied expertly. 'I beg your pardon.'

Then the touch of a hand on his arm; blood-red, illuminated gothic lettering, the Chapel of Rest; and the clunk-chunk of a heavy door closing. The silence of prayer and forgetfulness: bare pine, white buds and a mid-Atlantic voice ploughing through the cadences of the Anglican service, getting the name wrong.

On the way out he stopped the minister. 'Thank you,' he said. 'David would have been so happy.'

'I'm sure he was with us,' the pastor replied, looking at his watch. His lips were very red. 'Were you the 3.20 or the 3.40?' he queried anxiously again.

'The 3.20.'

'Thank God for that. At last I'm on schedule,' he sighed, pronouncing it sked-yule. Then, touched by Philip's gratitude, he became confidential. 'Those people upstairs, they never give you enough time.' The very red lips pursed in irritation. 'Christmas is always bad and just now it's worse than ever. We had a fire, yes, a fire would you believe, only last week. Chapel Three is out of service.' The voice giggled knowingly but Philip missed the point. 'It was rather awful really,' the minister went on. 'The fire brigade thought it was all a huge joke and, by the time we'd convinced them it was a bona fide call, Chapel Three was gutted. There's going to be a terrible backlog after the holiday.'

Outside, watching the empty hearse drive away, Philip felt the beginnings of relief coming over him. He remembered, from their baby, that he'd dealt with the worst part. After the hassles of the last few days, he could handle everything else from home. The car started at once; he let out the clutch and shot backwards into the shiny side of a Jaguar. He looked round. There was no one about. Time's winged chariots, he thought, and drove home at furious speed with gears grinding. He didn't have a biro on him anyway, he concluded in self-justification, feeling in his pocket for the door keys.

The doorbell rang while he was changing out of his dark suit, the one his mother had given him for interviews, years ago when it was clear that, like Daniel, he was not interested in Mayhew & Taylor after the take-over. His first reaction to the ringing was that after all someone had taken his number down and told the police. Careful not to make any noise, he went to the top of the landing. There was no sign of life in the rest of the house. Although it was almost dark he had not yet switched on any lights: with his weak eyes he always preferred the shadows. The bell pealed again, longer this time and more insistent. He crouched down inside the bedroom ridiculously, not moving. They must know he was around. The car was parked in the street outside. Then he heard the click of the gate and footsteps, light and feminine, tapping away down the street. He was getting what Stevie called paranoid. Several minutes passed before he went cautiously downstairs in his socks into the hall. It was quite dark now. No sound or movement disturbed the silence around him. He turned the latch and pulled gently. The door gave a slight thud but did not yield. He'd forgotten that after Jan had gone he'd taken to bolting it as well. He slid the bolts back and pulled again. Sitting on the doorstep was a large square parcel wrapped in Christmas paper.

There was a perky greetings card attached with tinselly string and, trying not to disturb the box, he gingerly prised it open with his forefinger. 'To Philip. Happy Christmas. Love Jan.'

It was not yet Christmas Day. He had always found the traditions comforting: so he put the gaudy parcel, unopened, on the table in the sitting-room. It was quite heavy, but, to his boyish curiosity, it did not stir or rattle in his hands.

'How nice. A present,' he said aloud; he would save unwrapping it until the morning, then Christmas would be like it always was. With all the complications of the past week – solicitors, bank managers and undertakers – he had quite forgotten about Christmas presents for anyone. He wondered if it would seem contrived to dash out and get Jan something in return. He knew he would be too embarrassed to deliver it. He hesitated. There was always flowers.

The woman in the Interflora was sorry, but the first date they could deliver was after the holiday, and besides there were no blooms worth speaking of at this stage.

'You've left it very late, dear,' she said, looking at Philip sadly. 'It is Christmas Eve, you know.'

'I know,' he said. 'It was only an afterthought,' he explained, backing out into the street. He hated shopping, especially when it seemed to expose his emotions; he was glad the undertakers had taken care of Daniel's wreath.

He came home through a gloomy fog. All the other houses in the street showed twinkling festive lighting, red and green and yellow, and when he slammed the car door he caught the distant sound of music and singing. The faint notes grew stronger. Carol singers were horsing about down the street, laughing and shouting. Philip stepped on to his doorstep to watch them go past. They did not seem to be stopping much and their voices were ragged and broken. When they came nearer he saw that it was a group of about a dozen, girls and men, bellowing tunelessly and shaking their money boxes like percussion instruments in time to the rhythm:

O come all ye faithful
Joyful and triumphant
O come ye, O come ye, to Bethlehem.

As they drew level, he saw that the carol singers were drunk, and stood in the shadows to avoid a confrontation. They staggered on down the street, shouting and singing.

At his desk again, there was the bureaucracy of untimely death to cope with: solicitors, hospital authorities, the police and documents from yesterday's coroner's court. All the assurances had been good; there were no complications. The eventual verdict would be a formality. Cardiac arrest. It had all gone more smoothly than he had feared, even though the most difficult responsibility, telling his father, he had yet to face. He had arranged for the notice to appear in *The Times* immediately after the holiday, by which time the rest of the family, including his father, would have been informed. He had already told the housekeeper that he would not be home before Boxing Day, but had not elaborated any reasons. Now he was leaving the 'phone off the hook to guard against any more of her blackmailing entreaties. Philip wanted to get things straightened out before he came home. Of course it would not break the old man's heart if he was away for Christmas. At the end of a lifetime of disappointments, his father could easily cope with the sadness of such a temporary rejection.

Philip was always thorough and methodical with his own bills and correspondence. He liked, if possible, to sustain an ordered world around himself. So in a way these new, funerary duties gave him a certain pleasure. He liked documents: unlike people, they could be labelled and evaluated according to rational procedures. But he did not immediately admit to himself the peculiar fascination of the work. He was afraid it was an admission of vulnerability, but the fact was that, as he sifted the paperwork, he hoped to discover some hint about where Daniel had been living. Or, to put it another way, where he might find Stevie. There was, it turned out, no obvious record of the house she had talked about. Daniel, it appeared, had died without leaving a will. The family solicitors had not done the conveyancing. Inquiries at Coutts in the Strand, where the Taylors had traditionally banked, showed that Daniel had closed his account there over five years ago. He had not been carrying a credit card when he was found in the street nor, apart from the out-of-date press card, any other means of identification. So there was no immediate way of finding his new bank; for the moment Philip had left the tracing of the house to his solicitors. He was aware, at his appointment there earlier in the week, that the articled clerk who was looking after his file could not understand the urgency of the search.

'You will do all you can, won't you?' Philip had said, reluctantly repeating himself.

'Of course, sir,' the clerk was taking notes in a looping Victorian hand. His letters filled every line and the old-fashioned calligraphy contrasted oddly with his appearance, swarthy and pot-bellied, like a minor rock star. 'There's usually no problem. I'll get started on it as soon as I can after the holiday.'

Philip was disappointed. 'You can't do anything about it before?'

The clerk began to sound irritated. 'Quite honestly, Mr. Taylor, I can't. It's not a priority in a case like this, is it? The house is not exactly going to walk away.'

Philip knew that he lacked the self-assertion to protest or to talk openly about his anxiety to find Stevie; he hardly dared admit it even to himself. The meeting ended with promises to talk on the telephone in the New Year.

After he had left the solicitor's offices, impelled by the vague hope of bumping into Stevie in the street, Philip found himself walking towards the Charing Cross Road. He knew he would not have the courage, even in his dark suit, to go near Harry's again. It was, he realised, pathetic to exhibit such weakness, so instead, to justify his presence in Trafalgar Square, he turned into the National Gallery.

But for the first time in his experience Philip found that the pictures only added to his sense of loneliness and desolation. A profile, a smile, a twist of a hand, eyes, a mouth, the bending of a neck, the texture of a particular colour, the tone of cream or brown or steel-grey: again and again he was reminded of Stevie. He hurried through the crowds of holiday children to the souvenir shop and spent a lot of money on postcard reproductions.

'I'm afraid you'll be a bit late for the last Christmas post now, sir,' said the assistant helpfully.

'Not to worry,' he said. 'Not to worry.' He sounded pleased.

He had put the postcards in front of him on his desk when he got home, a row of icons that gave him extraordinary satisfaction.

It was very late now. He had finished his paperwork for the night and was trying to get to grips with a short polemical piece for the press about his experience with the Bomb Squad. The thought that Stevie might read it was a great impetus to composition. He considered his first paragraph. 'The man was thirtyish, wearing an army surplus overcoat. The woman was the same age. The place was a run-down coffee bar in Charing Cross Road. Occasionally their talk was of the state of the nation, and the role of the army and the police.' He suspected that this was not the right kind of opening. Daniel would have known how to do it.

He yawned and, looking up at the clock, saw that it was after midnight – that it was in fact Christmas Day. He poured a generous last finger of Teachers into his glass and went up to bed. At least there was Jan's present to look forward to in the morning.

When he woke again the day had begun. He went to the window and looked out over his tiny back garden to the houses across the gap: a light-bulb sun was throwing opaque white light over the still, broken Christmas landscape. He felt as unrested as ever and his left eye was fluttering still with nervous exhaustion. He looked down at his slug-white body and shivered. When he had bathed and shaved, he would open Jan's present. Later, tomorrow perhaps, tonight if he was bored, he would think about getting back home to his father.

The percolator was wafting the savour of coffee through the kitchen when he set the box down among the breakfast things. Perhaps it was a trick, a joke . . . he'd heard of estranged wives who sent their husbands turds. Under the greetings card was a label he had not noticed before: This Way Up. Prompted by the clue he tore off the paper – pink and lavender and peacock blue – and found inside a plain cardboard box, thoroughly taped. Philip ran his thumbnail quite expertly along the creases and the lid sprang open. Inside, in a nest of damp peat and moss, was a perfect baby orchid, *Laelia harpophylla*, he saw at a glance, the one she knew he wanted for his collection. There were tears in his eyes when he saw what a perfect specimen it was, sepals and petals brilliant orange and joyfully edged with that distinctive sunny yellow lip.

The small greenhouse abutted on to the back of the kitchen. It was Philip's secret garden, with pots and hanging baskets overflowing in a profusion of greenery and colour. There, all the colours of nature became intensified in the exquisite petals of his orchid collection. The greenhouse had come with the house and when they first moved in it was dry, empty and dusty. Jan – she had an eye on entertaining in style – was the one who suggested growing what she called 'houseplants', and it was Philip who found, in the miniature perfection of orchids and their sensitivity to the climate of the world outside, a natural artistry to which he could respond with interest and sympathy. Interest soon turned to fascination and now not a morning or an evening passed when, if possible, he did not tend his plants – *Cymbidium* and *Angraecum sesquipedale*, moth orchids and *Coelogyne speciosa*, slipper orchids and cattleyas – fertilising, pruning and watering with complete absorption.

He passed through the familiar wall of humidity as he carried the precious *Laelia* to his workbench. He took the rotten branch on which it was living in his thin white fingers and held it to the light, marvelling at the perfection of the orchid. This was where he could forget the violence and indifference of the city and where the pace of change was rhythmic and unhurried. He tended to think of himself as in many ways clumsy, but with his orchids he was deft and accurate. Now he took the tiny plant in its new basket and hung it where, from experience, he knew it would do best, flourish and grow.

The sun was coming through quite strongly now, and pale patches of hazy blue were showing overhead. If it got any warmer he would open one of the greenhouse louvres and stir some fresh air through the staleness inside. The *Laelia harpophylla* swung free. It would be fine there. Philip brushed his hands together briskly to rub off the worst of the peat mould and stepped out through a small glass door at the side of his secret garden to check the outdoor temperature. His city casuals crunched on the concrete and he blinked in the sunny brightness. It was a perfect winter's day with the stillness breaking as the frost melted and a few birds began to twitter thinly between the houses. As he stood and listened in contented loneliness and felt the sun warm on the back of his head, he heard a seagull cry, with a single mournful shriek, as though cut off and separated forever from the sea downstream.

The poignant sound, locked in between the frozen trees and high windows, and his own private burden of sadness and worry, sent boisterous gangs of memory racing through his mind, carrying him back to long summer holidays on the west coast of Scotland, a huge family party, picnics, noisy games of hide-and-seek, and Daniel leaping through the bracken shouting, 'Seen you! Seen you all!', a tall boy, still in shorts, flushed, tousled, grubby and exultant.

In the evenings, when their parents and the other adults played chess or read the newspapers or library books, Daniel and Philip and their cousins and sometimes family friends (the boys in the party) would go off into the pine woods surrounding the house, so dry underfoot and frightening in the dark. They would light brushwood torches and rush into the velvet blackness, exploring the forest floor. It was on one of these nights that Philip first became conscious of Daniel's seniority. He was eight then. Standing in fear among the noisy shadows, in a small dry hollow, with his torch flaming wickedly and the other boys whooping nearby, he saw something on the ground, a shrivelled scrap of rubber, a balloon.

He shouted, 'Look what I've found – a balloon!'

He was far too young for them; they didn't believe him. 'A balloon?' The boys crowded round. 'Blow,' they said.

'No thank you,' said Philip, holding the dirty scrap of rubber away at arm's length. It was certainly an odd shape for a balloon, strangely coloured.

Daniel snatched it from him, examined it, became scornful. 'Who said it was a balloon?' he challenged, looking at his younger brother contemptuously. 'That's not a balloon – that's a rubber johnny.'

'What's that?' they said.

'Don't you know? Don't you know what it is?' The force of Daniel's derision suggested his own uncertainty.

'You don't either,' said Philip.

'I do – so.'

'What is it then? Go on!'

'I'm not telling squits like you.'

So Philip was banished, his pathetic trophy snatched away and the secret shared, with uneasy laughter, among the other boys. As he remembered that humiliating moment and the seagull, circling unseen above in the Christmas sunshine, cried again, Philip turned to go indoors. It was typical, he went on, worrying away at their relationship, typical of the way Daniel had always treated him, the condescension verging on contempt. Only when his brother wanted something out of you did his manner change. Then his casual and infuriating superiority was transformed into brotherly informality, salted with sly references to family obligation and effortlessly sustained in the face of every kind of truculence. Daniel could be so winning when he tried and was always a master at getting his own way; by contrast, Philip knew well that he was extraordinarily good at drawing the short straw. At times he had been tempted to play at failure to the full, drop out and give up, but the uncertainty, the risks, had always stopped him. Now, with that wrecked face still fresh in his mind, he saw it all differently. For all its inadequacies his had been a way, painful and mundane perhaps, of surviving. He poured the first drink of the day. He had been reminded by the unwelcome recollection of the past that he had still to break the news about Daniel to his father in the country.

He studied himself in the mirror and, indefinably proud for a moment, toasted his reflection. 'Happy Christmas,' he said, swallowing hard.

4

It was nearly midnight when Philip returned to the country. Christmas was almost over. He had spent the evening travelling north along deserted roads. The light had faded from a day of golden clarity and, when the route ran through towns, he could see what he was missing in the picture windows along the empty streets, animated scenes from an advent calendar.

Now he switched out the lights of the car and sat momentarily in the darkness listening to the engine as it contracted. Silent night, silent night, he whispered. His breath clouded in front of him. The frozen stillness of the land reasserted itself, and when he stood outside, the old house seemed like a model in a planetarium, dwarfed by the heavens. He let himself in through the back door and went straight up to his room where he fell, exhausted, into bed.

'How is your wife?' the housekeeper asked pointedly the next morning. There was a prurience about her manner that Philip found faintly disgusting.

He had almost forgotten his pretext, but managed to stammer tactically and change the subject. By way of retaliation when Miss Groom came to clear away the plates, he asked: 'How is father? Did he have a comfortable Christmas?'

She told him crisply that it had all gone very well and that one of the Elders had called for sherry as usual just before lunch. 'He missed you, of course,' she went on censoriously, 'but I think I managed to calm his anxiety about you.' She was obviously eaten up with curiosity herself and could not refrain from saying: 'I don't like to pry but you won't mind if I say I hope everything is all right,' stressing the words with great significance. He thanked her for her interest and said he should speak with the old man that afternoon.

So at teatime, when the sound of the Boxing Day guns in the copses had ceased and there were logs crackling in the fireplace, Philip sat down with his father in the drawing-room (he had given instructions for the covers to be taken off and for winter roses and holly berry sprays to be arranged in copper vases) and tried to kindle some conversation.

'Miss Groom said you had a good Christmas,' he began, and immediately regretted the allusion to his desertion. 'I –I –I'm sorry I was away – something came up unexpectedly, you know.' Philip looked at his father in the amber light of the winter afternoon. Only the low flicker of the fire in his eyes and the sound of rhythmic breathing, occasionally broken by a bronchial rumbling, gave away any sign of life. The old man was wearing his favourite brown tweeds and his habitual worsted tie and looked, even in the half-light, the picture of a country gentleman, full of taciturn contentment and ease, though Philip knew from his manner that he was nurturing a small resentment against his son for his sudden absence from the family hearth at the time of traditional festivities. The silence was oppressive; Philip was doubting whether his words had got through, but then the familiar voice grated in the shadows.

'Did you find her then?'

He was startled by the question. How could his father know about Stevie? Then, ashamed of his preoccupations, he grasped the meaning. 'Oh I see,' he replied. 'No – she hasn't come back. That's not –' He broke off, unable to elaborate the reason for his trip to London. He was frightened by what he had to say. He wondered if they would ever talk again when he had finished. He was beginning to discover a fierceness in his desire to talk openly about his brother's life, a life that seemed to have been thrown aside for no purpose, that was stronger than filial piety. For a moment longer he said nothing and his father's natural impatience surfaced.

'Not what?' he asked brusquely. 'Come on, Pip. Are you in trouble?'

'It's about Daniel, father.' The stillness in the room between them was so complete that Philip could hear the housekeeper chopping vegetables for dinner in the kitchen. He had broken the spell again, the unspoken family rule about Daniel. The old man was drumming his fingers on the arm of his high-backed club chair, waiting, it seemed, to see how far his son would go.

'When I came home a few days ago, father,' Philip went on, 'you were right. I was running away.' For a moment he teetered on the edge of an account of all that had happened in the Charing Cross Road, but then his candour seized up and he began to talk about himself instead. 'I'm thirty. My wife has left me. Mother is dead. I'm competent at my job, but the immediate prospect is more of the same.' As he began to articulate the thoughts in his mind, Philip, who had found it always so difficult to confide in his parents, discovered in this plain, self-critical tone the beginnings of a mode in which he could move slowly towards the subject of his brother, and out of his own grief, the courage to speak freely. 'It's absurd, I'm sure, but I find life stale, flat and unprofitable, a fact explained, no doubt, by my own inadequacies as a teacher and husband.' He paused and was surprised to have his monologue interrupted.

'Are you jealous of your brother?' his father asked. 'Is that what you're trying to say?'

Philip was shocked and excited by the question. His spirits quickened at the inquisitive turn to the conversation.

'At school, yes. When I was at university, less so. I suppose I was coming to terms with my own limitations by then. Now . . .' his voice faded, craven.

His father did not press his questions, as though he too wanted to avoid going deeper into what his son had to say. Philip poured some more tea and threw another log on the fire.

'Our lives have grown so far apart,' he said at last. 'He – he's a stranger to me now.' It was odd, this breaking of a taboo. The atmosphere between them was highly charged; it was a shared conspiracy and they were both conscious of the fact. Philip, who was also turning over in his mind the way to break the news, decided that this was quite a healthy preliminary. His father was speaking again.

'I'm afraid we neglected you; perhaps that was where it all

started to go wrong. Your mother of course had always hoped for a daughter.'

'I know.' Philip fixed his eyes on the flames. 'I have to admit it – I resented your favouritism. That's where the jealousy came in.'

'Do you dislike your . . . ?' His father hesitated still. 'Him?' he concluded abruptly, half trying to stop the conversation, even while his long-buried curiosity dragged it forward.

'No – that would be impossible.' Even now he couldn't admit everything. 'He was – is – is – always – too winning . . .' Philip paused, blinded by the memory of the face under the sheet.

'Oh yes – winning,' there was a note of sarcasm in his father's voice. 'He was very winning once upon a time, I'm sure. Winning was what we were good at – once. It's so long ago I've forgotten. And now – now that he's gone off the rails it all seems to be rather beside the point.'

'There was no crime in not wanting to follow you into the firm,' Philip responded with warmth. 'You could have appointed managers.'

His father glared at him. 'You claim to teach history, Philip, and you tell me that I could have appointed managers! Mayhew & Taylor has been run and owned by our family since it was established in the eighteenth century. It has passed,' he went on proudly, 'from father to son in strict descent ever since. I could no more hand the business over to managers than I could –'

'Sell it,' Philip put in.

The old man gave a precise, abbreviated grunt of annoyance. 'I was forced to sell. The world of medicine is not what it was. There are too many giants. We were undercapitalised. Our losses were appalling. Our rivals were trouncing us. If we couldn't beat them we had to join them, or go under.' He spoke with suppressed bitterness.

'In the circumstances, I don't see why you blame Daniel for his indifference.'

The old man was offended. 'But that's our history. We've had our backs to the wall before. He could have brought new blood to the company.'

'Perhaps he saw that the situation was lost.'

'Nothing is ever lost. We were just an old family firm that needed a shot in the arm. When I look back on it all, I see that the National Health caused half our problems. We simply didn't expand quickly enough to meet the demand. There was the wonder drug fiasco. In the end we were swept aside.'

'It was a bad time,' said Philip, remembering.

'Your mother was dying; I was not well. You – at seventeen – you were not ready for the job. Your brother was refusing to face up to his obligations. No, I had to sell out. There was no other way.'

'I think,' said Philip, trying to soften the candour of their talk, 'I think that we all felt betrayed in different ways. For all of us a number of expectations were dashed.' He was enjoying the unexpected turn to the conversation, partly because it postponed the need to come to the point.

'People said it was my fault; they said I should have seen the writing on the wall. But they don't understand. It's not in our past. I always imagined your brother would take over when my energies began to fail. I never questioned his motivation. Why should I? I assumed he would conform in the end. As I did.' He pointed irascibly at the framed testament over the fireplace. 'There is our charter. Every Taylor boy in the past lived up to it.'

In an old country, Philip thought, the past is like genes, programming its people. 'So you let Daniel go.'

'I couldn't stop him. I tried. You know that. I'd feared it of course and yet when it came – the rejection – it was still unexpected. We were stunned helpless. You were only a teenager. There was no one else I could trust.' His father sounded wistful. 'For generations there was the discipline of family loyalty. We took a pride in our work, in science, and we had optimism for the future. No wonder son followed father like day and night. There was everything to work for.'

The old man stirred in his chair, apparently moved by the achievements of the family business. Then his mood darkened again. 'With your brother,' he went on, 'something went wrong. Did we push him too hard? I don't know. He is obviously gifted. I only did what your grandfather had done to me as a boy. It seemed quite normal.' He sounded temporarily baffled. 'You say you haven't seen him recently. It would be nice to know what he's doing these days. Perhaps he and I could even talk it over together. Explain ourselves. It's gone on too long.'

The breadth of the confession left Philip bewildered. He did not know what to say, and was left only more apprehensive at the task he had still to carry out. His father was talking again, tracking back through the accumulation of misunderstanding and family discord.

'Perhaps that university was to blame. There was no sense of pride or decency in that place. He hadn't been there for more than a term or two when he started saying he was ashamed of his background.' The old man repeated the words with puzzled vehemence, working himself up. 'Ashamed of his background. What Taylor boy has ever said that before?'

Philip said nothing.

'I knew that some sort of poison had got to him when he and his friends began taking up with journalism.' He became contemptuous. 'Tell me, what good has the press ever done for the sick?'

'You have to admit that he was good at his job, father,' said Philip, appealing to the tradition of achievement in the family. 'He was quite a success.'

'Ace reporter.' His father was mocking and scornful. 'Young Journalist of the Year. A poor sort of success that was when his winning articles made me look a fool. National Health corruption. That went down well at the A.B.P.I. meetings, I can tell you. Yes,' he concluded, 'I do, I feel betrayed.'

Philip saw that what he had said earlier had lodged in his father's mind and was beginning to form the seed of a prejudice. That was always how it had been with him. He was too much the surviving custodian of the family tradition. Only the smallest cue from the heroic past was needed to remind him to find scapegoats for the inglorious present.

Philip said: 'He felt . . .' and began to stammer, 'f –f –feels rejected perhaps.'

'After what he's done to my life's work and the work of generations before him, Philip, he deserves to be rejected.' There was a surprising amount of passion left in the old man's voice. 'I know it's all over now, but . . .'

'It's hard to forget that sometimes he could behave very badly,' Philip volunteered, chiming in with the conversation. 'That used to annoy me and then I behaved badly myself,' he admitted. 'It was always a vicious circle.'

He remembered the Young Journalist of the Year award, the celebrations and excitement. There were speeches, wine and a scruffy press mob talking their heads off in a club somewhere in Fleet Street. Daniel had come to London only a few weeks before, a tall, fast-talking energetic person with all the self-confidence of someone who is on to a winning streak. But already, thinking about it now, there was the evidence of strain. The years in Newcastle had left their mark. Anyway, it was not as if, after his time in Africa, Daniel was in perfect health. His bloodstream, as he sometimes noted with a touch of pride, would be 'haunted by the fevers of the dark continent' for the rest of his life, and this, as Philip came to witness, meant brief but virulent bouts of malaria.

At this time Philip, who was just finishing his thesis in the British Library, kept a flat in Chalk Farm. Daniel, with a typical burst of fraternal dominance, made it clear that he was going to move in while he found somewhere to live. Philip, cowed by everything about his brother, his habits, his personality and lifestyle, did not argue.

They made a strange living unit. Philip was rather abstemious; Daniel smoked heavily, lighting the first cigarette over coffee, stubbing out the last dog-end as he drained a late-night Scotch. Philip was always reserved and thoughtful, lost in a world of saints and Latin manuscripts; Daniel talked non-stop about everything under the sun, especially his time in Newcastle, and left his quiet brother exhausted. Philip's sense of inferiority was subtly exacerbated. He would set off for the Reading Room with his card index every morning at eight-thirty, while Daniel lay in bed after a late night reading the papers and listening to the radio. Philip, who was about to start at the Poly, had no girlfriend then; Daniel seemed surrounded by women. The 'phone in the little flat was always ringing with invitations to dinner, to another party, to see a film or a play, to have a good time.

His brother had arrived from Newcastle with Kath, a round-faced, lugubrious blonde, also a journalist, who exerted a power-ful sexual fascination over Daniel and seemed herself to be completely absorbed by him. She was, in Daniel's words, 'easy on the eye, but not on any other part of my anatomy'. The cries and shrieks of their lovemaking was only one of many new sounds that Daniel's arrival had brought to Philip's tomb-like existence. But Kath, still on the local paper, had to commute down at weekends – Daniel said he would never go back to 'that rathole' – and quite soon he was launched into another affair with Sally, a publicity girl in a smart West End publishing house. Somehow he managed, by constant allusions to the hardships of inves-tigative journalism, to keep his weekday and week-end lives completely separate. Philip, a spectator in all this, found himself more and more in sympathy, at the weekends with Sally and, over the telephone, during the week with Kath. Looking back on it there was jealousy as well, a secret conflict that during Daniel's absence in the north had been dormant.

When the prize and the party were announced Kath insisted on coming south for the occasion. Daniel was not put out. All his plans to keep Sally away from the event and from the flat that night went smoothly. Philip watched his brother clear every hurdle with unhesitating confidence. On the evening of the celebration itself, with Kath's suitcase voluptuously open across Daniel's bed, Philip was just preparing to go out when the doorbell rang. It was Sally. She was standing in the hallway, her dark hair falling shyly across her face.

'Daniel's not –' he began.

'I know. He's away for the night. You're looking very smart.'

'I'm just off to a party. Would you like a quick drink?'

'Love one.' When she smiled her clear pale face lit up with disarming joy. She almost skipped through the doorway with a light bird-like movement that was so different from Kath's large-boned deliberate step.

Afterwards, he had no idea why he invited her in, or why he made no effort to close the bedroom door and conceal the evidence of Kath's visit. Perhaps, in the circumstances, the deceit was beyond him. Daniel's behaviour was suddenly too much. He half wanted to tell her straight out anyway. Daniel had certainly not confined his loyalties to the two girls and, Philip felt, had enjoyed taunting his brother with the evidence of his sexual power, nights out and cryptic telephone conversations. For some reason of genetic puritanism, Philip found himself offended. So now, without much prodding, he explained everything. Sally became angry and distraught. Though this was the response he expected, he did not know what to do. Her tears unmanned him. He was conscious that he was getting late for the party.

'You can stay here for a bit, if you like,' he said, panicking. 'We won't be back for quite a while I'm sure.' And then he fled, hardly thinking about the possible consequences.

The party went well and Daniel, in euphoric form, took all his friends and Philip out to dinner in Soho. It was June and there were sweaty-looking prostitutes waiting in the blue summer night. Philip was quieter even than usual at dinner, and when he got rather tipsy became morose and apprehensive.

'Cheer up, Pip,' Daniel teased him, 'it's not as bad as all that.'

He had smiled and smiled and had tried to keep up the appearance of good humour. Much later, he and Kath and Daniel found a cab and set off back to Chalk Farm. Kath was very drunk, kissing Daniel lasciviously round the neck. Philip had to pay for the taxi and was last up the stairs.

Blood and tears. That was all he remembered now of what happened next. Kath had become hysterical almost at once; Sally was as pale as ever, white with fear and anger. There had been no row, almost no words as far as Philip could tell, stepping nervous and weak-eyed into the bright light of his sitting room, just the sudden crash and tinkle of falling glass in the street below as Daniel, in a mad melodramatic gesture of self-destruction, plunged his bare arm through the window.

And then Kath was vomiting with fright, there was blood everywhere and Daniel moaning in pain on the floor with Sally pressing cushions, sheeting, anything to staunch the wounds. Eventually, a distant siren, and two ambulancemen calmly loaded Daniel on to a stretcher. They raced to the hospital through deserted streets. Only one vein was badly gashed; in a month or two he would be quite healed, if weaker in his hands, the doctor said. No one asked why it had happened and Philip was glad because he knew it had been all for his benefit. When Daniel came out of hospital, a friend collected his things from the flat. Philip, who had been privately looking for somewhere to live on his own, sold his lease and moved as far away as possible, to Baron's Court, only too glad to put the unhappy experience behind him. Shortly after that he had started his job at the college and met Jan. He had not seen his brother since.

Now he broke the silence that had fallen between him and his father, wedged in the frayed chair with age and sickness. The fire had burnt low and the room was cooling. In the hall the grandfather clock chimed the half-hour. He said, 'When did you last see Daniel, father?'

'Oh – I don't know. I forget. It doesn't matter.' The tone of voice was familiar, an authoritative note of warning.

But Philip was not put off. 'All that was years ago. Haven't you met since?'

'Why do you want to know – even if I did?' His father's defences were enfeebled.

'You can't hide these things for ever. We've kept too many

secrets in this family. There is more in the past than we care to admit.' The glassy face on the mortuary slab came to mind and the pain of it all pricked him on. 'What was he like when you last saw him?'

'I don't know what you mean.'

'Well – was he prosperous, happy, busy? Or was he,' Philip cast about for the words that would go with those wrecked features, 'dissatisfied, uncertain, a failure?'

'What are you saying, Pip? I don't understand.' Then an inspiration came. 'Has your brother been getting at you?'

Philip started. 'No – no,' he responded with a nervous stammer. 'It's just that I'm curious.' He gave an ineffectual laugh. 'I suppose it's loneliness that does it,' he disclaimed. He turned away to poke the fire. 'I've told you. I've not seen Daniel since he got that prize.' Then, feeling that he was protesting too much, he stopped. He couldn't go on. The embers in the grate blazed briefly, throwing lurid shadows across their faces. Then the old man was speaking, voluntarily, in a broken monotone, as though in a trance.

'Yes, I did see him. It's an occasion I'd rather forget, but if I tell you now, perhaps you'll leave the subject alone.' It was typical of his father to request a trade-off. 'It was after I sold out. I was still on the board, *ex officio*. The new people came to me. The press department was getting worried, they said. There were these stories appearing in the newspapers. It was . . . your brother's work of course, though most of it was unattributed. They asked me to intervene. I refused. The share value fell. I realised I had to do something. I wrote. He refused to talk. I wrote again. A telegram came. It said nothing, just a time to meet and the name of an hotel. A First Day.'

Philip listened without comment. He sensed in his father's old-fashioned usage the terrible humiliation of his brother's demand. His father was a devout, if mechanical Meeting House-goer and the idea of a Sunday rendezvous in the secular plastic lounge of a London tourist hotel was cruel and unthinkable. 'It was one of the worst moments in my life, Philip,' his father confirmed. 'We had coffee. The place was full of foreigners. He refused to compromise. He was not my son. He was so harsh and distant. He kept on blaming us – your mother and me – for what he said was on his conscience.'

'After his time in Africa,' said Philip remembering the days in

Chalk Farm, 'he sometimes talked about little else.'

'That's what I discovered. He said many hard things about the company. It was all lies and half-truths. Medical science has its risks; we all know that. You can't have progress without risk. Africa has its place in the advancement of science; besides, it's not as bad out there as people say. There are too many myths in our business. Your brother didn't know what he was talking about.' He turned his concentration on his son again. 'You ask Uncle Ronnie; he knows what I mean. There's someone with real experience.' He smiled fondly to himself.

Philip was not interested in his father's old friends. 'After this meeting . . .' he began hesitantly.

'Oh –' his father cut in, remembering the occasion with anger. 'There was nothing I could do. After that, I resigned from the board of course. That was the end.' He paused. 'I am a ruined, bitter old man, Philip, and I don't mind admitting it. I have nothing to hope for now but a peaceful death.' He looked at him with a pathetic smile that in its day had been very effective. 'But I'm grateful to you, Pip, for raising this –' he waved a distracted hand, 'this subject.' He might have been thanking a promising manager for an efficient memorandum. 'It's good to clear the air from time to time, you're right.' He tugged at the heavy cotton handkerchief tucked into his sleeve and coughed into it thickly. The smell of Vick hung, faint and soothing, between them. 'I'll leave it up to you to get your brother to make his peace with me.' He saw that Philip was looking at him with incomprehension, and became almost gentle. 'You understand, Pip, that I'm saying you have my blessing to invite him back here. His family home. Forgive and forget. Make peace, hm?'

His younger son sat in front of him, now quite chill with the fire almost out behind him, blind with misery. Everything had been misunderstood. They had only reached the beginning of what he had to say, not the end. He heard his voice speaking as though from across a vast distance.

'Fine, fine,' he muttered, wavering. 'I'll . . . t –t –try.' He was appalled at his own cowardice, and perhaps it was the evasiveness of his manner, after the reasonable candour of their conversation, that aroused the old man's suspicions.

'You're hesitating. What's the matter? Isn't this what you want – a reconciliation?'

For the first time in their talk Philip caught an urgency in his father's questions and, already distraught with his own duplicity, it strained him beyond his limit to speak at once. He got up stiffly and went into the cold by the windows, pulling the tall blue velvet curtains across to shut out the damp winter night that was crowding in on the old house. Then he switched on a standard lamp and returned to his seat on the conker-brown fender, taking as he did so his father's hand in his own.

'Daniel's dead, father,' he said.

He felt the hand stiffen in his grasp, and the black veins stood out like a crow's. He sensed in the old man's deep shudder the haemorrhage of pain he had released. There was panic in the faltering questions: 'My son? What do you mean? How? I don't understand.' He flinched with shock. 'Daniel?' he questioned in disbelief, the name torn from his lips at last by his emotion.

'That's why I had to go to London.'

The old man was defensive. 'You don't know what you're saying, What has . . . has London got to do with it?'

Philip marvelled at the vigour of his father's spirit and, for a moment, he hesitated, influenced as ever by the strength of the denial. Then, grasping reality again, he reasserted himself. 'I had to identify the body,' he said, doggedly repeating what had happened at the hospital to convince himself that it was all true. 'He's dead. I had to arrange the funeral. He was very sick . . . and old. I don't know why. Something had gone wrong.' He wanted to say comforting things about peace and repose, but he couldn't find words that were not shallow and meaningless.

'You never told me –' his father began in a crushed whisper, anger coming out of grief, 'you never . . .' His words dried up. Philip wanted to explain but saw that it was pointless. There was a final loss of communication between them that was like a curse. All he could do was hold the now limp fingers in his own, for he saw, through his own sorrow, that his father was crying. Oddly, he felt nothing but release, even though he knew he had broken his father's heart at last and had lost for ever the refuge of the family home.

Book Three

I

When Philip later looked back on his visit to Newcastle, the course of his short stay would seem predictable. At the time, the sequence of events took him by surprise. That was, he supposed, almost a definition of self-discovery, something, in turn, that he stumbled on – the trip had begun as a way of getting away from his father.

'I'm off to Newcastle,' he told the housekeeper, and explained about the promotion of his former tutor. 'There's some research to catch up on. Term starts again in a fortnight. I want to make the most of the holiday.' He knew she wanted to accuse him of indifference and added, 'I'll 'phone you as soon as I know where I'm staying and I'll stop by on my way back to London, just to make sure father's all right.' Miss Groom had been told about Daniel by now; the shock of the news restrained her habitual severity and Philip made his getaway with remarkably little disapproval. He shouldn't feel guilty, of course. His father was in good hands; there was little else he could do now.

Before he left he rang the solicitor's office, but there was only an answerphone to talk to. Then he remembered that the place was closed until after the New Year. He wondered why he was getting so flustered. He telephoned Directory Inquiries again and asked for J. D. Taylor and then Stevie, on the off chance. But there was no record of any number. Soon he was heading up the motorway.

The university was deserted. There were only cleaners and administrators about and the halls of residence were closed. Eventually he found furnished lodgings in Jesmond, not far from the city centre. His landlord, a crippled ship-welder, was obviously glad to find a short-term tenant for the yellowing Festival of Britain-style suite before he took what he called his 'winter jaunt' to the Canaries. The room, spacious for the money, backed on to a dingy basement yard, and there were radio and hoover noises from the houses opposite. It was early afternoon, grey and drizzling, but there were children and dogs playing in the space between. Now and then, as he unpacked his small suitcase and settled in, an ice-cream van jangled past like a mobile fairground, playing the theme for 'Match of the Day'.

The university library, when he came to it next day, was cold and empty but, as promised, the literature on the twelfth century was astonishingly up-to-date. His tutor, moving up there from the south, had obviously established his new department as the centre for study in this field with all the entrepreneurial skill that Philip remembered. Although the campus did not conform to his own idea of a university, he began to wonder how easy it would be to get a foot on the academic ladder here.

At the end of his first morning's work, he pushed back his notes and journals and strolled past the silent library stacks for lunch. The place, he noticed, sizing it up in his mind, was well-equipped too. There were all the necessary microfilm and microfiche projectors. Idly curious about what they had stored on film, he began to browse through the catalogue. Local history throughout the ages seemed to be a major subject up here. Almost every conceivable local document, written or printed, from parish registers to newspapers, was filed somewhere. Then he saw that they had a complete run of Daniel's old paper, right up to the December of the previous year.

He was oddly glad to have an excuse to forget about the twelfth century. Next morning, when his head was clear, he got up early, sparred with breakfast and then walked over, well muffled, to the library. He knew now that his recent ambitions had been unrealistic; he was not a first-class historian and never would be. He lacked the insights of gifted scholars and his prose was laboured, but he was a professional who knew how to quarry archives and that was enough for his purpose, the search through the newspaper archives of Newcastle in the seventies.

He took notes and made cross-references until lunchtime. Then, after a pint and a steak Canadian, to think about the story he was unearthing and for a mild form of exercise, he went for a walk. But, first, he map-read. He liked that. His weak eyes were soothed by the rainy pink and winter brown of the cartographer's palette, and his mind's taste for order was gratified by accurate renderings (faintly coloured) of the haphazard in cities and nature.

Philip drew inspiration from the place-names in front of him.

These were the streets that Daniel must have known. The names – Bigg Market, Grey Street, the High Level Bridge – gave meaning to the bare facts of the newspaper reports. And his walk itself gave physical shape to that meaning. In the next day or two he acquired quite an obsession for walking round this dispossessed place. For Newcastle was another kind of step back in time, a Victorian city of granite sinews, sweating with rain until the dirt came running down its steep grey contours into the sludgy guts of the old river. The houses bordering the Tyne seemed bunched together for comfort, like the trawlers crowded below the Swing Bridge during storms, while the people showed the suspicious intransigence of islanders, scornful of outward declarations, especially from a southerner. The maps and the walks that followed provided a refuge from such indifference. It was as though by trudging every backway and unconsidered thoroughfare he would somehow get closer to whatever it was that gave Daniel's journalism – the fiery words he traced each morning – such force and conviction.

One day he walked east along the Scotswood Road, tramping in amazement through the wrecked inner-city landscape, past boarded, derelict flats, past the crumbling riverside wharves and warehouses standing empty and silent behind rusty wire gates, past the islands of traditional slum, the bits of street and community that had escaped bombing and the planners' bulldozers, past the latest experiments in cheap housing, scarred with graffiti and the tattiness of ingrained poverty which ran as deep and unchangeable as the slow poisoned waters of the dead river at the bottom of the hill. Another time, he walked out across the Town Moor, scattering seagulls; and the next day went across the bridge into Gateshead, looking back at the proud monuments and houses and factories crammed together in the jumble of unforeseen industrial growth and decay, and still exhaling, here and there, yellow wisps of smoke, like an extinct volcano.

At night he returned to his rooms, voracious after his explorations, for the evening meal, served on the dot of six with incurious efficiency by the landlord's wife, a tiny mute woman with a death's head expression that bore witness to a married life of devoted subservience. Later, when the television blared downstairs (his landlord was rather deaf), Philip sat in his duffel-coat by the purring fire and tried to focus his concentration on the latest draft of his article, which had now become an essay on the nature of contemporary freedom, publishable, he hoped, in one of the political weeklies.

After two or three long sessions with the microfilm collection, he had formed quite an intriguing picture of his brother's career in Newcastle. The satisfaction it gave him was quite unexpected, and it was this curiosity, thus aroused, that prompted him to go one step further and try to talk to someone about it all, just for the colour of the thing. It was only a question of one telephone call (otherwise he probably would not have bothered); when it came to being in the know one name in particular cropped up again and again.

Mrs. Coventry was retired now (and Philip knew from his investigations that she had been widowed some years ago), but she was always welcoming. He'd guessed that even from her picture in the newspaper, which was another reason for taking the chance. Of course he could come and talk to her about her record in local government. She had nothing to hide, unlike some she could . . . Was it a book? Just some research. Only too pleased to help. What would the name be again? By any chance a relation of? 'Oh, but of course my love, whenever you like, Danny and I . . .' Philip knew he had made the right decision.

He was glad, the next afternoon, to leave the library, take his map in the car and drive up out of the heart of the city to have tea with Mrs. Coventry in the front room of her terraced house.

Ellen Coventry was as generous to meet as to talk to on the telephone. 'So here you are,' she said, almost before the door was open, and she gave him an affectionate kiss, like an actress, he thought. She was younger than he expected, plump and powdery and well cared for, a woman to open your heart to. A colour photograph in an ornate gilt frame on the piano celebrated her retirement from years of service on the local council; next to it was a monochrome studio shot of her late husband, and next to that, in maroon leather, was a rather wistful, soft-focus photograph of Daniel. He caught himself staring at it and switched his attention abruptly, ashamed to pry into Mrs. Coventry's emotions. But she, fussing over the tea spread out across the table, hadn't noticed, and plunged into conversation. 'You have the family look, if I may say so, dear.' Philip looked startled and, out of habit, half began to smooth his appearance with his hand. 'Now, don't get jumpy, there's a love; I'm not going to ask you all about Daniel and your papa – though I'm dying to of course – I used to know all about your family and I don't expect it's changed much.' She cocked her head inquisitively, as though for a prompt. Philip nodded. 'Oh –' she repeated, looking at him, short and dumpy and coquettish, 'but you do have the family look, you know. Now,' she rushed on breathlessly 'sit you down – that's right, that was Harold's favourite chair, God bless him – and I'm going to give you a proper Geordie tea. I can't get over it: Danny's kid brother. And how is the world treating him? He must be well into his thirties now.'

'I'm thirty,' said Philip, avoiding further comment.

'You know,' she went on, 'your brother was very good to me, a lonely old widow. He treated me like, oh like a mother.' Philip listened attentively, affirming his agreement with his usual tentative gestures. The pictures in the newspapers he'd seen showed Daniel, in his late twenties, a tall well-made figure, standing next to Mrs. Coventry in a proud official pose. 'He needed someone to love. You don't know how much he misses his family. Oh, I know he pretends, he's too strong to drop his guard in public, but underneath he's a sad young man. He always said he wanted to be understood and he said your father couldn't do that. It's a right old muddle and I don't expect it's any better now.' She gave a silvery laugh. 'There I go again leading you on. You've come to talk to me about local government. What are you? A sociologist? What can you want to know from an old widow like me?' She gave Philip a delicious wink and pursed her lips in mock concentration.

Philip realised that he was being invited to ignore her questions. He said: 'It must seem a long time since Daniel left.'

Mrs. Coventry's bright widow's face slackened in sadness and showed its age. 'Yes,' she murmured, almost to herself. 'It's been a long, long time.' Her eyes were round and grave. 'He's never come back, you see. Not once.'

Philip said, 'I'm afraid you're not the only one to feel abandoned by Daniel.' And then, to reassure her, he began cautiously to talk about his family and his father's hopes for his elder son. 'He feels betrayed too,' he concluded. 'It's not just that Daniel pulled out of the business, it's what he did afterwards,' he added, anxious to focus the conversation on the past.

'Listen, love,' Mrs. Coventry looked at him with an understanding smile. 'Danny's a fine young man with a lot to offer. Of course he wrote those stories. He was exploring his past, finding out about himself. I don't need to tell you of all people that when you come into the world with those advantages, you want to know if you deserve them – don't you?' Philip began to stammer, ashamed of his complacency. 'Your dear family took it all so personally. Now I suppose it's gone beyond reconciliation.'

'I'm afraid it has,' he said. 'But I'm afraid it's Daniel who has refused to compromise in the end.'

'Oh, but Danny is a child of his time, dear, don't you see? We all believed in investigating things then. No one took anything for granted. The world was a corrupt place that needed a spring-clean. I'm a silly old woman who knows nothing about anything, but I found it very refreshing. In those days he was always educating himself. He didn't take much thought for the consequences of his investigations but he got things done. They loved him round here you know. He never stopped wanting to know more. I've always thought he's like a small boy in that way.'

Philip thought this was rather an apt description of one side of Daniel's character as he remembered it. The account seemed to chime so well with the photographs he had seen recently. Daniel striking poses for an audience, like a child in dressing-up clothes. Daniel in his unsmiling investigative reporter expression. He wanted to ask Mrs. Coventry about it, but she wasn't paying attention; transported on a cloud of nostalgia she talked on, her voice articulating her sentences with perfect cadence. 'He became quite famous up in these parts. No wonder they gave him that prize. He was a winner up here, make no mistake. No –' she put up her hand in a stagey gesture, 'I'm not asking what went wrong since, why we don't see him writing in the nationals any more. I don't expect you to know anyway. Don't worry about me, dear, I'm just a nosey old widow. What was it you wanted to know?'

'What exactly did Daniel uncover up here?' he asked.

'It was a local affair, though I'm sure you could find it elsewhere. Corruption among local doctors. It was a great shock, much bigger than you can understand, to a tight-knit community like this. We all know each other in Newcastle. No one could believe it at first. Have you seen the poverty round here?' He nodded. 'Well, corruption is like stealing from your neighbour.'

'I understand it was in the Health Service.'

'That made it worse again – cheating the sick and all that. I remember when they started the National Health of course – such high hopes. You've no idea what it was like before . . .' She gave a little theatrical sigh. 'Now it's just another thing we can't afford.'

'Was it serious corruption?'

'Oh yes, it was. Not all of it came out, I'm afraid to say, but what they printed was bad enough – you've read that of course?'

'Yes,' he admitted. 'Though, for all the scandal, the reports sometimes seem rather short on details.'

'But that's the point, dear,' Mrs. Coventry made her emphasis husky for effect, 'vested interest tried to muzzle the story. That's where I came in – when your brother and his editor needed political help. We'd never met. I'd heard about him of course. Folk were beginning to talk, you see. The editor came to me and said, "Ellen we've got this case." I met Danny then. He was so impressive.'

'And after that . . . ?'

'They knew me, Philip. I'm a fighter. She doesn't look it, you're saying to yourself, but ask anyone in Newcastle. I've been in scraps all my life. I love a good fight if the truth is told, especially when I know I can win. When your brother showed me the documents I knew we had a winner.' She sat up in her chair proudly, bright as a robin. 'And we did. There was the usual business; the denials and retractions and all the rest of it. But in the end at least two went down and another half-dozen or so had their careers badly stopped.'

'Quite a big racket,' Philip commented.

'And that, my dear,' she added pertly, 'is not counting the employees of Mayhew & Taylor Ltd. who got their come-uppance. Which is where your family –'

'We'd sold it before, you know,' he countered, defensive.

'No offence, love, but there was still family interest. Your papa was still on the board. Anyway there were company reps doing a very brisk business greasing the palms of the hospital administrators.' Mrs. Coventry became suddenly indulgent. 'Now, Philip, don't go upsetting yourself. I'm only telling you because you asked. It's a while gone by, and why should the sins of the fathers . . . ?' She waved her hand airily and her bracelets jangled and her heavy Victorian rings flashed in the pink light of her parlour. 'I must say one thing though. Danny had a feel for that story. He really understood it – the jargon, all the issues. Plenty of people outside the Health Service couldn't understand it, thought it was boring. It wasn't boring for him. That's how the racket flourished of course, on the indifference. Oh, he did very well, did Daniel. He deserved that prize,' she repeated, then slid forward on to her feet rather unsteadily and went over to the table. 'Now come along, dear, have another slice of lardy cake.' Mrs. Coventry poured the tea and passed willow pattern tea plates piled with food. He helped himself with civilised noises of appreciation and watched his hostess carefully lifting sugar with a pair of fancy silver tongs. Silence fell for a moment. He looked around at the fussy, decorative interior, so neat and brightly burnished that it might have been the setting for a Victorian comedy. Mrs. Coventry tapped her cup deftly, the china rang and she said, on cue (with a teasing frankness), 'Oh – now I've offended you, blabbing my head off about silly old Mayhew & Taylor. Let's not think about that. Tell me about sociology. Are you very clever?'

But, before he could consider his reply, she was rushing on, turning vainly towards him as towards a spotlight, sizing him up flatteringly. 'I was wrong you know, you're not like Daniel at all.' She lowered her lashes coyly. 'You're much more refined and sensitive I think, a dreamer perhaps. Rather complicated under that plain manner you show the rest of the world.' He wondered if she was mocking him. 'You're not married, are you?' she challenged.

'No,' he said, not elaborating.

'I thought not,' she said decisively. 'You're too easily withdrawn, dear, though I can tell you have a warm heart underneath it all.' It was as if she was telling his fortune. 'I don't expect you see Daniel much these days.'

'No. I – I – I don't,' he said hesitantly, and fell silent, reproaching himself inwardly for the blankness of his thoughts.

'Oh, but that's such a shame, dear. He's such a lovely boy – well, he was before I lost him, if you know what I mean. I'm sure you'd be the best of friends if you didn't worry about what your papa thought. Don't you think?' She gave a girlish lilt to the question and tipped her head to await his response.

'I suppose so.' He found that her torrent of playfulness made him more than usually laconic and reserved. Nor had he resolved in his own mind whether to tell the truth about Daniel.

'I think,' she went on, appraising him deliberately, 'that you are more flexible than Daniel. You know dear, it's an odd thing, but in a curious way he's quite a puritan, is Daniel. I well remember one occasion – it was late – after a meeting in the parish hall, a question-and-answer session for the local people. We came back here and talked into the night, like students. I asked him then why he did it, what drove him, where it all came from. He always did seem driven, you see, people commented on that. And I do believe what he said was the truth.'

Mrs. Coventry was talking in flutters, and the memories were coming back in pieces, scattered by age and time. 'He was sitting in my husband's chair, as you are, dear. I was just two years widowed and needed the company. Your dear brother understood that and used to come and be with me, stay overnight if necessary – oh, he was so kind – and, as I say, he was sitting there that night in his jeans and his anorak and his scarf. It had been raining as usual and his hair was wet. Very brave and wet and strong-looking he was. The cold outside and all the talking we had done at the meeting gave his whole expression a what-do-you-call-it that was quite wonderful to see in a young man. Animation! That was it – a most wonderful animation. You'll remember how many young people in those days were so listless and feeble.'

Philip said he remembered, deciding he had probably been in that category. 'People were fed up with the system,' he defended.

'Listen, love,' Mrs. Coventry replied, crisply, 'Daniel has never been a one for the system, you know that, dear, but when I knew him he had fire in his belly. His eyes had this – this kind of animal glow when he talked about all the scandals he was going to uncover. He was very honest too; he didn't deny he was vindictive sometimes. He used to say there was a lot to be vindictive about. He would clench his fist and thump the air. He'd say, "Well, we got them, didn't we? We got them there!" '

'You were saying about his motives – that's very interesting to me . . .' Philip coaxed the conversation forward. He felt excited to be getting closer to the state of mind he was trying to understand.

'Oh yes – one thing I must say, he's always in such a hurry, your brother. I hope you're not like him, Philip. It'll wear him out, I'm sure, one of these days. I used to say to him, "Slow down. You've got a whole lifetime to set the world to rights." He wouldn't have it. "Time is short," he used to say. "Time is running out for all of us. I can't wait." You always have a great sense of doom with Danny and he's such a forceful personality it's hard to escape it.'

Philip tried again: 'And that night you talked together . . .' He waved his hand to encourage the recollection.

'Of course – I was forgetting. You know how he talks; his whole body goes tense. He leans forward, nervous, on edge.' Mrs. Coventry was relishing every minute of her narrative. 'After he'd gone I'd always feel exhausted. But he needed me. You don't know how much he needs to be loved.' Mrs. Coventry's lips quivered involuntarily and her pebble-green eyes became full and moist. 'He used to call me Flower.'

'Flower?'

'It was a joke between us. I've told you I'm a Geordie. In Newcastle we always say "Flower". He knew that of course. He has the most astonishing naturalness, your brother, do you know what I mean? He isn't always very sensitive to other people, but you have to forgive him because he is so spontaneous and open.' Philip smiled wanly. 'He discovered quite quickly that I was born and bred here, and one day, when we'd got to know each other, he said, "Thank you, Flower." Quite naturally. I could have kissed him there and then. He is a darling.'

There was a heavy banging on the door. Mrs. Coventry got up with an apology. 'That'll be the evening paper. Help yourself to whatever you want, dear. Danny's paper, I call it.' She exited with a flourish; Philip sipped at the remains of his tea.

'There you are,' she said, coming back, with the deliberate poise of one who wants to be noticed. 'Danny's paper,' she passed it with pride and then noticed the empty tea cups. 'Gracious,' she went on, 'how time flies. Time for a little sherry, dear?' He accepted politely. 'Look at it now.' She pointed to the headline scornfully. 'NEWCASTLE MAN SCOOPS POOLS.' What sort of a story is that! When Danny was making his big discoveries he was headline news – with a by-line. You see, I know all the jargon!' And she laughed her actressy laugh. 'The editor was delighted. This was the time of Watergate, you see. It was good for us to have a cover-up of our own to talk about. Mind you, Daniel had to stick to his guns. A lot of people were out to stop him. Of course that only made him more determined. Cheers.' She settled herself comfortably in her chair.

'Cheers.' The sherry was the best. Mrs. Coventry was a lady who paid attention to life's luxuries.

'Daniel,' she continued, 'was fond of saying that he came from a line of outsiders. He told me your family, the Taylors, were Quakers.'

'Yes – we were excluded from civil rights for generations.

That's why the first Daniel Taylor started as an apothecary. There were no other avenues. In those days a druggist was little better than a grocer.'

'Your brother is rather proud of the family past, you know. He used to talk about your great-grandfather, the one who was so far ahead of his time and had electricity in his laboratories.'

'When you look back on it, that was our finest hour.'

'There is a part of him that wants to get back to the simplicity and certainties of those old days. I know he always says he is an atheist – but that was to try and shock me. Deep down he has this longing for a Quaker lifestyle; he knows that something has been lost and it makes him quite hostile to the present.'

'He sounds rather confused,' Philip commented with some relief.

'He's not as certain as he sometimes seems. When I knew him he was very divided indeed about some of his beliefs.'

'So am I,' Philip admitted. He was taken aback by his own candour, hesitated briefly and then continued. 'With a family tradition like ours in which prosperity and faith have gone hand in hand so successfully for so long, if you withdraw from it, as he and I have done, you feel disorientated and rootless.'

'When he was here, he was secure,' said Mrs. Coventry with pride. 'If I do boast,' she added defiantly, and gave another sly wink, her rouge now naturally freshened with the sherry. 'And, when his journalistic instincts proved that the Health Service was fallible, he found an outlet for his zeal. He's always had this deep sense of injustice.'

'Did you ever find it odd that he should use it against his own family?'

She considered the point thoughtfully, looking into the half-empty crystal glass like a gipsy medium. 'No, I don't think so. It was a very natural act of rebellion.'

She broke off as though remembering something left in the oven: 'But I was telling you about the time – I can see it so clearly – we had that great heart-to-heart. After that . . .' She gave a wistful smile and looked across to the serried photographs on the sideboard. Philip, an amateur when it came to the nuances of emotions, was left to fathom her meaning as best he could. 'Oh – I remember it all so clearly –'. As she began to recall the conversation, long past midnight on that winter night when Daniel was still a young man with hope inside him, Philip, for the first time, caught the authentic voice of his lost brother. And when he thought about it afterwards (walking back down the long hill to his car) he realised that for all her council politics, Ellen Coventry was an actress at heart, a woman for whom memory was a form of theatre.

'There he was in my husband's old chair. He talked and talked. He started by saying how he could only speak his mind to me. "You see, Flower," he said, "I can't talk to anyone at home. All father can think about is the company. In the mornings, in the school holidays, I used to go down to breakfast in the dining-room and I'd find him talking to the family portraits, justifying himself. Of course he was joking, but sometimes I thought he was going mad with his responsibilities. He had been bullied by his father and gave in when he was young. I am in the same position, the only difference is that I won't give in." And he didn't,' she commented with a tiny laugh.

'That was always the battle,' said Philip, 'to kick the habits of tradition. It happened every generation. The eldest son always tried to break away and always failed. Daniel succeeded – in a way.'

Mrs. Coventry did not catch the hint and went on with her story. 'He was very bitter about what he called the hypocrisy of your family. He talked about your mother, as always. "Even when mother was sick – dying – no one admitted it," he said. "That's the sort of family we are, keeping up appearances even if it kills us. How well you're looking, mama, we'd say, and we knew we were lying all the time. And all father could think of was the bloody export drive, or the African market. Their marriage was over long before she died, but she never complained, just did her best to avoid disturbing father. If she had been better maybe she would have reconciled us all. As it was, she couldn't and I'm the casualty. Of course, there's Pip, but he's cowed. He'll always be pig in the middle." '

'Did Daniel say that?' he interrupted.

'His very words, dear. I look at you now, my love,' she went on candidly, 'and I see that Danny is right as usual.'

'Yes,' he admitted, 'he w – w – w – is right. I am torn. I went along with the family line on Daniel, but I also abandoned the business – not that it mattered by then.'

'Can I give you the other half?' Mrs. Coventry was already tipping the bottle. 'Perhaps when you go down south again you'll make amends and look up your darling brother for my sake.' Her free hand tapped his knee. 'Promise?' she inquired, with admonitory sternness.

'I – I – I – I'll try,' said Philip, stammering.

'On some things, of course, Danny was always quite sure where he stood. When his mind was made up it could be quite frightening, I remember. For instance, he didn't believe in the future, that's what he always said. "In medicine, our business," he told me, "the idea is that people are always getting better and that if they're sick the sickness can be cured. I can't take that. I look around this city and see too many lies. So much is rotten in this country. It's built on exploitation and misery, and after the damage has been done we try to find a remedy, a national health service or a free school system. After decades of ordinary people being sacrificed for the fat cats in the south, people like my family, it's just futile. I tell you, Flower, I feel guilty here like I've never felt guilty before. All I can do is dig up the facts that will shake the system at the roots." ' Mrs. Coventry nodded at her visitor, 'So you see how obsessed he was about corruption. It was his way of proving that the past had no future.'

'Not what father wanted him to think,' Philip commented.

'That's his problem,' she replied. 'It was eating him up, Philip. The past. The things that had happened before he was born. He'd seen what Mayhew & Taylor and all the others do overseas. He knew what went on in places like Africa –'

Philip interrupted. 'What do you mean?' he asked, genuinely interested.

Mrs. Coventry seemed put out to be distracted from her happy memories. 'Oh – the usual export caper – I don't know – ask Daniel if he hasn't told you already.' She lifted a cigarette from an onyx box on the table and, placing it in her cigarette holder, lit up with a flourish. 'You don't smoke, do you?' she said, almost as a reproach.

'N – n – n – no, thanks,' he stammered.

'Where was I?' she raised her painted eyebrow quizzically.

'Daniel's obsessions,' he prompted, apologetic.

'Thank you.' She inhaled strongly. 'In the end, his attempts to shake the system were rather, what's the word, quixotic. He knew that of course – he's no fool – and it was beginning to depress him, even before he'd left for London. I sometimes wonder – when I think about what he's up to now – if he's still in journalism.

People ask me occasionally. "Such a clever young man," they say. And I don't have an answer. Maybe he's ashamed to come back.' She looked at him meaningfully.

'I'm afraid I – I don't –' Philip began, dissembling as well as he could.

'I know. You've lost touch. It happens. It's probably his fault,' she went on in a way that suggested just the opposite. Behind the fluttery pink exterior was a certain toughness, Philip realised. 'I can't believe somehow,' she said, 'that he's settled down to be a newspaperman. We all had such hopes for him all those years ago. Of course I'm always afraid for him. He is always living on a knife edge with himself. When he left Newcastle he was already disillusioned with his profession, with the words. The last thing he said to me is something I've never forgotten, dear. I went down with him to the station to see him off. We were on the platform; it was crowded, dark, and the train was a few minutes late. He was wearing the tartan scarf I'd given him. A hunting tartan: I thought that was appropriate for an investigative reporter. I was standing there not wanting him to go and not knowing what to say. He turns to me and he says: "Don't worry – you don't have to say anything. You can't say things any more. No one can. No one really listens. You can't say things any more. You can only do them." In that marvellous intuitive way of his he understood exactly what I was thinking, but he said it as though it was for him as well. Then he kissed me and the train came. I've not seen him since. There was another girl in it somewhere, that was half the trouble.' She looked at him, pathetic with sadness and sherry. 'You will let me know, won't you, darling, when you see him?'

'Of course,' he said in a strangled murmur.

'So there you are. That's what he said, that's what he believed. It still frightens me to think where it might lead him.'

'He was always violent,' said Philip. 'People used other words. They said he was impetuous or energetic or headstrong, but that was not quite all they meant. Underneath there was this current of violence running through him like an electric charge, ready to jolt things that got in the way.'

'He's born for his time then, isn't he?' Mrs. Coventry gave a small nostalgic sigh. 'That's all we have nowadays – violence. Arson, muggings, and rape whenever I turn on the box. Pointless, pointless violence and Danny, for all his Quaker upbringing, in love with it all, it seems. Do you know: was he frustrated?'

Urgency sounded in her voice, a note of pain only half-suppressed. 'Where is he, Philip love? Have you no idea?'

Her question was like a refrain; he shifted evasively in the chair and looked down at his glass. 'I'm sorry,' he said miserably. 'I can't help; I would if –' He stopped, choked and confused by his own meanness. The power he felt in the anguish he could create before his own eyes appalled him, and he wished he had never come.

'Of course you would, dear.' And then with actressy self-consciousness she said: 'I'm just a silly old thing with the world on her mind.'

Suddenly Philip saw how deeply he had hurt her with his silence. There were tears shining angrily in the powdery folds of her painted eyes. He didn't know what to say: it was hard to ignore the sudden coolness in the atmosphere between them.

'You're right about the violence,' he said, for the sake of saying something. 'Only just before Christmas I was with a – a – a friend in a café and we were picked up by the Bomb Squad as suspects.'

He repeated an edited version of the story; as he spoke he knew there was one thing he'd forgotten to ask about, and when he had finished and Mrs. Coventry had expressed her view that 'the police are often the real bastards these days', he returned to the question. He said: 'My brother seems to have had few friends up here.' He was about to go on and ask about Stevie and Kath with some more oblique inquiries, but Mrs. Coventry broke in, surprised out of her mood. 'Don't you understand,' she was quite disarming, but also slightly shocked at his obtuseness. 'I was his friend.'

Philip, who had so many private confusions in his own life, looked at Mrs. Coventry and decided that it was all true. He guessed that she had been swayed out of retirement, back into politics, by an unexpected susceptibility for Daniel's raw, youthful idealism and energy.

'You're thinking that he was lonely and desperate,' she went on, almost laughing. 'Not at all; it was a marvellous springtime for me and a wonderful release for him. We were both in need, dear.' She sounded proud, and made him feel naïve and simpleminded. 'Won't you have some more?' She might have been talking to a four-year-old. 'I haven't said a word about local government.'

There was a warning in her tone, as though she knew that was only a pretext. Philip, nervous of any further scrutiny, heard himself refusing the hospitality with some excuse about running out of time and having to get back. When he stood up, awkwardly stretching his legs, he felt clumsy and oafish as though he was about to knock over one of the prized but worthless china ornaments that crowded every polished surface. There had been a rapport, but he had broken it: now he wanted to get out before he made things any worse, at least in his own mind. Mrs. Coventry struggled hastily to her feet, eager for the cue, disdainfully refusing help. All at once he was standing on her gritty doorstep, fumbling to adjust his raincoat and extending a hand to shake goodbye. But she, with superb composure, kissed him as before and he looked down with embarrassment. Contrasted with his own reticence, her apparently natural warmth made him ashamed for what he had done, for the way he had exploited an old woman's desires and traded nothing in return.

Mrs. Coventry's purple Turkish slippers were extraordinarily vain, but they completed the picture he had of her, the star of the municipal stage. She pressed his hand with practised sincerity.

'When you speak to him – you will, I'm sure – tell him to give his old girl-friend a little tinkle for her sake.' Her face was transformed momentarily with hopeful, indulgent smiles that faded only when he turned and clattered down the steps into the darkened street. The door banged behind him. He found that he was running, but he was unfit and in a few yards he stopped, leaning against a dark wall, breathing hard. There was street noise, the sound of an early disco and his own breath coming in steamy gasps. He had shocked himself at his manipulation of the lonely widow. The tears in her eyes at the end were real enough. He had given nothing away. Perhaps Jan was right after all: he had no heart. He buttoned his raincoat more closely and went on downhill towards his car. In the darkness, the sodium lights of the city centre glowed like an open furnace.

2

It was foggy and damp as Philip turned the car down the last road through the fields. There were deer browsing in the wet grass. He slowed as the phantom shapes came up at him through the mist like statues. In the depth of winter the country was perfectly still and dead, and it was as though the deer were the indifferent survivors of some natural catastrophe. The noise and dirt of the north seemed part of another planet.

The old house was gloomy. He parked immediately in front of the heavy stone portico and, not bothering to put the car away, went straight up the steps, relishing his trivial act of disobedience. As soon as he was inside the hall he knew he was right to have come at once. There was a hint of light filtering from the study and he could hear the sound of voices arguing indistinctly. He hurried down the passage towards the door, which was ajar.

At the sound of the booming footsteps on the bare pine, the voices stopped and the short, businesslike figure of the housekeeper, her heavy bottom absurdly profiled by the light behind her, appeared in front of him. She seemed at first almost welcoming, but her manner changed when she saw who it was. Her face was in deep shadow but he could imagine her reproachful expression only too easily.

'Oh –' she said in her sharp way. 'I thought it was Dr. Young.' Her mind moved into its usual attitude towards Philip. 'Why are you so late?' she demanded. 'You know your father is not well. I need help.' The panic in her voice explained her rudeness, he thought.

'I came as soon as I could,' he explained, brushing past her with his own kind of indifference. 'Your telegram only arrived at breakfast. I drove straight down. What's the matter with him?' he asked over his shoulder, crossing into the familiar room.

The mess in the study was emphasised by the extraordinary brilliance of the lighting. The chandelier was on; the dusty brackets on the wall were lit; and three or four standard lamps, running on long flexes from power in the wainscot, added extra wattage, illuminating the heaps of documents and newsprint scattered, at random it seemed, across the floor, spilling out of filing cabinets and spread across the desk behind which, seated in his faded green dressing-gown and reading by two lamps, was his father. The old man had not noticed his arrival. Philip contemplated him as a dismayed spectator, and, though the circumstances were so different, for him the sensation was oddly reminiscent of those painful moments watching Jan in childbirth, she so oblivious to his scrutiny, he tortured by the tragedy happening in front of him. Now, the figure of the man for whom throughout childhood and adolescence he had been schooled in deference was sitting there before him, distracted and incoherent, pyjamaed like a lunatic. He put his hand to his forehead and realised he was sweating from the lights.

As Philip stood there he became aware of the housekeeper behind him. 'You must not disturb him. I have help coming.'

He took in the scene and said: 'He looks quite disturbed already if you ask me.' He gestured at the paper. 'These files – where do they come from?'

Miss Groom shook her head with disapproval. 'I don't know. They must have been here all the time in those cabinets,' she pointed at the open racks behind the desk. 'I'm afraid he's beyond my care now, Mr. Taylor. He was here when I came down this morning. I think he was up all night. He refused to go to bed or do anything I say.'

'What are all these lights?'

'He says he can't see properly. I'm terrified it'll blow a fuse, but if I try to switch them off he shouts at me and says he must have lights. He says he's looking for something.'

'I'm glad that you got in touch with my godfather,' said Philip. He sensed she badly needed reassuring.

'Yes, I rang Dr. Young's surgery this morning,' she managed to sound very disapproving. 'I said it was urgent. It's old Mr. Taylor, I said. They promised to tell him as soon as he came in. But he still hasn't come. I don't know what the world is coming to these days.' She looked at Philip as though it was his fault. 'In my young days, doctors looked after their patients, especially the private ones.' Her superior smile was curiously unappealing, but Philip, out of sympathy for her predicament, said: 'If he doesn't come in the next few minutes, I'll drive over and get him. It's not far.' He looked at the absorbed, silent figure of his father again. 'I'm sorry it's come to this,' he said, to make some conversation.

'I did what I could. I've tried to cope.' There was tension in her voice, the fear of professional incompetence. 'I didn't want to give in, but in the end, I had to talk to someone. He was driving me mad. At first I thought he was drinking secretly, but now . . .' She shrugged. 'Once he'd put the announcement in the *Telegraph* he seemed to go to pieces.'

'What announcement?'

'The usual notice of death.'

Philip did not comment. It was fitting, he reflected wryly, that

Daniel who had held the stage so much in his lifetime, should need to be seen off it with a double fanfare. Miss Groom detected but did not understand his surprise and began to justify herself.

'He ordered me to do it. After that, things have gone from bad to worse. He talks about . . .' she paused uncertainly, wary of the sensitivities of grief, 'about Daniel all the time.'

At the mention of the name his father (who had paid no attention to the intrusion) pushed his reading glasses back on his head and looked up with a disturbed stare.

'Daniel? Is that Daniel? What are you doing here? They told me you were dead. It was all lies of course. Lies, lies, lies,' he repeated to himself and tossed a sheaf of notes on to the floor.

'Father – it's me, Philip.'

His father dismissed the remark. 'Philip left last week,' he said with decisiveness. 'Who are you? Are you from the press? What do you want?'

The housekeeper interrupted like an interpreter. 'He's been like this all morning. He imagines he's being interviewed. You must try not to excite him. Dr. Young will administer the appropriate sedative.'

Philip went over to the desk, and, very carefully, began to shuffle the papers together into bundles.

'What are you doing?' the old man shouted. 'You won't understand. It's not my company any more. I don't know what went wrong. Africa was a mistake, of course I know that. Nothing to do with me. Next question?' Philip looked up from his attempts to collate the material. His father stared hard. 'You remind me of my son, young man. Do you know him? Daniel Taylor. I hear they talk about him in Fleet Street. What?'

'Father,' he repeated. 'This is your son, Philip. Daniel's not here.' He took the old man's hand, it was cold and ancient and there was very little life in it. The gesture seemed to soothe him. He looked into his father's eyes in the blazing white light of the desk lamp but they were unfocussed like a baby's and slightly bloodshot. A trail of saliva was shining at the side of his mouth. Philip felt for a handkerchief and dabbed carefully at his father's lips. There was no resistance. He reached out with his free hand and turned out one of the lamps and then the other. The old man's eyes went dim and aimless. He sat slumped behind the desk, his fury exhausted. As Philip straightened up and motioned to the housekeeper to turn out the other lights, footsteps sounded in the shadowy corridor. It was his godfather.

Timothy Young was the family doctor and a friend of long-standing, a large simple man with astonishingly smooth skin, neatly parted, sandy grey hair and large clumsy feet. He looked, Philip always thought, as though he had just been boiled, or as if he was about to lead a party of wolf-cubs on a weekend expedition. Traditionally dressed in tweed jacket and grey flannels, the country tones asserted with a subdued tartan tie or silk handkerchief, his unfailing conservative manner was matched by an accommodating, unassertive mind. His irrepressible friendliness and anxiety to please expressed itself in almost every word and gesture. He was so nice, as Daniel had once said, that you wanted to hit him. In his godson, Timothy Young's good nature often induced a morose defiance, but, seeing him now, Philip remembered that Young had seen the Taylor family through the worst moments of its decline, especially Mrs. Taylor's prolonged dying, and he resolved to be polite. His godfather was in many ways the perfect companion, steadfast, genuinely innocent of political consciousness, enthusiastic about the achievements of Mayhew & Taylor Ltd, and, as a regular Christian, unsparingly devoted to the relief of human suffering.

'Hello, Tim' said Philip, smiling a welcome.

Young seemed surprised to see him. 'Oh, hullo there,' he said, automatically putting out his hand. 'Glad you could make it too.'

'It was good of you to come over at such short notice.' Philip always found himself falling into rather formal courtesies with his godfather.

'No – no, not at all. Anything I can do. One cannot pass by on the other side.'

'Yes,' said Philip, meaning no.

'Well,' Young went on, folding his overcoat on a chair and adopting the doctor's manner. 'How is the patient, Miss Groom?'

In the presence of a bona fide member of the medical profession the housekeeper did her best to become winsome and deferential. Even before she had completed her account of the last few days, Young was moving efficiently towards the sick man, now virtually motionless in his chair. Philip watched in admiration while, in a few gentle but firm moves, the doctor took charge of his father, arranged for him to be put to bed, and assigned the appropriate treatment. Turning briefly to his godson, he promised to arrange proper nursing home facilities as soon as possible.

'Christmas and New Year,' he said wearily. 'Always the worst time to find a bed. After Epiphany . . .' He touched his palms lightly together, parting them like a priest to show how easy it would be. Young had brought a collapsible wheel chair in his car, and together he and the housekeeper – who now looked very relieved – took the old man between them like a dummy and trundled him out down the corridor.

Philip stayed behind and began to collect the papers scattered across the room into regular piles. Curiously, he browsed through the documents. There were newspaper clippings, letters and publicity hand-outs from the Mayhew & Taylor press office. Most of it seemed to date back to the early sixties when he was still a boy. All the main references seemed to be to the pharmaceutical breakthroughs of the Mayhew & Taylor laboratories. Some of the headlines described a 'wonder drug'. Then he heard Timothy Young's voice in the hall and he went quickly to the study door, calling out, 'Have you a moment, Tim?'

'My dear chap,' Young turned towards him with a pontifical gesture. 'Of course.' He came into the study.

'I want to talk about Daniel,' Philip said bluntly.

Young bowed his head. 'Terrible news, terrible news,' he repeated. 'A dreadful thing to hear, dreadful.' He widened his great doggy eyes in sadness and said soothingly, 'If it's any help, Philip, you should tell me about it.' He ran his soft fingers over his chin. 'A problem shared is a problem halved, as they say.'

Philip sat down in one of the study chairs in which, as a bored teenager on holiday, he had read his father's books, the Kipling, Hardy and Stevenson in uniform bindings, often uncut, high-minded editions bought for display not pleasure.

'There's so little to say. He died just before Christmas,' he said. 'They picked him off the street. Cardiac arrest, finally. I had to identify him. He was finished, worn-out, wrecked.' He checked the note of bitterness in his voice. 'I still can't believe it. He was only thirty-five.'

'It can happen, I'm afraid. People do go to pieces like that. Your brother always drove himself hard.' Young sighed. 'God bless him,' he said slowly. 'He was a troubled soul.'

For a moment Philip felt angry at the benign absolution. It seemed pointless. He said, trying to suppress his irritation, 'But that's meaningless, Tim. He's dead.' Philip saw that his words had embarrassed his godfather. Young's faith had no adequate response for unbelievers and no sufficient vocabulary for those, like Philip, who were indifferent to the solace of eternity.

'Look,' Young said, changing the subject, picking up a silver frame on the mantelpiece. 'Here you are as boys together, do you remember?'

Philip took the frame and noted with surprise that there were other pictures – snapshots – spread out unevenly along the mantel, as though in a hurry. He had not seen photographs of Daniel there in seven years. He looked at the brown picture. Of course he remembered. It was a seaside photograph, Camber sands, or was it Hayling Island; a huge sandcastle and a large group of people in summer clothes spread out across the beach having a picnic lunch. Philip, in an aertex shirt and baggy swimming trunks, was at one side looking cold; Daniel was standing, very proud, on the top of the castle.

'It was the company outing, wasn't it? I remember coming down in coaches. In those days everyone came and father knew them all. There were wives and children, hampers and buckets and spades. Daniel was impossible, a bumptious schoolboy. He stood on the sandcastle shouting, "I'm the king of the castle, I'm the king of the castle," and annoying everyone.'

'But it was the fifties,' said Young, hurriedly shifting the conversation into a more general key, 'people were still deferential to the boss's son. Macmillan was Prime Minister.' He looked across the room with sadness. 'The years of plenty,' he reflected.

'That was in the summer of '59 – long and hot,' said Philip. 'The swimming pool went green. Daniel was twelve.'

'He was very immature.'

'The year of the election.'

'Do you remember that?'

'Oh yes. And I sort of remember Suez, I think. We were sent to Scotland, and I remember lying in the heather and Daniel telling me the end of the world was coming.'

'There was no outing that year.'

'And '59 was almost the last.' Philip looked at the photograph. 'Daniel was still trying to pretend he was a child, running about on the sand annoying people. That was why we built the sand-castle I think. I was seven. But he was too old for that sort of thing

116

really. He pretended he wasn't. All the company people resented him. He was very cocky.' Philip found the memories coming back in fragments. 'That outing was not a success. Father tried to make a speech. He used to play his banjo in the bus going home and the men at the back always sang the dirty version.'

'And there was that row.'

'Oh yes,' he stared into the floor. 'Daniel was shouting, "I'm the king of the castle," and someone told him to shut up. He jumped off in a fury and said "Fuck off" very loudly.' Young started, and began to blush. Philip caught his nervous smile of shame, and went on quickly: 'Father was furious. He beat him in front of the staff.' He remembered wondering why exactly his father had been so cross, walloping him like that.

'It was the beginning of the end,' said Young, rather withdrawn.

Philip realised he had shocked his godfather. 'I'm sorry,' he said. 'I've offended you. I didn't mean to.'

'Please,' Young put up a hand. 'Among men . . . I know those words.' He looked at his godson. 'You're different, Philip. Is it Daniel?' He sounded concerned. 'This bitterness – it's not like you.'

'I'm still getting used to what's happened,' he admitted. He gestured to the mess of papers. 'We all are.' Young nodded sympathetically: Philip turned away from the row of photographs. 'It's the last nail in the Taylor family coffin,' he added with an ironic laugh.

Young looked at him, rather didactic. 'There is no place for families in big business now, Philip, not if they want old-fashioned roles. There are dynasties being squeezed out of industry all over the world. In his own muddled way Daniel was right to reject your father's career. As you were. There is no guaranteed place for either of you in the Mayhew & Taylor of the future, whatever that future might be. Your father should have accepted that it was time for the family to retire gracefully. I myself tried to tell him this, but you know your father,' he smiled affectionately. 'He was going to fight to the finish whatever anyone said.' He pointed to the empty chair behind the desk. 'I remember him sitting there one evening at the end of the Fifties. Things were going badly. "I'm fighting like a tiger, Timothy," he said. That's him all over.'

Philip shook his head. 'I don't believe it was inevitable like that. You make it sound like –' he hesitated, 'oh, the loss of an empire.'

'Well, so it was in a way.'

Philip glanced at the cuttings on the floor. 'Mayhew & Taylor Go For Broke', 'Will Wonder Drug Cure M. & T.?', 'Research Breakthro' Says Drug Chief.' These high hopes had been dashed by a string of failures. Philip had never known much about the ins and outs of all this: thanks to Daniel his father did not bother with his younger son. Without his brother's stomach for battle, Philip himself had subconsciously suppressed any natural interest of his own. Now his curiosity surfaced and he asked, 'Why did Daniel take on the company like that? Something must have triggered his attack.'

'Your brother's journalism in the seventies was one thing – that had its own source I think. But there was already all that bitterness during his university days. That was when it all started – when it was obvious that there was no real future for Mayhew & Taylor.'

Philip nodded. A lot of us, he thought, have been brought up with expectations that have not materialised, educated to play parts that are no longer written in a drama that is no longer performed. Daniel's rebellion was not just a crude rejection of the family tradition: Young's words showed that deeper down, where unadmitted truths are concealed, it was also a protest that the appointed role no longer existed. Now, thinking about it all, he remembered the family rows.

'It was absurd,' he said. 'Everything was Daniel's fault: the losses, the problems with the research programme, even the fact that we had become hopelessly undercapitalised.'

'Your father provoked things, I'm afraid to say.' Young was self-conscious about his criticisms of his patient. 'Even when your brother was still at university, he was openly blaming his difficulties – the company problems – on Daniel's indifference. He would break off in conversation with remarks like, "How can I expect to compete with so-and-so when they know my own family is against me." He became obsessed by it. Tragic really.'

Philip was less sympathetic. 'It was ridiculous.' Momentarily he identified with Daniel's predicament. 'There's no other word for it.'

'I suppose it was. Your father would have had to sell out or go under in the end. Yet, even after he'd been taken over and had managed to bully his way on to the new board, he was still blaming Daniel.'

Young smiled and faltered, as though taken unawares by his own outburst. 'It's a funny thing, but doctors hear a lot of secrets. Must have treated most of your father's chaps at one time or another. One picks things up, you know.'

'I can imagine,' said Philip. 'I know he could arouse very mixed feelings within the company. Some of them worshipped him of course, and always would. Others . . .' He began to stutter, 'h – h – hated him. Even when I was still at school he had become quite erratic and tyrannical. His memory was failing and he got obsessed with small details. Once I remember he tried to fire a rep. who stayed in such-and-such a hotel. And all because it had been four-star in the fifties. Now it was one of the cheapest in wherever it was and he didn't know that.'

'A great pity,' said Young, 'a great pity. Have to say this, Philip, but I'm not surprised to find him a bit distraught, not entirely with us, if you know what I mean.'

'Like just now, this week.'

'Well, yes. It's not new, you see. Even when he was still on the board he was getting pretty . . . well, mad really.' He shifted uncertainly. 'Sorry about that, terribly sorry.' He put his hands together. 'Old age can be horribly cruel.'

Philip nodded his head in agreement. 'You're right, Tim,' he said to reassure him. 'I don't deny it. And the older he got and the worse things got, the more he relied on the traditional ways, on my grandfather's strategies and practices. It was crazy. No wonder the firm was going down the drain.'

'I used to have his chaps in my surgery and they were getting frightfully shirty about it all, actually.'

'Your patients?'

Philip's mild query elicited a surprisingly defensive response. 'I know I shouldn't be telling tales out of school, as it were,' said Young hastily, 'but it's a long time ago, if you know what I mean.' He laughed nervously, as though conscious that he had revealed something of himself in an unprofessional light. 'They were never well paid, you know, and they knew it. What was bad was that they thought it was all your father's fault.' He sighed. 'It's a sorry business, Philip.'

'Particularly the corruption,' he replied, focussing the conversation on Daniel again.

Young was plainly discomfited by the word. 'Well, well, yes. There was that. One can't avoid it. I always maintain that it wouldn't have happened if they'd all been better paid.' He became confidential. 'I'll tell you something else.' He leaned forward. 'For your private ear, you understand.' Philip nodded. 'Well,' said Young, 'Daniel was used. You realise that, don't you.' Philip looked at him, not fully understanding. 'I'm afraid,' his godfather went on, 'your father had his enemies. When they discovered that Daniel was interested in medical politics, it was a golden opportunity for them to pay off old scores.'

'Using the boss's son as an instrument of revenge.'

'I don't think he knew it, but Daniel was being fairly ruthlessly exploited by some very disgruntled chaps.'

Philip said: 'No, I'm sure he wasn't aware that was happening. When I saw him last – it was at that press party for his Young Journalist's prize – he was boasting about his sources of information.' Suddenly Mrs. Coventry's recollections appeared in quite a different light. 'Are you saying that he was living in a fool's p – p – paradise . . .?'

Young became defensive; he seemed anxious not to draw too many logical conclusions. 'No,' he contradicted, 'I'm not saying that in many ways Daniel wasn't a very good investigative journalist. But the fact is that he was being used. 'He seemed distressed at his own indiscretions. Silence fell briefly. Around them the house creaked like an old tree.

'Was father aware of what was going on?'

'Yes. He was. But he wouldn't believe it. I tried to tell him on one occasion, as a family friend. He accused me of being disloyal. He simply couldn't understand how anyone from the old Mayhew & Taylor could do such a thing. He was mesmerised by his son's influence.' Young gave Philip an odd look. 'D'you know, I think there was an element of pride of – of masochistic pride in what he thought of as his son's ability to destroy him.'

Philip was not surprised. He was beginning to appreciate the complicated emotions of people who suffer, in addition to the usual discords of father and son, the burdens of family and historical responsibility in their relations towards one another. In public, his father had always appeared so confident, strong and decisive, the model of a benevolent captain of industry; yet in private he had been tyrannical and obsessive, the constant prey to doubts and fears for the future. Perhaps in some subconscious way he had become grateful to Daniel for relieving him of those dynastic preoccupations, even when in public he was bound to keep up his guard and sustain the family feud. That, too, put his father's hotel rendezvous with Daniel in a different perspective as perhaps a botched attempt to begin a reconciliation. Thinking of this, Philip said: 'You know father tried to intervene and actually made an arrangement to see Daniel in the middle of the crisis?'

Young smiled, almost beatific. 'That was my initiative, though I say it myself. The shares were falling. The board was insisting that your father do something. As an old friend, they deputed me to talk to him. I suggested he had that meeting. It was very awkward, I can tell you, telling him what to do.' Young passed his hand over his chin nervously. 'And when it failed he was very cool towards me for months afterwards.'

'I heard from father that Daniel humiliated him,' Philip said. 'So perhaps that was understandable.'

Young sighed deeply, strained by the memory of it all. 'All I can say now is that it's a family tragedy, and – looking back on it – it's one I'd rather not have had anything to do with. The past should be past, shouldn't it, but somehow . . .' he gestured vainly.

'It always haunts us.' Philip completed the sentence for him. 'I'll be honest with you, Tim, this thing has spooked me too. He was only thirty-five, for Christ's sake . . . sorry,' he apologised. Young turned his head aside with understanding.

'You're taking it on to yourself too much, Philip. If I may say so, as your godfather,' he smiled, 'you will do well to leave well alone. It's happened. That's all there is to it. I've known men and women die of broken hearts, of boredom, even of shame sometimes. Daniel just gave up. But he had a choice – once. You should not feel guilty. It may have been the best alternative in the end. Grief we all have to live with. Blame doesn't come into it.'

Neither said anything for a few minutes. The steady tick of the clock on the mantelpiece regulated their thoughts. Then, picking up the thread of the conversation, Young went on. 'You know, if anything, I'm the one who should feel at fault.'

'What do you mean?' Philip asked sharply.

'Well, occasionally I wonder if it would all have been different if he had never gone to Africa. That was very important to him, you know.'

'I suppose it was. He never told me much about it. I wasn't very interested.'

'You remember how he came down without a job,' said Young, launching into another set of recollections, 'and without much of a degree either. Student power was at its height. The Vietnam war was at its worst. There were demonstrations and protests. Daniel had hair down to his shoulders and seemed to be mixing with a lot of undesirables. You remember he went off hitch-hiking round the United States for several months with that girl, what was her name . . .'

'Alice,' said Philip automatically. He'd forgotten all about Alice; spaced-out, barefoot, bra-less Alice, the scandal of the neighbourhood.

Young seemed disconcerted by the memory too, and moved on quickly. 'And then he got involved with some draft-dodging organisation out in California. He was quite the Quaker when it suited him.' He smiled weakly, apologising for his censure of the dead. 'Your father was frankly rather appalled by him, I know, and after that disastrous experiment with law school was in total despair about the whole situation.'

'Looking back on it,' Philip commented thoughtfully, 'it's hard to see why father hoped that Daniel would take to the law after rejecting every other aspect of – of bourgeois life.'

'Well, the funny thing is that for a month or two Daniel actually accepted the idea. He had his hair cut, and bought a suit. I think he saw himself as a radical lawyer fighting injustice on behalf of the oppressed.'

'I see,' said Philip. He had been away when all this was happening, engrossed in his first year at university, going to all the lectures, the first into the library in the morning, sweating for the first-class degree that finally eluded him.

'Once he realised that he would be doing no such thing, he quickly dropped out again and said he was going to travel, take a minibus to the Far East, Afghanistan etc., etc.' Young sounded uncharacteristically sceptical of youthful idealism. 'But your mother was dying and she was frightened that her eldest son would be murdered by bandits. I persuaded your father to offer him a trip to Africa.'

'I remember that.'

'The idea was to work towards a reconciliation that way. Africa appealed to Daniel. It was fashionable with his left-wing friends. Your father got Ronnie Appleby to organise the trip. Of course, being your father he couldn't resist arranging for his eldest son to have a V.I.P. tour of the Nairobi offices and the labs in Johannesburg and so on.' Young smiled. 'That didn't worry me at the time. Frankly, I hoped it would get your brother interested in the company's business.'

'Ronnie Appleby?' Philip queried. 'I was never very clear about him.'

'Ah, but no one was, Philip. Appleby's rôle in things was always rather too dark for my taste. The first time he showed up at Mayhew & Taylor they said it was to help out with some overseas publicity material, brochures and such. I imagine it was for Africa. I forget. He was called a consultant and the company was told he had a lot of press experience. There was quite a bit of resentment from the old hands I remember.' Young seemed to be searching for an elusive recollection, and then said, rather abruptly: 'Apparently he knew it all – but that's another story.'

Philip had vivid childhood memories of Ronald Appleby. 'When Daniel and I were small we used to call him Uncle Ronnie,' he said. How clearly he could still see those clear blue eyes twinkling as he told a tall story or perpetrated some outrageous practical joke. 'All we knew at home, I remember,' he went on, 'was that he was an old friend of father's from the war. We were told he'd been in camouflage. I'll never forget that explosive laugh of his. Sometimes you thought he'd die laughing. He used to pop up out of the blue. Mother said he had fallen on hard times and that father was being kind to him. He always behaved like an uncle and brought us exotic presents, tribal masks, wooden dolls and things.'

'No mistaking he was an extraordinary chap,' Young remarked, with obvious reservations. 'I'm afraid I always felt out of my depth with him. He was very much in with some of the régimes out there, and used to name-drop terribly. He sold things – weapons, supplies and medicines. At times he called himself a government relief agent. I often wondered if he was in security. He does careers advisory work at your old university now, doesn't he?' He paused to take stock of his thoughts; he was nothing if not deliberate. 'I think he was one of those few for whom the Empire never really stopped. He was always fixing deals.'

Philip smiled. 'As children he was always very impressive to us in the way he would pick up the telephone and say, "Operator, get me Cape Town." '

They both laughed.

'Anyway,' Young continued, 'it was Appleby who fixed Daniel's trip. Of course Daniel travelled pretty much as he pleased, but at that stage he wasn't above using addresses and contacts. Appleby provided all those. So did I – missionaries, old friends and so on – that was why he came to see me when he got back and that was how I heard all about his travels.'

'I imagine you were one of the few people he told about his time out there. He was always reluctant to discuss it with me. I always assumed it had been in some way a painful experience.'

'Well,' Young frowned to himself, 'it made him more hostile than ever to Mayhew & Taylor, or rather to the conglomerate that had taken over. Daniel got involved with the V.S.O. and Peace Corps people. Many of them were very radical and filled him up with plenty of propaganda about big business in Africa.'

'So the plan failed.'

'I'm afraid so. The idea was to encourage Daniel to travel – taking in a bit of company life on the quiet – in the hope that he would get interested in the international dimensions of the business. Instead, he came back more than ever against it. Of course he was not the first university graduate to be put off by trade, though to hear your father talk you'd have thought otherwise.'

'In retrospect,' Philip commented, judiciously, 'I suppose it was hardly surprising that Daniel, a fairly typical student Marxist, should have failed to be impressed by a company that had the kind of trading relations Mayhew & Taylor have, I mean had, with . . .' He searched for the words, 'well, the old Empire.'

Young looked rueful. 'I suppose not. You're right, I should have forseen it.' He seemed quite depressed.

'Please,' Philip was genuinely disconcerted. 'It was not a criticism. I was only reflecting with the benefit of hindsight. You couldn't have known.'

The clock on the mantelpiece chimed three slowly, like a toy. 'Well,' said Young in his amiable way, 'I suppose I'd better shoot upstairs and see how the patient's settled.' He took Philip's arm, even though his words expressed a distance of understanding between them. 'Don't worry,' he reassured him, 'I'll find a place in a nursing home. I'm afraid dear Miss Whatshername can't cope much longer.'

Philip wanted to tell him that he was quite indifferent to most of this, but, diplomatic, he agreed and thanked him for his kindness. Then something that Stevie Beck had said came back to him. 'One thing, Tim –'

'By all means; what's that?'

'You mentioned that when he was in Africa Daniel got to know people in V.S.O. – where was that?'

Young almost chuckled. 'Still on Daniel,' he patronised, and then saw Philip's expression sharpen. 'Now where was it?' he flustered. 'Tanzania, I think.'

'Did he ever talk about them,' Philip continued, suddenly almost implacable. 'The people that he knew out there?'

'No – no. I don't think so.' He did not seem inclined to say any more. Philip thanked him again. He thinks I'm unbalanced, he said to himself. He doesn't want me to brood on what's happened. He realised that if he stayed any longer his godfather would invite him to stay. 'See you later, Tim,' he said briskly, moving towards the front door. They shook hands and, as Timothy Young climbed slowly up the sweeping staircase to the first floor, Philip pushed out through the front door into the twilight.

All his life he had been lonely, but he had never known loneliness like this. As a child, overshadowed by Daniel, he had learnt to play his own solitary games; in adolescence, when his brother's battle with his father was just beginning to hot up, he was often ignored. Introspection became his armour against the indifference of the world. In his marriage, reluctantly incorporated into the flux of Jan's social life, what he called his 'independence' became another kind of defence, another way to minimise the risk of rejection. When Jan left him the isolation that followed was not unfamiliar, though, because she had provided, temporarily, a love he had never had, the pain of it had been hard to bear. At least then, he could retreat to the family home and the old certainties. Now, even that door seemed to have been slammed in his face.

He found he was standing in a little copse of wet trees when he heard the front door open. Timothy Young was coming out with the housekeeper. His godfather's bulky middle-aged shape was outlined against the light. Philip, like a snooper, watched them shaking hands and observed that, in the English manner, they were taking a long time to say goodbye. Then Young climbed into his estate car with one last word of farewell, and Philip tracked his tail lights through the trees as he drove away down the drive. The front door banged; he realised he was alone again. He brushed off the dew that had formed on his moustache and walked slowly back towards the house.

The housekeeper was tidying up in the study. 'Well, Miss Groom,' he said, rubbing his hands together. 'Is everything okay then? I must be on my way now, I'm afraid.'

He detected the flicker of worry, almost of fear, in her eyes, and for a moment he hesitated. He was very bad at causing pain, and like people who lack the nerve of selfishness was often best at doing it inadvertently. But he had made up his mind, out there in the dank solitude of the winter afternoon. He had tried, feebly, to fight off his desire to know more, his hope of seeing Stevie Beck again, and had failed. Uncharacteristically, the urge to follow up one more loose end was strong and decisive, and already, in a latent puritan way, he was promising it to himself in exchange for another filial visit, perhaps to the nursing home, at the end of the following week. Besides, he realised that if he didn't catch Ronald Appleby before the week-end, the term would have started again and there would be no time to spare. He had a new course to teach – Colonialism – and it was high time he completed his unfinished lecture on the consequences of the Paris Peace Conference. That was one of the agonies of bereavement, the awareness that ordinary life prevented the observance of the proper obsequies. Visiting Appleby could be seen as part of his duty. So he found the ruthlessness to say:

'I'm sorry, Miss Groom. I have to go and see an old family friend. About my – my – my brother. Father will understand.' He stuttered weakly. 'It's all the little d – d – d – details that take the time, isn't it?'

The housekeeper was trying to get out something about the nursing home. Philip pressed on, his voice buzzing oddly in his ears, not wanting to hear her pleading.

'I'll give you my 'phone number, just in case,' he prevaricated. 'I don't need to tell you that Tim Young is a marvellous doctor. He'll make all the arrangements. Look,' he said in desperation, giving away his private deal with himself. 'I'll be back next week-end anyway.'

She named the date, anxious to pin down the commitment.

'Yes,' he said, calculating quickly. 'Less than ten days. Father's okay for now. You'll be fine.'

'We'll see you next week-end, then,' she repeated, as though sealing a contract.

'Next week-end,' he said. 'Bye.' The front door shut behind him with the usual ominous booming.

3

When Ronald Appleby said, 'Africa changed your brother. It always frightens me what that continent can do to people,' Philip knew that his instincts about Daniel were still right: somewhere in that unknown landscape something had happened to convert truculent antipathy towards the Taylor family and its business into open rebellion. Now, in January, when the pulse of the English year was at its slowest, it was hard to imagine the African vastness, where the even rhythm of the white man's blood was disturbed, it seemed, by tremors from the heart of the earth itself. Typically, Philip had only wanted to travel to India (like most of his student friends); Africa remained an enigma, a place of dry white bones and violent skies. Above the desk, on Appleby's wall, there was terror scored across a tribal mask. And on the book-cases, crammed with periodicals and abstracts, there were Christmas cards, reminding visitors of the bland certainties of white faith.

Philip said, 'I see.' His intuition knotted his stomach. He was conscious of stepping out of the known world. Appleby's room was hung and cluttered with the trophies of his years on the Equator; it was like a colonial museum. Skins, rugs, antlers, masks, drums and spears and a tourist board photograph of Kilimanjaro gave the high-ceilinged office an air of imperial wantonness, of things uprooted and abandoned. But there was also a raw edge to these wounded pieces: Philip's eye jumped from drumhead to spear point to the broken stare of masks, and his gaze flinched back to Appleby.

The erstwhile foreign correspondent was now, on the brink of retirement, the director of Philip's university careers office, a Victorian stucco mansion standing at the end of a short gravel drive surrounded by cedar trees. He had aged perceptibly in the last few years, Philip thought. There was something punctured about him, a loss of confidence and a certain defensive bonhomie, as of a con-man whose bluff is about to be called. Still, his appearance was authentic, if old-fashioned. Appleby was a stout, crumpled gentleman, with a fondness for snuff and hot jazz, a keen supporter of the university rugby club whose matches, home and away, he attended as religiously as he did the local pub, striding up and down the touchline, bellowing encouragement to the players, 'young men', as he called them. He had drifted into the safe harbour of university bureaucracy after half a lifetime spent as a roving journalist, mainly in Africa, with whose leaders he still kept in regular and friendly contact, taking safari holidays with the Minister of this or that, returning home with slides and gossip. As a much-loved bachelor, he would regale the Women's Institute with the slides, but save the gossip for those high tables where he still had dining rights. In this way he contrived to seem well-informed, amusing and attractive to either sex, eligible widows or lonely old dons. Appleby had written a number of second-rate books on Africa (cobbled together from his cuttings file), and though often referred to (in radio broadcasts) as 'the doyen of foreign correspondents', he had been consistently wrong about decolonisation. But his paper had kept him on in Africa throughout the fifties – now in Accra, now in Nairobi – not so much because he was a good analyst, as because he loved the continent and its people and, as one basically unaware of the true nature of the political situation, a Western commentator much courted by African presidents and dictators. It was for this last reason, too, that after his visits he was invariably debriefed, very informally of course, over dinner or a drink, by someone from the Foreign Office. All this he did for his love of the place and of his own self-importance. His many deals would come to fruition later; and then the money would spurt into his bank account, and he would buy another white Jaguar.

It was the heartiness of the sporty man of leisure that greeted Philip on his arrival. 'P. R. Taylor!' he exclaimed in his schoolmasterly way, and shook hands with what Philip took to be suspicious warmth, as though there was already something not quite admitted between them. 'Well, well, well,' he went on automatically, 'so what brings you here? You don't want me to find you a job surely!' He began to laugh volcanically, spluttering and flushing in complete self-absorption. Suddenly, seeing Philip's seriousness, he switched moods with disconcerting completeness, gravely offered him a chair, and said: 'I heard all about Daniel.' Only a slight hoarseness of expression betrayed his former mirth. 'It was a terrible shock.'

Something in the trite formula and in the way he said it told Philip that the avuncular interest Appleby had once taken in Daniel's career was now dead. He waited patiently, letting him run through the routine expression of concern for his father's health, and wondered how long it would be before the mask would drop and he could begin to probe the bonhomie.

Belatedly, Appleby asked: 'And yourself, Philip? How's yourself?'

'So-so,' he replied without enthusiasm. He could feel the atmosphere sobering; it would only be a distraction to add that Jan had deserted him. 'Frankly, I've got into a bit of a rut at the college. I find the teaching's become a routine.'

'You know what I always say, old thing, you can't get out of a rut until you've got into one. The young men who come here are all scared stiff of the so-called rut. Half of them nowadays don't know the meaning of work. Solid routine, solid achievement. That's what this country needs now. Sorry –' he laughed, self-deprecating. 'Just one of my hobby-horses.'

Philip nodded, but said nothing. The twinkling glance in front of him was unfaltering, but he held it.

'Come now, Philip,' Appleby chided, half peremptorily, sitting back in his old cane chair. 'What is it? You have something on your mind.' Like the doctor who refuses to accept the ostensible illness as the cause of the visit, he pressed forward with an encouraging chuckle.

Philip was determined to test him. 'I feel we all have to have something to answer for,' he began, 'myself more than most.'

Appleby began to bluster. 'But, my dear chap, of course it's a terrible tragedy, I mean I don't want you to misunderstand me, but Daniel . . .' he made a little grunting sound and started to feed his briar.

'But Daniel . . . ?' Philip quizzed him, angered by the way his brother was being ignored.

'What I'm saying, Philip,' his eyes were darting here and there for inspiration, 'is that it's all history. You can't bring him back to life, you know. It's something we all have to live with.' A thought occurred to him, and he went on to the offensive. 'It's not as though you had much to do with your brother these last few years.' Appleby sounded almost callous, and then the match flared at the end of his fingers and he began to draw on his pipe, a reasonable, contented Englishman of the old school giving good advice to a young friend.

'So he stays lost in a memory hole,' Philip replied, bitterness creeping into his voice. 'We cut Daniel out of our lives, and when I see what that did to him I feel ashamed.'

'What did it do to him?'

'It wrecked him, Ronnie. I – I –' He could not go on. All at once the cluttered office seemed close and inhospitable.

'But, my dear boy – it was Daniel who wrecked himself. Your father did everything for him, as I well know,' he concluded with significant emphasis.

'Of course,' said Philip, in mock surprise, 'I'd forgotten the help you gave father about fixing up Daniel's African trip.'

'Well, I did what I could,' said Appleby. 'I mean your old man had been incredibly good to me in a tight corner. I was only too glad to give him a hand myself where I could.' He paused to frown and pull on his pipe. The flavour of strong tobacco thickened the air. 'As you know,' he went on, 'one way or another, I have spent all my life in Africa. My folks had a farm in Tanganyika – as it was then – in the good old days before the war. They hacked it out of the bush, out of the bush,' he repeated. 'Wonderfully courageous people, my folks. I was brought up there. Africa is my country. I loved the place. When I became a journalist all I wanted to do was go back there to live and work; and of course in those days that was possible. I had a marvellous time, travelling around all over the place, filing stories and getting on the right side of the colonial civil service. I knew them all. We whites were always the smallest tribe. Then the wind of change blew me away. After independence, there was no role for me. Suddenly I was out of a job. Of course, I could have come back and edited the *Bogshire Chronicle*, but when you've been out in the field nothing is the same again. You always want to go back. That was where your old man came up trumps,' he sucked the ancient stem with a contented popping sound, 'absolutely came up trumps.'

Philip let him talk on, listening attentively.

'Your old man knew I knew all the locals and knew how to butter them up and what not. One thing led to another and I became a general oiler of wheels, you **know** what I mean, for Mayhew & Taylor. I flatter myself but I did the firm a lot of useful business.' He winked. 'I'll tell you something I've never let on about before. You won't believe it, but I even managed to turn the corruption of the system to the company's advantage.' Philip's expression betrayed nothing. 'As I expect you know, salesmen in that part of the world are always expected to accept a bribe or two. There's nothing unusual about that. It's just the way they do things there. If you don't conform you just don't get anywhere.' Philip nodded his acceptance of this rather laboured self-justification. 'Well,' Appleby continued, 'the usual way the smooth men from the multinationals do it is with a double invoice. They pay the money into a Swiss bank account. No one back at head office is any the wiser and the smoothies are a great deal richer. Simple, eh? Well, I did the same – but I went one better. My bank account was linked directly to the firm's.' He chuckled with satisfaction. 'And only your father knew. God knows how much research those bribes funded,' he concluded self-righteously.

Philip smiled his commendation, wondering privately why he was being told all this. He said: 'Father was always rather inspired when it came to unconventional appointments.'

Appleby swallowed the compliment like a performing dog, with a little snort of pleasure; he preened himself in front of his visitor with shocking immodesty.

'But then,' Philip chipped in, almost off-hand, 'you had to come home, didn't you?'

'Indeed yes,' Appleby responded, oddly nervous. 'I got sick. I suppose a lifetime in the Tropics didn't do the old ticker much good. Anyway, I had to slow down. Quite a blow for a chap in his late forties. Quite a blow. I have to thank my stars that your old man got me a job in the publicity office while I sorted myself out.' He sounded at once grateful and dismissive. The evasive tone was uncharacteristic.

'After those years writing for the newspapers it must have been easy work,' Philip commented.

Appleby snatched eagerly at the remark. 'Easy work!' he exclaimed. 'I should say so. It was very ordinary, routine stuff,' he emphasised. 'The usual press office nonsense, you know. It only lasted a year, but it did tide me over till I got a good job here. As I say I have a lot to thank your father for.'

'But when you fixed up Daniel's trip for him,' said Philip, returning to the subject, 'you still had your contacts.'

'Absolutely. We old Africa hands stick together. Ha! The bad old days.' There was discomfort in Appleby's thin loud laugh but Philip could not decide what it was he had said.

'Daniel had a lot to be grateful to you for,' said Philip, flattering. 'I mean, thanks to you he became a journalist.' He spoke without irony, but Appleby went on to the defensive.

'Now,' he protested, interrupting with a donnish forefinger, 'that was never my idea.'

'But you fixed it up.'

Appleby looked at him as though he did not expect such a peremptory challenge; not for the first time recently, Philip realised that his manner was getting shorter and more pointed. It was as though he was acquiring something of Daniel's old style.

'Quite honestly,' Appleby was saying, 'I was the only one who could have done. It's a complicated story and I wasn't happy about it in many ways, but if your dear father wanted it, then who was I to argue?' He gestured emptily with his pipe; Philip realised that he was looking into the face of a man who would agree with whoever suited his purpose at the time. Appleby sat back in his chair and tried to broaden the conversation. 'Ah,' he said, 'how well I remember Daniel in those days. He was so intense and energetic, like a coiled spring. There was such passion in his desire to be a reporter. When he was talking, it seemed almost a noble profession,' he laughed and then checked his cynicism. 'Mind you, I'm not saying my work in Africa was – well, you know, unrewarding . . .' He stopped, confused by his own train of thought, and then went on with new vigour. 'What always interested me was the country, the people, the people,' he repeated, realised his repetition and halted, embarrassed. 'When Daniel went up north,' he continued, backtracking, 'he continued, backtracking, 'he had such·ideals. Of course everyone wanted to be a TV producer or some damn glamorous thing in the media. Daniel was different. He really cared. I'm *parti pris*, but I believe he did.'

'That's what his friends in Newcastle say, the ones that still remember him.'

'When he won that prize he was good. I'll admit I didn't much like what he was writing, but it had something about it. That was something you had to recognise.'

Surprisingly, Philip could not recall if Appleby had been at the party. He would have been indistinguishable among the mob of baggy-suited journalists. Daniel had been back in England nearly four years then.

He said, 'He was very logical. He always followed the reasoning in a situation to the end.'

'I remember,' said Appleby, nostalgic. 'Later . . .' he shrugged. 'His judgement failed perhaps.' He didn't seem inclined to say more.

'After that party, I never saw him again.' There were moments recently when Philip found his words running on indifferent to the thread of the conversation, confessional private statements that somehow floated to the surface of dialogue. He checked abruptly. 'I imagine you kept in touch.'

'We chatted on the 'phone a few times.' He looked quickly at Philip. 'It was right and proper that he should go his own way. He had no need of me by then.' Appleby evaded the invitation to enlarge on those years. 'I did hear that he was getting flak from his editor. But he was never very good at compromise, was he?'

'It would make him a good investigative journalist, though, especially when there was something for him to get his teeth into. On the other hand,' Philip found himself ashamed by a sudden insight, 'it would make him frustrated and bitter when he was getting nowhere.'

'The talk was that he left himself a bit out on a limb at the paper.' Appleby focussed a direct look at Philip. 'The truth is that Daniel was excited by human suffering. He had this craving for terrible things. That was what he was really interested in writing about.'

Philip was silenced for a moment by this sudden burst of candour. 'You mean it turned him on – things like sickness and poverty?' Appleby nodded. 'Well,' said Philip quietly, 'he was in the perfect field for that.'

'At another time he would have been a war correspondent,' said Appleby. 'Even in peace he was always looking for combat zones, so to speak.' He laughed. 'Africa certainly answered those needs. But I don't think he realised how much he was being influenced. Once you've been there you see things differently somehow.'

Philip broke in before the moment was lost. 'So you do think he was deeply affected by that trip he made?'

Appleby seemed aware that he had admitted something he didn't intend about Africa. He fiddled with his pipe. He hesitated, and then he looked at his visitor with a patronising elderly steadiness that Philip disliked. 'Yes,' he said, after a long pondering. 'Africa changed your brother. It always frightens me what that continent can do to people.'

'I see.' Philip looked at Appleby's undaunted, weatherbeaten expression, the tilt of his silvery moustache, the relentless twinkle in his eye, as though about to repeat the oldest joke in the world, and realised that here was a man for whom double-talk and glad-handing was a way of life. Truly, he decided, Appleby does not know who he is.

'You survived,' he commented.

'But, my dear chap, I was born there. That makes all the difference. It was always the world I knew. Besides, it's a question of temperament. I don't make waves, never have done. Even when the Union Jack was tumbling down about our ears, and all the whites could hear was the sound of the Last Post, I accepted the situation. I filed my copy and did what I could to get on terms with the new rulers. It was the only way to salvage some profit from my folks' place for instance.'

He looked at him disarmingly after this admission, and Philip found, despite himself, this honesty rather winning.

'I know what you're thinking,' Appleby pursued, 'a trimmer, you're saying to yourself. But the white man in Africa has to trim to survive. It's not his country; he has to adapt. People claim that the whites exploit their status. They talk a lot about the black man's loss of dignity. It's not true. The black man is the native; it's his land; he is there on it, always has been, always will be. He has more dignity than the white man ever can have. It's true the ex-pats are treated like gods, but the more superior the whites feel, even now, the more ridiculous they become. All the evidence shows that they still do not understand the country. Your family's old company sells aspirin and tranquillizers to the new régimes. It's Mayhew & Taylor that lacks dignity.'

'But you did that sort of work, too,' said Philip, wondering what it was that Appleby had in mind.

'I had to. I was broke when I quit the paper. I've compromised all my life, Philip. It's second nature and I'm not ashamed. I'm English. If I have a loyalty it is to myself and to what I own. Myself, of course, is the society in which I live, the class to which I belong, my friends and colleagues, but ultimately I'm loyal to all these for selfish ends – I want a quiet life, the freedom of self-sufficiency. I'm like most Englishmen in that respect. Your brother was different; oblivious to personal discomfort and the consequences for himself of any given action. He was a true zealot. I'm afraid we disagreed totally. His reaction to a situation was always extreme.'

'And Africa was an extreme situation, I suppose,' said Philip.

'That's how he saw it. I was surprised at his reaction, I must admit. I suppose I should have warned your father about the risks of his trip. Africa, you see, is full of shameful secrets, mainly from the past. So much more happens out there than most people know – or even want to. There are wars that nobody knows about; famines that never reach the newspapers. For someone with your brother's curiosity it was inexhaustibly fascinating. Naturally he soon gravitated towards the most controversial areas. When Daniel went there it didn't take him long to get in with the V.S.O. crowd, the bleeding heart liberals and suchlike. I suppose he heard more than was good for him.'

He saw Philip ready to challenge him. 'Now,' he went on, pointing the stem of his pipe imperiously across the desk, 'don't misunderstand me. The point is that those development agency types have quite a different view of things. It's easy to get worked up about issues which, in context, are quite normal – business practices in general, the politics of aid, that sort of thing.' Appleby was not wanting to elaborate. 'Much more than all that was the impact of the place itself, the power of Africa.'

'It made him . . .' Philip searched for the word.

'Violent.' Appleby spoke without hesitation. Philip was surprised at his quick certainty. 'Violent in thought and word of course. I've seen it happen a dozen times. With your brother it was more noticeable because of his nature. He was already a very strong-minded young man.'

'But when he became a real journalist he started doing things that made life very difficult for the company,' Philip commented. 'He must have picked up a lot of information in Africa.'

'You've got to see it in perspective, Philip. He'd seen quite a slice of the family business in operation out there, more than most of his newspaper colleagues.' Appleby explained, in laborious detail, how, when Daniel started writing stories about the politics of medicine, his previous experience had given his work a certain authenticity.

135

'Timothy Young told me that the board begged father to stop him.'

'Oh,' said Appleby with a snort. 'It was only the publicity people as usual.' Scorn clouded his avuncular manner in a way that offered a brief insight into his personality. 'You know what those people live on – the ever-ready smile, the half-truth, the sugared lie – that's their currency. They always want a sunny sky and a calm sea. Anything that disturbs the picture is a threat. If Daniel had written to the local paper saying he was in favour of hang-gliding the press office people would have been worried. That's their job. As I'm sure you know,' he concluded, enlisting Philip's support. Appleby always said what he thought you wanted to hear, Philip realised, and always offered a mixture of acquiescence and reassurance that made him at once both vulnerable and encouraging.

Philip was uneasy at all this. He realised his recollections were imperfect; his attention at that time had been monopolised by his thesis. Self-conscious and rather priggish, he had distanced himself from the family troubles, pulled up the drawbridge and retreated into his books and notes. Now he regretted his scrappy memory of that time. It was not as though the dates and statistics he had mastered then were of any use to him now.

He said: 'Only the other day, father said I should ask you about what happened in Africa. He obviously has happy memories of what you did, for him, out there.'

As he expected, Appleby mellowed. 'That's nice. On the African end, I suppose I was some use. Yes, of course. Your brother, very frankly, got a bee in his bonnet about the way the pharmaceutical industry works in Africa and he started to ask a lot of impertinent questions, impertinent questions,' he repeated, not elaborating. 'As I say, he was half-informed by his radical friends in the maize fields, who filled his head with Fanon and the African Marxists. I'd fixed up a number of introductions for him and he was going around ruffling feathers and putting people's backs up. Obviously it had to stop. I knew all the dealers, the reps, the civil servants and so on – I was the obvious choice. Also, I'd set up the trip. I was responsible.'

Appleby became suddenly rather abrupt and mysterious; Philip remembered that this was his way of inviting more questions, of exciting curiosity. 'So he came home. You know all about that. And went to Newcastle.' He affected an expression of great confidentiality. 'I want you to know, Philip, that I lost a lot of sympathy with Daniel after that episode. Africa had influenced him more than I had realised: all he seemed to want to do was to poison the family wells, as it were. It was a cheap, mean thing to want to do and it always stuck in my throat.'

Appleby smiled. His face was in the sun; the foxy, scarred features were lit up by a winter whiteness from outside. Philip turned, blinking scholastically, and looked briefly away out of the window into the pale stratospheric blue sky darkening over rooftops with the hint of smog.

'I don't apologise for this,' Appleby was still smiling, a row of perfect teeth gleamed in the shadowless midday light, predatory and ingratiating. 'We remained on good terms. I like to think we were still friends. There was just this small reservation I always had after that.'

'It sounds as though Daniel gave you a hard time,' Philip challenged, guessing.

'As I say, old thing,' Appleby tried to win his sympathy, 'his thoughts became violent, very violent,' he repeated. 'There was an irrational side I could never quite get to the bottom of, too. It was as though Africa unlocked something in his personality that had been sealed up before.'

'It sounds as though everyone needs to go out there sometime,' murmured Philip intransigently.

Appleby appeared not to have heard him. 'When he was there,' he said, engrossed in his own narrative, 'he got in with some very odd types, I can tell you.' Philip recognised the signs of a burgeoning anecdote. 'He was hanging around the villages and the hospitals – this is Tanzania I'm talking about now. Remember, by this time he'd been out there for quite a while. He'd moved from the South, where I sent him originally, to the West. He'd got sick there not surprisingly, and gone across to the East – for the politics of course. Like so many people at that time he wanted to see the showcase black republic for himself.' Philip noticed that Appleby always sounded both bitter and nostalgic when he was talking about the home he had lost.

'African socialism,' said Philip quietly, recalling some of Daniel's excited phrases all those years ago in Chalk Farm. Perceptions sharpened by grief, he could see the lost face too, older now, but still the face of a young man with causes to fight for, restless eyes searching anxiously to find a fellow idealist in a world that was getting grey and cynical. Philip remembered now that his lukewarm pragmatism had been a serious disappointment to his brother.

'Balls to African socialism,' said Appleby. His amiable smile did not disguise his sarcasm. 'Tanzania is a fantasy land for all kinds of Western nutcases. You don't know, Philip, you don't know how it hurts someone like me who loves Africa. These people go out there with a bundle of preconceptions, half-digested Marxist tracts. They treat the country, worse, the Africans, as an empty canvas on which they can colour in a version of their own ideals. It's sick, Philip, it's sick.'

'And even Daniel –' Philip concurred, doubtfully. 'It's a shame that even he could not see what he was doing.'

'But no one,' Appleby rammed his words home with dogmatic gestures, 'no one realises what Africa is doing to them. They go out there, out into the midday sun – and they go mad. Yes. Literally. Mad. Westerners are just as likely to crack up in Africa as blacks are in – in –' he cast around for an example, 'in Lewisham.' Appleby was quite indignant. 'We're so vulnerable, you and I. And so was Daniel – all the more so for his unaware-ness of the fact. Africa called him out there – and then took its vengeance.' He paused in thought; then his mood lifted and he became the Uncle Ronnie of memory, though still slightly dis-turbing in manner. 'Is that what your dear father wanted me to tell you? Of course, I'm talking with hindsight. I never expected it to affect your brother like that. In fact it was Daniel – Daniel more than anyone – who taught me what Africa can do to people.'

'And then he came back,' Philip said, to complete the story from his own experience. 'One day I got this letter from father to say Daniel was in England. Although we had got on badly in the past I was very excited: after more than two years I still wanted to see him. He'd done something that hadn't been done before. He'd broken the family tradition and I wanted to know what it was like. But when I got to the end I realised why father was writing. Daniel was back, but he hadn't come home. Even his convales-cence was in London; after that he sulked in private, away from the family.'

'That's right. Your father was very shocked when he realised.' Appleby sounded superior. 'But at least Daniel was back in the country and back on the rails again, so to speak, getting ready to go to Newcastle.' He sounded self-important, consciously alluding to his own role in Daniel's career. 'If we hadn't acted quickly he might have stayed out there indefinitely, living off his radical friends.'

Philip found himself becoming defensive on his brother's behalf. 'You're forgetting,' he said with some irritation, 'that he was still getting over mother's death. That must have been a terrible shock to him, even though he knew it was coming. You know how much she meant to him especially. He'd missed the funeral. He probably wasn't ready to make the transition.'

Appleby looked sternly at him. 'Daniel didn't miss the funeral, Philip, whatever your father told the family. In fact, he offered him money to fly back, but he refused it.' He modified his censorious tone slightly. 'In many ways that's when the real estrangement happened. Daniel said some very hard things to your father on the telephone about your mother.'

Philip said nothing. There were too many secrets in the family. After a moment, a thought occurred to him. 'What brought him home in the end, then?'

Appleby chuckled proudly. He made a disagreeably self-satisfied picture, sprawled back in his chair, his belly swelling under his maroon jersey. 'I did,' he said. 'Look,' he went on, to dispel Philip's confusion. 'Daniel got very sick. He was already low on money and living in dreadful conditions. So he cabled your father a blackmailing message to say that he would die if he didn't get some more cash at once. Your father had been bailing him out for months. God knows how many final payments he'd threatened. Each time he capitulated and sent some more. He was still very upset about Daniel's reaction to your mother, and couldn't face another crisis. As you know, beneath that fierce exterior, there's quite a soft heart. But finally when this message came, his patience snapped and I was dispatched to bring Daniel home by hook or crook.'

'That must have been difficult.'

'It was. Your father decided that the only way to get him back was to give in and to offer him the journalism course he wanted. That was my job – to sell him the deal.'

Philip nodded, encouraging the story.

'It wasn't one of my best experiences. First of all I had to track him down like a private dick. That wasn't very nice. He was living in Tanga, a fly-blown seaside rathole if ever there was one, in this appalling bungalow with two girls from one of the overseas aid programmes. God knows where they both fitted in, but they seemed fond of him. He had been trying to live more or less native and had got sick. Then he had run out of money. That was the point he cabled your father and asked for more to pay for a doctor. When I found him he was in this . . . this squalid building, in bed, sweating with a fever, very pale and thin. There were piles of books and pamphlets all over the floor. Think what your father would have said!' Appleby exclaimed. 'After all, when Daniel set out I'd got him fixed up with perfect introductions to all the embassies.' He still seemed genuinely astonished. 'He offered very little resistance. The two girls didn't seem to take in what was happening; they were probably on drugs. Well anyway, I had a taxi waiting and an old houseboy of mine from the old days with me. We shovelled all his things into suitcases and drove hell for leather to Dar. There I took him straight to my hotel for a bath and some treatment. We caught the plane the next morning. If he hadn't been so demoralised and sick it would have been impossible. Even though he was exhausted with the fever and the heat and no food, he was still hating it all. We had a terrible row on the plane. He was very torn of course. He was glad he had won the battle to become a journalist, but he didn't like the price he was having to pay. I could see his point, and I told him so. It was very humiliating.'

Philip concentrated on the details of the scene. 'Those two girls he was living with – can you remember anything about them?'

'Well,' Appleby laughed. 'They were girls,' he said facetiously. 'White, of course. Thank goodness.' He frowned. 'They were student types – thin, fair-haired, scraggy-looking. They were quite alike I think. I really didn't pay much attention – so I suppose they weren't terribly attractive.' He smiled.

'You don't remember anything else about them, or their names perhaps?' He was trying to see the room in his mind's eye, and imagined he was watching the action remotely, in silence, as though behind thick glass.

'Oh – I'm no good with names. They were ordinary middle-class kids like Daniel, running away from their responsibilities. That was what it was like then. They were like all students at that time. I didn't pay much attention. I was only there for a couple of hours – less perhaps. They just sat on the floor, smoking and looking at me. I told you there was no resistance.'

Although Appleby's story was unexpected, adding yet another

dimension to the shape of Daniel's hidden life, Philip was still disappointed. He had hoped for more detail, and might indeed have expected it from an ex-journalist. But Appleby was plainly more impressed by his own performance as a troubleshooter. His preoccupation had been to jet in, track down his friend's wayward son, and pull out as swiftly as possible. Appleby seemed aware of his visitor's unfulfilled expectations.

'You think I'm hiding something from you, I can see that,' he said candidly.

'N – n – not at all,' Philip protested. 'I'm just curious. It doesn't matter. It's all in the past now.'

'It's a thing you notice in this job,' said Appleby, turning to genial self-explanation. 'There are some young men – and women too – whose faces could melt into any crowd, who seem quite classless, detached, neutral.'

'Like those girls,' Philip commented, thinking of Stevie.

'I suppose so,' he frowned. 'They made no impression.'

With most people, Philip thought to himself, death simplifies; obscurities are explained, mysteries exposed, and secrets given away. Everything that Ronald Appleby had said this morning had only given the portrait of his brother new subtlety and depth, perhaps because it had been such a blank slate to start with.

And now the old fixer was talking on, reassuring, planning and evaluating. In due course he would suggest a pub lunch, a walk, more easy talk, etc. But nothing he said now could distract Philip from the belief that he had not heard everything there was to know about Daniel's time in Africa, or even Appleby's own shrouded career. Uncle Ronnie (even now it was hard to think of this matey veteran in any other terms) was a dealer, a man of yarns and gossip, hot tips, know-how and political savvy; he was a buttonholer of unsuspecting travellers, a man who traded everything, especially information, three times over if possible, keeping the rate of exchange in his head or on dirty screws of paper in his capacious pockets, a man whose ready flow of talk would inexplicably dry up if the conversational traffic didn't go both ways. He had bartered freely this morning, swopping some scraps for others, sacrificing trifles to save up his trumps and aces. When a man like Appleby yielded an admission or gave away a confidence it was for a basic purpose: the preservation of his freedom of manoeuvre. This in turn was given such roomy definition as to allow for contradictions, small flaws and minor peccadilloes. 'No one's perfect,' as he was fond of saying. And Appleby played the game of being a good fellow, one of the boys, so well that everyone made precisely these allowances. Nothing he had said to Philip had seriously compromised the open record of his career. But Philip knew that it was part of his style to use this loose-fitting personality like a cloak, to hide in it, to show to the inquisitive outsider the profile that he chose to show. There had been too many rhetorical silences, queries unacknowledged, and evasions disguised as ignorance, for him to think otherwise. He didn't expect to get any more out of this fine corrupt old figure, but at least he could test him one last time.

'Ronnie,' he said, interrupting, 'I'm going to need your help with father, you know.' He paused slightly. 'He's very sick. Quite honestly, there's no one else I can turn to.'

Appleby sprang boyishly to his feet, slapping his thigh. 'But why didn't you say so before, old thing.' He put his arm round Philip in his most avuncular way. 'You are a funny chap. All that stuff about Daniel and all the time you're eating your heart out worrying about your dear old father. Of course I'd be only too delighted to do anything I can to help. Don't pull your punches, Philip, what is it you want me to do?'

Appleby's face was alive with relief. There was no mistaking his delight that the subject of Daniel and Africa had been pushed aside.

Philip heard his own voice in the background of his thoughts. He heard himself asking Appleby to visit his father over the week-end, while his mind was compulsively re-shaping its image of Daniel, seeing him differently now, yellow and sweating, with the thin, wasted look of the sick and abandoned, living in a fly-blown bungalow, distinguished by his long damp hair and cut-off jeans, the local English boy with the dollars and the craving for hashish, a modern white settler going native in his own way.

Philip had expected that the meeting with Appleby would satisfy the need that he had to go on looking for his brother. Instead he was now beginning to realise that his curiosity was only feeding his sense of loss. To call the emotion he felt grief, after those years of misunderstanding and resentment, was perhaps to adopt too readily the symptoms that people like Appleby expected him to exhibit, but still he recognised within himself a yearning to know more and a willingness to be drawn into

Daniel's footsteps as a way of atonement. As ever sceptical and divided in his self-analysis, he knew that there was an aspect of all this that was merely a surrogate for his growing obsession with Stevie.

He listened to himself talking about his father. '. . . He's taken bereavement very badly, as though . . .' His thought-process got confused and he hesitated . . . 'as though Daniel was a lover not a son.' He blushed to hear his subconscious surface in real conversation and tried, with deepening embarrassment, to explain away the simile. 'I mean, even I – you know – I've found that the emotion of – grief in the family, with me at any rate – things like restlessness, loss of appetite – insomnia, bad dreams and lack . . . lack of concentration – it's like when I was just a teenager – you know – first love and all that.' His smile was as halting and uncertain as his words and Appleby, who was listening with a startled expression of concern, nodded apparently in sympathy. Philip's eyes filled with spontaneous tears. 'Don't worry, Ronnie, I'm okay, really. I'll be gone soon. I'm okay.'

'Don't worry, old chap, don't worry about a thing. A dreadful blow, I know. A dreadful blow. What you need is a good stiff drink and a bite to eat.'

It's normal, said Philip to himself, it's quite normal; no need to be ashamed of tears. He pulled on his coat and began to hum a little tune to demonstrate his mental equipoise.

Appleby laughed uneasily. 'Land of Hope and Glory,' he identified, showing Philip through the door into the icy hallway. 'It's funny to think that people used to believe those words.'

'It's not funny,' said Philip, suddenly acid, 'it's bloody tragic.'

'Come along, old fellow; pub's just down the road,' Appleby went on, humouring him; his breathless elderly steps crunched fussily on the gravel.

Drink to me only with thine eyes, Philip quoted to himself, back on Stevie in his mind again.

4

Philip knew someone had been in the house as soon as he unlocked the front door and stepped into what the estate agent had once called the small parquet vestibule. The letters he expected to find drifted by the door on to the mat were stacked on the table; doors he had left closed were open; his fastidious eye picked out a tread of mud on the stair carpet.

'Jan,' he called out in a throttled, tentative voice. He caught sight of himself in the hall mirror and saw what he already knew: that his expression betrayed no enthusiasm at the prospect of his wife's return. He looked tired and slightly disarrayed. He wanted a hot bath, time to wash his hair, and clip his moustache. Travelling, he had not had time or energy to pay much attention to these details. He was aware that he had let himself go, and it disturbed him. Now, with the new term in prospect, he would have to smarten up and get down to some serious preparation for his lecture course.

There was no reply, no answering creak or footfall. The silence in the twilight was all-embracing. He went through into the living room, as still as a county museum, and flopped into an armchair with the post clutched in his left hand. He switched on the anglepoise. The yellow bulb gave warmth to the shadows.

The accumulation of mail was mainly bills and circulars, but there were also a few painful reminders of the odds and ends from Daniel's unfinished life that remained to be settled. The crematorium told him in unctuous prose that his brother's ashes were now awaiting collection. Dust to dust, he whispered, wondering where Daniel would like to be scattered. That thought set him checking whether the solicitors had found a will, or better, any trace of Daniel's house, the one that Stevie had mentioned. But the stack of envelopes did not include the heavy cream paper favoured by his lawyers and he could only make a mental note to 'phone on Monday. So next it was natural to pick up the receiver and dial the familiar number. He couldn't suppress a little flutter of hope, but he was not surprised to draw a blank again. This voice was more officious than the others. 'You know,' it said, 'I can't help you if you don't have the address. Those are the regulations.'

'Thank you,' he replied nervously, and rang off.

There were one or two torn envelopes crumpled in the grate; he went over, mildly curious, and picked them out. For a moment, dizzy with bending, he hallucinated, saw Dan Taylor on the address and flushed in shock. But then he looked closer, squinting in the half darkness, and saw, as he anticipated, that the letters had been directed to Mrs. Jan Taylor. He threw them back into the cold fire-place with the thought that it was high time he changed the locks on the house, and then walked through to inspect his orchids.

He didn't realise until he scraped back the door into his magic garden how agitated he had become by the evidence of Jan's latest interference in his life. In the damp fragrant atmosphere of the little greenhouse he began to reassert control over himself, proudly marvelling at the perfection of his flowers, gratified that the precautions he had taken before going home had worked. The colours were as pure and brilliant as ever; the fantastic entanglement of fleshy stems and exotic blooms was not wilting. Only one or two plants showed signs of needing attention. He walked round his lean-to Eden pruning, fertilising and watering with an almost childish innocence, humming quietly. When he came to Jan's *Laelia harpophylla*, swinging in its basket, he reached up to test its welfare with his long white fingers. But he snatched his hand back in shock: entwined among the roots was a small ebony statuette. Gingerly he prised it loose and held the voodoo figure in his hand. It was a primitive carving of a black child. Daniel had sent it to them both as a wedding present, and, turning it over in his palm, Philip remembered the shock and disappointment they had felt, unwrapping it after the honeymoon.

Jan, in a printed Greek skirt and matching cornflower blouse, sitting on the floor of her dream house, surrounded by tissue and cardboard and red ribbon and wrapping paper, had the temporary brown glow of a Mediterranean holiday burning in her cheeks, she whose northern pallor was always rouged not bronzed by a hot day in the English sun.

'Oh look – darling – he didn't forget us after all.' The pleasure in her voice betrayed her fascination with Philip's remote and enigmatic brother.

Her new husband was absorbed in a long letter from his god-mother. 'What?'

'It's Daniel. He's sent us a present.' She held up the small brown parcel.

'How do you know?'

'I recognise the writing. No one else writes that way. You know, strong and black like he was using a chisel.' She smiled. 'Isn't that nice of him.'

Philip said, 'We don't know what it is yet.' He sounded recalcitrant, but that was only to disguise his inward pleasure at his brother's unexpected gesture. 'Well, go on,' he urged. 'Open it up.'

He still remembered her face, a sudden seriousness breaking the mood of irresponsible gaiety. 'Oh,' she said, tearing the last twist of paper. 'It's a doll.' She hesitated, crestfallen. 'A black doll.'

Philip took it from her hastily, almost grabbing it.

'Darling!' she protested. 'Don't snatch.'

He ignored her. 'It's an African charm,' he explained. Then he got annoyed. 'Well, I think he might have done better than that. What a miserable present.' They were surrounded by salad bowls and china, toasters, bread-boards and cut-glass, quiche dishes and dainty Irish linen tea towels.

'It's very – original,' she said doubtfully.

'No, it's not,' he replied with vigour. 'He's got loads of these, I know. I've seen them. They're two a penny at Lagos airport. That's just typical of Daniel. It's a sick joke.' He was angry, though he had not quite known why. Looking back, with Ronnie Appleby's words in mind, he could see now that even then Daniel had been making a statement about himself.

Then, quite pointlessly, they had a row about it, she defending her brother-in-law; he, already irritated by the plainness of her mind, trying to get it across to her why it was little better than an insult. And now, here it was again, deliberately planted in his backyard paradise in a similarly calculated gesture. Jan had come a long way since those early married days.

'Bitch', he said aloud and, bolting the front-door, went upstairs to unpack. But he took the black baby with him, rubbing the dirt out of its sexless crevices and corners, and put it by his bedside before he went to sleep. He had his recurrent dream about Jan's childbirth again that night.

He was awakened by a distant rattle from below. Then the bell pealed loud and long. He went down into the hallway in his dressing-gown and slippers as quietly as he could and stepped cautiously up to the security peephole. It was Jan. Her keys had been frustrated by the bolts. Philip stood there, pressing his face up against the wood (it was quite a smart oak door, installed when, as newlyweds, they had moved into the house), spying on his wife. He heard himself breathing hard as he looked at her for the first time in three months, and with the privilege of privacy that reminded him of the times when, in the first flush of their love, he would wake up in the early morning and gaze like a parent on the sleeping face beside him in bed. She'd done her long mousy hair differently, he noticed, and had bought the sort of clothes his students were wearing, though her figure wasn't really up to it. People sometimes said that those close-set lake-green eyes suggested a jealous nature, and perhaps that explained her former possessiveness towards him in the heyday of their relationship. Studying the independent, upward turn of her face, the determined, fractionally apprehensive licking of lips, it was hard to recall that side of her nature. She had obviously been walking hard and her unexercised lungs clouded the picture that was standing so nakedly before him with soft foggy breaths. Otherwise, he couldn't help thinking as he contemplated the familiar features, she was looking very well on their separation: healthy, rested and relaxed. She had never needed much make-up and now her clear English complexion was almost girlish again. He peeped at her with curiosity, admitting to himself that he wanted to know more about her, what she'd been doing and how she was getting on. He wanted to know if she was in love with anyone, but despite her freshness he was surprised to find that his own sexual interest was not aroused. She leant forward to press the bell again and then, amazingly, caught her own reflection in a scrap of brass on the door and began vainly to adjust her appearance. Oddly detached, Philip watched, astonished at his own objectivity. She had come back, but he didn't care and he didn't know why. It cost him nothing to pull his dressing-gown together, slide the bolt back and jerk open the door.

'Hello,' she said. 'You've been peering at me through the door. I heard you.'

'I – I – I – of course not,' he protested feebly. He knew he was colouring.

'Well, I haven't come back if that's what you're thinking,' she went on, businesslike, ignoring his hopeless denial.

'No – of course not – I didn't imagine y – y – you . . .' he stammered, thinking why does she always push me around. 'Was that supposed to be a joke?' he challenged, getting down to things.

'What?'

He knew her innocent mock-puzzlement so well but resolved not to react to it. 'Daniel's wedding present,' he said mildly.

'No,' she replied, rather cold. 'It was not a joke.'

'It gave me quite a shock, I can tell you.' He attempted a small laugh.

'Good,' she said, unmoved. 'You know you never even thanked me for my Christmas present.'

'Oh my Go —' He was genuinely confused and began to stutter his apologies.

'Forget it,' she dismissed him with contempt. 'You're so thoughtless sometimes.'

'I tried to get you some flowers as well, but they couldn't deliver in time, and anyway the woman said they'd run out.'

'So what's new?' Her sarcasm was wounding and final.

He stepped back, almost recoiling. A frosty wind was chilling him to the bone. His wife moved as well and the door swung to behind them with a faint click.

'I came here yesterday,' Jan went on. 'You were not at home, but I still have my keys, so I let myself in. Sorry about the intrusion. There are things I need. I wanted to say I'd called — I admit I disturbed your precious privacy — but there was nothing I could think to put on paper to you. I imagined that even you would telephone when you saw I'd been here. I was wrong of course. I'd forgotten you don't know how to use the 'phone these days.'

'What do you mean?' Philip was suddenly out of his depth.

'You know perfectly well what I mean,' she replied, rather tart. 'I tried to ring you just before Christmas. I watched you come home and then I called you from that 'phone box on the corner, just to wish you well. You hung up on me. Remember?

'I — I — I didn't know it was —' He could never confess that his thoughts had been monopolised by another woman. For a start, Jan would never believe him. Lately she had always scorned his appeal to the opposite sex, had even hinted that he was probably a bit confused.

'I wanted to prove to you I wasn't quite as cruel as you think. I needn't have bothered. I suppose I should have realised —'

'I was exhausted.' He cast his mind back to the moment he had run away from Stevie Beck. 'I'd had a hard day. Quite honestly I couldn't face anything more just then, even a wrong number.'

'Don't worry about it.' She shifted her feet and looked past him into the kitchen. 'We're going to have to sell this place to make the settlement. You do realise that, don't you?' She looked into his hollow eyes. 'Is something the matter? You look terrible.'

'It's nothing. Why don't you come in. I'll get dressed. Would you like some coffee?' He stepped back, stumbling awkwardly over a ruck in the mat.

'No – don't bother. I don't want to stay.' She stopped. They stood uneasily in the tiny hallway. Philip fiddled with his dressing-gown cord. He didn't know what to say.

She said: 'I only came . . . It was just to make sure you realised I wanted a divorce.'

The hateful thing, he said to himself, is how messy this is. I can't even look at her without flinching; she's standing like a guest in her own house; if I touch her she'll probably hit me; she's asking for the end of our marriage in the way she might ask for a foreign holiday, using words like 'divorce' and 'settlement' as if she was a travel agent fixing up a package tour. He could feel himself bottling up his emotion and guessed that she, with her even speech and steady gaze, was doing the same. In a minute, he thought, she will fumble in her bag for a cigarette.

'Yes, I understand that,' he said in a very quiet disintegrating voice. 'I'm not trying to stop you. I've never made any demands, have I?' She didn't say anything, anxious it seemed, to avoid a row. 'You look very well,' he said, feeling foolish and exposed.

'Thank you.' She smiled for the first time, but he knew it was because she was getting her own way. Philip looked at his silly white ankles. Standing there in pyjamas and dressing-gown, having a difficult conversation with a smartly-dressed adult woman, was like being a convalescent in a hospital. He felt ridiculously vulnerable. He said: 'I want to sell the house too, you know. My life has changed a lot recently.' He faltered, unable to elaborate the complications.

'I know,' she said. 'I heard about Daniel,' she murmured. 'I'm very sorry.' She looked at him with an expression of pity that for the first time had warmth in it, like a flush of colour in stone. 'A terrible loss . . .'

'Thank you,' he said, not knowing why. 'I'm going to be all

right. I could do with a holiday.' She ignored the hint. 'Perhaps I'll arrange a sabbatical after Easter. I can't say I relish the prospect of the new term. Father's not at all well.'

'What about matron?' she asked in the private language they had once shared.

'It's worse than that. We're having to put him in a nursing home. I think the news is going to kill him in the end.'

'I'm sorry,' she said again, sounding wooden. Incongruously, for a moment his mind flashed back to their wedding day and her toneless intonation. '. . . I take this my Friend, Philip Taylor, to be my husband, promising through divine assistance, to be unto him a loving and faithful wife . . .'

'It's okay. Things will sort themselves out. It could have been worse.'

'Philip Taylor's had a rough time.' She spoke about him impersonally, a consultant discussing a patient.

'Yes, he has.' He almost wanted to cry.

'Tell me about Daniel,' she said, fully sympathetic for the first time.

He felt so grateful, a sense of almost physical release. 'You're sure you wouldn't like some coffee? I've not had breakfast. Look, I won't be a minute.' He ran upstairs, and while he was pulling on his clothes he heard the familiar reassuring sound of Jan moving about in the kitchen, filling the kettle, looking for mugs and opening the fridge.

They sat down at the kitchen table. Jan opened her bag and took out a cigarette with a nervous hand. 'Do you mind?' she asked. He shook his head with a smile and got her an ashtray. When they were living together he had tried to get her to give up. He watched the lighter flare, the indrawn breath of satisfaction, and a calmness coming over her.

'In a funny way,' he said, very candid, 'I'm glad you left when you did.'

'Why?' She was intrigued.

'I've been able to cope with the Daniel thing best on my own, in my own way. It's very personal, an amputation. The solitude has been a help, oddly.'

But she was not interested in Philip's internal predicament. 'What happened?' she inquired briskly.

'He was picked up off the street and died in hospital shortly afterwards.' He saw she was shocked and it gave him a queer pleasure to elaborate for her. 'He was very rundown, he'd let himself go terribly. It was as if he just gave up, lost all heart to go on . . .' He paused, drew a deep breath to control himself and arched his eyebrows to move back the tears of stress. After a moment he went on, 'I hardly recognised him. He looked so old.'

'Only thirty-five it said in the paper.'

'He might have been fifty.' He stared into his coffee cup and the steam clouded into his contact lenses. 'You remember what he was like.' She nodded. 'Well, the change was extraordinary.'

'Does anyone know why . . .?' She seemed to be unable to say any more. He noticed, not for the first time, how unwilling everyone was to confront the reality of failure, struck inarticulate as though they lacked a vocabulary to encompass the disappointment of early promise.

'No,' he said shortly. And then regretted his bluntness. 'All I know is that he was working freelance on some big investigative story.' He heard himself talk about Daniel in a way that now seemed irrelevant. He was using the language of careers and success; somehow it seemed an inappropriate means of interpreting the mystery. Daniel had just given up and gone to pieces. He had died of something intangible, like a tribesman spellbound by a witch doctor. But he didn't expect Jan to understand what he meant and didn't mention it.

'Where did you pick that up?' She was as inquisitive as ever, hungry for the gossip.

'Oh – from a friend of his.' He knew he sounded evasive, and regretted it: she always complained about his secretiveness towards her.

'May I ask who that was?' she replied with more formality. He was grateful at least that she did not chide him for his evasion.

'Someone called Stevie Beck,' he found real pleasure pronouncing her name openly. 'I don't expect –'

'Stevie Beck!' Her exclamation of course confirmed all his reservations about his reserve. 'That's extraordinary. What were you doing with her?'

Philip was astonished. 'You don't know her?' He'd forgotten how Jan's gregarious tentacles stretched out across London, the names and numbers stored in a disintegrating notebook, grubbily interleaved with cards, snapshots, receipts and clippings.

'I don't know about "know her",' she replied, almost playful.

'You see, Stevie and I shared the same boyfriend once . . .' For the first time there was humour in her voice. '. . . though of course we didn't know it to start with.' She lit another cigarette. 'This bloke and I were at the university together. Stevie was living down the hill in the town, though she had some links with one of the faculties, I think. She was doing an external degree in politics, as far as I remember. She was very extreme and rather odd. No, I didn't know her exactly, at least not until we found we were having treatment together, if you understand what I'm saying.'

Philip nodded, stoically, digesting the implications.

'It's quite funny, in retrospect. We got talking over coffee one day. She was very frank. So then I was – and then we discovered about John.' She laughed. 'Stevie Beck,' she repeated. 'There's a blast from the past. She was known as Red Stevie, mainly because she stood outside the supermarket on Saturday mornings and distributed copies of *Socialist Worker* and such like. She was into everything. It was as though she was ashamed to have missed the sixties. Where did you run into her?' Jan's eyes sparkled with curiosity.

'Oh,' he lied, 'at a party. She knew Daniel apparently, or knew of him,' he added carefully. 'She'd heard he was working on a big story. That's all I know.'

'It doesn't sound as though he was up to working on a big story – from your description.'

'I know. It's odd to think that once upon a time he won this prize and everyone was after him. I would like to know more, I really would.' He was surprised at his own animation and lowered his voice to a note of mere curiosity. 'So when did you last see Stevie Beck?'

'Years ago now. I mean when I was at college. It was only this . . . accident that brought us together. Fortunately we didn't much care for the guy so there was no hassle – I mean we were pissed off with him but not offended by each other. Actually, it was quite a laugh. I think we confronted him together. I remember she enjoyed embarrassing him. Stevie was in with this women's group, a radical co-operative living in a big house out on the southern edge of the town. She invited me along to one of the meetings. We argued about our rights and practised anti-rapist judo.'

Philip was intrigued. 'Did you go often?'

Philip noticed, as she spoke, a perceptible stiffening of her morale. 'Not perhaps as regularly as I should have – the meetings were twice a week. Stevie was the main inspiration of that place. She seemed a bit older than most of the others, and always sounded as though she'd had heaps of experience in Africa and places.'

'I believe she was with the V.S.O.,' said Philip.

'It was in the family. Her parents were missionaries. She certainly had missionary fervour when it came to politics. As a feminist she was completely uncompromising.'

Philip looked directly at his wife. 'You never told me about this before.'

'There was no point,' she sounded more resigned than angry. 'When I married you it was deliberate regression. God knows why I did it. I suppose I wanted to please my father. Anyway, married to Philip Taylor I had to forget all about most of what I learnt from Stevie.' She looked down at her coffee. 'I don't mind admitting I could do with her around now. She always made me feel courageous, you know, positive, and in a strange way free.' She flashed him a vulnerable smile. 'That was quite an achievement, wasn't it? You know what I was like then, Phil, with my card indexes and bibliographies and all the usual hang-ups.'

He was embarrassed by her candour. 'Well,' he flustered, 'she – Stevie, I mean – is here – in London. I don't know where.'

'I never saw her after I left the campus. There was no reason. We weren't friends really. It was hard to know her. She was a lonely figure in many ways. I could never tell her how much I owed her. I wish I had done now.' She sighed. 'It seems a long time ago.' Then she brightened. 'But how funny you meeting her. What's she up to these days?'

'I don't know. I didn't ask. There wasn't time. We talked about Daniel mostly. There was a whole crowd of people.' The lies came easily and naturally: he felt as though he was defending private territory.

'She's changed if she's going to your sort of parties,' Jan commented. 'She was very strange. She hated men, she said, yet she was compulsively drawn to them. She had quite a reputation, you know.' She looked at him meaningfully.

He found her attitude unexpectedly offensive. He tried to stay calm and neutral. 'I thought she was rather attractive,' he said, wondering if she had already begun to suspect his emotions towards Stevie.

'I didn't know she was your type.' There was an edge of uncertainty to her banter. 'I suppose she's quite desirable in a bolshy sort of way. I can't imagine that she'd let you screw her,' she added, and laughed.

'Jan,' he protested. 'Please.' He sensed an argument beginning to break, and because he was now a host not a husband he apologised. Jan lit another cigarette, asserting her independence. He changed the subject. 'What's it like with . . . Jessica?'

'Yes. It's fine. Great.' Jan recovered her original mood, and became once more chilly and self-possessed. Perhaps, he thought, she has also given too much away.

'That's good.' His preoccupations rushed in again, ruthlessly crushing the resurgence of his feelings for a woman he hardly knew. He said: 'When I've sorted this Daniel business out we'll get an estate agent round and –'

She broke in. 'Why can't we do that now?'

'Well – I've got a lot to do – you know. Daniel. Father. It won't be long, I promise you. I'm not stalling. Please don't think that. You don't think that, do you?' He heard himself become almost pathetic in his desire to please.

'No.'

'It's just that I feel I somehow owe it to Daniel to straighten things out, to . . . to . . .' He began to stammer and smiled at her, ashamed and watery with emotion.

'Poor Philip,' she said. 'I expect you feel guilty about it now.' She said it so casually he wondered if she was aware what she had said. He blushed with suspicion and anger.

'Guilty about what?'

'Please don't get upset. I'm not attacking you. It doesn't matter. I didn't mean it.' She became decisive with irritation. 'Look, I must go.' She pushed her half-finished cup away and Philip reproached himself with another failure in communication.

'Okay,' he capitulated. 'When I'm sorted out I'll be in touch about all this,' he gestured around him.

'Fine.'

'Well. Goodbye.' He got up uncertainly, wondering if she expected a kiss.

'Please don't move. I'll let myself out.'

'Fine.'

'See you, then.'

'Nice talking to you.' She was at the door, hardly looking back. He felt something slipping away from him and vanishing into a terrible abyss.

'Goodbye,' he said, strangled.

'Bye.'

Jan's footsteps faded and for a long while Philip stayed at the kitchen table letting his private world re-compose itself after her peremptory invasion. In the silence that he liked best, the cadences of winter – flurries of rain on glass and the wind blowing at the top of the chimney like a child on a milk bottle – restored a sense of security within.

But the mood was transient. The words that Jan had used – guilt, loss and divorce – were lodged like splinters in his brain. The things she had said only induced his natural tendency to self-recrimination. His behaviour towards Daniel should have been more mature. An objective witness would say that Daniel had partly died of neglect. But then, on reflection, Jan, who was always so quick to apportion blame, had quite a lot to answer for herself. It was she who had taken the lead in excluding Daniel from their lives. Bitch, he said, silently shaping the word in solitude. He felt his fingers clenching and a modest fury racing in his head. It was typical of her to have known Stevie. There was nothing, it seemed, that he could call his own. Whatever it was that had once been his was now more or less gone; whatever it was he had acquired for himself was now lost. For a moment, it seemed hardly worth going on. His restless curiosity about Daniel was almost certainly pointless, leading nowhere. The carefully-made stability of his life had been uprooted. The passing sense of identity he felt with Daniel was unnerving, like seeing a familiar face unexpectedly in a crowd. Suddenly, he badly wanted distractions. He picked up the newspaper: it would be nice to go out this afternoon and see a film that gave him a good laugh. He could not remember the last time he had laughed spontaneously. His father had a phrase: laugh and the world is with you, he used to say. Alternatively, there was his revised piece for the newspapers to type up. The neatly written pages were on the desk by the window. He went over to it, and began to re-read his opening paragraph: 'Officers of the anti-terrorist bomb squad have been interrogating innocent citizens picked up in the cafés and streets around Central London. Just before Christmas last year, I and an acquaintance, S.B. . . .'

His attention was distracted by a blur of colour in the corner of his eye, and he found himself contemplating his carefully-spaced row of postcard reproductions like a worshipper.

Book Four

I

'Are you saying that this is the key to the door?' Philip swung the Yale on its string, feeling suddenly light-headed, almost deranged, and waited while his solicitor, sluggish and bloodshot after the holiday, leafed through the file.

The Christmas vacation was nearly over and he was back in Chancery Lane, trying to wrap up the formalities before carried away by the commitments of the new term. There was still his course on Colonialism to finish. Fortunately, only the final inquest and the sale and distribution of assets remained to be settled. Philip was privately indifferent to all this. Finding Daniel's house was all that mattered to him now; in this respect his solicitor had been unexpectedly efficient.

'As you are no doubt aware, sir, it is the key that was found with Mr. Taylor,' the lawyer was saying. He seemed to be enjoying his client's anxiety, exploiting his obligation to skirt round the painful details to keep Philip on tenterhooks. 'I am pleased to say,' he went on, 'that our inquiries have now revealed that the deceased is recorded as the owner of a freehold property in North London; as far as we can ascertain, a terraced house in good repair.'

Philip's dark suit was matched by an unassertive tie; in the street he would pass for a clerk. Now he was twisting his long fingers together with nerves. 'And this is the key to the door?' he asked again.

'That is our assumption, sir.' The voice ignored Philip's expression of relief and began to read abstractly from the file about enclosing the address in the letter herewith, and advising him to make an inspection of the property at his earliest convenience with a view to the speedy and advantageous disposal of the freehold to the mutual benefit of the immediate family.

'I think I'll decide what to do with the place when I've had a look,' said Philip assertively.

'Very good, Mr. Taylor. An excellent plan in my judgment.' The unemotional response did not vary. Philip had the impression that if he said he was going to assault five secretaries on his way out and give Daniel's house to charity, the lawyer would still have concurred.

He came away into the street. It was raining hard; cars and taxis were jammed, wipers going, lights shining in the wet, red on white on red all the way up the hill; people under umbrellas were slushing up the pavement, gaining ground against the traffic. Philip felt his hands getting raw; an icy shiver of rain went down his neck. He hurried to reach the shelter of his own car; there, insatiably curious, he tore open the envelope and was soon cross-checking the reference in the *A-Z*. Daniel's house was not far from his own, in North London, an address in Barnesbury. He knew instinctively that he should go and look it over without delay. Tomorrow would be too late.

Tomorrow there were the faculty and his students to face. He would have his heart freshly wrung in public by those who knew about Daniel and said so, halting through the unfamiliar vocabulary of condolence; by those who knew but could manage nothing, not even half-stated unwitting solecisms; and, worst of all, by the embarrassment of those who discovered that they did not know but ought to. He knew he would have to steel himself for a kind of social espionage: whispered asides and glancing looks, the surreptitious scrutiny of friends and colleagues. With Jan's departure now common knowledge, he would be seen as doubly unfortunate, the victim, he sensed, of a fascinated sympathy, and, elsewhere, the subject of no doubt frank and brutal dissection in a dozen conversations. Perhaps, he queried wryly to himself, it would make him more attractive to a certain kind of woman, this helpless vulnerability. He did not know, and the thought did not, in any event, fill him with much anticipation. He guessed his emotions to be secretly mortgaged, though he could hardly bear to bring himself to articulate those feelings, even in thought.

The rain stopped and the short day lightened briefly. He put the car into gear and moved away from the parking space with an indefinable reluctance, as though starting out on a journey both longed-for and yet intimidating. Driving slowly through the afternoon traffic, he knew he was wanting an excuse to postpone the visit. He began to day-dream. The street-map open on the seat beside him brought back memories of those days when, after Daniel had moved in, unnerved by his brother's lifestyle, he had searched for somewhere else to live.

The flat in Baron's Court had appealed twice over; it was equidistant between the college and Kew Gardens. On summer afternoons, when there was no teaching or lecturing to do, he would take the District Line, and rattle out to the toy station by the side entrance and then, sometimes hurrying, sometimes strolling, pass through the turnstile into the soft-coloured spaces of the park, a cool, shady contrast to the dust and noise of West Kensington. After he met Jan, he attempted without success to retain the solitary and uncomplicated pleasure he found among the trees and flowers, but she had no patience for that. She was always wanting to hurry away to meet her friends for a drink in a pub. After a couple of visits, broken off in this way, they stopped going. Once they had moved, Philip's passion for his orchid house became a natural substitute. It would be nice, he thought with relief, even in winter, to wander down a few leafless paths and avenues.

'Gardens close at four today, sir,' said the park-keeper as Philip pushed through the wet iron gate.

'I won't be long,' He was almost alone. He walked over the ragged winter lawns, black with worm-casts, and when he caught sight of the Palm House his spirits lifted. He paced slowly round the ornamental lake, watching the ducks ruffled by the cold wind and the sickly goldfish moving like fallen leaves in the icy water. His thoughts turned inexorably to Jan again. She had exacted many other submissions as well. His flat, for instance, did not fit her idea of a suitable residence for a married woman. They would have to buy a house, she said, and then refused to consider property in the cheaper parts of Brixton, Clapham and the fashionable East End on the grounds of street violence.

'One of the girls at work,' she said, wide-eyed, 'has a friend who was raped at knife-point there.'

In those comparatively early days of their relationship Philip always acquiesced: their house was found in Belsize Park, with the help of a generous loan from his father, one that both sides knew could never be repaid. Daniel, he imagined, had raised a similar loan. It was one of the curiosities of his brother's rejection of his father that Daniel had never been disinherited. Reflecting, as he had recently, on the ramifications of this relationship, he had come to believe that in some ways his father had needed a family problem like Daniel to distract him from the others –

marital and entrepreneurial – which threatened him more personally. And so, for both of them, the money had always been there.

Now he watched a mother and her daughter throwing bread to the ducks; the woman was bending over the excited child, talking to her with that peculiarly parental absorption, steadying with a gloved hand to stop her falling into the water. Philip wondered idly if Jan would ever know the satisfactions of motherhood, or indeed if now she wanted to. Here, on their first visit, she had posed against this stone lion for a photograph. They had known each other then for barely a month; everything they did and everything they said was monopolised by sexual curiosity. It was early autumn on that occasion, with the heat and colour of an Indian summer, and she was looking, to his eyes, very desirable in close-fitting tee shirt and jeans under an Afghan coat. Her hair was longer in those days, and pulled back from her forehead, severe but striking.

And then he had given her the camera, and she snapped him, careless with laughter, bullying him playfully. 'Don't look so serious,' she said.

He, pale and myopic in the radiant sunshine, did his best to make a natural smile.

'What sign are you?' she asked.

'Why do you want to know?'

'Well, look,' she pointed to the stone lion. 'A leo. It would be nice if you were a leo too.'

'What are you?' he parried.

'Virgo of course.' She sounded proud. 'And you?'

He hesitated.

'When's your birthday?' she quizzed him.

'St. Swithin's Day. July the fifteenth.'

'Oh. Cancer. That makes you very sensitive, you know. And home-loving. Say cheese.' And she clicked again. He never told her that the camera case had blocked the lens and ruined her picture. When the film was processed she was only interested in his shots of her, photographs he had thrown away in his recent spring-clean.

He stood on the edge, on the paving, and looked down into the water. His peaked white face stared back at him, distorted.

'What a funny nose you've got,' Jan had said. And he had smiled and wrinkled his face. From his daily consultations with the mirror, he knew he had aged since then.

It was almost dark when he left the gardens. Soon he was steering back into London through the rush-hour like an automaton. It was only when he slammed the car door and drew in the late winter air that he took stock of the fact that this was finally the place, the street in which Daniel had lived.

The road, running downhill, was quiet, almost deserted, and badly lit. At the bottom, the heart of the old city was spread out in front of him, a scatter of white lights sparkling in the cold new year darkness like the crystals of a broken windscreen. As he began to pick his way over the litter on the pavement, checking off the numbers on the doors, Philip saw that the houses on the right hand, some of which were roofless and derelict, backed on to a vast space that seemed to stretch flat and empty across to a row of lighted windows two or three hundred yards away. On the opposite side of the street, where he was walking, stood a terrace, tall, solid and Victorian, with wrought-iron balconies.

A car, with headlights on full beam, came bouncing up the hill. He carried on walking but shielded his eyes with his arm, and when they had recovered from the blinding, he looked up to orientate himself and stopped still. He was standing at a small junction; the building on the corner was his destination, number eighty-seven, Daniel's house.

Perhaps it was his nerves, but, from the first, the place struck him as distinctly odd. The flight of steps to the front door, for instance, was flanked by a pair of plaster sphinxes. He puzzled briefly about which long-forgotten popular event had prompted the architect to add these strange, imposing figures to his design. Looking back up the street, he saw that on this side at any rate each house was guarded in the same way.

'How do you do?' he said playfully to the silent faces in front of him. He felt a fluttering of excitement now, but also an awareness of making a move that was final and irreversible. After Daniel's house there would, he guessed, be nowhere else to take his search.

Then, unable to contradict his movements, he climbed slowly past the sphinxes up the steps.

The house was dark; standing under the lintel, it seemed deserted and uncared for, though the door was freshly painted and solid-looking. He was twisting the key string nervously in his fingers, but superstition said that he should ring first. He did so, conscious of the absurdity, but could hear no answering bell inside. A man, walking very slowly, came down the street, looked at him and carried on with deliberation towards the main road at the bottom. Philip pressed the bell and again there was no answer. It was very quiet. The street was out of the way to most traffic. As he listened attentively to the silence within, his ear up against the door, plucking up the courage to use his keys, he became aware of the faint sound of typing. At first it seemed to come from the house across the road and he thought his hearing was playing tricks with him because that too was darkened and empty. Suddenly, there was an audible click and a light came on in an upstairs room, lifting the shadows from the area basement. He strained for the sound of footsteps inside but there was only the faint steady clatter of the typewriter. There was no door knocker. He stepped back into the street and looked up at the lighted window. As he did so the curtain closed, automatically it seemed, shutting out a glimpse of a high ceiling and bright paint.

Confused, he ran up the steps again, and pressed his ear to the door. The noise of the typewriter continued. He put the key in the lock, turned it and pushed. The door opened with a slight booming sound. Inside, it was pitch dark like a cellar. 'Daniel,' he said, quite loud; his head pounded with apprehension. 'Daniel,' he repeated, louder still. The typing stopped and the sphinxes behind him darkened as the light upstairs went out. He heard footsteps coming downstairs in a slow shuffle. He was about to say 'Daniel' again when the steps stopped and a woman's voice said, 'Greg, is that you?'

Philip's mind went empty with confusion and embarrassment; for a moment he imagined he had made a mistake and come to the wrong number.

'It's m – m – me,' he stammered. 'Philip Taylor. I've c – c – come.' He felt suddenly like an intruder; he looked up instinctively to see if he could make her out in the darkness.

'How did you find this place? What do you want?' Stevie Beck was speaking in a suppressed and furious whisper, though there was no apparent danger of her being overheard.

He hesitated; secretly, he had always hoped for this scene, but had dared not imagine it. Now that it was being played out, he did not know how to begin. Half of him wanted to apologise for everything and run wildly away down the street towards the crystal lights, run until he became a stick, a straw, a thing merging with the outside air. She paid no attention to his inarticulacy and started quizzing him again.

'What are you doing here, for Christ's sake?' Another car went past and a parallelogram of light picked up the fierce gleam in Stevie's eye, staring down at him from the turn of the stairs. 'What do you want?'

He dropped his voice. 'When you rang me before – before Christmas – you said you had to see me about Daniel. Now it's my turn.' He paused. 'I'm sorry about what happened –'

'Don't say anything,' she ordered. 'Just shut the door and come upstairs.' He obeyed without question; the house echoed and he stood paralysed by total darkness. Then a light came up on the landing and he began to climb the stairs, wishing he did not feel so anxious and divided. After the decay of the exterior, Philip was surprised to find wall-to-wall carpet underfoot. The house appeared to be well heated and, as he reached the landing, a light in the hall came on without warning. He started and, briefly disorientated, looked about for Stevie. But she was standing in front of him, grey eyes steady with concentration, in the half-open door leading to the spacious front room upstairs. Philip looked about. The landing, the rooms opening off it – everything was furnished in colour-supplement luxury, with matching fabrics, blended tones of wallpaper and paint, sofas, armchairs, a stereo system, a colour television, and even an unopened bottle of Glenfiddich on the bookcase. To his astonishment, Philip found his sober suit and well-polished shoes rather in keeping.

'Won't you sit down?' said Stevie, but he couldn't decide if she was mocking.

'It's very nice,' he commented conventionally. 'Did you have it done for you – by a designer, I mean?' It struck him that Jan might even have revised her opinion of Daniel if she could have seen all this.

'It has its points,' Stevie commented obscurely, as though she did not altogether approve.

'It's nice,' he repeated. He regretted his inane conversation, but he was still feeling profoundly disconcerted.

There was all the self-deception to cope with first. He had never admitted to himself that he was likely to find Stevie here, though he was well aware that she had already told him she shared Daniel's house. Self-consciously scrutinising himself now, he knew he had never acknowledged the hidden motive in his search for Daniel's house. The solicitor, who had not referred to any other residents, had abetted these secret evasions of the heart. To justify his inner confusion Philip found himself blaming the shock of the unexpected. Even when he had dared to anticipate this visit in his mind, he had never imagined Daniel's house quite like this. Relaxing slightly, he noticed the heavy calico-patterned curtains drawn across the window, and he half-expected Stevie to offer him a whisky-and-soda in a magenta cocktail glass.

Stevie herself was a surprise too. She had become so much a part of the life in his head these last few weeks that the reality of that snub-nosed, boyish, slightly arrogant expression was fractionally at odds with the ideal of his dreams and fantasies. Jan had talked about 'Red Stevie', but here was a woman in jeans and a heavy Aran sweater, sitting back on cushions printed after William Morris. Now she was looking at him with that steady inquisitive gaze he had found so intimidating last time. It occurred to him then that from her manner she did not know about what had happened and he drew back from serious conversation, afraid.

It was nice to be warm again. 'It's cold out, isn't it?' he said.

'I don't know. I've been in all day.'

He looked about him. 'So this is the house that Daniel bought,' he said uneasily. 'Are you alone here now?'

'At the moment.'

He remembered her first words on the staircase. 'Who is Greg?' he asked.

'Greg is none of your business,' she said, not rudely.

'Oh. Sorry.'

'Don't apologise. You couldn't know.'

He was surprised how quickly he was getting used to her bluntness again. It made him more forthright himself. 'I'm glad I found you here –' he began, and then feebly tried to make a preemptive strike. 'I mean I wanted to talk to you about . . .' He waved vaguely with his hand to indicate the episode with the Bomb Squad.

'So do I.' Her expression hardened with characteristic suddenness. 'What happened?' She demanded. 'I asked the guy at the desk on the way out where you'd got to. "Oh, he left hours ago," he said. Why did you just piss off like that?'

This was the accusation he feared. He looked away. 'I was

afraid.' It sounded feeble. 'I'm sorry – it was an unforgivable thing to do.'

'I'll say.'

Her indignation – expressed in the way she straightened sharply, sitting as she was, cross-legged in one of the armchairs – shamed him and he went on: 'They gave me a hard time; I lost my nerve. I'm not used to that sort of thing.'

'Nor am I,' she replied half-heartedly.

He sensed in her denial a confusion in her own mind about the appropriate response. 'Well,' he said, referring shyly to their former conversation. 'At least I wasn't completely unprepared.' He attempted a smile of gratitude. 'Thanks to you.'

Stevie was uneasy with praise. 'Did they interrogate you about me?'

'Yes.' He wondered if she wanted details and remembered with shame that he had seemed to incriminate her. He fell silent.

'They claimed you were part of an active bombing unit,' she said. 'It was ridiculous. They wanted to know why we'd talked about the Army.'

'They asked me that, too. It was very disturbing to be accused of things you haven't done.'

'That's their method.'

'In the end they realised it was all a mistake, I suppose, and let me go. I'm sorry: all I wanted to do was get away. I should have stayed,' he added, contrite.

'Okay.' She cut him short. 'Don't overdo it.' She appeared irritated by his efforts at conciliation. 'I can look after myself. Anyway, it was no big deal, just the usual cock-up.'

'Do you believe that?' Philip was reassured to think that she did not have any darker suspicions.

'Of course. They're always raiding those places. It's routine. You just happened to get caught.' Stevie narrowed her eyes reflectively. 'They soon found out what my politics are. Then they really got started. I didn't give in,' she concluded, rather nervously, he thought, watching with secret admiration.

Philip remembered the screams. 'I was searched,' he said, hoping to lead the conversation forward.

'Oh, so was I.' She seemed anxious not to be outdone. 'Stripped and searched,' she said, and quivered involuntarily. 'Bastards,' she whispered. Philip imagined she was going through the scene again in her mind. 'It's all good training,' she went on didactically. 'I told you the State is falling apart. It's the crisis of capitalism, isn't it?'

'It was also an invasion of the rights of the individual,' said Philip in his donnish way. 'I've written an article about that, actually, for one of the newspapers. I think people ought to be told. Would you like to see it?'

'An article?' She seemed intrigued by him, then scornful of the idea. 'What's the point? I've told you just now. It's happening all the time. It's not news – whatever you feel about it. Besides the Tory press would never print it.' Her manner softened as if she did not care to be so dismissive. 'Why did you decide to write an article?' she inquired.

'Because I thought you might read it,' he said candidly. 'I didn't know where you were. I wanted to find Daniel's house.' He spoke in a nervous falter, afraid of her reaction. 'Do you know about Daniel?' he asked tentatively.

He saw her flinch in her chair, as though electrocuted, and waited miserably for what he expected to be the fury of her reaction. But to his amazement she managed to sound casual and relaxed. 'Yes,' she said. 'I know about Daniel.' Her eyes shone brightly and she held herself steady as a mast, staring away from Philip towards the window. He watched, with tears in his own eyes.

'I'm sorry,' he said quietly. He had underestimated the desolating loss of Daniel's death for Stevie. After a minute he tried to go on. 'I didn't mean to hurt you . . .' he began.

'Don't say that,' she retorted as though he was spoiling things, affronting her with his consideration for her finer feelings. 'It's happened now. We can't escape it. It wasn't unexpected, you know.'

'When we met,' he started, 'did you –?'

'I was desperate, Philip,' she broke in shortly, using his name in a way that suggested his failings of the past were forgiven. 'I don't mind admitting that. Your number was the last chance, I thought.' She hugged her arms round her thin chest. 'By that time I was really getting afraid.' Silence grew between them like the approach of darkness and they sat quite still for some minutes, observing, it seemed to Philip, a mute requiem for his brother. Finally, a new mood of calmness settled between them and Philip found that they were talking quietly like old friends, at ease in the conversation. As if it answered a buried need, Stevie talked about

Daniel and Philip tuned in and out of her words like a radio ham, listening to her when not distracted by his own thoughts. '. . . in the end he became impossible to live with, very suicidal actually. But then he was very run-down and wild, and relying on tons of drugs to get him through each day.' Stevie's conversation was full of hints and suggestions. He wanted time to tease out the information that was buried beneath the surface of her allusions, but it was hard to know where to start.

She got up, very agile, and began to pace across the carpet. He noticed for the first time that she was wearing only thick patterned ski socks on her tiny feet.

'I suppose this is all yours now,' she said with resignation, gesturing across the room towards the stair-head. 'When do you want me out?' she went on, reinforcing her question with a plain blunt look.

'I – I – I don't know just yet,' he stammered. 'N – n – nobody knows you're living here, you see. I mean the solicitors didn't mention you.' He began to struggle to pull the crumpled letter out of his coat pocket, and then, suddenly conscious of his self-respect, broke off. It annoyed him to think that he wanted to justify and explain everything he said, as though he did not trust himself not to lie to her about his intentions.

'I've been away,' she said abruptly. 'When I heard about Daniel I just couldn't stand it here. So I closed the house and went to Amsterdam for the New Year. An old boyfriend. I only got back this weekend.'

'Why did you come back?'

'I had a date,' she said quickly and then seemed to regret what she had said.

'With Greg?' he queried playfully. He realised as soon as he spoke that he had gone too far and risked too much familiarity between them.

'That's none of your business.' The look of defensiveness was unmistakable.

Philip, embarrassed, looked about him at the vulgar affluence of the fittings and said, attempting to change the subject: 'There's s – s – something odd about this house.'

'What do you mean?' she challenged. Philip was muddled. A small tremor of curiosity shivered in his mind.

'I – I don't know. It's just not what I expected.'

Stevie stopped her pacing. 'Was I what you expected?' she

demanded. He found that she was looking at him with humorous mischief, exposing for the first time yet another side of her character he had not seen before. Everything about her when she was in her element like this seemed only to sharpen his sense of desolation and longing.

'Well, no,' he said, wondering how much more he dared to say. 'No, you weren't,' he repeated lamely. Out of sheer nerves he looked at his watch. It was eight o'clock. Tomorrow there was an early start to make, the final preparations for the new term to round off. After his walk in the winter air and his driving he was hungry; he could do with a takeaway before he went to bed. He hesitated with indecision. He could hardly go now and leave this chance meeting unexplored. But he didn't want to risk antagonising her as well; his fear of rejection was as great as his fear of acceptance. She seemed to have forgotten about his behaviour before Christmas, but if he stayed longer, he worried that those events would be brought up for more scrutiny. He could not think of that without serious anxiety. As usual, Philip sat there completely divided about the best and safest course of action. Parting is such sweet sorrow, he thought, and was then amazed at his own pretension. It was as though he was watching himself from the outside, like a spectator.

As if to emphasise the fortuitous nature of the situation, the light in the middle of the room suddenly went out and plunged them both into shadow. Philip turned round, but Stevie seemed unsurprised. She walked to the door and pulled it open. A shaft of light from the previously darkened landing fell into the room. Stevie fiddled with the switch.

'What are you doing?' he asked, grateful to have a harmless question to prolong his stay.

'Adjusting the time switch,' she replied, slightly nasal with absorption.

Once more, Philip was surprised. 'Daniel certainly went in for some sophisticated equipment.'

'Oh,' she sounded quite off-hand, 'it's just a precaution. This way the house looks lived in – even when I'm not here.' Philip had the impression that she was trying to tell him something. The light clicked on again. 'There.' She gave a little skip in her coloured socks and leant back against the wall, looking at him.

He didn't know what to say, but managed to stammer something about the decoration being untypical of Daniel's style. 'I suppose that's what I meant about the house being rather odd,' he added, labouring an explanation.

'Oh,' she replied with an animated bounce in her voice, with its slightly breathless catch. 'Daniel never had any taste. Surely you know that. I don't think he ever took the slightest notice of his surroundings. His clothes were always jeans and sweaters. The pictures he liked best were advertisements.' She sized up the garbled furniture. 'This isn't bad for Daniel, this stuff.'

Philip grew bolder; this was a conversation he could understand. Besides, it seemed to have no risks. 'I didn't know you were bothered with bourgeois design.'

'The main thing,' she said, smiling enigmatically, 'is that the neighbours should treat us as one of them.'

'Even in clothes.' He pointed at her surprisingly fashionable jeans.

This time Stevie did not seem to mind the implication of familiarity. 'Oh' – again that asthmatic lilt – 'I don't know.' She put her arms out like a scarecrow in a sudden and childish gesture, planting her thin legs apart under the overhead light. 'Look.' The shadow distorted her expression strangely and made it at once menacing and sexy. 'Once upon a time I thought I wanted to be a model.' She sighed. 'It was only a teenage day-dream.'

Philip looked up at her from the sofa with helpless fascination, and tried to find the energy to get going and leave. Behind the low cropped fringe of her hair, now black in the angle of the light, she was watching him, arrogant and teasing. He was glad that the austerity of her mind was softening. In a few minutes she might even start to gossip. She dropped her outstretched arms to her sides with an exhausted gasp.

'Well?' she said inquisitively.

He sat forward in the sofa, responding defensively to the invitation for more talk. As he did so, there was a slight hum from the window and the heavy patterned curtain pulled back automatically revealing cold white stars like splinters in the blue winter sky.

Everything went wrong for Philip's new term. He overslept and left half his notes at home in his hurry to make up lost time. The traffic was heavier than usual; at Hyde Park Corner an articulated lorry had skidded and overturned; columns of vehicles, slowed down by the accident, steamed in the rain. So he arrived late for the faculty meeting, breathless with confusion and apologies, scattering drops of rainwater across the committee's memoranda and timetables. Afterwards, as he anticipated, the other staff talked about him in cagey murmurs while affecting mild sorrow for his bereavement. Someone said, 'Why don't you take a sabbatical, Phil?' and he didn't know what to reply. At the moment he couldn't imagine anything he would like more. But there wasn't the time to worry about what his colleagues were saying or thinking, and he dashed off to see the students who had turned up at his office. He had never found himself racing through his work like this before. In general, he was known to be painfully conscientious, thorough, unhurried and devoted; he would always take trouble with the lame ducks and encourage extra reading for the enthusiasts. In his own work he never felt confident unless he had covered every eventuality, and checked every reference. Now, in his eagerness to get the day over with, he skipped his usual cafeteria lunch, broke his habit of reading the paper over coffee, and conducted a sequence of increasingly attenuated conversations as he saw the afternoon light fading outside. At four-thirty he crammed everything on his desk into his briefcase and ran to the car park.

Half an hour later, calmer but still apprehensive, he pushed open the front door of Daniel's house. 'Stevie,' he called. The silence was complete. He imagined she would be back before long, banged the door shut and walked through to the open kitchen at the back. It was, like the room upstairs, furnished with the best of everything. He found the kettle and went to the sink. He turned the tap. The water ran over his fingers. He dabbed his eyelids and his face stung with the cold. His tiredness was catching up with him again. He put the kettle on the gas and felt the warmth rising into his face as he stood over it, waiting. There was nothing else to do.

A draught stirred through the kitchen, dancing with the steam from the kettle, and causing the dried herbs, hanging in fists from the wall, to rustle against the pinework. Stevie was standing in the doorway. She was wearing a shapeless tent of bright Indian cotton that flowed around her as she moved. Philip saw that her face was furrowed and crumpled after a deep sleep and her hair messed like a schoolboy's. She looked hot and sticky-eyed, leaning her head wearily against the door frame, watching his movements with silent attention. Despite her lazy stance, she had not lost her poise of motion and, when he turned to glimpse her, she moved into the kitchen, prowling vigilantly. He found the latent energy in her movements, even the smallest gesture of her hand or deliberate placing of her bare, sandalled feet, intensely erotic. Stevie herself seemed relaxed, less hostile, more accustomed to his presence.

'Would you like some coffee?' he began, feeling inadequate yet anxious to please. 'I'm just boiling the kettle.'

Ignoring his question, she watched him make his coffee. 'Don't waste that coffee. 'It's all I've got –'

'Oh. I've got plenty of money with me,' he replied.

'How nice for you,' he heard her say before the glass door into the hallway slammed and her footsteps thumped angrily up the stairs. Philip shrugged, finding her change of mood unfathomable. Nonetheless he put two mugs of coffee on a tray and carried them up. Stevie was sitting cross-legged in one of the soft armchairs in the upper front room staring at nothing. She looked at him indifferently.

'Here's —,' he began.

'I told you I don't –' she began with crisp fury, then stopped and put out her hand to the tray. 'Thank you,' she said. It came out like an apology. Philip, encouraged, said: 'I enjoyed last night. It's nice to have someone who understands what I'm talking about.' She did not reply and he realised that he had given too much of himself away to make her easy; there was nothing, it seemed, she feared more than having to expose her own feelings to someone she did not completely trust.

'You were late for work, weren't you?' Her question sounded amused; he was relieved not to have provoked another outburst.

'How do you know?'

'You're wearing odd socks.'

He looked down. 'So I am.' Involuntarily he began to justify

173

himself. 'At this time of the year it's so dark you can hardly see a thing when you get up in the morning – especially if you're blind like me.'

'Don't they have electricity in your part of London?'

'I don't like artificial light in the early morning,' he confessed. 'It hurts my eyes.' He looked down at his feet. 'Odd socks,' he repeated. 'How dreadful.'

She looked at him curiously. 'You really get uptight about small things.'

'It's my nature,' he admitted. 'I'm quite different from Daniel.'

'In some ways,' she commented. Philip wanted her to elaborate, but he was afraid to pry too closely. It was enough, he felt, to enjoy the satisfaction of her company, paradoxical though that might seem.

'Well, you both like talking all night,' she said.

'You don't have to believe me,' he replied with sincerity, 'but I haven't talked like that since I was a student.'

'I'm glad you found it interesting,' she said coldly, concentrating on her coffee. She seemed to distrust his confidences. Her shy prickly nature had a primitive quality to it.

'Oh yes,' he said with quiet enthusiasm. 'There's so much about my brother I don't know. You may think it's strange, but I need to know how it all went wrong – I think it's something to do with the sense of loss I feel.'

'Yes,' she said gravely. 'I can understand.' He was about to become grateful, but she added a tiny cruel coda. 'Quite rightly, you feel guilty.'

He began to stammer and then simply fell silent, cowed by the hopelessness of the misunderstandings and antagonisms that seemed to spring up like snares in their conversation. He wondered temporarily whether it was his obsession with Daniel that was provoking Stevie's temper, but they had discussed all that last night and he felt sure that, in fact, she was as anxious to talk about it all as he was, and was certainly more experienced in the agonies of grief.

'I don't know why you trust me like this,' he had said, as the curtain had drawn back, half-longing for an excuse to make his escape. She was studying him objectively. Her frown lightened magically and she almost smiled. 'Do I?' Philip had fluttered nervously, but she interrupted. 'I don't think you could lie to me. You wouldn't succeed; you don't know how to. You see, you're a coward, and you haven't the courage to lie well. You're quite good at deceptions to save your skin, but that's a sort of coward's courage, isn't it? So,' she had concluded, with a disarming change of mood, 'even if I can't trust you completely, I don't need to fear you.'

Philip had been hypnotised by the accuracy of her assessment. It was as though he had been opened down the middle and deftly filleted of all his secrets. But there was also a generosity in the way she saw through everything and told you about it. It made him feel ashamed of his fears and of the mean collusions of his own mind.

'I'm probably quite honest,' he had said, with his customary self-awareness 'but that's only because I have no imagination.' He spoke without irony, staring in front of him sadly. 'I'm too ordinary really to do anything but stick more or less to the truth, whatever that is. I'm not inventive enough to cope with duplicity. I can't improvise like Daniel. But, as you say, I'm also a coward, so I can accept a situation, even if I know it stinks. I've always been a coward like that,' he admitted, 'and I've always been bullied, from Daniel onwards.' He checked himself, conscious that he was talking too much. She was strangely sympathetic, despite her fierceness; he felt a new confidence and noticed that his stammer had stopped. It was odd how he wanted to tell her about himself, to share his thoughts so freely with her. He supposed it was only because she seemed to know them already. Many times, as the conversation had gone back and forward, he noticed how she became suddenly remote, as though her mind had become momentarily disembodied. Philip, sensitive as always to his effect on people, had thought at first that she disliked the gaucheness of his open-hearted spontaneity and had lapsed into silence.

After one such interval she had said, 'Would you like to see the house?' It was untypical for Stevie to play the hostess, but she became insistent and he did not resist. Each room carried the hint of fresh paint; it was all tidy and carefully furnished.

Philip said, following like a tourist: 'Daniel did a thorough job.'

'We paid someone to do it,' she explained. 'He wasn't well – and I wanted to get it finished quickly. The house was going to be a new start for him.'

'What kind of new start?'

'Oh –' she sounded vague. 'A break with the past.' She hurried on. 'It was my idea – the house.' She ushered him past a small door halfway up the staircase. 'No need to go in there, it's just junk.' She reverted to her theme, 'I thought that it would give him something to concentrate on. But –' She stopped and Philip did not want to press her further. 'But he never finished . . .' Her voice faded. 'There are one or two things you'll have to fix if you're going to sell it.'

They were back in the upstairs front room again.

'I – I – don't – I – haven't decided about that,' he stuttered, and took refuge in practicality. 'What's got to be done?'

'The back garden – you can't see it in the dark – is full of rubble. The hall hasn't been papered. And the balcony out there,' she waved at the window, 'needs restoring.'

'I love these balconies,' he said, indicating the rest of the street.

'The ledge is okay, but the ironwork needs replacing. At the moment it's missing – I think the builders nicked it – and it spoils the look of the house.' She smiled at the irony. 'From the property point of view.'

'Those sphinxes,' he said, warming with enthusiasm. 'They're amazing.'

'Yes – aren't they. That's why Daniel and I bought the place,' she said with a wide smile. 'It's what the agent called a special feature, but for us it had a private meaning,' she paused enigmatically.

'What was that?'

'Oh.' Conscious that he was fascinated, she became inaccessible again. 'A private thing.' She seemed to enjoy her riddling replies. He hated to feel humiliated by the suggestion of something shared only by Daniel. Eventually Stevie broke the silence. 'You're very gloomy. Speak,' she commanded.

The conversation had gone on. Talking about Daniel and his house was a way of coming to terms with an event not yet fully assimilated into their lives, a way of transforming the pain of bereavement into the ache of loss and finally to the steady, acceptable pulse of memory.

Now, almost a day later, Stevie modified her initial harshness with a rapid and characteristic shift of mood. 'To be fair, Daniel felt guilty as well. Your problem is the problem of being born into the Taylor family. It was like this with Daniel, and now it's the same with you.' She sounded almost sympathetic and her lips parted in a magical expression of private laughter. 'So, you see, you're not as different as you think.' She spoke as though she had just successfully demonstrated a complicated geometric theorem.

'Perhaps.' He felt ashamed. 'I've never taken risks like Daniel. I never went to Africa for instance.'

'Oh – you came quite close to Africa last night,' she said with an odd look, 'though you probably don't recognise it yet.'

He felt uncomfortable with what she was saying, as though she had some mantic powers; it became his turn to parry. 'Daniel was more at home there, of course, than I would ever be. He was always so . . .' he searched for the word, 'wild.'

'That wasn't my first impression.'

'When you met in Africa?'

She nodded. 'Tanga. On the coast.' She lit a cigarette slowly and exhaled. 'The beginning of the seventies, that was. It all seems a long time ago now and a long long way away.' She was dreaming of the past, Philip could see; her eyes danced. 'South of the port it's glorious. Beaches and blue skies. Amazing seas you get there. Daniel and I used to walk along the shore, looking out across the ocean towards the East, pointing at China or Australia, and playing games with the waves. He was very childish sometimes.'

Philip smiled. 'Not the serious-minded rebel.'

'Your brother was like an adolescent; sometimes I wondered if he would ever grow up,' she was almost scornful. 'At first I thought it was incredible, how green he was. I was younger than him, but he was so naïve he made me feel like his aunt.'

'This was his first trip there.' Philip was surprised to hear himself defending his brother.

'Like a lot of young Englishmen from your class it was obvious he'd had a very sheltered upbringing. I know he'd been to university by this time but none of that had given him much maturity, at least as far as I was concerned. Listening to him talk about the parties and the games and the eating and drinking, it was as though he was describing a rather good finishing school.'

Philip recognised the picture she was painting for him. 'I didn't realise you knew him so well before he came to London.'

'Tanga is a small place. The Europeans tended to stick together. There wasn't much to do after the day's school was over except swim in the harbour, drink and screw and play poker. We shared a bungalow for a while; or rather, to put it more accurately, he moved into the one I was renting.'

Philip identified what he considered to be the familiar pattern of his brother's behaviour.

She noticed the quickening of his interest. 'No,' she went on, 'we weren't lovers then. I was having this very heavy affair with a Tanzanian government official. There was another girl in the flat; I think they slept together a few times. All Daniel was interested in was what I knew about the drugs racket. I think it was the first time someone had told him something really bad about your family's business.'

'How did he react?'

'He was shocked at first. When he realised it gave him a good reason to hate his father and not to go into the company, he got very excited. I thought he just wanted to use what I told him for his own ends. Later, of course, it was different – when he became a journalist, I mean.'

'He came home quite soon, didn't he?'

'He got sick and he ran out of money and all your Daddy's people were running around with their hands in the air saying, Get this kid out of here, he's making a nuisance of himself. So this old fart arrived to bring him home. He came to the house. Daniel was in bed, quite sick. This bloke just took him away in a taxi. He was a shit.' She lit another cigarette. 'I didn't see Daniel for a while after that.'

'And by then he'd done his Newcastle stuff,' he hazarded.

She smiled, genuinely pleased with herself. 'The tiny little seed that was sown in Africa had borne fruit. He could never look at the drug business in the same way again.'

Philip nodded and said: 'The old fart you mentioned is a guy called Appleby. I went to see him recently. He told me that Africa changed Daniel.' He faced her questioningly. 'But he wasn't very specific about what it was that had such an effect on him.'

Stevie did not ignore his invitation. 'The truth about Mayhew & Taylor,' she announced with mock theatricality. 'That was what disturbed him most.'

Philip said something about truth being a difficult concept in such a dubious moral area like the behaviour of Western pharmaceutical companies in the Third World.

'It's not difficult at all,' she said sharply. 'There was nothing dubious about it – it was fucking blatant.' And she laughed like she had laughed once before with Philip, throwing her head back and filling the room with a peculiarly harsh merriment. 'For a start, the company salesmen were being encouraged, unofficially of course, to export risky and out-of-date stock to the governments of the Commonwealth. If you want it another way,' she said with sarcasm, 'they were dumping the kind of pills they couldn't sell in England and other so-called civilised countries, on the ignorant niggers of the old Empire.' She sounded bored and off-hand about it all, as though the information would be wasted on someone like Philip.

'My father was always obsessed by Africa,' said Philip, mainly to himself. 'He was always very defensive about what happened there. Recently, he admitted that he thought it was a mistake.' He looked at her with gratitude. 'I've never really understood what he meant – until now.' He rubbed his eye nervously. 'I've had a pretty sheltered upbringing too.' He didn't want to admit that his students had done their best to educate him in these facts.

'I don't know. You'd be surprised how many people don't know about this.'

'I can't believe that our . . . the Mayhew & Taylor staff were any worse than their rivals.'

'No, that's true.' She spoke as though she was only humouring him. 'Everyone does it. It's a sick story and the further you get into it the sicker it gets. That was Daniel's problem.'

'He never had that sort of difficulty with investigative reporting before, did he?'

'Perhaps not. But in the end he couldn't see the point of printing a long piece in one of the Sunday newspapers and leaving it at that. He was writing quite a bit for the alternative press, like me, but it wasn't the same. No real impact where it matters. Anyway it's not exactly news, not in the abstract. There are one or two case studies . . .' She left the sentence unfinished and returned hurriedly to her theme. 'The press has known about all this for quite a while, even if they don't bother to report it properly.'

Philip hesitated, slightly uncertain. 'Are you saying Daniel couldn't bring himself to do it or that they wouldn't print it for him?'

Stevie did not answer him at once. He had apparently stepped into an area of her life where once again her responses were censored. Finally **she** said: 'It's true there was a part of him that couldn't cope with the whole thing. Like you, he'd been brought up with all the privileges money can buy. He was only too aware that the money had been made out of a corrupt business. His sense of guilt was appalling. He couldn't forget his Quaker up-bringing completely. He talked about his conscience all the time. But that wasn't the whole story.'

After a moment Philip realised he would have to lead her on with a small personal admission. 'I know what you're going to say,' he said. 'I felt it myself when I was a student. There's this feeling that I shouldn't ruin the company – and the past – to which I owe so much. There are some things you can't betray, however tarnished they've become.'

She looked at him teasingly. 'Didn't I tell you that you and Daniel are quite similar?'

He laughed.

She continued. 'So there was this endless conflict in his mind. And the more he delayed the more alienated he became. Which is why he ended up here, Alienation Hall.'

'You make it sound as though he was turning away from con-ventional society,' he prompted, 'towards something . . .' Bits of his conversation with Mrs. Coventry came into his head and he stifled the sentence introspectively.

'Meaning?' she challenged.

'That's what you can tell me, isn't it?'

Her sour, hesitating reply triggered his own uncertainty about himself and he began to apologise for his insistence, blaming the chemistry of grief again.

Stevie cut him short. 'This is not just about gratifying your curiosity, Philip. You have to understand that if you come here it's serious. Unlike the other people in this street I'm committed in what I do. What happens in this house is for real. Daniel and I made certain decisions and if he had lived they would have had important consequences.'

Philip's mood deepened. 'This place,' he said, going back to something he had mentioned before. 'It worries me. I know I'm easily worried, but all these automatic devices you've got are disturbing. It's as though the place is being used for something other than living.'

'Who told you that?' Stevie questioned him sharply.

He was genuinely disconcerted. 'N – n – n – no one.'

She pressed her head in her hands as if to stimulate and com-press her thoughts; her fingers glowed white. 'Daniel had got to a point that he could see no future in this society we live in and which had given him such a ringside seat. In fact, he was in the process of rejecting it completely. That's why I persuaded him to move here.'

Philip's sense that she was cutting a long story short was confirmed by the decisive way Stevie consulted the heavy large-faced watch on her wrist.

She jumped up. 'I have to go.'

Philip felt his peace of mind suddenly threatened. He didn't know how to say what he wanted. 'Can we –?' he began.

'It's your house,' she said, quite unaffected. 'Come when you like.'

He began to mumble something about how he had teaching to do tomorrow, but could he come in the evening as before?

'Sure,' she said. 'See you. I'm late.' Then a thought occurred to her. 'I tell you something,' she went on hurriedly. 'When you come tomorrow I'll have Daniel's cuttings and notes if you're interested. They're with someone else for safety. I'll get them over. Okay?'

She did not stop to hear his thank you, slipped through the door and lightly down the stairs. He heard the door bang and then she was gone down the street, vanishing into the city darkness.

3

Philip had just parked in front of his brother's house and switched off the lights, when he saw the front door open; someone, a man in a donkey jacket but otherwise indistinguishable, ran down the steps and walked quickly away down the street. Philip waited for a few moments, then, slightly apprehensive, let himself in with his latchkey. He heard the jingle of the radio coming from the kitchen. Stevie was there, in jeans and a powder-blue smock, clearing away mugs. She hardly paid any notice.

'I see you've been entertaining visitors,' he said, drawing attention to his re-appearance.

'So you've met Greg,' she replied, unconcerned.

'We didn't exactly meet: I just saw this mysterious figure coming down the steps when I arrived.'

She seemed amused. 'I hope he didn't scare you.'

He was discouraged by the lack of feeling in her voice. 'He didn't get the chance,' he replied, off-hand but inwardly desperate. He turned down the volume on the radio a fraction. 'Who is he?' he asked, as casually as he could manage.

'Greg's all right.' She seemed lost in thought, uninterested in his curiosity. 'He was jealous of Daniel,' she said, returning to the conversation, 'that's his problem.' She had a faraway look in her eyes as though she wished she was elsewhere. 'Greg's a lone wolf.' She turned back to the sink, closing the discussion. The tap-water drummed on the aluminium; after a minute or two she stopped the washing-up and dried her hands. 'Look,' she pointed at a battered suitcase; her distant mood softened. 'I've got hold of Daniel's cuttings for you.' She pulled the case across the table. 'Here it all is, Daniel's obsession.' She flipped the top. 'You'll see here that it's not just a question of pharmaceutical companies behaving unethically. It's all linked: the National Health, the drug scandals, and the ripping off of the Third World. It's a huge international scandal and all to do with greed. It starts with a family business like Mayhew & Taylor, extends into local health authorities and finally includes the real victims – the people in places like Africa. Professionally speaking, Daniel never wrote about anything else, hardly.'

'But –' Philip interrupted, 'even though my brother had this great scoop in Newcastle, afterwards there was nothing.' He sliced the air with his hand. 'And yet he had a prestigious job in Fleet Street?'

Stevie was curious. 'Who told you he had a prestigious job in Fleet Street?'

'Oh, I don't know. Everyone. It was common knowledge. People were talking about it at that party. There was this celebration. I mentioned it before, didn't I? I was there.'

'Then you don't know that the whole thing was a disaster,' she said simply. Philip stared at her in astonishment. 'Listen,' Stevie went on, 'Daniel, the wonder from the North, got taken up by this editor and was brought in as the blue-eyed boy. He got bowled over by it – knowing Daniel you'll know how that happened. So he came in on the crest of his own wave and the first thing was that all the other journalists resented him. It seemed as though he had the editor's ear and could write what he liked. It was fine while he had the editor's favour. They couldn't touch him. But when the man at the top lost interest in his Christmas puppy because it wasn't being quite as provocative as he expected, then Daniel was in trouble.'

'And so he turned to you.'

'He was desperate to prove himself. Typically, he over-compensated: he was determined to convince his editor that there were still plenty of good stories in the pharmaceutical business. He started to get on the 'phone to all his old contacts. It was tragic. This was when he got in touch with me.'

Philip recognised that, while he was getting married, Daniel had been miles from his thoughts. 'This was when –' he began, recalling the conversation in Harry's bar.

'Oh yes,' she responded, mocking his circumspection. 'This was when.' She wrinkled her sandy-brown forehead. 'If I'd known . . . if I'd known how long it was going to last and where it was all going . . .' She gave a tired smile. 'He got very obsessed.'

'I imagine the more his stuff was spiked, the more he refused to give in – being Daniel.'

'Right. He started to say it was all a conspiracy. He blamed everyone in sight: your father, big business, the editor, everyone. He was getting wild. He used to rant on about the British people. "No one cares about important things any more," he used to say. "We are only interested in the tiny problems on our doorstep. We've lost our vision." That sort of thing.'

'Wild stuff,' said Philip.

'The worst thing about it all was that the editor kept him on the payroll, even though he wouldn't give him any space.'

'Why?'

'He was embarrassed, I think. He liked Daniel.' She paused to make a point. 'Your brother could still be very charming when he wanted to be.'

'I know,' said Philip, remembering the better moments of Daniel's invasion of Chalk Farm.

'The editor kept asking for stories on other subjects, but Daniel wasn't interested. He'd got his big break doing what he believed in and nothing would make him compromise.'

'I assume this was why he got interested in other kinds of newspapers,' said Philip, referring to her earlier conversation.

'For a guy with his pride, it was pathetic really. He would do things for fringe newspapers and magazines, but no one took any notice. He joined a number of radical organisations, but they couldn't relate to what he was saying. It was all too technical, and it wasn't what they understood, not even when he quoted Fanon at them.'

'I suppose he rubbed those sort of people up the wrong way.'

'He simply couldn't understand why they didn't share his enthusiasm.'

'A lot of English radicalism is very insular and chauvinist, you know,' Philip commented, in his lecturing manner.

Stevie ignored him. 'So then he started going on marches, distributing his own leaflets, carrying his own banners. He was getting more and more eccentric. He got picked up a couple of times. He hated the police, hated them,' she repeated. 'I'm telling you all I know. There may be things I didn't hear. He didn't tell me everything by any means.' She sighed and drained her coffee.

'Don't go on if you don't want to,' he said, suddenly aware of the painfulness of this particular memory.

She seemed surprised by the warmth of his concern. 'Thank you,' she said. 'There's little more to say. None of these fights with the authorities did him any good at work. I always thought it was a miracle the editor didn't fire him, but I suppose the editor always protects his staff. I don't know. I think the man recognised his own fault in all this – the way he'd taken Daniel up like a mascot. In the end, though, there was a big row. After that it got very bad with Daniel.'

Stevie retreated into silence. Philip almost regretted he had pushed her this far. It still amazed him how deeply suppressed this strange, aloof woman kept her feelings. Throughout her narrative she had barely expressed a single personal regret or anxiety that gave anything of herself away. He was fascinated to know if anyone, including Daniel, had ever come fully close to her. Her independence of mind and spirit left him awed and silent. The radio muttered in the background.

Suddenly she looked up from the depths of her own thought. 'I've never spoken like this about Daniel to anyone before, Philip,' she said. She spoke quite spontaneously, but with an intuitive naturalness that, after his own thoughts, was almost uncanny. He stared at the sound of his own name, and she smiled, boyish and quizzical, as though asking him to declare himself.

'Your smile – I like it,' he said, gambling.

She made a face and turned half-heartedly away, and at the moment that she hesitated he knew that if he wanted he could say anything to her. If I were her lover like Daniel, he thought, I would put out my hand and touch hers (it was at rest on the table, there was a nicotine stain, he noticed, and the nails were chewed) and she would respond to my touch. His hand jerked with the intensity of the fantasy and she noticed his preoccupation.

'You're worried about something, aren't you?'

'No,' he said truthfully. 'I'm more relaxed.' He spoke so deliberately it was clear he meant it, and she nodded with acceptance.

'I believe you,' she said, and got up. 'I want to sleep now. I'm tired. I expect you'll stay and go through all this.' She pointed at the suitcase.

'Well, now I have a reason to,' he said, and then realised she might not have understood exactly what he meant.

He must have looked a bit vulnerable, he thought, pink-eyed and exhausted, sitting hunched in his old brown sweater at the kitchen table, the picture of a minor academic, because, as an afterthought, she added: 'Don't worry if Greg comes back.' She was poised confidently on the step into the kitchen. 'He's okay really.'

'Who is Greg?' He was bolder now about repeating his question. 'Just in case we're not introduced.'

'Even I don't really know,' she said, disregarding his efforts to modify his inquisitiveness. 'Just someone I've come across recently, and who's got a use for this place.'

Philip's intuition about the oddness of Daniel's house returned, worrying his subconscious mind like a familiar but forgotten face. 'But Greg isn't living here. You told me you were alone.'

She considered him levelly for quite a few seconds and then, seeming to make a decision, she sighed and signalled to him across the room. 'Come here for a second.' She walked into the hall and Philip followed. After the kitchen it was cool in the darkness at the foot of the stairs. 'There are houses and houses,' she said, speaking in a whisper as though afraid of an eavesdropper. 'Some are safer than others, you know,' she murmured, with a playful lilt. Then she opened the door leading to what he knew was the cellar and flashed on the light. 'Look,' she ordered. 'What do you see?'

The bulb threw an old yellow glow up the steps. 'Rubble. Boxes. Plastic bags, blue ones. They look like cement bags.'

Stevie flicked the switch, and the cellar went dark again. 'Not cement,' she said, banging the door. 'Explosives.'

Suddenly, everything became clear in Philip's mind: it was like being told the maddeningly obvious solution to a brainteaser. 'I see,' he said, enlightened. 'That's why –' he waved at the junkroom up the stairs.

She nodded and in the twilight he saw her put two right-hand fingers to her temple. He followed her back to the kitchen. 'So this is the riddle of the sphinx,' he said, joking to cover his anxiety. He was awed by the matter-of-fact way she had introduced him to Daniel's secret life.

'If you like,' she replied without humour. 'This house was my last throw for Daniel,' she explained softly. 'A bid to make a place for him in the world.' She yawned. 'After he left the paper I thought he would lose heart completely without something like this to engage his interest.'

'It's ironic that he should still be a landlord not a tenant,' Philip commented.

'There are lots of ironies,' she replied briskly. 'You realise that Greg is only the first to use it since we've moved in. Now you've turned up,' she went on without bitterness, 'he'll be the last as well.'

Philip reflected that he was winding up more of his brother's life than he intended. 'Was this –' he gestured around him, 'a rôle he wanted?'

'At first I thought so. It seemed to appeal to him. But I was wrong. He'd given up long before we moved in, really. Perhaps it's only my fantasy in the end,' she admitted with candour. 'Now, I'll never know.'

'What do you mean?'

'Oh – in a few weeks it will be sold again, I suppose, and then it will be all over – finally.' She did not sound bitter towards him, just resigned.

'What's Greg doing exactly?'

It seemed for a moment as if some suppressed anger was about to bubble up in a characteristically acid put-down, but instead she yawned again, pressing her small pale hand to her mouth. 'Oh – oh – what does it matter: he's moving that stuff through London.'

'So this was your date.'

She nodded. 'He came here with his bags and suitcases at the week-end. From Amsterdam, I think.'

'To – ?'

'I don't ask.' She smiled. 'Ireland? I don't know. All Daniel and I planned to offer was security.' Her forehead puckered. 'I could do with some security myself right now. That guy – Greg – kept me up half the night last night – he came here after you'd gone. He prefers the small hours.' She sounded annoyed. 'Just because we share the same political views doesn't mean I'm going to let him sleep with me.' Philip couldn't disguise his startled expression. 'Oh – he's been trying to get me into bed for days,' she muttered with irritation. 'That's the only way he sees women.'

'As objects,' he suggested, using Jan's standard vocabulary.

'Right.' She was speaking in her breathless violent way. 'Pure sexual jealousy on his part – Daniel and I first met him last autumn at a meeting. He couldn't see why I was living with this premature wreck.'

'If I was you, I'd keep him out.'

Her reaction was incredulous. 'With all that stuff here?' Her face clenched in another yawn and she continued sleepily. 'No – I can look after myself. It's all supposed to be over by next week. There's nothing to worry about. You'll just have to let it take its course. Once the stuff's on its way and he's gone then you can sell it. I don't mind. I'll find somewhere to live.'

He was about to make a heart-felt offer of at least a temporary roof, but before he had time even to say sleep well, she had gone.

For some minutes, while he heard Stevie moving about upstairs, and the water creaked in the pipes, Philip found himself pacing the kitchen floor, working out the tension in his mind. His first predictable thought was to give the whole thing up and go to the police, despite his antipathy. Stevie's story had carried him to the very edge of the known world. Daniel's surrender was much more complete than he had realised. Beyond was only fear and violence . . . But if he went to the authorities, his modest achievements, the rapport with Stevie, the unravelling of Daniel's past, and the tiny surges of self-confidence he was now experiencing for the first time in years, these would be snatched away from him. The impersonal rigour of the law would take over. There would be explanations to make, embarrassment and publicity. All he had to do now was to shepherd the mysterious Greg and his lethal contraband out of the house; then he could sell up as Stevie suggested and be free forever of Daniel's last, desperate refuge. Listening to Stevie's account of his brother's last months, he had realised how much Daniel had been escaping from. In the end, giving up was all that was left to do. As the crisis in Daniel's life came closer, Stevie's role was a story of real loving, he imagined. She must have been everything to Daniel, like a young woman to a much older man; mind, body and soul, the breath of life. He saw them in his imagination, walking and talking together, Daniel not well, touching and turning towards each other, side by side. The thought of that lost relationship only helped to stir his own incoherent longings. He couldn't decide how much of his modest declaration, the admission of interest, had been acknowledged. Not a lot, he imagined.

He wished for greater strength of character and purpose to make a bolder move, though to be honest with himself, even if he tried that approach he would probably botch it. As always, he could not cope with the uncertainty of risk, and preferred the silent torture of the few slight certainties between them. He moved up and down, turning the conversation round in his head, analysing and evaluating and becoming, like a chess-player in a losing position, more and more confused even about the advantages that remained his.

After a time, there was no more noise above him and he sat down at the kitchen table to examine the pile of papers in the suitcase. Outside, the night thickened and went still, but to Philip, poring over the cuttings and xeroxes in the artificial warmth and light of Daniel's house, the sequences of time had become irrelevant. The place itself contributed to the sensation of timelessness. In the other rooms, shadows and shafts of light, controlled by the automatic blinds and programmed electrical circuits, came on and off, apparently at random and without obvious reference to the time. Daniel's security system was on the blink and no adjustment that Stevie could make seemed to override its indifference to the revolutions of the earth.

Turning the pages with curiosity, Philip speculated whether the interest in Daniel that he and Stevie had together was drawing them closer or whether there was now something between them that had a life of its own, something that was not fired by the occasional spark of shared memory. He was puzzled by her sudden announcement of Greg's sexual jealousy. It had nothing much to do with their conversation. The emotional frankness was unexpected. He pondered what interpretation, if any, her remark could stand. After their talk he openly admitted to himself that he was feeding on his love for Stevie like a life support system. This thought and the fear of ultimate rejection brought its own agonies and he discovered that he had been leafing through the documents like a zombie, dazed and preoccupied. Overhead, the neon strip kept up its monotonous whine; the light glared; waking and dozing seemed to have become the same and, in the end, without moving, he slept.

He was roused, with a jolt, by a cry (long into the small hours) and by the sound of someone rushing across the landing towards the front room. He hurried into the hall and at the turn of the stairs caught a frightening glimpse of a figure scratching at the window, apparently trying to throw it open. It was Stevie, a milky-white blur in the shadows, her tears suffocated and stifled by some intangible constriction. Philip felt completely calm. He said, 'Stevie, it's all right. Lie down again. It's all right. Go back to bed.' She shrank from the sound of his words and continued to fight the window, shivering and muttering. He remembered there was something about not shocking people out of bad dreams and he dared not touch her naked white body. He stood and watched, and as he did so she became calmer and calmer and went back and lay down on her own bed. He followed and covered her up with the blankets. She seemed to be asleep already, but her breathing was uneven and disturbed and she was whispering to herself under her breath. He felt an ache of pity for this strong-willed, tantalising woman whose bottled-up instability and passions only surfaced under cover of darkness. She gave another shudder and began to talk again. Gingerly, feeling it creak and give beneath his weight, he lay down on the mattress beside her, tense with apprehension, and put his arm around her like a brother, saying, 'It's all right. You're not alone. You can sleep now.' Slowly, without her waking, the nightmare subsided and her breathing became even and undisturbed. Philip lay outside the blanket, not moving, hardly breathing himself except in cautious attenuated gasps from his sudden exertion, with his arm thrown awkwardly across her in a gesture of protection. He heard his heart pounding out a wild rhythm. In a while he began to doze again. Once, there was a noise in the street and he woke with a start. But it was only a late party breaking up and going home.

Gradually the shadows on the ceiling turned grey and then the greyness turned to pink, and, like a photographic print, his hand, which had been ghostly white and then a neutral shadow, developed colour with the light.

He had feared, lying there, that Stevie would wake and find him asleep beside her, but he was the first to hear the splutter and mumble of the central heating and the gushing of early morning taps next door, the chatter of radios and the distant pipping of the time signal. It was the cold that had woken him, and he got up exhausted and drained. Stevie was deeply asleep, on her back, her face relaxed and deathly in the morning light. Philip walked across to the front window and looked out. It was brilliantly cold and clear and the sun was exploding bright as silver in the cobalt sky. People on their way to work, invigorated by the nip in the air, were hurrying along the frosty broken pavement. A skip across the street had been ransacked during the night and papers, plaster and bits of wood, frozen to the road, were scattered like jetsam in the wake of a barge. He stepped back from the window. As he did so a voice behind him said: 'You slept with me last night.' Her matter-of-fact statement cut the stillness like a knife.

But Stevie never stated anything flat. He felt impaled by her accusation, unable to turn round to look at her. He said, 'You had a nightmare. I tried to comfort you. It was all I could do.'

'Come here,' she commanded. She was propped up on an elbow on the mattress, the blanket had slipped off her shoulder, there was a shadow of auburn hair under her armpit and the nipple on her exposed breast was firm and rosy in the cold. She seemed unconscious of her sexuality and her expression was focussed on him with an extraordinary, provocative intensity, pointed, severe and inquisitive. It was as though she was demanding an apology. But, though he obeyed, he said nothing. He noticed that her skin was incredibly white in the new sunshine. 'Sit down,' she patted the mattress invitingly. He did so, bending down to ease himself beside her, putting a discreet, slightly formal, distance between them. He dropped his eyes briefly and thought he wanted to smile at her, a nervous, shy, attentive statement of affection and loyalty.

Then she hit him, once, hard across the mouth and cheek with the flat and heel of her right hand. He grunted at the blow, began to bleed from his nose and upper lip, and tasted metal in his mouth. Involuntary tears came into his eyes, he bowed his head in pain, ineffectually wiping away the blood with his sleeve, waiting for her to hit him again, just sitting there, crying and bleeding like a punch-drunk boxer, but not flinching. The shock and the betrayal left him speechless.

Then he realised she was shouting at him, kneeling on the bed, unaware of the cold, taunting him with his stubbornness. 'Where are your feelings? Can't you react? You're a donkey, an ox. You sit there. You do nothing. You're dumb. Do something.' He wanted to stop her, but couldn't rouse himself. In her frenzy it was as though she was now ashamed of what she had done. Finally he managed to say, 'I love you, Stevie. I love you. That's why I'm here.' Then his tears bubbled up, very deep and suppressed, and he found that she was crying as well, kissing him with her strong lips, the blood from his face running between them and she crazily mopping up with things she had by her, a handkerchief, a piece of the sheet, her fingers and her hair.

4

When he looked at himself in the steamy bathroom mirror at midday, Philip, always so fastidious about his appearance, was sickened and repelled by the dark yellow and purple bruise that spread upwards from his lips and cheek. He had bathed his aching body in a hot bath, dabbing his cut with cotton-wool, and had found a new relaxing suppleness in the warm water.

'Ugly duckling,' said Stevie, appearing behind him in the glass and running her forefinger experimentally down his bare spine. He turned and smiled. Their bare toes touched and she crowded close to him, standing on his instep, her pinched brown face straining to kiss him. Their lips came together and he winced in pain; then he knelt down on the bathroom matting and kissed her belly, tracing with his tongue the soft fishbone of hair that grew on the seam of her body. When he got unsteadily to his feet, he bent and took a nipple in his mouth, sucking childishly and looking up into her eyes.

'Baby,' she said.

'I'm cold.'

'Well, get dressed then.' She gave him the intent appraising stare with which he was now so familiar. Intolerance was burning inside her as ever like a fever: he, who was so weak and indecisive, cherished her for it with unqualified admiration.

After the intimacy they had shared all morning, her renewed sharpishness awed him and made him flinch, even though she had already apologised for her violence.

'Why did you do it?' he had asked, his head throbbing on the pillow.

'Because . . . because you asked for it,' she said without elaboration. He could make nothing of that and she saw it. 'You insulted me last night; you said I was the object of sexual jealousy.' She seemed to know he felt cheated of explanation, and he recognised that it was not in her nature to go further without prompting. Guessing, he said: 'You wanted me to be like Daniel, but I'm not, is that it?'

'You can think that if you like.' She was content to remain enigmatic. 'It's funny, but you're like him in more ways than you realise. I can tell, you know.' He saw at once from her expression that the memory of Daniel provoked complicated emotions. 'Did he hurt you?' he had asked.

'Oh, no – when we were together he was usually very attentive. Gallant – is that the word?'

'It's *a* word,' said Philip. 'But does it describe Daniel?' He paused. 'Yes, I can imagine him as gallant,' and he gave raffish stress to the final syllable.

Stevie seemed disturbed by the memories. 'There was always a part of his mind that belonged to no one.'

'I know,' said Philip. 'I know what you're saying.'

'It made living together very difficult sometimes. Especially after he'd been away. But you don't know how I miss him. There was always something going on when he was around.'

Philip thought he saw the relationship quite clearly. He said: 'He was no longer the gauche student of Tanga days.'

'There was still the wildness, but now it was about serious things. After Africa I could respect him, love him, sometimes in spite of myself.'

'Were you afraid of giving yourself away?'

'Of selling myself cheap,' she countered tersely.

'I meant that Daniel was the kind of person who could mono-
polise and engulf you if you weren't careful.' He smiled in self-
deprecation. 'Like he did to me.'

'Exploitation is what you're talking about,' her voice had gone
cold again, 'even if you won't recognise it.'

He didn't look at her. 'Part of you distrusts men very deeply,
doesn't it?'

The silence between them that followed was isolating and
profound. But though he felt he had said something unforgivably
cruel, somewhere he found the courage to believe in what he had
said and not shrink from it as before. In the end, he realised it was
her love that gave him the confidence, and the irony shocked and
excited him.

'Philip,' she said at last, 'you don't know how hurt I've been
. . . by men.' Then she talked of her first love, a fellow student,
brilliant and radical, who believed in the simple, ruthless solutions of the ideological left. They had lived together, and she,
hardly nineteen, had become pregnant just before her first year
exams. Her lover, who was in the middle of his finals, behaved as
she had feared he would. For him the unwanted child was an
abstraction, to be thrown away like a failed experiment. Emotion-
ally immature, he had only been able to handle the complexity of
the issue at a philosophical level. Stevie went through the abortion more or less abandoned by her lover, and going through the
beginnings of a nervous collapse.

'You can hardly blame me for loathing men after that,' she
asserted, without self-pity.

'N – n – no. Of course not.' He knew he did not sound convinced, but it was not in his nature to attempt to unravel such
mysteries in cold blood. Always a coward, he waited for her to fill
the void between them with words of her own choosing.

Stevie was immersed in her thoughts. Finally, she drawled one
word. 'Men.'

'Selfish, rough, arrogant . . .' he began.

'Well, it's always on your own terms, isn't it? You never have to
give anything. Never seem to want to. For us, giving is the only
fulfilment – and the biggest risk in the world. But, without it, we
are denied in a way you never are.'

'You make it sound like a tragic predicament,' Philip commented. 'Is that how you feel?'

She came back at him abruptly. 'Of course it is. I don't say things I don't feel.' Her pride asserted itself as usual. 'I just don't trust anyone,' she said reflectively.

'What about me?' He was becoming egotistic. 'You know I've surrendered.'

'You think you have,' she replied darkly. 'I'm sorry – it's something I'm not used to and I can't quite believe it. I'll tell you,' she went on, 'it's been my whole life – giving and getting nothing back.'

She admitted, then, that her fears and suspicions went back far into childhood, like hooks in the brain. Her parents – both missionaries – had died in a Mau-Mau atrocity and she, a baby in England, had been brought up an orphan by aunts and godparents. She was lying on her back next to him, blowing cigarette smoke thoughtfully up to the ceiling, watching the faint warmth of the white sunshine swirl its grey shadow in tiny eddies. Philip, glancing sideways, caught her lips in a tulip profile against the bare white wall. 'I was a lonely child,' she said reflectively. 'I can't tell you how much I missed my father. I used to sit at home in the school holidays poring over the family album trying to imagine what he was like.'

'And not your mother?'

'Mother was easier. She and her sisters – my aunts – were quite similar. But my father was an only child. Like me. Because he spent almost all his life in Africa he didn't even have any close men friends I could talk to about him.' Her only source of information about this gentle smiling-faced man in the Brownie snapshots, she explained, was the rest of her mother's family who in some obscure way blamed him for what had happened.

'Sometimes people are so ridiculous like that.'

'You can say that again.'

'It's odd: I've felt it myself with Daniel's death. Irrational prejudices against people I used to respect. You see the world differently all of a sudden.'

'I suppose so. When my father died I was only two and a half. By the time I was conscious, all I knew was that I wanted him alive again very badly. At the same time, perhaps because of the loneliness and the kind of education I was getting, I had this extraordinary sense of who I was, a woman with a life of her own. I felt very solitary but also intensely aware of my individuality. I needed men, but at the same time I didn't. I didn't trust anyone, even when I gave myself to them. Does that make sense?'

Philip said, yes, he understood what she was saying. He felt subdued and moved by her self-analysis.

Apparently, when it happened, the monstrous regiment of aunts and godparents could not cope with the abortion. At the end of a stormy adolescence in which they saw her repudiate all the faiths and truths of her parents, with which, as they saw it, they had been entrusted, that was the final betrayal. Stevie was exiled from what little family security had been hers. She had barely got over her nervous breakdown when she had gone, at the age of twenty, to Africa. 'I wrote to my parents' old friends, and simply said I was coming. I remember celebrating my twenty-first birthday being chatted up by my father's solicitor, a colonial drunk, in this bar in Nairobi.' She laughed. 'And I had gone all that way to find the answer to my problems. To start with, it seemed no different from England really.' She paused, digesting the painful memory. 'In the end, total disaster,' she said. 'As your brother found, Africa is not the place you take your problems to. It only makes a whole lot more. In fact, you can end up wrecked like him.'

Philip wondered how she had extricated herself from the situation. She replied with unexpected, almost guilty, brevity. 'I suppose I have to thank that guy who came and took Daniel away. I suddenly saw how low I'd got. So I came home.' A note of sarcasm crept into her voice. 'I'm not totally without willpower, you know.'

'Not a very pleasant homecoming,' Philip commented.

'Right. For the first few weeks I was suicidal. I thought I'd made the worst decision of my life. I was completely alone and bored out of my mind. This country seems like an old shoe-box when you've been away for a bit.'

Gradually, she had picked up the threads, took up her studies again, at another university this time, away from all the bad memories. She thought the students, even the post-graduates of her own age, tedious and immature, and found herself having a series of affairs with older men. 'Mostly married,' she said with satisfaction. 'Christ,' she murmured. 'Those days.' She became indignant. 'Middle-aged men are cold lechers. They only want to do it when they're pissed and all they can talk about is their fucking sons and daughters.' She gave a little kick of irritation under the blanket. 'Thank God for the women's movement. I think I would have gone to pieces otherwise.'

Philip told her what Jan had told him. 'She said you were very impressive,' he concluded, slightly patronising.

Stevie was not offended. 'Janice Grant – I remember Janice Grant –'

'My ex-wife . . .' said Philip, nervously repeating what he had already told her.

'How funny.' Now that she was interested, she examined him with new curiosity. 'I wouldn't have thought – well, perhaps I might. She was a little mouse.'

'I think you'd find she's changed. She admired your strength, she said.'

'It was all done with mirrors – no kidding. Inside, I thought I was going to crack up.'

Philip laughed uneasily, embarrassed by her frankness. He considered all that she had just told him. 'No,' he said, answering his own thoughts. 'I don't expect I'll ever quite understand what you've been through. No man can.' He gave her his nervous winning smile. 'Have patience with me,' he pleaded.

'I will,' she had kissed him then: it was like a promise. She sat astride him in her bed, which sagged hot and tousled in the middle, and bent low to soothe him, arousing him in a gesture that was like an act of homage. She knew instinctively how exhausted he was and made love to him with unselfish devotion; it was for her astonishing sense of the appropriate touch or word or gesture that he knew he loved her.

'When we made love . . .' she whispered, speaking in snatches. 'I've not known it – like that before – it was as though – something inside me – was breaking down.'

She had said nothing more then, but later, after he had 'phoned the faculty office to explain that he would be late (still fighting in his mind the way he was selling his job short for this girl), when they were drinking tea together in the kitchen, she returned to something he had confessed in bed.

'Do I still alarm you?' she asked.

He was surprised. 'Why do you say that?'

'This morning I had this feeling that a part of you was tense: I felt you weren't giving yourself completely. It was as though you were keeping part of yourself back from me.'

'Is that from fear?'

'It could be – with you. You're a very nervous person.'

His mood became more sombre. 'Perhaps it's this house. Now

that I know . . . it frightens me.' He turned his head awkwardly towards the hall.

'Hey,' she tried to encourage him. 'Don't worry. Okay? By next week all the stuff will have gone. Greg will have gone. There's no problem, okay.'

He told her that, after his experience with her before, he was afraid. 'It's not you, it's the world you live in that alarms me,' he said. 'Someone could be watching.'

'No one knows about this place. Believe me.'

'You can't be sure.' He was surprised by his own doubts. His imagination was getting as suspicious as Stevie's.

Her confidence came back at him like a rubber ball. 'But that's why, with you here, it's fine. You're just an ordinary guy no one's ever heard of who's come to take over his brother's house. You don't look like one of us. It's great.'

He touched his face carefully. The bruise was painful. He considered the sober lines of his clothes, his conservative haircut. 'No,' he admitted, 'I don't suppose I do look like one of your people.' He was worrying what he was going to tell his students about the bruise later that afternoon. He was convinced they would never accept that he had walked into a door.

'So that's okay,' she concluded.

Philip found himself slightly preoccupied with his neglected preparations for the lecture course on Colonialism. He pulled his attention back to her remarks, painfully divided by his various loyalties.

'And where do you stand in all this?' he asked, with concern. 'It sounds as though you're going to lose a whole way of life next week.'

Stevie shrugged. 'Well, perhaps I am.' Her cigarette quivered in her fingers. 'Yes, I did have hopes for this place. It could have been good.' In the rich afternoon shadows, her eyes were shining with excitement; the light gave a soft contour to her features. 'Violence and politics.' She sighed. 'Now I'll go back to where I was before Daniel.'

'Back to college?' He began to plan in his head.

'Shit, no.' She made a noise of contempt in her throat. 'I'll go on like now – somewhere else. I'll stay on the dole. I have a few friends. I've got a life that suits me. It's not hard. There's this bookshop down the road where I work when I want to. It has everything I want to read. I can go to meetings, demonstrate. I won't starve. Living outside the system is not what it was.' She frowned.

'You'd like it all to be more heroic.'

'Listen,' a note of warning sounded in her voice, but milder than before. 'I've told you already, this is not a game I'm playing here. The situation is too serious for that.'

'You're talking about violence, I suppose, and things like inflation and unemployment.'

Stevie was flicking her fingers with irritation. She made Philip feel naïve and out of touch. 'Those are just newspaper words. Symptoms not causes. I'm going deeper than that. There's something very corrupt about the peace the West has made. We're still living off the places we used to call the Empire. The flag is down but the cheques are still rolling in.'

'I know,' said Philip, 'that's how Mayhew & Taylor made their big profits.'

'Ripping off the Third World to keep the old country on its feet,' Stevie commented savagely.

'Once you get used to a lifestyle it's hard to kick the habit.' Philip thought of his own family and the accumulated traditions of the past. He remembered the shock when his father sold out.

'I remember once with Daniel,' Stevie went on after a moment. 'A year back. We went to this big country house for a walk in the gardens. Just outside London. Something House. Daniel had been there as a kid and wanted to see it again. He got very worked up about the state of things. It was a lovely day. Spring, with a few crocuses and no one much about. There was a caretaker with a hook hand, and peacocks in the garden. Peacocks everywhere. For some reason it made him angry.'

'Perhaps he was reminded of home.'

'Actually, I think it was the peacocks.' She seemed to enjoy the idea. 'He started to talk about England. He said it was just like a large country house fallen on hard times. Half the rooms are empty, most of the servants have been sacked, the heirlooms have been auctioned off to settle the debts and the butler is probably screwing the daughter of the house in her boudoir, and yet –'

She paused to catch her breath and they both laughed. 'Go on,' he said.

'And yet everyone still dresses for dinner and pretends that nothing had changed.'

'And if,' said Philip, joining in, 'the eldest son finds a cache of diamonds in the attic, they will order up Dom Perignon, celebrate their good fortune and carry on just as before.'

Stevie lit a cigarette, and changed tack. 'As far as he was concerned, it was all finished. For him this society was a capitalist junkie that had gone mainlining on profits for years and, now bankrupt, was faced with the prospect of agonising withdrawal symptoms.'

Philip said quietly, 'It's hard not to agree with that view – historically speaking.' His attention was distracted again briefly by his teaching commitments. His approaching departure filled him with anxiety.

'Recently,' she went on, 'he started relating everything – the state of politics, England, the English – to his own story, the big investigation. In the end, some people thought he was a total screwball. Even I thought he was a little bit crazy.'

Philip nodded, encouraging.

'The final catastrophe happened in the middle of last year,' she said, launching unprompted into the more recent past. 'He was quite paranoid really.'

'Last summer?' said Philip, keying the events in his mind.

'You remember how wet it was and how green, so vivid it was sick. We used to sit in the pub on the corner, talking and drinking till closing time. Daniel was heavily on the bottle by then. I tried to stop him but it was no use. I suppose you could say he was an alcoholic. God it was wet; it seemed like the sun was never going to shine.' He remembered well, the land had been sodden and cold. 'Daniel used to drink his way through jugfuls of red wine and beer, getting angrier and angrier. Sometimes I was very frightened.'

Casting his mind back to that time last year, Philip remembered that it was the moment when his marriage collapsed. It was in June that Jan finally gave up the effort of disguising her infidelity after the loss of her baby. It pained him to think of the way he had become an outsider in his own home. 'Don't you understand,' she had said. 'It's post-natal depression.' 'You mean screwing around,' he had fired back angrily. He was still ashamed of his reponse, and appalled by the viciousness between people who, five years before, had pledged themselves 'loving and faithful so long as we both shall live'.

'There was a violent streak in Daniel,' he said.

'Well, one day – it was after a row – he came back home – this was in our previous flat of course – and he was in this wonderful mood. There was something in the way he was. Just different.' Philip remembered what he had been like in the early days: charming, witty, bubbling over with funny stories, ideas . . . 'Just very good company,' said Stevie. 'It was early morning when he came in. I was sitting outside on the step typing something on my portable. It was one of those few fine days and I was making the most of it. The sun was still low. He came through and squatted down beside me so that we were level. "I'm sorry," he said, touching my leg, "it was my fault. It's been very difficult, but now I've got what I want. I've got the evidence I need." '

Philip pictured them together; Stevie in a loose cheese-cloth shirt and jeans, the typewriter balanced unsteadily on her stick-like legs; Daniel, an imposing dark figure with the restless eyes and pouchy defeated face of the alcoholic, bending over her in a clumsy inadequate gesture of apology.

'Are you going to tell me what it was he was after?' He looked across at the battered suitcase on the table. 'I couldn't find much in those papers, at least, not anything I could understand. Perhaps I don't know how to read them.'

'Probably not. No –' she sighed, as though under great pressure. 'The whole thing was in his head.'

'You mean it was a fantasy?'

'No. It was real enough. He just hadn't written it down.'

'How do you know?'

'Because it was my experience he was investigating.' She looked at him with a proud half-smile. 'I've told you something about Africa. My parents were missionaries. I was sent home when I was very small. They had had enough and wanted to get out. Then they were killed. You can't know how much I wanted to see the country that had destroyed them. It may seem odd, but when I went back to Africa all I wanted to do was work in a mission hospital. I mean, screw religion, I wanted to look after blacks.'

'This was when you were recovering from your –' Philip stumbled on the word, 'your –'

'Breakdown,' she prompted briskly. 'Yes. I've told you already I thought Africa would help. Anyway, people took care of me – they remembered my parents – and I worked up-country in this amazing bush hospital. No running water. Kids with worms. Cancers the size of footballs. That was when I first got to know about the drug scandal. I remember one day a black woman and her baby coming to the hospital. Her child was very sick, vomiting and hardly breathing. She couldn't understand it: she'd been given some pills by a dispensary out in the bush and she assumed they would cure her child of anything. Of course we looked at the instructions on the packet. They were only written in English. It was a dangerous drug that is only administered under strict supervision in the West. Not surprisingly the baby died.' She sounded very matter of fact. 'Even in a country where death is commonplace that baby's death affected me terribly. I can still see the mother holding the multicoloured packet with the tears streaming down her face. She simply couldn't understand.'

'Nor could you, I imagine – I mean that this sort of thing can be allowed to happen.'

'Not really. I was very inexperienced still. I did not see the pattern until much later.' She turned over a page of the photograph album in her mind. 'After several months out in the bush I drifted back to the city. I'd found the loneliness too much to bear. I wanted a change.'

'This was Tanga.'

She nodded. 'One of the seediest places on earth. That was where I first met Daniel.'

'Getting his head together,' Philip commented ironically.

'That's what he thought I suppose. In fact, looking back on it, we were both very depressed. We drifted together in the way you do in those situations. Although I wasn't actually part of the programme, too young still, I was in with the V.S.O. crowd. Naturally, so was he. I expect we discovered we knew friends of friends. The English always do. Considering how much we had in common it's surprising we weren't closer.'

'Were you glad to find someone who was keen to hear what you had to say about the drug business?'

'Not at first. I didn't think of it like that. But when I found out he was a Taylor from Mayhew & Taylor, I got a real kick out of that. I don't know why, but I really wanted to upset him as much as I could.' She seemed exhausted by the thought. 'I suppose I succeeded in the end.'

She stopped, as if she wondered quite how to go on. Then she leant across the table and kissed Philip gently on the end of his nose. 'This morning – when we were talking about this – I didn't quite give you the full story.'

'But you've never given me the full story.' He did not sound resentful. 'I know that as well as you do.' He sounded quite amused by the idea. 'If anyone's been holding out . . .'

'I didn't trust you,' she said, unsmiling and self-justifying. 'What was I saying?'

He apologised for interrupting her, anxious to coax her memories. 'The full story,' he said with a smile.

Stevie's face was long and serious as she began to talk, pausing frequently for breath, and working her thin hands as the nuances and ramifications began to take a grip of the narrative. 'After Daniel came home – after that guy Appleby had been and gone – I made one more long trip into the bush. Thanks to one thing and another, I'd got interested in the details of what happens to some of the drugs that get shipped into Africa through ports like Tanga.'

Philip asked her to describe the town to him more fully, and she did so in a few plain hard sentences, recalling with disgust a place of harsh climate that had destroyed her illusion, as an impressionable white student, that Africa was a continent she could expect to understand.

'I found,' she continued, 'that the more I was shown to be out of my depth, the more I wanted to know. So, you see, I wanted to know what happened to these drugs when they got distributed to the people, the ordinary, illiterate African villagers. Of course, thanks to my family background, I could go places Daniel would never have known about. I was proud of the advantage,' she admitted. Her voice became subdued. 'You know, there are parts of that continent where no Westerner has stopped for more than two minutes. Villages in the scrub, just off the highway where the trucks grind through the dirt ferrying out the raw materials. That's where you see the real Africa; that's where you see the things we've done to those people.' Her voice was shaking with indignation. 'Take the drug business. The drugs are distributed by district. There's a lot of bribery and corruption as you'd expect. If the district medical officer is corrupt, all kinds of things can go wrong.'

Philip, half listening, heard again his father's familiar argument that Africa had a vital role to play in the development of medicine. He watched Stevie; she was speaking deliberately, almost with violence.

'There's one place I came across by chance,' she said. 'An out-of-the-way district.' She was breathing more asthmatically

202

than before; the tension between them was one of anticipation on his part, indignation on hers. 'All the children – all the children,' she repeated, slower than ever, 'of a certain age – the ones that survived – were deformed. Hideously deformed. Thanks to a tranquillizer for pregnant mothers. Banned in the West. Dumped in Africa. Made by Mayhew & Taylor.'

'The wonder drug,' Philip murmured. 'The wonder drug that ruined the company. The hope for the future that cost a million pounds to develop and was withdrawn before it was on the market.' He had read about all this in Daniel's cuttings file; only now did it all make sense.

'Exactly,' she obviously knew all the details; she sounded extraordinarily satisfied.

'How did it happen? I cannot believe it was merely a desperate search for profits.'

'But that's just what it was, Philip.' Her indignation flooded over. 'Of course, when the kids were born, the bureaucrats stepped in and did what they could to stop the trade. The story has been totally covered up. The people at the top out there are being bribed. Nothing will ever get out. No one knows how many children were affected. Or how many died. No one cares about Africa in the way they care about the West. I've heard that the foreign correspondents who bothered to ask were told that the deformities were the result of malnutrition during pregnancy. Even from obscure tribal customs. What shit!' Her sense of outrage was as strong as ever. 'But I knew. Your brother – Daniel knew. That was the story he wanted to tell.' She lit a cigarette.

'And this was the reason you came home,' Philip guessed, breaking out of a shocked reverie.

'Right. I was sickened. I couldn't stay. It made me want to destroy everything to do with the West. I came back. Later on – when I was still wondering what to do about it – I saw in the paper that Daniel had won this prize. What I told you before isn't quite true either. I wrote to him to say I had a story for him. That was how we met again. He got very excited of course – even though he was appalled. But he needed more than my report. He needed hard evidence, photographs and so on. That was where the difficulty started.'

'Why?'

'Well, most of the evidence – as it was – had died by the time he got on to the story. The children were thought of as devils by the villagers from the moment they were born. Several were killed off very quickly by the midwives. The ones that survived had a terrible life. Many committed suicide or were left to die. The mothers, who were treated as lepers, did what they could to kill them off. The ones I saw were only a minority and even they didn't have a chance in the long run. No one in the villages realised that it was the pills that were to blame. They saw it as God's will. They are incredibly fatalistic in that way. Now, if you go out there and if you speak the right dialect, you could probably get at the tribal memory of the "devil children". One or two of the kids who got off lightly probably hang on here and there. But you have to know where to look.'

'And Daniel failed,' he commented.

'Looking back, it was inevitable. At first he went after the story with such enthusiasm and fury that everyone knew what he was after. This made it very difficult later on. The defences were up. In Africa, which he visited two or three more times, the officials stonewalled him. There were some unreliable statements which he could take down as evidence of a sort, but there was nothing on paper which linked the drug –'

'Which no longer existed, of course,' he interjected.

'Right. With Mayhew & Taylor. Also there were no reliable documents to prove the shipment had been distributed either in the country or in that district. And, the more he tried and failed, the more frustrated he got. He'd succeeded in Newcastle and he couldn't believe he couldn't do it again. The contacts who'd helped him in the north just shut down on him. Vested interest again,' she said, fiercely stubbing out her cigarette. 'What was worse was that Daniel came across less dramatic cases which told a similar story: Mayhew & Taylor, in the years before they sold out, were increasingly corrupt and dangerous. I told you before,' she went on, 'he got alienated. Then he got violent. There was also the problem he was having with himself: he was paralysed by the knowledge that it was your father's firm that had done this. In the end he was wrecked by it. He went to pieces. He just didn't have the heart to go on. It's as simple as that.'

Philip looked across the table at her. The short winter day had ended while she was speaking and now she sat motionless in deep shadow, only the points of her eyes shining, piercing and steady at him. He realised she was crying. She was phrasing something; the words were broken and choked, but he thought he heard her say 'no more secrets, no more revelations', with an air of melancholy finality.

His own reply was buzzing unbidden in his head, but he rose stiffly to his feet without a word. He began to stammer his getaway line. 'I – I –'

She mercifully cut him short. 'See you tomorrow – after class.' She seemed to understand that he wanted to stay, but couldn't; there was no reproach in her tone.

He slammed the front door behind him and paused in the sudden fresh air. It was painful to turn away from the company he needed most, but he also needed familiar loneliness to grapple with what Stevie had just told him. 'Those whom the gods destroy they first made mad,' he said out loud. It was a phrase that he had planned to use in his imminent lecture on the Paris Peace Conference.

As he hurried down the slippery broken steps to the street he noticed a man and a woman, almost identical in army surplus greatcoats, looking curiously up at Stevie's lighted window.

'Daniel doesn't live here any more,' he said as he passed them.

'Oh,' they said, their uncertainty answered, and like him they began to walk down the street towards the sparkling lights of the city in winter.

5

Philip rehearsed his words all the way from the class, weaving loquaciously through the traffic. 'This is for you,' he said to the driving mirror, painfully exercising his bruised lips on the sentence. 'I've brought this for you.' At least his students had accepted his explanations about bad light and doors and congenital clumsiness without obvious scepticism. It was impossible to gauge their response but his perfunctory cancellation of the afternoon seminar had provoked approval rather than suspicion, he felt. He had perpetrated another, more serious, deceit that same morning, telephoning his father's housekeeper to announce that, thanks to 'pressure of work' and 'unavoidable commitments at the college', it was going to be impossible for him to visit the old man that week-end as he had promised. He had made another arrangement for the next week-end, but it was not the same. He knew from her manner that she profoundly distrusted his statements of good intention. 'You're getting as bad as your brother,' she had commented sharply. Too bad, he thought, and returned to the present. 'I thought you might like this,' he experimented, smiling lopsidedly at a startled taxi-driver in the outside lane. 'This is for you.' His face was aching; he couldn't shave easily and he knew his moustache was going to get horribly ragged. 'Here is a little something for you, Stevie.' He planned to underline this careful tribute with a gesture of devotion. He had rarely felt such strength of commitment; perhaps what he envisaged as out-stretched arms and an open smile would be all the eloquence he needed.

It was an early Friday afternoon and still light. The week-end traffic had not yet started. As he coasted, humming softly, down the hill, he anticipated that Stevie would be at work as usual, habitually smoking a cigarette, and typing something polemical on the kitchen table about the Government.

In the short time he had known her, he had come to respect the seriousness of her journalism. Each day, he noticed, she would spend at least a couple of hours tapping away on the kitchen table, not stopping until she had two or three sheets of neatly-typed foolscap to put in the post. With her help, his own piece about their arrest had been transformed into a publishable article, and was now on its way to one of Stevie's contacts in Fleet Street. Upstairs in her room, stacks of newspapers and magazines, the alternative press she wrote for, were crowded together on the floor, each copy carrying its contribution – feature articles, letters, reviews, leaders – above the laconic signature, S. Beck.

As he prepared to park the car, he saw that there was someone outside number eighty-seven and, coming closer, focussing with concentration, he realised that it was Stevie, bending over a shovel, clearing some of the weeds and debris from around the sphinxes.

'Hi.' She straightened up, flushed with the exercise. Her faded jeans were tucked into a pair of wellington boots and she was wearing the parka he remembered from their first encounter. The demands for Peace and Liberation and Nuclear Disarmament clashed oddly with the picture of her leaning rustically on her shovel, a slight, elfin figure quizzing him with her smile of greeting.

'Guess what?' she said.

'I give up.'

'I've had a call from Greg,' she said. 'He's planning to come here tomorrow to shift the stuff.'

He began to stutter, but did not manage much of a sentence. He had been wondering about the meaning of her work out here. It was too much to hope that she, too, was glad to be seeing the back of her mysterious visitor.

'So next week this will be all yours.' She sounded sad as she looked up at the peeling façade with nostalgic fondness. 'I suppose you'll want to sell. I'm trying to improve what they call "the aspect" for you,' she explained sarcastically, raking the shovel across the stone.

'No,' he said gently, 'I won't sell. I want you to stay here,' he went on. 'With me.' He shook his head. 'This is all that Daniel left behind him. I can't sell it. Not for the moment.'

She came up to him, stepping over a pile of rubbish, and kissed him on the lips.

He found himself excited to be planning for the future. 'The first thing to do,' he said, pointing up at the balcony in a business-like way, 'is to get that ironwork fixed. It looks a mess.' He turned his eye up the street, comparing Daniel's house with the others in the terrace. The sun was out and it was warm, almost springlike, on their faces. 'Smell the air,' he said, breathing deeply.

She inhaled with longing.

He faced out across the street, like a cliff-top sailor. The house opposite was occupied; but next to it was the empty shell of a mansion that had once been a desirable residence for a middle-class Victorian family, optimistic, assured and prosperous. Through the blackened window-frames Philip could see that extraordinary expanse of wasteland, the flattened rubble of bull-dozed streets, stretching perhaps for a quarter of a mile to another row of houses in the distance. The only sign of activity was a rusty mechanical digger and a few rolls of barbed wire.

'Desolate view,' he said, mostly to himself.

'It got half bombed in the war,' said Stevie, answering his query. 'And then for a generation no one bothered to do anything about it. Last year they pulled the rest of it down.' She sighed. 'A whole way of life obliterated in a few weeks. The people moved away. It will never be the same again.'

She noticed he was struggling with his bits and pieces, his suitcase, briefcase and his parcel. She took the briefcase and led the way up the steps. 'I'm glad you've come back,' she said, going through the hall into the kitchen. She spoke as though she had not fully expected his return. Then she saw the present in his hand. 'What's this?'

'It's for you,' he mumbled. 'A present.' In his diffident way he was proud; Stevie tore hastily at the wrapping paper.

'It's beautiful,' she said slowly. The poinsettia stood uncovered on the table between them. She smiled, uncertain what more to say. 'It's beautiful,' she repeated. 'It's one of yours, I can tell.' He had told her about his secret garden.

'Actually,' he said rather shyly, 'I bought it in a shop.' The Interflora woman had remembered him, and studied his bruise surreptitiously as she wrapped the plant. The embarrassment had been appalling.

'It needs a mixture of warmth and shade,' he said now. 'I think it will do best upstairs in – in your bedroom.' After his rehearsal he was worried that it all sounded too premeditated, but she did not seem to be conscious of that.

He did not tell her why he wanted to have it near him, this perfectly-formed thing.

In his spare hand he held the suitcase with his things for the week-end. He would never be able to explain how comforted he was to know that the plant was there, and would still be there tomorrow when he woke up. They went upstairs and Philip fussed about like a pensioner. Stevie became irritated. 'Come here,' she instructed. She put her hands gently round his swollen cheeks and kissed him slowly. He closed his eyes and enjoyed the taste of her tongue, making an involuntary noise of pleasure.

'Does it hurt?'

'No, no. It's wonderful.' But he flinched when she kissed him harder and she drew back. She said: 'I'm sorry.' She ran the tip of her tongue down the bridge of his nose. 'I love you,' she said. He saw his own hollow-socketed expression shining at him out of her clear grey eyes. 'Narcissus,' she said.

'Do you love me?'

'I love you.' The automatic note in her voice sent doubt running through him.

'Like Daniel?' He was curious.

There was a small portable radio on the mantelshelf and she began fiddling with the tuner, not saying anything. He put out his hand to touch hers and the pressure of his fingers told her that he wanted an answer. 'No,' she said, somewhat displeased. 'With Daniel it was different.' She twisted free of his embrace. 'It was sex mainly and the fascination of the bloke.' She smiled. 'But you're something else. You wouldn't touch a fly. You know about other people's feelings. Daniel never did.' The radio squeaked and whined. Suddenly there was a burst of music.

'That's nice,' he said. 'Leave it.'

'What is it?'

'Elgar,' he said, without hesitation.

'Imperialist,' she laughed, and bounced on to the bed with a mock salute. 'Land of soap and water,' she sang in a tuneless alto. 'Mother's in the bath.'

Philip protested earnestly. 'He was misunderstood. People only think of "Pomp and Circumstance". He's not like that at all.'

'Do you like classical music?'

'I'm afraid so.' He sounded shy and old-fashioned. 'It's all I know really. I've never been much of a one for pop.'

'Pop,' she mimicked.

'Well, there you are.' The music reached a tinny crescendo. 'This was my favourite piece when I was about fourteen. I used to lie in bed and try to imagine the England of the old days, the England of my grandfather when all was well. You can hear it all in Elgar.'

Stevie interrupted, joining his mood. 'It's funny you should say that. This stuff makes me think of Malvern. We used to have outings in the hills there. When I was a kid my aunt occasionally took me there at half-term. We'd have a rather plain picnic and afterwards explore the Beacon, clambering over tussocks and mole-hills. I was a very sporty child. I loved to scramble up on my own. To the top of the world it seemed like.'

Philip imagined it: the counties spread below like a quilt and a high, wide sky opening out overhead.

'I remember auntie,' Stevie continued, 'struggling up behind me very fat and red and out of breath. She used to take me there from boarding school for the day. It seemed like freedom.'

They sat silently, secluded in their own thoughts, listening to the ebb and flow of the music. All of a sudden there was a crackle on the radio and a man's voice rang out sharply, talking very fast in the jargon of the short-wave intercom. Philip started at the sudden staccato burst. Stevie jumped up and ran to the front room. She looked out into the street. 'It's only a taxi,' she shouted back in reassurance. Philip had come up behind her. 'It happens sometimes,' she went on when she saw him. 'They get on the same frequency. Once I heard the police on it that way.'

'It doesn't do much for the nerves,' said Philip.

'I've told you,' she instructed him, 'they know nothing about this place – and never will. Next week Greg will go away and it will become an ordinary house again,' she tilted her head appraisingly, 'the property, by inheritance, of Philip Taylor, college lecturer.'

'You don't seem to have any regrets,' he said.

'Why should I?' she demanded provocatively. 'Deep down, when I meet people like Greg – you'll see him tomorrow I expect – I realise that people like me don't count any more. We haven't got what it takes.' She was talking in an insistent, humdrum murmur. 'In my way, I'm as outmoded as your brother, I don't make any impact where it matters.'

Philip protested. 'What about your writing?'

'Oh.' She sounded contemptuous. 'I shouldn't think a single sentence of what I write has ever changed the world one bit. And that's all that's important now.' She was opening herself to him; he was conscious of the compliment. 'I try to disguise it, but I'm basically a liberal activist – and there's no place for those any more. Greg and his people are right. The only thing left is militant action.' She sounded enthralled. 'Violence.'

'Then you must have some regrets.'

'None at all,' she was defiant.

'Why?'

'I've explained already –' she was angered to be goaded by him. 'Because –' She choked on the confession. 'Because I can't face it. I love the idea of this world here, but the reality frightens me. I have to admit it – I'm not that extreme.' She held his gaze briefly. 'When they searched me in that cell, I was terrified. I screamed. You must have heard it.'

He nodded dumbly.

'For the first time in my life I was forced to recognise my limits. The only act of violence I can manage is against someone . . . someone I love.' Her voice was very small and strangled. 'I thought this house would be what I'd always wanted, a marvellous fulfilment.' Her voice was fierce and unforgiving. 'But it's been a fucking nightmare. I'm glad you turned up when you did. I think I'd have gone out of my mind on my own.' Her head was bowed as if in defeat.

'Stevie,' he said, holding her strongly. Her behaviour in the last few days was becoming clearer.

They moved back into the bedroom. Elgar's music was playing on triumphantly, but Stevie was sobered by the intrusion of her own suppressed inadequacies into her private idyll. They stood together under the light, touching and kissing to recover their intimacy. Stevie shivered and held his hand firmly. He felt a hole yawning in his stomach as though he was about to be sick.

'Lie down,' she commanded. He stretched out on his back. She knelt at the far end and pulled off his shoes, and then peeled back his socks, unbuttoned his shirt, and then slowly, deliberately (piling his clothes lazily on the floor), stripped him with silent, slightly breathless absorption. She climbed off the bed with a light skip and went to the window, half-drawing the curtain. She kicked her shoes under the bed. Then he watched her pull off her own boyish clothes – sweater, jeans and faded black tee-shirt. They began to move together in a slow build-up of first one breath laid on another, and then faster, kisses meeting and parting, and the thudding of their heartbeats drumming them forward until the crescendo of breaths, lips and blood carried Stevie to the infinitesimal moment of stillness after she had arched her body in its final spasm, like a woman at the point of childbirth. Philip, caught between pleasure and pain, thought he would cry out. Blinded with tears of joy and lust, he glimpsed Stevie's lips, swollen with blood, parted in childish delight. Finally they lay, heaving breathlessly under the prickly blanket; Philip's face was bleeding again and there were little bloody pink kisses all over Stevie's thin white body.

As a lover, after the faithful, boring years of his marriage, and recently his floundering attempts to acquire some more sexual experience, he felt clumsy and inadequate. His way of compensation was passive compliance. He admitted this. 'It's nice,' she said. 'It's sincere. I prefer that.'

In his mind he guessed that Daniel was – had been – unsophisticated about it too, though by contrast instinctive and unrefined. Stevie herself lost her shyness in voracity: she told

Philip that, for her, there was a satisfying of a profound and inarticulate need for something that confirmed her view of man's brute sexuality. But Philip intrigued her. He was different, she said, much more considerate than other lovers, more private and hesitant than his brother. He aroused a certain protective warmth in her that she did not know well. Gradually she realised that there were no repressed primitive longings to be uncovered or released. The frenzy of her passion gave in to something more intense and lasting. There was no fight, only a slow ripple of movement shared between them that carried them both forward with a shudder, mutually absorbed.

Still awed by their own emotions, they began to talk, as much to distract from the ebb of feeling. Stevie was pillowed on his arm; the intimacy of their conversation was wrapped round them like a blanket. In a while, Philip was back in Africa. All day he had been worrying in his mind about what had happened there.

'You said yesterday that our company was getting more and more corrupt. What does that mean when you come down to it?'

'It means a lot of things that subconsciously you've always run away from.'

He did not deny that this used to be the case. 'But now it's different,' he continued. 'I want to understand what it was that destroyed Daniel.'

She winced, as though she found his directness painful. 'The worst thing about it all,' she began, 'is the way in which the drug companies pretend to take the welfare of the Third World seriously and yet, in fact, do fuck-all to help the basic problems of – of a continent like Africa.' She raised her eyes. 'What do you think most people die of in the bush country around Tanga?'

After all their recent talk, he felt quite at home with the answer. 'Tropical diseases, bacteria, common viruses . . .'

'It's simpler than that. They die of things like measles. The people are often so weak with worms and malnutrition that they catch anything that's going. There's never enough clean water and no sanitation to speak of. Children die from the kind of diseases we got rid of in – in –' she was stumbling with indignation.

'The days of Elgar.'

'Right.' She raised herself on her elbow. 'And yet companies like Mayhew & Taylor export drugs that have nothing to do with these basic problems. Africa gets treated like just another market for painkillers and sedatives, drugs that are quite useless out there. The mothers and children I saw in the bush hospital didn't need tranquillizers, they needed basic medicines.'

'Don't they get basic medicines?'

'That's the whole point. The health service administrators have got so overstocked with irrelevant drugs, that they in their turn have to dump them on the illiterate peasants in the countryside.'

'You can't blame Mayhew & Taylor's salesmen for that sort of bad management,' Philip riposted.

'If only it was bad management . . .' she frowned. 'There's no way these officials can avoid buying tons and tons of drugs that nobody wants.'

'Why don't they refuse the stuff?' He knew he sounded naive, but she answered him seriously nevertheless.

'Bribes,' she said simply. 'They come in all shapes and sizes, cars, holidays, discounts and gifts, but they all add up to the same thing.'

'And that's what Mayhew & Taylor were up to?'

'Right. The company was in trouble. They desperately needed to improve their sales. As usual in England, exports was the obvious way to do it. It's a well-known fact out there that your father's salesmen had a particularly bad record when it came to pressure like that. They must have taken their orders from head office.'

Philip remembered Appleby's unaccountable nervousness about his work for the company and his self-serving version of African corruption. Stevie was still talking.

'But that's not the whole story. It's not just a question of the wrong drug for the wrong situation.'

He knew instinctively what she was going to say. 'It's what you've described before, isn't it? Pharmaceuticals that have been banned in the West.'

She nodded significantly. 'The story of what happened to Mayhew & Taylor's so-called wonder drug is only one of the worst out of dozens of cases. Sophisticated drugs with dangerous side-effects got sold across the counter in the Third World like they were throat pastilles.'

'Presumably with no indication of the risks,' Philip added.

'Right. In the West we don't even let Olympic athletes take

anabolic steroids, but in Africa if you want to be in good shape for the village rain dance, you can get a drug like that as if it was aspirin.'

'Mayhew & Taylor have come a long way from their heroic philanthropic beginnings,' he commented bitterly.

'That's what Daniel felt most of all, I think. He felt responsible for decades of this kind of commercial crime. I've told you he had this appalling sense of guilt. In the end it was stronger than that. He just didn't believe he had any right to exist,' she concluded with finality.

Philip pondered her remarks. 'When I started work at the college,' he told her, in a sombre whisper, 'the students protested against my appointment. At the time I couldn't understand it. Now I can see why they objected so strongly to my family connections.' He recalled the embarrassment of those weeks. 'There were some quite violent demonstrations.'

'I remember,' she said calmly.

'Were you . . .?'

She grinned wickedly in affirmation. 'I told you I was a liberal activist. I'd only just come back from Tanga. I had friends at the college. Of course I got involved.'

'So when you rang you knew exactly who I was . . .'

'I thought I did,' she kissed him affectionately.

He reflected on those days. A lot of water under the bridge, he thought, platitudinous as ever.

'But the students never mentioned the things you've been telling me.'

'Oh, yes they did. You just didn't bother to read what they wrote.'

He was silenced temporarily, acknowledging the fact. 'I'm sure they didn't know about the dumping of the wonder drug.'

She paused. 'No,' she admitted. 'I kept that for Daniel.'

Philip's thoughts turned to Daniel and the last few months of his life. Yesterday Stevie had broken off her own account of the crisis in Daniel's career. Now he took her back again in memory to that cool summer morning.

'He apologised for being away,' she said softly, turning in his arms. 'I didn't know what to say. He was so pathetic. Whatever there had been between us was pretty well over. And then he said that it was all going to be all right in the future. As though he knew what I was thinking. He said there were no more problems with his story. He now had all the information he needed to get it published.' She sat up under the blanket, quite animated. 'And then he behaved rather strangely, like a mechanical doll that has been wound up and let go.'

'What happened?'

'He jumped into the air and did this extraordinary dance. It was almost a war dance. He was shrieking at the top of his voice, singing bits of songs he remembered from the Sixties. Like he was high.'

'It amused him to act mad,' Philip commented. 'When we were children he did it to attract attention. He liked adults to comment on his behaviour.'

'He was very crazy.' Stevie seemed only half to be listening, lost in her recollections. 'When he had calmed down he told me he was going straight to see his editor. You realise he hadn't been near the paper in months, even though they were still paying him. "I'm going to see that bastard," he said, "and I'm going to give his newspaper the scoop of its lifetime. They'll have to do a special feature, no, an exclusive, by-line and all, and I'll get a fucking Pulitzer, that's what I'll get." '

'But that's an American prize,' Philip corrected.

'Right. It just shows you how crazy he was getting.' Stevie went back to her story. 'He was shouting all this at the top of his voice. "And when I've done that, I'll go and look up my old man and give him the shock of his life." He was so excited. He was waving this sheaf of papers, dancing round, singing, "I'm a winner, I'm a star." ' She sighed. 'I tried to get him to tell me about his big breakthrough, but all he could say was that it would be in type by the end of the day and I could read it on the front page tomorrow morning. Although it was only ten o'clock in the morning, he already looked exhausted. He was sweating heavily and he had to have a large whisky before he went off to the office, "for medicinal purposes, you understand," he said, toasting me.'

'I don't remember anything dramatic about drugs in the press last summer,' said Philip.

'Well, of course it never happened. I remember sitting and praying that it wasn't a fantasy. It was very quiet. By mid-day it was drizzling again. You could hear the rise and fall of children's voices in the street and the sound of telephones in houses four or five doors away. Someone was listening to a French radio station in the flat upstairs. It's funny what comes back. I can see that day quite vividly, I suppose because I was so hopeful. I thought if the story was published then it would break the spell. He'd really screwed me up, you see. Perhaps he didn't mean to, but he did. So all my hopes for him were selfish really.'

Philip said nothing. He listened intently, his head on his hands.

'Daniel came back around seven. He seemed totally defeated; it was only when he started talking that I realised how angry he was. I thought he would break down. The editor had said no. Daniel had often threatened to walk out, but had never really meant it and I don't think he ever took the idea very seriously. Now he'd resigned on the spot and old whatshisname had accepted it then and there. That was it. Daniel was out. He was finished. He was wet from walking in the rain and he said he wanted a drink, so we went off to the pub. Then we went to another, and then another. He got totally pissed. He said he wanted to celebrate his new freedom – *celebrate*, I ask you – in Soho, have dinner, go dancing. Later we went to this roller-disco, but he fell over and hurt himself. Suddenly he seemed very old. I said we should go home. Finally he agreed. He insisted on driving. We got stopped by the police around one. They breathalysed him of course and he was arrested. They were vicious and rude, as you'd expect. He shouted and swore at them. Then they took him away and this young guy drove our car – I can't – with me to the police station. He tried to chat me up and I nearly hit him. The bastard. So I sat in this waiting-room until three in the morning while they took his details and did all those tests. They were bringing in junkies and strippers off the streets. It was terrible. When they let him out he was exhausted. As soon as he caught sight of me he started shouting again, but he was hoarse and tired and unsteady on his feet. All I remember now is sitting down on the steps outside the police station and crying, while he walked up and down shouting at me. In the end we got a taxi and I brought him back here and put him to bed. Things were never the same after that. He went downhill very fast.'

In his mind Philip saw the old man's face on the mortuary table, the dank wet hair streaked with grey and the lines of dissipation scored across his brother's cheeks. 'Yes,' he said, 'I know.'

'It was after he left the paper that I decided we had to get this house. He'd tried before to make contact with some of my friends and other more extreme groups, but they'd never really accepted him. He gave away money. That didn't work either of course. They always distrusted him. They knew all about his background, you see.'

'So this place really was the end of the road.'

'Right. It was to be for anyone who wanted it. We only moved in last October. Greg is the first – and the last.'

Stevie talked on, compulsively working the corner of the sheet with her fingers, staring trance-like at the ceiling, lost in bad memories whose fascination she could not quite resist. But Philip was only half hearing her; more and more clearly he was imagining his brother without her help. He could see Daniel in his mid-thirties, hating his own identity, uncertain where to go, in his mind betrayed and rejected, turning to more and more radical solutions, living just across the border from his own life, spending hours in pubs or half-empty cinemas, talking late into the night with people (students mostly, much younger than himself) he hardly knew.

To these, who saw him for the first time, he would seem slightly wild, rather erratic in thought and speech, and obviously lonely; always on the edge of meetings, showing his age by the clothes he wore and the style of the words he used, unfamiliar with the newest ideas, slightly on the fringe of any group, though anxious to be the centre of attraction, recognised as a once-gifted, slightly intimidating talker, remote and inaccessible, liable to violent outbursts of surprising lucidity and penetration.

Philip pictured him during that last summer, a lonely figure, tall, gaunt and wasted, with failure written all over his expression, showing in the nervous watchfulness of those once-steady brown eyes, and in the suspicious vulnerability to a slighting word or gesture. He imagined Daniel as in a permanent state of suppressed anger, often the worse for drink, habitually in filthy clothes, a shambling, defeated shell with only the inspiration of his own thoughts to keep him going.

Daniel had been an optimist and Philip realised that, when his brother found no hope in the future, this would be the end. He was dismayed at his growing sense of identity with his brother's predicament. He became aware that Stevie was questioning him. She had stopped her monologue, the flux of recollection, and was challenging him.

'I said: are you definite about keeping the house on?' she repeated.

'Yes,' he said. 'You must trust what I say now – always.' He kissed her on the mouth. She did not move. A single tear ran down her cheek and she put out her hand in a gesture of solidarity.

Philip could hear mice scuttering about between the roof beams in the ceiling overhead. Although the day was fading fast outside, and the hooting and revving of the rush-hour had started in the foggy late-winter gloom, the noise of the mice for some reason reminded him of early morning. This is like a holiday, he thought. Something that Stevie had said came back to nag him.

'With all this, why was Daniel so distrusted by the people he wanted to accept him?'

'They couldn't believe it was genuine, knowing his background, and nothing he did would convince them. That made Daniel wild, of course. He would do terrible things to prove himself. He had an enormous capacity for self-inflicted pain.'

Philip asked what she meant.

'Well, he always volunteered to do the things that no one else wanted to do. One day I remember he sold copies of one of the papers in the bookshop on the street for twelve hours. And there were only two takers, I think. There were times when I thought he actually wanted to get himself arrested, as though to prove that he was a rebel like the rest of them. Of course, the wilder he became, the more of an eccentric he seemed to everyone else. There was something pathetic in his eagerness to win approval.'

'And you?' What did you think?' He looked deep into her shadowy grey eyes, searching for an answer but finding nothing. She affected unconcern and her eyes did not give her away. 'When you're sleeping with someone . . .' She shrugged. 'You know things that other people don't know. So I was always more sympathetic.'

Sympathy, he thought to himself, was not a quality he would have suspected in her at their first meeting. She was too definite in herself and too mistrustful of motive to want to risk sympathy. Yet now it was part of whatever it was that was between them, a characteristic of their love both fierce and unifying. Philip, who had not known this meaning to the word (over-educated in the nuances of the liberal vocabulary of Victorian England) and who was always in the past grateful for the smallest glimmer of interest from other people, felt proud and grateful, as if, like a dedicated astronomer, he had made a discovery that was not previously recognised. He thought to himself then that endless love was all he wanted.

6

It was after dark. The house had begun to make its usual unexplained noises and Philip, wakefully turning over the thoughts in his head, could hear the automatic circuits clicking and whirring out of sync. Stevie, childlike, was drowsing next to him.

The telephone rang in the front room. 'I'll get it,' he said and loped through. The receiver was in his hand. Pip, pip, pip, pip. A call box. His first reaction was to wonder how Jan had found out.

'Hello,' he said, trying to sound neutral.

But the line had already gone dead. He waited for a minute or two but nothing happened and he went back to the bedroom.

'Who was that?' she asked sleepily.

'Someone in a 'phone box. A wrong number probably.' Apprehensions began to form again in his mind. 'When's Greg coming tomorrow?'

'He didn't say.' Stevie rolled towards him. 'You're getting tense again. Don't worry. Greg's okay.' He knew she was trying to reassure him. 'I haven't told him who you are.'

'Is that important?'

'Well –' she seemed aware of her mistake. 'He was jealous of Daniel. You know that.' She scowled. 'So it's probably better if he doesn't know. That's all.'

'You might have told me before.' He turned away and concentrated on the poinsettia by the bedside table. After only a few hours the plant was already getting past its best. Tomorrow it would begin to wilt; the leaves would flutter to the floor.

'You're pissed off with me,' she said. 'I'm sorry.'

'No, I'm not,' he lied. 'I'm looking at your plant. I don't think it's going to last here. I'll have to take it back home to the greenhouse on Monday.'

'Home,' she repeated shyly.

He caught her meaning. 'Yes,' he admitted. 'I'm still a bit divided. Give me time.'

He looked around him. The little room had already become their own private territory; and lying together under the blanket they traced adventures across the cracks in the ceiling.

'Love, can you see there,' she said, 'I'm walking by the sea. There are rocks in the water, a headland. I think the tide is coming in. Can you smell it?'

'I love the sea,' said Philip. 'Yes, I can smell it.' He blew in her ear. 'You can hear it too.'

She laughed. 'There are seagulls. You can hear them cry.'

'You can see them swoop towards each other.'

'Dive together.'

'Kiss.'

'How *do* seagulls kiss?' she asked, sitting up.

'Like this,' he said and did so, mockingly.

Stevie pulled back, excited. 'No, no – it's like this.' Philip closed his eyes and saw the sun break through the clouds and a sharp sea wind scurry over flat watery sands. 'Now I'm a worm,' she said, burying herself under the blanket crouching and huddling in the darkness between his legs.

Philip had a momentary flash of his first months with Jan, before they were married, laughing together in the early morning in the little room in Barons Court, crowded with clothes and make-up, his work piled on the table under the window, and the bed, heavy with the smell of sex, jammed behind the door with the rusty hook. The blood-red leaves by the bedside reminded him that he used to buy her flowers from a stall in Oxford Circus (daffodils, irises, tulips, roses and Michaelmas daisies as the seasons passed), bring her breakfast in bed, read the Sunday papers with her there, furnishing dream houses from the pages of the colour magazines, and then perhaps go walking out for the afternoon down the towpath and along the river past Kew Gardens. He shuddered involuntarily.

'What's the matter?' She lifted her head.

'Nothing.'

'You were holding your breath. I thought you were dead.'

'Don't say that.' He surprised himself at the vehemence of his words. His heart bumped unevenly.

'I was only joking,' she ran her hand across his forehead in a soothing gesture. 'You're sweating,' she said, and touched his lips with her fingers. He tasted the salt and said nothing. When he thought about it, the present scared him. This house was full of strange noises.

He tightened his embrace round Stevie and put his face into her breasts for comfort. She pushed him away with irony. 'My first boy-friend said I was flat-chested. I was upset then. I don't mind now: I realise that most Englishmen like their women to look like boys.'

'They say men who like boyish women are latent homo-sexuals.'

'Well –' she said, amused. 'Look at your relationship with your brother.'

He was defensive. 'What do you mean?'

'Oh – don't worry. What do you mean, anyway, saying I'm boyish?'

'Your clothes for a start.'

'It's all I can afford.' He lay in silence for a while, thinking. Stevie was half-asleep on his shoulder. He sighed very deeply. 'You're not relaxed,' she said. 'What is it?'

'I love you, Stevie, but I'm afraid. I don't know why.' He turned sharply towards her. 'Stevie – please – why don't we have a holiday, go somewhere for a bit. To the country perhaps.'

She gripped him with sudden fierceness, as though his admis-sion was a failure that threatened them both. 'You mustn't let this place frighten you.'

'It's not just the house,' he admitted quickly. 'It's you. You say you're not extreme, but to me you are. You live in another state, I feel sometimes. I'm not used to houses like this . . .' He made an incoherent gesture with his free hand and then said, more quietly, 'I want a quiet life, my things about me, flowers to look after.' He saw that she was studying him like an intruder. 'You don't know what I mean, do you?'

She stopped his hand in mid-air and held it strongly in her own thin fingers. He felt her faded porcelain ring digging into his knuckle.

'You've got nothing to fear,' she whispered.

'What about Greg?' he asked, rather ashamed to expose his fears again.

'For Christ's sake, I've told you a dozen times. Greg's okay.'

'Don't you think it would be better if I wasn't here tomorrow? I've got plenty of other things to do at – at my house.'

'Fine – why don't you piss off now if you're worried. I don't give a shit.'

'I'm sorry, Stevie, I know I'm letting you down. It's just something I feel.'

She turned away, spurning him with her shoulder. He crawled up to her and rested his chin on her elbow.

'Don't.'

He was hurt. 'Stevie.'

'Oh, fuck off.' He had forgotten in the idyllic moments of the last few days how intolerant and unforgiving she could be, and he saw that her disappointment in him made her angry. It was as though she was always challenging him to match her own free spirits and daring. At first he had promised that; now, when he weakened and became vulnerable again, she lost interest, found him like other ordinary men, lustful and selfish. She resented the emotional plea that said, 'Help me,' because it reminded her that she too was vulnerable. He knew she hated to look into the mirror of another person's face.

'Of course I'm going to stay,' he said. 'Tomorrow, perhaps, we can go . . . to the sea,' he added with happy inspiration.

'Perhaps,' she commented cryptically.

He took Stevie in his arms, using his strength to turn her towards him, kissing and soothing her with his swollen lips. Gradually her body, which had become cold and distant, seemed to relax, despite the tensions of their conversation.

But then she broke in. 'I'm sorry. I'm not with you.'

He fell back beside her, hurt and disappointed, and he thought how quickly the real world intrudes on dreams. He sensed that Stevie felt confused and guilty as well. 'Don't worry,' he said. 'This is the way it is.'

'I know,' she replied in a sad whisper. 'Getting it wrong when you want to get it right.'

They slept, it seemed, for hours. He lost all sense of time. His dreams were rare and vivid. When he woke again it was night; Stevie was lying there listening to the radio, tuned in to the classical music station that Philip liked, beating time with a thumping left arm and humming as the glorious sound echoed and reverberated round the bare room like a poem in a lunatic asylum.

'Do you like Beethoven?' he asked.

'It's . . . fantastic,' she said, seeming to choose her words with care. 'I don't understand it, but it's fantastic.'

'His last symphony,' he said.

'Ludwig van Beethoven,' she said slowly, savouring the name. 'This stuff is amazing. Keep at it, Ludwig old boy,' she said, parodying Philip's accent.

Philip felt his heart break open with love for her and for the unexpected intrusion of the pure sound of Beethoven. The first movement came to an end, the radio audience shuffled and coughed, and, because the batteries were low, the speaker hissed and crackled. Then the jaunty rhythm of the second movement began.

Listening to the music he had a deep sense of estrangement. There was a world where people in well-cut suits went to concerts and restaurants that seemed irretrievably remote. There was nowhere for him to go now that did not seem pointless and unreal, and yet the place in which he found himself, while it satisfied his grief's need to get closer to his brother, only seemed to mock his search for straightforwardness by its alienated and inaccessible code. He supposed that Stevie claimed not to understand Beethoven because she hated the society that played Beethoven. He rolled over in bed. 'When I was a student,' he said, 'this music used to make me feel free, happy and excited; better somehow; now it only make me feel sad.'

'You're funny,' she said. 'You're always looking to have yourself relaxed and satisfied. You want your nerve ends deadened, don't you? You don't like discord. You want answers, you want patterns, order, peace. You want things to happen according to the timetable. I don't understand that.' She saw that he was about to question her as he always did and went on, almost tumbling over her words, with that familiar provocative catch in her voice. 'I want to feel things as they are, not as they're made or interpreted. I want to be able to say things how I want, how I see them. Okay, I prefer uncertainty, what you'd call a messy situation, because that's what it's like out there. People like you have spent too long building fences to keep out the chaos. You call building these fences providing answers. That's a lie. All you want, you say, is a quiet life. For God's sake, there are no answers, not now. The world is too fucked up. All the problems now are bigger than any possible solutions. But you – Philip – you're like Daniel, like a lot of middle-class schoolboys – you like games, puzzles, exams – you want to solve things.' She thumped the bed petulantly. 'That's why you're here, for Christ's sake.'

223

'I'm here because I love you. I told you that before,' he protested.

'Perhaps. You're here also because you wanted, as you would say, to get to the bottom of things. Right?'

'I've told you that already.'

'But there is no mystery; no correct solution and a ten pound book token. Can't you see that?' She flicked her fingers with irritation. 'There's a human tragedy as always, but that is something else and far too complicated for your sort of mind, I'd say.'

Philip felt disturbed by the force of her words, and his silence said that he was compelled to recognise the truth in them. Knowledge of Daniel was also self-knowledge and he, who had always had a taste for ruthless self-criticism, wanted Stevie to instruct him in both. He could listen to Stevie's urgent, deep-drawn voice all day, for hours at a time. It had a hypnotic quality, nothing to do with her words, which was earthy and at the same time refined. And when, to command attention to what she had to say, she put her finger to his lips, or to soothe him ran her hand through his thinning hair, blowing on it childishly and caressing his bald patch, his senses caved in and asked only for satisfaction and release. He was enchanted.

'I love you,' he said. It was a poor answer, but he was admitting that there was now no other focus of his loyalty left. He said to himself, I have lost my wife, left my house, cheated on my job, withdrawn from my friends and surrendered myself to a woman who fears and hates the society in which I grew up and was nurtured. He saw that she was smiling at him with her slow enigmatic smile and thought he was being gently taunted.

'It's true,' he said. 'You think I'm a dull, old-fashioned lecturer; but I share your anger and Daniel's anger – you have both taught me that. Yes, I can believe this is going to be my home. It scares me but I'm happy here.'

She kissed him. 'There you are again,' she teased, 'you're only happy when you're being happy.'

'I believe in happiness,' he said without irony. 'What do you believe in?'

'You've asked me that before. I don't know. Nothing much.'

The adagio ended. There was more shuffling on the radio. In the distance, outside, Philip thought he heard the shriek of a car cornering at speed, but sleep had clouded and dulled his reactions and he experienced none of his usual anxieties. Now he surrendered to the syncopated rhythms of the fourth movement and the intimate warmth of Stevie's body. He rolled closer towards her like a baby and drowsed in the thick smell of their bodies together. Then the Ode to Joy began, a clarion call that roused Stevie and had her thumping her arm wildly in time to the beat. 'Come on, listen, join in!' she shouted. 'Freedom! Freedom! Freedom!' She tore away from his arms and stood up unsteadily on the bed, jumping up and down like a punk dancer in a wobbly frenzy, shouting and exhorting. Philip lay back on the pillow watching her in awe and amazement. 'You're mad,' he said with a smile, and she collapsed, laughing and speechless on top of him. Her heart was thudding against his chest and then he became aware of another hammering sound, a violent banging from downstairs in the street. He pushed Stevie off with a panicky thrust and staggered unevenly on to the floor, pulling on his jeans in a fumbling movement of apprehension. Stevie's expression changed; she shouted at him in anger. 'Can't you hear,' he shouted back. 'People. At the door.' She got up in a hurry. He was trying to button his shirt. His fingers were thick and unco-ordinated. He was shaking. She grabbed her sweater and a loose Indian skirt. He ran to the stairhead. The hammering and shouting outside continued louder than ever. He thought the door would splinter.

Stevie was next to him suddenly. 'It's Greg,' she said. 'Let him in.' He did not move. 'Go on. Let him in.' He ran downstairs, as though he was being shoved, slipping the last few steps. The bolts seemed incredibly stiff. He tore a nail and began to bleed but didn't feel any pain. Suddenly the door sprang open and Philip found himself carried backwards as fast as he had arrived, on a tide of movement, with a stump of metal rammed against his chest, winding his words.

The man was shouting. Philip saw sweat pouring down his face, a sudden close-up that lost all significance when he realised that the thing butting into him was a gun, and that the open barrel was facing him, a small black hole that transfixed his attention. He wanted to say, 'Leave me alone,' but the words would not come. After the shouting and the slamming and bolting of the door came the approach of police sirens, several, heavy feet drumming on the pavement, running downhill fast. And, then, a jabber of noise outside. He found himself pushed in a huddle upstairs, backing away from the tiny piercing eye of steel in front

225

of him, and as he rounded on to the landing he caught sight of Stevie's white face, framed in the darkness of her bedroom doorway, looking at him, as though across a chasm.

The man who had grabbed him was yelling at him now in fear, but nothing he said had meaning. Philip found he had an irrational desire for his socks. It was so ridiculous that he almost laughed out loud. Then, almost at once it seemed, the sirens outside stopped, and someone began talking at the house through a loud-hailer. Philip heard the phrases he had heard on news bulletins so often in the past, but couldn't focus on the reality. This isn't happening to me, he repeated, this isn't happening to me. Then the noises and the voice stopped; there was an intense moment of silence broken by the last chords of the fourth movement and the tumultuous and ecstatic applause of the audience in the Festival Hall.

Book Five

I

Nothing made sense. Everything was uncertain and unexplained. Philip found himself watching what was happening as though it had nothing to do with him, like looking at the world through the wrong end of a telescope. He could see his hand was shaking, but he felt so numb and disorientated that it registered nothing. To his surprise he discovered that his immediate reaction was to worry about the week-end ahead. Not a very good start, he thought, watching the man pile furniture – a bed, chairs, the mattress and a clothes horse – across the top of the staircase. He was about to point out that he was cutting them off from the food in the kitchen downstairs when it occurred to him that without food this situation wouldn't last very long. With luck he will go away soon and it will all be over by Sunday, he thought. (He had been looking forward to surprising Stevie with breakfast in bed on Sunday morning as he used to with Jan). Perhaps it would speed things up if he offered to help. 'Just keep quiet.' The man who was slight and sandy-haired, almost dapper in his plain brown suit, was sweating and gasping with the effort of dragging a heavy wardrobe to reinforce the home-made barricade.

Everything was unreal. He had been pressed against the garish wallpaper at the top of the stairs, like a suspect, threatened intermittently while the man wrestled the things into place. He felt his torn nail throbbing and saw that it was bleeding. Someone was in the front room at the end of the landing, fiddling with the radio, skidding the tuner across the wavebands. It was like an hallucination, and Philip did not immediately realise that it was Stevie until he glimpsed her through the crack in the door, characteristically crouched in a corner. Suddenly, civilised voices, talking about the money supply, came over the air.

When he heard the talking, the man stopped what he was doing, grabbed Philip by the shirt and shoved him with careless strength into the spacious front room. 'Who's that?' he demanded. His voice was vicious, as though it was used to getting its own way only through the hint of violence. 'Who's talking?'

Close to, the impression of a bank clerk running amok was not sustained. There were stains on the man's suit and his jaw was hard and cruel, shadowed with stubble. But the effect was of a demobilised trooper not of a gangster. Philip found the air of unreality testing his mental equilibrium and he tried to centre his concentration on the things he understood. With the man's question still unanswered, he watched Stevie and noticed with pride that, although she was obviously frightened, she was managing to stay insolent.

'It's only the radio,' she replied.

'Bring it over here,' the man ordered, giving a peremptory shake to his gun.

She saw at once that he wanted to smash it, and refused with a gesture at once possessive and sensible. 'Don't,' she warned, 'you've got to stay in touch.' It sounded to Philip as though she was quoting from a handbook. That was all she said; then she switched it off and put it down beside her. Her hand was shaking; but, despite this, she stared up at the man with a slightly coquettish smile; he shuddered with thwarted rage and jerked the barrel of his pistol at Philip, who, though the thing looked like a toy, jumped back in terror.

'Don't move.' The man was enjoying the exercise of power after Stevie's tiny victory, 'or I'll blow your fucking head off.'

'Don't be silly, Greg,' Stevie commented from the side, almost patronising. 'We're all in this now.'

It was part of the absurdity of what was happening that Philip's immediate reaction was one of gratitude to her for having sorted out the minor query about the invader's identity that had been nagging in his mind. At first – it seemed already hours ago – he had heard, or thought he remembered, Stevie talking about Greg. Yet Greg was expected tomorrow and she appeared totally indifferent to the arrival of this athletic, sweat-streaked figure. Philip, alert to her behaviour even in the middle of his own fear, had been wondering if she hadn't made a mistake of identification. In fact, he had begun to assume that this was one of Stevie's other contacts, an unexpected manifestation of the shy but violent subculture about which she was so divided. But now – he told himself, making another mechanical connection in his mind – it was all straightened out: it was Greg. Philip found it oddly reassuring to know this. It was why, he assumed, Greg was strangely so responsive to Stevie's commonsense suggestions. His fears began to recede. It will all be over quite soon, I expect, he reiterated to himself; at least there was quite a bit of the week-end to look forward to, and with luck a day by the sea.

Philip was becoming gradually aware of the outside world; he could hear more sirens in the distance, dogs barking, and a confused hubbub from the street below mixed with a remote banging from the front door. Greg was squatting by the chimney, his pistol on the floor, a wary eye on his prisoners, emptying his pockets and setting fire to small scraps of paper torn out of a neat black notebook. The flames flared in his face and Philip wondered if he was distracted enough to risk a dive for the gun.

'Careful,' said Stevie. 'You'll make a mess of the carpet.'

'Oh,' said Greg. 'Sorry,' he added incongruously, and made sure that the little flags of fire fell harmlessly on to the dun-coloured porcelain tiles round the grate. The knocking down-stairs was repeated and there was, Philip thought, a shouted sentence that resounded obscurely against the sturdy wooden panelling of Daniel's front door.

'What did they say?' asked Greg, looking up. A match blazed in his finger and he flicked it aside with a quirk of pain.

'They said, "Come out, you're trapped," ' said Stevie with composure. 'What are you going to do about it?' she inquired, finely calculating her challenge.

'Tell the bastards to fuck off,' said Greg. But the non-committal tone of his words was betrayed by the anxiety with which he stood up and went carefully over towards the open door. He waved his gun vaguely at Philip. 'Don't move or try anything. Okay?' He peered over the bannister into the darkened hall below and then, not trusting his hostages, swung back into the room. There was a pathetic arrogance about his expression that showed his deter-mination to appear in command.

Philip looked surreptitiously at his watch. It was ten-forty-five. It was the first moment he had thought about time since it had all started and he realised with a flush of disappointment that so far these events had taken about ten minutes.

Suddenly the automatic timing device went crazily into action and the heavy curtain was pulled back with a creak and a hum. In his confused state of mind, Philip found himself wondering again whether there wasn't someone else in the room. His initial paralysis briefly took hold of him as he wrestled to control his perceptions.

He found himself surprised by the urgency of events. Greg was shouting to Stevie to draw the curtain. At the same time he was slamming his hand down on the light switch by the door and plunging the room into darkness. By the pale light filtering up from the kitchen downstairs, Philip could see Greg's slender silhouette against the open door-frame, rigid with fear and alertness. The street lights outside, suddenly exposed, filled the room with a hard yellow glare, and for some reason all three of them were temporarily checked and silenced, immobilised by the undefined scrutiny and menace of the forces gathering in the road.

Involuntarily, to give shape and focus to the paradoxical fear he felt towards the external world, Philip turned and looked out of the window across to the familiar houses over the street. The derelict buildings were black and skull-like as usual, but, where the renovation was finished, one or two showed a welcoming light. As he looked, he glimpsed in the house opposite, the figure of a small girl with fresh-scrubbed cheeks and flaxen curls appearing at one of the windows in front of him. Her pyjamas were spotted with a nursery motif and she was in a state of high curiosity. Philip experienced an intense surge of nostalgia. The baby-child studied the scene very seriously for a moment and then, half-distracted from behind, gave a quick naughty wave. Philip flinched and might have waved back, but the little girl turned as if summoned more urgently than before, hesitated disobediently, and then ran back out of sight. The light was switched out; he became aware with foreboding that all the other houses opposite had become blank and hostile. Stevie was now drawing their own curtain and the room returned to deeper shadow.

Once the view was blocked, Greg flicked the light on again. He stood by the door looking at Philip and Stevie, the gun loosely clasped in his left hand. The frowning heaviness of his eyebrows was accentuated across the room, and this, together with the rigid slope of his body against the door frame, emphasised his suspicion and isolation. Philip eyed him sensing an advantage. This is like school, he thought, I'll stare him out. It was something to do, but he couldn't keep it up. After a few seconds, disturbed by the hostility of Greg's response, he shifted his gaze away to neutral territory, but he found he couldn't relax there either. The impression of Greg's malevolent scrutiny was fixed too graphically in his mind's eye. For all the sweat, it was an unemotional, slightly frozen face, with a straw-coloured quiff falling across the pale forehead, an appropriate mask, Philip thought, for a man with no one to trust. He had the look of a persistent, slightly belligerent, mature student from one of Philip's history seminars, but, despite the disorientation, Philip realised that this was going to last more than three hours with a break for coffee. Next week we shall discuss the invasion of the Rhineland . . . He began to worry about having enough time to prepare his next presentation. Then he became aware that Greg was watching him closely; his impassive expression was almost bloodless. Philip realised, when Greg shifted the tilt of his body, that this was the man who had been trying to get Stevie into bed. Somehow, from her comments, he had expected his uninvited visitor to be less attractive. Now, when there was time to pause and think about it, real apprehensions about the immediate future began to take hold of his imagination. The commando vigilance of Greg's attitude suggested that perhaps it might be more than a few hours before they sorted things out. It was lucky, Philip thought, that they had the whole week-end ahead of them. He wanted to be out by Sunday at the latest. There was a lot of teaching he had to prepare for.

He realised his mind was turning on a treadmill, and he transferred his worries to Stevie's poinsettia. It needed attention. But this man, Greg, didn't look like someone who was very interested in flowers. But, then, you never knew. People had the strangest tastes. He began to fantasise about Stevie's relationship with his brother.

Then the telephone rang. The bell sounded downstairs in the hall as usual. 'Where is it?' Greg demanded, menacing them both. Stevie pointed casually. Greg switched the light off before he picked it up. Almost at once he began shouting obscenities into the mouthpiece, then slammed it back into the cradle.

This time he left the room in darkness and turned on the overhead light with the Japanese shade on the landing, fumbling behind his back for the switch.

'Who was that?' Philip was astonished at the mild note of interest in Stevie's voice.

'A bloody newspaper,' said Greg. 'Bastards – they wanted to

know if they could help.' He thumped the thickly carpeted floor with his boot. 'Help? Christ, no!'

The telephone rang again. Philip, who had found it so difficult to trace the number, was puzzled. This time Greg jumped in and grabbed the flex, whirling the 'phone around his head so that the plastic casing splintered against the wall. The receiver flew off, dangling like a torn limb, and the ringing stopped. Then he put his foot against the bits that were left and tugged until the multi-coloured wires were wrenched free. Pieces of cream bakelite were scattered across the floor like a broken egg.

'How do they know you're here?' Greg sounded desperate. 'This is supposed to be a safe house.'

'It isn't a safe house if you bring half the force in London to the doorstep, for Christ's sake!' She was angry. 'I have my contacts in the press. News travels fast. There are still some journalists who can put two and two together.'

A little learning is a dangerous thing, Philip thought to himself.

After that, Stevie seemed calmer, temporarily more secure, and inwardly satisfied by the release of her tensions. Greg on the other hand appeared for the first time disturbed by what had happened. He took off his jacket and threw it carelessly on the floor. Philip could see the muscles in his forearm flexing with anxiety. Greg's slight figure had the kind of visible strength that suggested brutal experiences. Philip's sense of vulnerability and isolation suddenly became claustrophobic and, without knowing it, he stood up.

Greg jumped and took up a marksman's stance. 'What are you doing?'

Philip shook his head, shocked at his own unconscious thoughtlessness and sat down again on the sofa, stammering his apologies. He looked down at the floor in shame. When he heard Greg say, 'Take your tights off,' very cold and unemotional, he didn't understand at first. He looked up at Stevie and the blood began to pound in his head. He wondered vaguely what chance he would have if Greg tried to rape her. But Stevie seemed unconcerned. She kicked off her faded plimsolls, reached up her skirt, peeled the tights off and threw them across the room without comment. It was only then, when Greg started stretching the little ball of nylon in his fingers, that Philip realised he was going to be tied up.

234

'Who are you?' Greg demanded, grunting as he jammed the last knot.

'Philip,' he answered back. 'Who are you?' He was aware that this uncharacteristic show of bravado had caught Stevie's attention. He did not look at her, though, but concentrated on Greg who examined him curiously for a moment and then straightened up.

'Mind your own business,' he said. 'Ask her if you like.' It was as though he was daring his captive to take a risk.

Philip checked the invitation to recklessness just in time and suppressed a further comment: after Stevie's description of the relationship between Greg and his brother, he did not want him to discover that he too was a member of the Taylor family. He was aware, from her expression, that this was Stevie's worry also. Greg's casual question added another dimension to the instability of the situation and it started a new murmur of disquiet in Philip's mind.

Outside it went very dead. The sirens were silent, the noise of cars revving urgently down the street had stopped, and the police had given up trying to talk to them through the megaphone. Only the occasional shout of warning broke the quiet. Philip imagined that the other houses in the vicinity were being evacuated and he saw the girl with the golden curls, full of unanswerable questions about what was going on in the house over the road, being settled down for the night in a hotel or a church hall. He himself sat on the floor, his back resting against the sofa, trying not to elaborate the implications of what was happening. The knots on his ankles chafed slightly. Stevie was slumped in the corner, her head on her knees, apparently overwhelmed by depression. With Greg the tension showed in his restless prowling movement round the room, his curious prying into cupboards and behind pictures, and in the way his head darted from side to side like a party-goer on the cocktail circuit.

Now that Philip had had time to acclimatise to the details of the siege he became aware that the curtains had begun to glow with a silvery lunar light. Stevie and Greg had noticed this almost simultaneously, and they all realised – looking at each other in the new grey shadow, not speaking but understanding – that arc lights had been turned on.

'Perhaps we're on T.V.,' said Stevie at last.

Greg did not comment. Philip said nothing and hoped that Stevie's attempt at conversation would falter. His heart was

235

beating with fear again: he had become conscious of a noise at the window, a muted irregular bump that he was straining to hear. Hope and anxiety were mixed together as he twisted his neck (discreetly to avoid drawing attention to his curiosity), trying to catch the mysterious sound. But Greg had heard it too. Still pointing his gun at Philip, he moved crabwise across the room, crunching on the broken plastic, towards the curtain. He stood at the side of the window and flicked at the heavy folds with his free hand. A shaft of light broke in suddenly and the megaphone outside issued a sudden burst of instructions.

Greg jerked back as though shot, the curtain folded together again, the room went shadowy and, almost as abruptly, the noise in the street stopped. It was as though light and sound and action were all synchronised by some unseen film-maker. Philip found himself bitterly resentful of this intrusion by the outside world.

'It's a telephone,' said Greg. 'On a rope. They're lowering a telephone on a rope. They must be on the roof.' He was thinking aloud very fast, hyped up with apprehension.

'They want to talk to you,' said Stevie from her corner. 'They want to negotiate.' Philip knew what she was going to say next. 'What are you going to do about it?' she challenged.

Greg seemed to be able to make up his mind without difficulty. 'I won't do it,' he said. 'I know what they do. They've got psychologists and things. They end up controlling your mind.' He turned on Stevie with frustration. 'You know that as well as I do.' It was the first time he had spoken so freely with them and his voice, low and bitter, had a slight Liverpudlian edge to it.

For all that the shared experience of the siege had brought the three of them involuntarily together, Philip observed that they were all getting locked into a profound inner loneliness provoked by the isolation and the fear of sudden violence. He saw that Greg's solitary rôle was forcing him to adopt uncompromising responses. The man was completely alone, under the spotlight. There was no one he could talk to or discuss tactics with. He would not be able to hurt Stevie; his mind was probably divided towards her. All he had was one good hostage. He was living in his head with a cacophony of intolerable voices. As time passed his fears and doubts would grow more and more terrifying. Philip knew that: he was having the same experience. Any one of them might crack up or go berserk. He realised that, while there was the absolute necessity of doing nothing to antagonise Greg, he had to talk to him to remind him of the rational world. Quite deliberately he began to do so, even though he was privately forced to admit a small adjustment to the optimism of his first hopes. The thing looked as though it would last until morning at least.

'I want you to understand, Greg,' he began, very quiet, 'that I'm not violent, I won't –'

'Keep quiet.' But he said it so half-heartedly that it was almost an encouragement.

'I won't try to escape.' Philip went on with determination. 'I won't. As Stevie says,' he added, invoking her name, 'we're all on the same side really.' He began to improvise a monologue of reassurance and self-justification with desperate ingenuity.

He heard his own voice, smooth and civilised, purring away in the dark like a hypnotist. The luminous hands of his watch glowed on his wrist and the slightest gesture described a magic arc in the shadows. Greg broke the spell.

'Is there an attic in this house?' he demanded. Something was on his mind. He turned towards Stevie and she seemed to be aware, although she was still bowed in her corner, that the question was for her.

'I don't know.' Her manner was listless and grudging. 'There's a trapdoor in the ceiling out there,' she waved vaguely at the landing. 'I suppose there must be then.' Scorn came into her voice and she came to life. 'What are you worrying about now? I want to get some sleep.'

Greg became clipped and tense with anger. 'Look,' he chopped with his free hand for emphasis. 'Outside the window. On a rope. There was a telephone. From above.' He glared at her as though he had demonstrated an important proposition.

'You're right,' said Stevie in a tone that Philip recognised to signify ironic approval. 'The roof slopes. They must have climbed into the attic from next door.' Again she adopted her calculated taunting. 'What are you going to do about it?'

Greg hesitated. He was balanced like a dancer on the balls of his feet. Philip noticed that, there too, even the unobtrusive detail of shoes – Marks and Spencer, plastic soles – had been meticulously attended to. In the street, this man would be anonymous in the flowing crowds of the city. He watched Greg move uneasily out to the landing, looking back nervously at his hostages, and crane up at the trapdoor. There was no sound, no movement overhead, just the faint whistle of a cistern. It was clear

that another threat had been added in Greg's mind to the insecurities with which they were already surrounded. He came
back into the front room, petulantly ramming the door back on its
hinges to that he had a better line of sight on to the landing and
blocked staircase.

Philip did not start speaking again. He could not concentrate.
Rational, calming sentences would not form. He found he had a
kind of mental stammer that scrambled his reactions to his multi-
plying dangers.

'What time is it?' Stevie asked. Philip told her. It soothed him
even to share a mundane exchange like that, and temporarily the
tide of panic in his head was stemmed. Stevie suggested tentatively that they could watch the late news headlines on the television.

'I couldn't give a monkeys,' said Greg, but made no move to
stop as she darted forward to switch it on.

Then she came and sat cross-legged next to Philip on the floor,
a move of child-like companionship, touching him lightly on the
nose with her finger as she did so. The almost imperceptible
gesture of affection amplified a thousand times the debate in
Philip's mind about where her loyalties lay in such a crisis.

There was a burst of noise from the set. 'Turn it down,' Greg
yelled, looking up apprehensively at the trapdoor again. Under
cover of the distraction she said, 'Don't worry.' Philip felt happy.
He smiled (turning his head away from Greg); his swollen lip
cracked and began to bleed a bit. But he was strangely grateful, as
he licked the tiny wound and tasted the blood on his tongue, for
something personal and private on which to concentrate.

'What are you talking about?' Greg demanded, his voice un-
naturally loud, as though he were deaf. Stevie turned the volume
down and moved swiftly to his side in reassurance. 'Greg,' she
said, almost cooing. He started back as she put her hand on his
arm, waving the gun unsteadily.

'Get away,' he said, still very loud. Philip was selfishly glad to
see that he was treating her with hostility: he felt more secure to
have Stevie treated as a hostage. When the signature tune for the
news started Greg suddenly lost his nerve, went over to the set
and turned it off. He raised the butt of his gun over the screen.

'Don't smash,' said Stevie, half getting to her feet. 'Don't.
We've got to know what's happening.'

Greg put his arm down (Philip saw that it was jerking uncontrollably) and turned aside, scowling. 'You can watch the news tomorrow,' he conceded, and shoved the television set against the wall as though he hoped it would break. Philip had the sense of another small victory. At least Greg was talking about the future.

Time flowed. Philip took out his contact lenses, grateful that his hands were still free, and put them carefully in his pocket. The outline of the room softened and his aching eyes were soothed. Greg seemed much calmer. The sudden flurry of words and action was now followed by inactivity and silence. The restricted landscape was becoming familiar at last. And when the outside world was quiet, when the little noises it made did not seem to threaten sudden violence, the disturbances in Philip's mind throbbed with a weaker pulse. He was almost accepting the situation.

He tried to sleep but found it difficult, with his legs stretched awkwardly out in front of him, to get a comfortable position. Stevie was sitting next to him on the floor, her head on his shoulder, unblinking. He took her hand and played with her fingers; she did not resist. Her skin was warm and moist. In an odd way he felt that the harsh nature of the circumstances in which they suddenly found themselves had softened and relaxed her usual mood of vigilance. Psychologically, she had always suspected her surroundings of obscure and subtle dangers; it was as though she was relieved to be in an environment that lived up to her worst expectations. Philip himself was less alert; he had the drowsy numb headache of one suddenly roused from sleep and he was beginning to want something to drink. This set off another chain of speculations in his head. He knew there was water for Stevie's houseplants in the scarlet tin jug on the window-sill. Of course there was also water in the bathroom down the passage, but that seemed incredibly remote. Then again, there was the bottle of Glenfiddich, unopened, in the bookcase. At first he decided he would only ask for a drink when he actually craved it; then he thought that Greg might get pleasure out of exploiting his suffering, and refuse. The best insurance might be to start negotiating at once. On the other hand if he appeared to make a nuisance of himself with too many requests that would be counter-productive.

Then Greg spoke, breaking this treadmill of anxieties. He said, slightly slurred. 'Stevie, I want to talk to you.' He gestured at the landing and she moved obediently towards the shadows outside, quick and light-footed as ever, a faun, thought Philip, even in a waste-land, a faun. Then Greg bent down towards him, very close so that Philip could smell him and look into his china-blue eyes. The rims were already red with tiredness. When he spoke Philip could see his te~th, broken and discoloured like an old dog's; a new skin of sweat was forming under his thatchy hair. Helpless in Greg's shadow and staring into his hard, glassy eyes, Philip felt thin and weak, a straw that could be snapped in the man's fingers. 'Who are you, shit-face?' said Greg, very tense and low. 'What are you doing here?'

Philip started to stammer. He knew, incongruously, that he was blushing. There was another fear in his mind as well. Stupidly, without his socks, he was afraid Greg would stamp on his bare toes. Greg's breath was stale, he menaced his captive for a moment with his sheer size and then said, 'Shithead,' with compressed venom and spat into his face. Philip recoiled and bowed his head, sickened and embarrassed, and rubbed with his sleeve on the raw surface of his cheeks. He told himself angrily that he was falling into the rôle of victim again. It's the same story, he thought, I'm getting pushed about. Greg walked away from him backwards, slightly ludicrous, toting the gun at him, steering himself uncertainly towards the landing where Stevie was waiting.

Philip watched the two of them through the door, noticed that the tidy vulgarity of the room was disintegrating. The impression was dirt and chaos: mud from Greg's shoes, disarranged chairs, and the tangle of wire from the telephone. Outside, they were talking in low murmurs. He strained to catch their words, but it was no good, there was only the tone to go on. A whisper of suspicion echoed in his head and he shut his eyes to concentrate. They seemed to be arguing or bargaining. He wondered how much Greg knew about their relationship, and how much she would tell him. Whose side was she on when it came down to it? The contradictory nature of her behaviour was characteristic, but it frightened him even more in these circumstances. Would she shield his identity? Would she give him away? Would she crack under pressure like before? His skin was smarting where Greg had spat at him and he winced again at the indignity, telling himself that he must not lose his temper. Then the conversation outside stopped and Greg and Stevie came back into the room.

Philip thought at once from the exaggerated, casual way that she joined him again on the floor that she had betrayed him. He looked at Greg lolling in the doorway: he too seemed less nervous, as though he had achieved a significant tactical advantage and perhaps some other kind of encouragement as well. Neither Stevie nor Greg looked at him for a moment and then Greg, obviously pleased with the new arrangement, rumbled his throat and spat again, on to the carpet this time.

'There are so many other ways we can get them to give in,' he said. The vague menace of his words and the sense that they were part of a conversation in which an important deal had already been struck was doubly frightening to Philip. Suddenly he was vulnerable and alone.

The silence that followed between the three of them was loaded; Philip felt the embarrassment of the outsider at a party who cannot think of anything to say, or worse, the awkwardness of the third person in a group. His attitude to the outside world was now totally reversed: he listened keenly for unexplained noises, the fall of dry plaster in the wall cavity or perhaps the nearly inaudible whine of a high-speed drill, as evidence that he was not to be abandoned here without some effort of release. Such random signals of activity around the house would be reassuring where formerly they had been threatening, an intrusion on a close-knit group. He wondered if there were still people on the roof and what had happened to the telephone outside the window. When there was a muffled thud behind the fireplace from next door he did not regret the clumsiness of the cordon as before, but hoped that it indicated perhaps the preparations for a dawn raid. All at once, the situation in Daniel's house seemed hopeless. The false buoyancy of Stevie's movements filled him with despair.

'Why did you do it?' he asked, not bothering to hide his alarm and bitterness.

She motioned to him to keep quiet and then looked away; Philip thought he saw her signal to Greg to move on to the landing. Or perhaps Greg had already stepped back into the shadows before she'd turned. He didn't know for sure. He was conscious that with his tiredness his reactions were getting slower. At least there was the certainty that they were comparatively alone. He became less aggressive.

'Can we talk?' he whispered, articulating his words carefully.

'Yes,' she said in her low, grave voice. Greg turned again at the word, but Stevie nodded towards him and he took two or three paces back on to the landing. 'He's in a bad way,' she went on very low and fast as though she did not want to answer Philip's questions. 'He's terrified of course.' She shook her head with disapproval at his weakness. 'Absolutely terrified. It doesn't help that he's getting tired.'

'How long can we talk like this? What's the deal you've made?'

She ignored him and went on with her own train of thought. 'I've explained to Greg that you're not a threat,' she said magnanimously.

'Did you tell him who I am?'

She looked scornful. 'No – of course not.'

'He'll turn on me if things go wrong, or if he finds out.'

She became defenceless and vulnerable. 'Don't say that – no – don't think that.' She was imploring him, reaching out her hands to his. 'Please, please.' When he saw how fragile her confidence in his safety was, he felt his own fears growing again.

'Why did you do it?' he repeated. She seemed not to understand. 'Why did you talk to him?' he demanded. 'We should have stuck together. We're separated now. He can do what he likes. Divide and rule. We'll never get out alive now, do you see that? Not unless they manage to break in.' He had wanted not to lose his sense of equilibrium but his defences were breaking down and his preoccupations were coming to the surface despite himself.

'It's going to be all right,' she went on, reassuring. 'I had a talk to him. He's calmer now. He was getting very crazy. I didn't give anything away. It's not a betrayal. For God's sake, trust me.' She too was sounding frantic. He had not heard her make this kind of appeal before. 'He'll threaten a bit and the people out there will give in. We're not foreigners, for God's sake. They can't let us kill each other. They'll give us a car. We'll fly . . .'

'Where to?'

'To . . . to Libya, or . . . or Cuba . . .' It was obvious that she had not thought about this at all. Her confession of weakness was true. This was not a situation for which she had any relish or experience.

He smiled weakly. 'I don't want to fly to Libya – or Cuba.'

She seemed disappointed with his response and began to talk urgently and businesslike. 'Once he gets on the plane we'll be released. You'll have done your bit. I'll come with you. It's like before. They've nothing against us.'

An earlier question stirred sluggishly in his thoughts. 'What happened . . . ? Why . . . ?' He shrugged in the direction of the window. She brushed that aside.

'I'll tell you later. It doesn't matter at the moment.' She was speaking as though time was short and there was something very important on her mind. 'Listen, Greg needs all the help we can give him. You'll have to let yourself be used by him for a day or two.'

'A day or two.' Philip was shocked.

'That's all.' She affected not to notice his surprise and pressed his arm confidentially. 'They can't do anything to him if you're with us. He may have to threaten you a bit. It will all be all right. We'll give them a deadline for a car to the airport and . . . and . . . a plane to . . .'

'Libya,' said Philip. 'Or possibly Cuba.'

But she missed his irony. Her face was serious. 'It's brinkmanship, that's all.'

'What happens if they ignore the deadline?'

The simple question seemed to confuse and startle her. 'But you do accept your rôle, don't you?' It was all she could say. Her urgency and pleading gave her away and she knew it.

She was crouching next to him; he saw her toes flexing on the deep pile. She had pulled one of his donnish sweaters over her tee-shirt, her skirt flounced over her knees, and, in the half-darkness, the expression of feeling was disguised by the shadowy contours of her face, but all the same he realised that she was ashamed of what she had said to Greg and of what she had agreed to do. He took her hand very gently and played with the limp fingers and felt the stickiness in her palm.

'Why don't you admit it, Stevie? Greg asked you to get my co-operation. I know it. It's obvious really. You don't want any violence and he doesn't want any trouble.' He had never known her so submissive and became less hostile in his words himself. 'You thought he was offering you a choice – the chance to have his sympathy. None of us has a choice here. Greg's gun is the only thing between us and the rest of the world. Violence rules O.K. I accept that. I have to. But so do you. If the deadline doesn't work –' he felt suddenly inarticulate and started another sentence. 'You and I are both hostages in the end. Whatever the deal. Don't kid yourself.' He sounded hurt. 'You didn't have to come and get my support – exploiting our relationship like that. Don't you see: you're the one that's being used and that's not like you. Not at all.'

He became upset at the circumstances that had done this to her and genuinely angry. His nail was hurting. He raised his voice and called out: 'It's all right, Greg. You've got what you wanted. You can use me, kick me about. I won't complain, okay.' Greg came back down the landing in a hurry. 'Just one thing,' said Philip, 'don't use Stevie like that any more. I can't stand it.'

When he realised what he was saying he recognised that he had betrayed himself with his own words and admitted that he was a victim. A mood of resignation was burning inside him, made more incoherent and bitter by the consciousness of something lost between himself and Stevie. He gave a private sigh of disappointment.

Greg looked at him through the door, a curious spectator at a drama of emotions from which he was separated. 'You can sleep if you like,' he said.

2

Philip was woken by a steady tap-tap-tap that was at first a part of unremembered dreams, then an indeterminate noise at the edge of his consciousness and finally the sound of something banging against the window-pane. The reality of the siege and its dangers came back with a shock; he yawned deeply and became aware that Greg, sitting against the doorpost, was equally alert to the sound. As Philip stirred, trying to repress his panic at the possibility of violence, he disturbed Stevie who was asleep on the floor beside him. They were both in a distorted sprawl across the carpet like the victims of street violence. The central heating was off and it had become very cold; he shivered, though partly at the unwelcome return of anxiety.

'What time is it?' Stevie whispered, bleary. Her face grew more substantial as she looked towards him and her expression was caught by a thin shaft of light shining through a slit in the curtain. Philip, who had eventually put his contact lenses on top of the television when he went to sleep, brought the watch close to his face and studied the luminous dial.

'Five o'clock,' he murmured. They had slept about four hours, he calculated; he felt refreshed and more optimistic again. He stretched out and picked up his lenses, licked them and put them in his eyes. The whole room came sharply into focus.

Greg paid no attention to their exchange of words. He was obviously considering what to do about the noise at the window. 'It's that bloody telephone again,' he guessed, thinking aloud. 'Why don't they realise I'm not communicating?'

After a few minutes the noise stopped; presumably they had given up the latest attempt to make contact. Philip wondered how long Greg had been fighting his response to the problem, hours perhaps. Exhaustion would be beating in his head. He was now staring suspiciously at the trapdoor but there were no tell-tale noises overhead. It was very still, it seemed, and the arc lights were still on.

Philip ran his hand over his chin. He felt dirty and unshaven; he knew he wanted to wash his hair and clean his teeth. He tested his tongue against his lips; the inside of his mouth was dry and furry.

'I want a drink,' he said, quite unpremeditated.

Greg made no objection, perhaps he felt benevolent once the threat of the telephone had been overcome, and asked Stevie to fetch some water from the bathroom. Philip heard the splashing of the tap and he began to imagine what it would be like to have a hot bath, to have warm soap slipping in his hands, steam rising in his face and the skin on his feet and fingers puckering in the piping water. Stevie was back again with a tooth-mug which she passed over to him without a word.

'Do you want some?' he asked.

'After you.'

He drank: it was incredibly cold and he discovered that it had quite a taste to it after all these hours. His mind was loosened by the refreshment and his mouth no longer felt rusty and painful.

'It's very quiet.' The sky outside was still dark, though with a hint of indigo.

'Perhaps they've all gone away,' she said, lyrical. 'Perhaps they've left us alone.'

It's like waking from a dream, he thought, and wondering whether it was all true, a lover returned or a wish fulfilled, a death averted. 'If only it was a dream,' he said.

She rocked backwards and forwards on her heels. 'If only . . .'

She teased his fanciful speculation and her own mood hardened. 'History is full of ifs.' She had this habit of sketching herself on to the largest canvas, as though anxious to cast herself in a major rôle.

Philip, not altogether mocking, asked: 'What will history say about Stevie Beck?' He wanted to resist the temptation to plead for her support but was unable to avoid the twist. 'Will history say she was loyal to her cause?'

'Don't test me,' she warned, alert to his meaning. 'You have your loyalties. I have mine . . . They have their own logic. They don't always happen to coincide.' There was a cold edge to her words.

'Why don't you ever trust yourself?' he challenged.

'Because I'm divided of course.' She was angry. 'I'm still torn between you – and him.' She pointed her cigarette at Greg, who was staring indifferently into space. 'Or, rather, what he stands for in my mind.' Greg seemed to be paying no attention to the conversation. Philip imagined that he was already dazed with tiredness. So he found the courage to question Stevie confidentially in the darkness.

'What's that?' he asked. 'I mean, what does he stand for exactly?'

'Oh, you know. I've told you. An end to the fucking boredom of it all. Fulfilment of my crazy dreams.'

'Everyone has to dream,' he protested, seeking companionship.

'But when your dreams turn into nightmares . . . what then?'

He knew that she was in love with the idea of reality and said, to please her, 'At least this is real.'

'It was never meant to be quite like this.' She sounded rueful. 'It was supposed to be safe as well as real. If you know what I mean.'

'But this is the sort of risk you have to run – in the real world you're talking about.' He was surprised to hear himself so much more practical.

Her face made a wry smile of self-admission. 'That's what I don't like, isn't it?'

Another doubt reawakened in his mind. 'What happened today – I mean yesterday?' He nodded in Greg's direction.

'Something went wrong. They keep a watch on everyone coming into the country. They were on to him, but he didn't realise it – not until it was too late.'

'That doesn't explain why he's come here early.' She queried him with a look. 'You said he was coming to pick up the stuff –' he paused, painfully acknowledging that all this was not a fantasy, 'today.' He indicated the chaos. 'Why did he have to arrive early?'

'Apparently he only found out that he was being followed yesterday afternoon. He tried to 'phone me – remember? – but when you answered he lost his nerve. Still, he knew they'd be watching the bedsitter he's in. So he decided to come here instead.'

'I see.' It all made sense. 'He thought he would be safe.'

'Right. In fact, it turns out that it must have been what they wanted.'

'I don't understand.'

She began to speak in a hurry, linking all the details in a monotone. 'He thought he'd come here once he'd thrown off the guys on his tail. So he goes into the Underground and thinks he's done it. Takes a bus. Then another tube, and then finally a cab. Walks the last bit down the hill. He gets into the street here and two cars are racing towards him. They'd followed him all the time. I suppose that was the connection with Daniel's house they needed. What they didn't expect was this.' She gestured at the room and the squalor. 'If he wanted he could blow the place sky high.'

The conversation flagged while she rummaged for another cigarette; the yellow flame illuminated her clear white concentrated features. Philip leant towards her, straining for a kiss. She drew away; he understood from the indrawn way in which she dragged on her cigarette that she was only in a mood for talk.

'So,' he murmured, swallowing his vowels carefully, 'he's not much of a courier after all.'

Stevie reacted as if to a personal criticism. 'How could I know that? When he came here first he seemed okay. Anyway, it's not my business to interfere.'

'What did Daniel think?'

'There was nothing Daniel could have done about it – even if he had wanted to.' She seemed to be aware that she was talking in riddles. 'I said earlier that it was my idea to use Daniel's house for –' she faltered.

'This?' he said.

'If you like.' She apparently resented the implication of failure,

247

but carried on. 'That's only half-true. Actually it wasn't my idea. Not at first.'

Philip encouraged her to continue.

'Daniel had bought the place. That was my suggestion. We were moving in. I was working part-time in the bookshop. Most days they had meetings there in the evenings. Daniel and I used to go and join in. I've told you they thought Daniel a bit strange the way he was always going on about the drug companies. But they all knew who I was and what I did. One day this guy in a suit came into the shop. Not Greg. He looked like a tax inspector. He asked for me. He said could we talk about Daniel's house. So, we went for a walk. Round and round the Angel. He had money, he said. He wanted somewhere nice and quiet to stay when he and his associates were in London. Associates. That was the word he used. Like a businessman. He said he'd made inquiries. He knew I was committed. He had this plan for Daniel's house. If we agreed . . .'

Stevie drew on her cigarette.

'Enter the real world,' said Philip, very low.

'Right. Looking back, it was something I thought I'd been wanting all along. The chance to do something that really mattered. It all fell into place. The house. A job for Daniel that wouldn't exhaust him and made him feel good. An action to match his words. And something for me. When I said goodbye to the man in the suit it was all fixed. I even had the money to make the alterations he wanted.'

'Alterations to what?'

'Oh. The house.' She indicated the room. 'He wanted these security devices we've got, and all this bourgeois anonymity.'

'But –'

'I know. I said it was Daniel. It wasn't – but there was no way I could tell you about this other arrangement, was there? Not until now?' He could see she didn't like to admit the deceit. 'Now you see why I wanted to know if you really meant to sell it or not.'

Philip's mind went into a whirl at the thought of these complications. He turned back to the present. 'When did –' he indicated Greg – 'appear on the scene?'

'At the end of last year. Not long before Daniel walked out. First of all he came to see what we'd done to the place. He must have given a good report. The next thing we were told was that he was going to be moving some stuff through here over the New

248

Year. It was supposed to be a safe time. But after Daniel went, and I didn't know what was happening, I got frightened. I realised I'd made a mistake. And then I rang you.'

'What happened in the café must have been incredibly disturbing,' Philip commented.

'Right. I thought they'd sussed. On top of my own second-thoughts about it all, it was too much. I was ready to freak out. Even when I realised that they thought they'd made a mistake.'

'It's ironic that they've probably no idea that you and I are here now,' he interpolated.

'It doesn't make any difference,' she concluded, with grim introspection. She was thinking aloud. 'This is the end.'

'Is it?' he asked apprehensive. He nodded at Greg. 'Won't his nerve hold?'

'Well, at least they won't shoot if you're with us,' she commented, evading his question. She laughed faintly, with slight malice. 'He said he would have forced me to fuck him if I didn't get you to co-operate last night.' Her voice was quite steady, almost bored; but her words hurt him like a razor. He didn't know how to respond at first. 'You – you – you couldn't have done that?' he stammered in amazement.

She laughed aloud. 'The guy's got a gun,' she said with scorn. 'As you said yourself, that's what counts. I'm not bothered about any other sort of thing.'

Greg was distracted from his reverie by her laughter and looked across at them. 'Keep quiet,' he said. He sounded very tired and listless.

Philip appealed to Stevie with panic in his eyes. 'Isn't there anything – anything between us? You said . . .' he stopped, embarrassed to be talking about the memory of their intimacy.

'What did I say?' she challenged.

He knew she was testing him: he decided to go on, though he knew she would hate him for the reminder of her vulnerability. 'The first time . . . you said something about something inside you breaking down the first time . . . the first time we made love.' He paused. 'I believed you.'

She was staring past him, not seeing, and her words were slow and even. 'That was the first time we made love. Now it's different. That's all I can say.'

'Stevie,' he protested, 'what are you saying? What are you

doing? Why?' His appeal did nothing to fluster her indifference. It seemed there was nothing he could do to stop the manipulation that she managed so effortlessly. His voice was rising with tension. He checked and looked anxiously at Greg. He had stood up and was now framed in the doorway, staring across the room at them. There was natural light beginning to show through the skylight in the hallway. Philip stopped: he had become disorientated by Stevie's assertion of shifting loyalties. He had given himself to her without shame or reserve and now discovered in a crisis that at heart there was a part of her he had never known, a part of her that apparently delighted in humiliating his love. Paradoxically, the realization only intensified his feelings towards her. He studied her with a shivering heartbeat and wondered why it was that he liked her to push him around.

Stevie sat like a Buddha, her proud, neat profile showed in outline against the curtain. She seemed characteristically locked into her own thoughts and as inscrutable as when they had first met. I have learnt from you, he thought; I have learnt about feelings I have never had. Stevie always seemed youthful, passionate, unquenchable, uncompromising in the defence of ideals, and anxious to experiment with everything. Yet with all the vitality she had a poise and intelligence that, even now, made the emotion catch in his throat.

'I love you,' he said involuntarily, despite his thoughts, and despite Greg. 'I do.'

There was a metallic click. 'Kiss her,' said a voice. Philip, not understanding, thought he has hallucinating. Then he saw Greg levelling his gun at him across the room. 'Go on,' he ordered, cruel and lascivious, 'kiss her.'

'W – w – w – what are you saying?' Philip was bewildered.

'Go on –' Greg was excited. 'Do it to her. Do what you do. Now.'

Stevie looked at Greg in astonishment. He was leaning back against the wall, very arrogant, with his feet firmly planted apart, the pistol held in both hands taut in front of him. He was enjoying the power but it was his eyes that gave away his real emotions; sunk deep into their hollow sockets, they were alert and voyeuristic. They shone like wet stone in the grey early morning light. Stevie hesitated and then got up from where she was sitting. The floorboards creaked. The tension was at its pitch. Greg did not move, just watched with pleasure. Philip, who was sitting helplessly on the floor wondering what to do, held his breath as he always did when he was nervous.

'I can't,' he complained. 'I can't move.' His ankles were rough and sore from the chafing of Stevie's tights.

'Do it,' Greg ordered. 'Don't argue.'

Philip, helpless on the floor, twitched ineffectually, jerking his body as if mortally wounded. All at once Stevie was next to him; her hair, when she bent over him, brushed the base of his neck like a caress. 'Please,' he said. 'Don't do it. Don't give in.' The shame that was fighting against his need for her made him hesitate and panic. He looked over his shoulder. Greg had lowered his gun and was watching them with fascination.

Stevie seemed quite oblivious to the vicarious gratification that Greg was getting. All the remoteness of their last conversation had been forgotten. Obviously she had felt slighted in a way that he, and perhaps even she herself, could never understand. The springs of her responses were buried deeper than in anyone he had ever known. But now she was merely instinctive. She knelt down in front of Philip and spoke to him in the voice that he remembered.

'I love you. Kiss.' The whisper of her conclusion caught him like nausea in the pit of his stomach. For a moment, Stevie drew away from him; her mouth was half-open and swollen and her words were getting blurred. 'I don't give a fuck about him,' her breath was on his face, warm and dry. As always, she was so proud, casual and instinctive about her desires. He discovered that he too had forgotten about the voyeur in the doorway. She kissed him again; he closed his eyes and felt himself plunging into an empty universe. Something opened wide in his head; silver and black exploded in his eyes. He thought he was crying but then, with the shudder of a swimmer in icy water, understood that it was Stevie's face, wet with her tears. Drawing back, he glimpsed his own bare toes and feet, white in the darkness, and went into a vivid fantasy, seeing Stevie, naked white, wet and sticky, her tee-shirt rucked above her belly in a kind of teasing pin-up nudity, heaving and crying ecstatically on top of him.

A voice. 'Get up, you fucker.' Greg was standing over them, the thrill in his mind had turned sour and he had suddenly become furious with disgust and frustration. Philip struggled to get himself to his feet, but his arms were numb, he could not find the strength. Greg stood over with the gun. He raised the butt in the air. Stevie screamed. Philip flinched and tensed himself, but nothing happened. Then he felt Greg's shoe against his side and he was rolled over on his back again like a corpse. Greg stared at him speechless and furious with sexual jealousy. When he was able to speak he said, 'It's disgusting.' He turned away, unable quite to bring himself to use the brutality Philip feared.

Greg was bending down again. He had picked something up from Philip's side, and, though he was flinching with fear and confusion, Philip could see that what Greg had in his hands looked like a wallet. He scrabbled wildly in the back pocket of his jeans. Greg had opened it out and was studying it by the grey light from the landing. It was beginning to dawn.

There was a short pause and then he got violent. He shouted and raged at Stevie, slammed the gun into the wall with fury and kicked the door so hard that it jumped back, splintering on its hinges. Then he grabbed Philip by the shirt and pulled him to his feet. He was flushed with anger and there was a froth of saliva at the corner of his mouth.

'Philip Taylor,' Greg yelled at him, his face screwed up with fury. But he did not seem to expect an answer and Philip said nothing. He found himself being dragged along the landing, barking his shins on the furniture cluttered at the head of the stairs, towards the tiny lavatory. He was forced to kneel down with his neck on the rim and his head, throbbing with exhaustion and pain, hanging in the bowl. Greg tied his ankles to a new knot at his wrists and left, crashing the door shut behind him. Philip could hear him shouting again at Stevie in the front room, her indignant replies, and the sound of loud slaps. Then there was the sound of Stevie crying, convulsive and uncontrollable, and he strained at his ropes, bellowing with frustration. But Greg did not bother with him and suddenly it was very quiet in the house. Philip heard the police, alerted by the dramatic burst of activity from inside, stirring at their posts, and caught the noise of cars revving and turning and the chatter of short-wave radios.

He ran over in his mind what Greg would do, all the violence and degradation that was possible. Greg must always have suspected that Stevie and the man in the house were lovers. Now he would feel doubly threatened by Philip's presence. When he considered all this, he found that thoughts of escape returned inexorably. He indulged wild fantasies that filled him with false hope. It was no good. He remembered from somewhere that despair was the best counsel in desperate circumstances. Then things could only get better. He said out loud, 'There is no hope, there is no hope,' and yawned painfully. Suddenly, out of sheer nerves, he was retching into the water and though his head throbbed with the pain of it he was oddly grateful for the distraction.

Slowly, as he waited, kneeling, humiliated, the wall in the lavatory turned from a shadow of grey to white. The second day of the siege began. He strained like a blind man to interpret the growing babble of sounds outside. Methodically, he eliminated the noises that had nothing to do with the events in the house, the whining of a jet decelerating over London, the tap of a branch on the window and, very faint and far, a church bell chiming. He forced himself to count the strokes (holding his breath with concentration), and said aloud to the lavatory: 'I can count to nine. I am not going mad.' Then the more immediate sounds in the house claimed his attention. Greg and Stevie appeared to be talking. He heard scraps of conversation, attenuated hints of violence that made him stare and stare at the wall in an attempt to void his mind. He heard the police megaphone again. They were offering food and from the clash of voices from the front room Stevie and Greg were arguing about that as well.

Food had not been in his mind at all until this moment; now for the first time since it had all begun he started to notice his hunger, a sensation that added to his growing emptiness. Light-headed, he said aloud to the lavatory. Light-headed: the word danced in front of him and the bird in the eaves twittered close by. The poignancy of birdsong in winter only underlined his desolation. Somewhere next-door came the sound of flushing water and by the usual ridiculous association he found he wanted to pee. He tried to put the need out of his mind and went back to composing a picture of the outside world.

The police night-shift, he imagined, would by now have handed over their duties of marksmanship and surveillance to the day-shift. The ones that had watched through the night would be high with tiredness standing outside the mobile canteen discussing the events of the night, drinking gritty cups of coffee out of plastic cups. He assumed that they could eavesdrop on almost everything that went on in the room at the end of the landing. Probably they would think Greg was a bit crazy to do the things he was doing. The kissing, for instance. He invented conversations between two or three stereotype policemen, TV series coppers, and for them, he decided, Greg was a nutter. 'We've got a right one here,' he said aloud. Uncontrollably he found he was pissing then, kneeling helpless with his face in the lavatory bowl, a hot stream of urine running down his leg on to the floor. When it was finished he tried to balance the relief against the new discomfort of his trousers. It shocked him how easily he accepted the encroaching squalor, he whom Jan had always called a fusspot.

There were sudden footsteps and Philip thought with elation, they're giving in; they're taking the food. But the steps stopped outside, the lavatory door swung open and his wrists and ankles were untied. Greg pulled him roughly to his feet, at the same time jamming the gun against his spine. A belch of sick came into his mouth. At first he could hardly stand, but when the circulation returned he stumbled, blinking in the full daylight, back into the front room. His head felt as though it was made of lead, and crossing the threshold he tripped in his usual clumsy way on a snag in the carpet, falling in an ungainly sprawl into the middle of the room and breaking the skin on his thigh against a jagged piece of the wrecked telephone. But in fact he was relieved to be on the ground again and lay there trying to ignore the soreness in his body. Greg was bending over him, talking at random, untangling all the knots from his feet and arms. Philip did not realise that the words were addressed to him until he heard him say '. . . going to give them a deadline. A car and a plane at midday, or we knock you off, okay?'

He made a dumb query in his mind, failing stupidly to put a construction on the words. He struggled on to an elbow and looked up at Greg who was standing over him, slight but intimidating. Greg saw the fear in the hostage's eyes and, partly to give himself courage, began to taunt him. 'Yes, Mr. Taylor. I mean that. In your language, just in case you don't understand me because I didn't go to the right school as it happens or a nice little university, that means bang, bang, bye, bye, curtains.' Philip slid off his elbow back on to the floor. Greg touched him with his boot and managed half a laugh of encouragement. 'Don't worry, Mr. Taylor. It won't happen. It's only bluff. They'll give in. They always do in the end.'

'You don't know that, Greg,' said Stevie nervously from the window. 'You don't know that.' Greg looked at her bitterly but said nothing. Philip, fighting a claw of nausea, got himself into a sitting position. He looked across at Stevie (he had hardly noticed her when he came back in), but she avoided his glance. She was in the same gipsy skirt but had pulled on a duffle coat against the cold. Her thin, pinched face was sallow as usual, but blotched with red marks where Greg had hit her. Her eyes which were normally cool-white and steady were inflamed with crying. But with the hood of the coat half-covered behind she managed to look petite and attractive.

She challenged Greg. 'So what are you going to do?'

'Open the window,' he commanded. She did not move, but looked at him, furious and defiant, challenging him to do it himself. 'Open the window,' he repeated, gesturing with a flick of his gun. When she refused again, he stormed across and, pulling the curtain aside, fumbled with his free hand for the catch. The sudden crack of light showed a bright day outside and touched the room with colour. Greg rammed the sash and it flew up with a shriek. The cold wind bounced in, stirring the thick smell of bodies and urine, tossing the curtains and soothing Philip's burning face. The field telephone had gone. The effort to make contact was probably abandoned. He wondered vaguely if that was good or bad.

'Hold the curtain,' Greg shouted and this time Stevie obeyed, trance-like. Then he took from his pocket a white lump which he threw over the balcony into the street. He stepped back from the line of sight. 'Now – shut it,' he ordered and again Stevie obeyed him with mute concentration. When the wind was gone, and with the sudden activity completed, the room became calm again. The next development had taken place. Now, until noon, there was only waiting.

No one spoke. After some minutes there was the sound of someone talking through a megaphone. Philip could make no sense of the words. He panicked. 'What's he saying?' he asked, looking urgently at Stevie.

'If you shut up we'll hear,' she said and turned away. The voice of the megaphone rose and fell in a rhythm. Philip realised, feeling stupid, that it was simply the repetition of a simple message to surrender and come out.

'Listen, they think we are going to give in,' said Stevie.

'Not at midday they won't,' Greg replied.

'What did your message say? Has there been a misunderstanding?'

'It said what we agreed it would say,' said Greg, looking from Stevie to Philip, and back to Stevie, marking the alliance with his eyes.

The megaphone outside stopped. Stevie changed the subject. 'Would you like some whisky?' Philip noticed that the bottle in the bookcase had been opened. He shifted his position on the floor with anticipation, but did not know how to reply. Greg had taken a seat on a hard wooden chair by the window, facing his hostage. He was looking at him with contempt and loathing. After a minute or two he spoke, as much to himself as to Philip. 'I know all about your brother, Mr. Taylor.'

'What do you mean?' Philip was nervous at the hard menace in his voice.

Stevie interrupted. Philip heard the panic in her words and his hand began to shake unstoppably. 'You're wrong, Greg,' she was saying, 'he walked out because of me. He was sick. Dying, really. He'd given up. The only thing the police ever did with him was pick him up off the street and call an ambulance. Why in the world should he want to tell them about you, for Christ's sake?'

'He fucking grassed,' said Greg. 'It's obvious. That's why we're here now.' He spat. 'Your brother, Mr. Taylor, was a shifty lying bastard and so are you, shitface.' He waved his gun. 'I don't trust you, shitface. Get up. Up. Up against the fucking wall.'

Philip obeyed slowly and with great difficulty. His damp trousers clung, chafing, to his legs and he found he was trembling with cold and fear, tensed for a sudden, unexpected blow and cowed by the bullying tone of Greg's voice. He took up the prisoner's pose, arms outstretched up against the wall and his head hanging painfully down between his shoulders. He jumped when Greg poked him with his gun. 'At least your brother wasn't a coward,' he said.

Stevie was holding the whisky bottle like a hospital attendant. 'Shall I give him some?' She spoke as though he was not in the room.

'He'll pass out if you don't. He's shitting himself.' He came up close to Philip's ear, 'Isn't he?' he said, prodding the barrel of the gun into the cold damp stain on Philip's trousers. He seemed to be enjoying his power. Stevie passed the bottle over and as he took it he caught the time on his watch. It was eleven-fifty.

'Okay,' said Greg. 'Drink it.' Philip stepped back painfully from the wall and slumped down against the skirting. He clenched his

256

fingers painfully round the neck of the bottle and brought the glass mouth to his swollen lips. He swallowed one gulp and choked. Greg snatched the bottle back and gave it to Stevie, not drinking himself. The whisky revived Philip's spirits a fraction and put warmth in his veins. He realised he was still very hungry. 'Is there anything to eat?' he asked in a small voice.

But Stevie and Greg ignored him. He heard them whispering together in dispute. He knew they were discussing the deadline. He was amazed at the easy way in which Stevie seemed able to transfer her loyalties backwards and forwards. It was as though she were schizophrenic. He noticed the chaos that was slowly enveloping the room, the mess of clothes and broken things. The air was getting thick. In one corner, there was a small, rather perfect, heap of excrement, like a Christmas joke. All at once the megaphone started again. Greg moved across to the window. 'What's going on,' he shouted, panic in his voice, peering through the curtain. 'I'll shoot if they try anything.'

Stevie reassured him: 'It's only the same message.'

There was a new note of hysteria in Greg's voice. 'What time is it now?'

'Four minutes to twelve.' She sounded excited. 'Perhaps their nerve will break. They'll give in and we'll be free.' She gave an odd little laugh. 'We're going to be all right.' Philip found her outburst irrational. We're all going mad, he thought. Mad as hell. Greg was yelling something; he broke off in mid-sentence to grab Philip by the arm and wrench him to his feet.

Philip stared at him, unable to make sense of what he saw. Again the fear of hallucinations crept into his mind; this time he forced his perceptions mechanically to work. He realised that Greg was now using Stevie's tights to make a rough stocking mask that smoothed his features into plastic and unnatural contours. He looked like a disaster victim. Greg's words were getting baffled by the nylon but Philip found that he could not concentrate on what he was saying. The threats boomed uselessly inside his head and the nylon lips mouthed phrases that made no sense.

Greg had the gun against his ear, he could feel it cold and hard against his skin. Philip found his mouth suddenly full of spittle and his head seemed to be bursting with blood and falling off. He heard Stevie say something as though from the bottom of a well and realised that the curtain had been drawn back. Then the room

257

capsized, the window came towards him, very white and cold, and a wave of silence swept him out of consciousness.

3

It was so quiet when he woke up, he thought for a moment he was still dreaming. He had slept pillowed on his hands and his wrist-watch was sounding a rhythmic tocsin against his head. He opened his eyes; the dial glowed in a blur. The room was perceptibly darker and very quiet. Perhaps another day had passed and it was dawn again. These were strange experiences: could he sell his story to a Sunday newspaper? Psychiatrists would be keen to interview him. He could go on the lecture circuit.

'Mr. Taylor, were you aware of the passage of time?'

'Thank you. That's an interesting question, madam. It was very disorientating. You'd wake, look at your watch and see six o'clock. For a moment you'd be glad, you'd slept a whole day; it was another day gone. Then you'd realise it was six in the evening and you'd only slept a few hours. It was a very monotonous existence in many ways, punctuated by moments of complete terror. Next question.'

'In your very interesting talk, Mr. Taylor, you mentioned that you had nothing to eat throughout the siege. Do you think this was a significant factor in the eventual resolution of the situation?'

'In this case I don't think it was, no. There was running water and a bottle of whisky, as I've described. I've discussed human food requirements with nutritionists and their experience suggests that in a siege both hostages and hostage-takers can go several days without food and not suffer any noticeable physical harm. Of course this kind of deprivation does affect mental attitudes but, fortunately in this instance, it was all over before that became a factor.'

'Did you lose a lot of weight, Mr. Taylor?'

'About a stone in three days. I always say that it was a weight-watcher's paradise.'

Laughter.

'Mr. Taylor, I've read somewhere that in a siege situation a strange sort of affection grows up between the victims and the people who are holding them prisoner. I think it's called the Stockholm Syndrome –'

'That's right.'

'Can you confirm this in your own experience?'

'Certainly not. I never felt anything but fear and disgust towards the man who was holding me against my will. As I've described I was very badly, perhaps brutally, treated by him and it was a great relief when it was all over. I should add this, though. I never had any affection for Greg, but when it seemed as if the police might try to rush the room I was not afraid of him. I was much more scared about what they might do – accidentally of course. I never thought that Greg would actually use his gun on me.'

This time there was applause. It appeared to come from close at hand. He was not dreaming. Stevie had turned on the television for the six o'clock news bulletin. Out of the corner of his eye Philip glimpsed a shot of supporters at a party rally. Then the picture changed and the newscaster announced 'the main points of the news again'.

'Are we famous?' Philip asked ironically, speaking for the first time. Greg and Stevie looked at him. Greg scowled. The tiny screen flickered in their faces as they sat crouched in front of it like tribesmen by a fire.

'We are famous,' said Philip, as a picture of Daniel's house flashed on to the screen.

'Right,' said Stevie, cold and sarcastic. She leant forward and punched the on-off button. The picture imploded to a white dot, small and hard like a knot of anger. He felt withered by her annoyance and looked wordlessly away at the window. Stevie had become wounded and inaccessible again, easily provoked by his feeble attempt at self-confidence.

Then, strangely, in her unpredictable way she tried a gesture of reconciliation. 'I can't take it,' she admitted, nodding at the television. 'The strain is getting me down. I'm so tired.' She seemed indifferent to the effect of her words on Greg, who was sitting withdrawn and silent on the sofa. The gun was in his hand and he was holding himself upright like a robot, rocking slightly, fighting exhaustion. His mouth was half open and his cold secret eyes had become dull and heavy-lidded. The shadow on his chin had darkened like a bruise. Philip noticed that the whisky bottle was on the cushion beside him, still barely touched.

'He's been taking pep pills all afternoon,' said Stevie, speaking as though Greg was somewhere else. 'He's got incredible stamina. He'll never give in.'

Greg seemed to appreciate that she was talking about him and a broken smile of satisfaction alleviated his sallow features.

Despite himself Philip was impressed by the man's courage and self-discipline. He almost felt sorry for him. It was a losing battle. Whatever Stevie said about his stamina, he would surely have to capitulate in the end. In an odd way he found he wanted to help Greg stick it out. He said, attempting sympathy, but speaking to no one in particular, 'I'm sorry about this morning.'

Greg said nothing. Philip wondered if he had heard. But Stevie glared at him scornfully. 'Don't apologise. It wasn't your fault. Anyone would have passed out in that situation. I would have done, I know. For Christ's sake don't start apologising.'

Philip started to stammer his regrets and then stopped, ashamed. His fugitive eyes darted this way and that with anxiety. He wanted to ask what was going to happen next. After his long sleep he had forgotten temporarily about the boredom of waiting. The interval of oblivion had refreshed his optimism and given him a new lease of naïvety, it seemed. He had to re-adjust to the deepening despair of the others.

The grip of the forces around the house had obviously tightened while he had slept. He imagined the black vans and the camera-crews and the marksmen. All at once a bit of an old conversation came into his head, a phrase that had stuck. "They let me do a lot of shooting." And he had expressed surprised. "For sport?" he had asked nervously. Then he remembered the scene. Mountjoy in the country. He wondered if he was out there now, squinting like a Sioux down the barrel of a high-velocity rifle. Why hadn't they had a go at Greg this morning? He'd made a good enough target for a sniper, surely?

He was puzzling over this when, after some minutes of silence in the room, Greg suddenly sat forward and, as though to clear his throat, spat on to the floor. Philip started out of his reverie. Greg clenched his gun in a white-knuckled fist. 'Don't move, you bastard,' he said. He was fumbling with his free hand for the whisky, staring fixedly at Philip as he did so. It was as though he was embarrassed by that he was doing. Then he jammed the bottle between his knees, unscrewed the cap, took a deep hasty swallow, half-choked, screwed the cap on again and tossed it, still almost full, with a gurgle and clunk on to the sofa. The noise reminded Philip of the cloop of water between boats on the sea, and, prompted in his habit of quotation by his thirst, he said 'water water everywhere, nor any drop to drink' to himself in a low, pedantic murmur. He noticed Stevie bending towards him, slender and alert, trying to catch his words.

'I was thinking of the sea,' he explained.

'Daniel liked the sea,' she said, calm again. 'I associate him with it in a way, the restlessness and the power.'

Philip never ceased to be amazed at her mercurial nature. The highs and lows of her moods, the switchback of hostility and affection, seemed to be exacerbated by the tensions of the siege. Now he tried to make the most of the sunshine in her conversation. 'I wanted to take you down to the sea, you know,' he said shyly. He was going to add that perhaps he would still do it one day, but decided that this would be needlessly provocative in Greg's hearing.

'I did that with Daniel once.' There was a faraway smile on her lips. 'We went to Brighton for the day. Shortly after we met up again in England. It was January. There were a lot of old people in heavy coats having winter holidays, buffeting into the wind on the promenade. The sun was shining and the light was incredibly clear and blue. We walked for miles and the sea wind drew tears from our eyes. All the way we walked and talked and talked. It was so cold my lips became numb until I could hardly speak. We made pigs of ourselves in a fish and chip bar, spent lots of money on the slot machines, and then we caught the last train back to Victoria. I didn't have a proper coat, I remember, and Daniel lent me his. We felt so much better afterwards. It's funny, when I think of Daniel I think of walking by the sea. It was the same in Africa.'

'Near Tanga?'

'Yes, near Tanga,' she pronounced the word like a pledge and again that other-worldly smile passed across her face. He knew she was back in the past again.

'A wasted life,' said Philip, moved with a sense of tragedy. 'It's as though he had never lived.'

Even in the violent circumstances of the siege, the force of Stevie's reply was startling. 'How can you say that!' she exclaimed, taking his hand, incredulous. 'Look at you now: the only reason you're here is because of Daniel.' She flexed her fingers persuasively.

'That's not altogether true,' he said softly, looking at her with warmth.

She brushed this attempt at intimacy aside with a dismissive gesture. 'Oh, but leaving aside the bullshit, don't you see what Daniel's done for you. Don't you see that?' she repeated. And when she put it like that Philip, looking at her, passionate and tense in the shadows, supposed that she was right.

'Yes,' he admitted. 'Something has happened to me. I'm different.'

'For a life that failed, it's probably been his greatest achievement.' Her mood shifted. She pulled up her sweater with childish pride. Her belly was milky white in the gloom and her eyes gleamed fiercely with expectation. 'Touch me,' she said.

Greg started when he saw what was happening. He seemed to have difficulty in deciding how to react to the situation. 'Listen, Philip Taylor,' he said hoarsely when Philip stretched out his hand, 'don't try anything with my friend here, whatever she says.' He laid stress on 'friend' and watched suspiciously across the room.

Philip was not cowed. He laid his hand gently over the taut white skin; Stevie flinched with the cold touch and closed her hand over his. 'One day you'll do something for me Daniel never could,' she said, as if paying him a compliment.

'What do you mean?' He was baffled by her gratitude.

'Oh,' she became offhand, and drew gently away from him, tugging her jersey back into place, 'I wanted your brother's child. But he wouldn't. He said it was unjustified. Not once he knew what had happened in Africa.'

Philip thought of the possibility of a child growing inside her and his mind turned remorselessly to Jan and his own dead son. He wondered if his ex-wife had seen the news on the television. It intrigued him to think that there was no way she or anyone else he knew could realise that he was one of the hostages.

'Jan, my ex-wife, was pregnant once,' he said. 'He died in childbirth.'

'Oh.'

'I still think about it.' He frowned. 'There was a shortage of intensive care facilities. So the baby died.'

'Yes.' She did not seem interested and he realised that he was being incredibly insensitive. 'I'm sorry,' he said.

'Why is it that you always keep apologising?' she snapped. He recognised that she was channelling her upset feelings and did not react. After a moment he changed the subject and went back to the future. 'What's going to happen next?'

'You'll be okay,' she replied glibly. Greg seemed to be ignoring the discussion.

'In Libya,' he said, teasing.

'Or Cuba,' she answered, catching his mood. But there was no relaxation in his nervous flutter of laughter.

'D – d – do you think – ?' He dared not go on.

She began to lose patience; her own strain was showing. 'How do I know?' she replied with irritation. 'All I know is that he's going to try another deadline tomorrow,' she indicated Greg, unblinking on the sofa.

'Tomorrow is Sunday,' he said vacantly. There's still a chance, he thought, that we'll be out in time for class on Monday.

'It's nearly today,' she said.

He felt suddenly dejected and resigned and trapped. Looking at the bare feet in front of him (still privately deploring his lack of socks) and reflecting on his situation, he said aloud: 'Nothing.' Then he glanced up, embarrassed to have exposed some personal thoughts so candidly; Stevie had been studying him frankly from her seat.

'What do you mean?' she asked. He tried to look puzzled but knew very well what she was getting at. 'You said "Nothing",' she prompted.

'Oh –' he sighed. 'It's just that there seems to be nothing left. I was thinking about my family, Daniel, my house, Jan, my job and so on. After what you've told me, none of these things has any meaning. I honestly don't care about anything now.'

'You don't mean that,' she disagreed with him sternly. 'You're just depressed, that's all.'

'No, it's worse than that. I can explain how I feel if I say I'm conscious of being irrelevant and outmoded. We – the Taylor family – have failed. We had the power and responsibility and we misused it. Dramatically. When I say I don't care, I mean I don't think I have any right to care.'

Stevie considered him thoughtfully for a moment. 'Before Christmas, when we talked together in that café, I remember you said you wanted more to your life than you were getting –' He protested at the memory but she went on. 'You told me yourself only two or three days ago – you told me that at least Daniel's death had given you something to do that mattered.'

He shook his head, disconcerted by the accuracy of her remarks. 'In a funny way, I'm grateful.'

'But it's more than that, Philip; you know what I mean.'

'It's true,' he admitted. 'I've lost a brother, but I've gained something else.' He studied her reflectively. 'There's a kind of anger you feel after a death like this. That's a new experience for me.'

'Right. You do things you'd never dream of. You find out things about yourself.' She looked at him. 'You – for instance. You've discovered things you didn't know about – things you should have known about, but probably didn't want to.'

'And now I do know, there's nothing left. I've been betrayed by the system I used to believe in.'

'The system?'

'The search for answers, intellectual curiosity, investigation, research . . .' He shrugged. 'All that.'

'Betrayed?' she sounded quizzical. 'It's given you the answer you needed.'

'Did I need it?' he queried, slightly disappointed by her coolness towards his predicament. 'I don't want to trace a way through the maze like a rat in a laboratory and find myself running towards extinction.' He looked at her sharply. 'I feel as though I'm living on a slag heap with nothing to look forward to.'

She smiled. 'Not if you were a rat.'

Philip made a rat face and twitched his nostrils. Stevie laughed aloud. Greg stared at them both as if they were mad and took another cautious gulp of whisky. He shook his head in their direction, benevolent with drink but still vigilant.

'In that case,' Stevie went on seriously, 'you want the system to give you reassurance not truth. You don't want to be confronted with unwelcome answers. Look, Philip, you've had a glimpse into the future and you think it holds nothing for you. Well then,' she sounded approving, 'the system works for you. You have discovered a truth about your situation that is so accurate it hurts. You should be pleased.'

Philip ran his fingers through the strands of his hair, damp with cold. 'Stevie, I don't know. I don't know what I think any more. All I know is that nothing has much meaning. The only things you can trust are actions.' He sounded angry and defeated. 'And I'm not exactly in the best position for that now.'

Stevie looked at him oddly. 'If only you knew –' she began.

'Knew what?'

'How close you are to Daniel when you say that.' She hesitated. 'I remember one of the things he said to me towards the end of our relationship, here, in this very room. I was trying to get him to publish at least some of his stuff. I thought he had a kind of writer's block and had an idea that if he got something, it didn't matter what, into print then he would be calmer. He turned on me and shouted almost these very words. "You can't say things any more. What's the point; no one listens. You can only act – with violence." Melodramatic stuff. Typical of Daniel in the end. Just words. I think he knew that. A few weeks later he was dead.'

'With hindsight it's easy to say that was the only statement left for him to make,' said Philip quietly. 'It's all so sick and rotten, in some ways there's no point going on.'

'Don't lose heart,' she encouraged.

'But when you know some of the things you've told me, and when you know that it's your family, in this case your own father, who has let things happen that would be called crimes in the West, you can't just brush it aside. It's not as if it was even a mistake or a temporary aberration. You've shown me, and Daniel's work has shown me, that it was a policy, planned in cold blood.'

There was excitement in her steel-grey eyes; it gave her obvious pleasure to hear him talk like that. 'All right. But Mayhew & Taylor weren't alone. They all do it.' She ran through the familiar roll-call. 'In different ways, they all do it. They're all guilty in the end.' She danced to her feet. 'So don't give up,' she whispered. Every move was an affirmation. Greg stiffened expectantly. 'You'll make it,' she said optimistically and kissed Philip lightly on the forehead. He looked up into her eyes. It was like an absolution. He marvelled at the perfect simplicity of her gesture. 'What time is it?' she asked.

He knew she was trying to distract him.

'Sunday,' he said, croaking slightly after their conversation. He ran his tongue round the inside of his mouth which was as furry and dry as ever and tried to ignore the steady ache of hunger. He closed his eyes again and threw his thoughts as far away as possible to the land of dreams and memories and the cool depths of the English countryside. But the picture never held, and his mind turned to the anonymous glass and brick laboratories of Mayhew & Taylor and the dry brown African scrub, with village children, feared and rejected by their families, crawling through the dusk on smooth hideous stumps.

4

'I heard all what you said,' Greg's broken sentence surprised them from the shadows by the open door.

It was the beginning of first light and they were all exhausted. Philip had positioned himself opposite a crack in the curtain. He could glimpse a thin wedge of sky broken in half by a hard tile horizon. Now, as the light seeped in from the east, he began to distinguish the contours of the pelted slate roof. The sky above was hard and clear; he imagined a few late stars glittering faintly like silver dust. In the blue morning streets outside there would be the beginnings of movement, Sunday workers catching the first underground, night-shifts bicycling home, hospital chimneys smoking black and sooty before day-break and paper-round boys getting ready for their deliveries. He could not see this perfect metropolitan dawn, but the splinter of light in the middle of the window captured it for him as if he held the morning in his hands like a precious stone.

As he watched, the arc lights that had bathed the room in lunar half-shadows all night long went out. In due course, the daytime twilight of life behind blinds would strengthen and show the squalor of the place in more detail. The atmosphere had thickened and deteriorated badly. Stevie's cigarette smoke, body odour and the smell of excrement now composed a stench that was getting almost unbearable. Philip was afraid he would have to vomit if it got much worse.

Greg had not slept for two nights and was only able to move about with great exertion. His strong taut frame seemed to have dwindled inside his city clothes. The creased brown folds of his suit flapped loose as he moved unsteadily about the room, like the last guest to leave a Christmas office beano. As exhaustion took over, the more his fears seemed to have grown. For some time now he had been afraid to let his hostages use the bathroom at the other end of the landing. Stevie had been forced to squat behind the sofa to relieve herself on the carpet. Philip peed in the corner behind the television. Greg watched their indignity and suffering with the satisfaction of someone for whom events are conforming to expectations.

From where he was sitting, Greg had a clear line of sight down the landing and also up to the trap-door into the attic, though it was clear in Philip's mind that the watchers outside had abandoned their attempts to communicate either via the field telephone from the roof or with the megaphone in the street. Greg had not swerved from his policy of non-communication, and in a peculiar way Philip admired him for that, even though it meant other restrictions as well. In the beginning Greg had shared the bottle of whisky. Now it was less than half-full and he kept it close by his side. Philip and Stevie had to make do with the diminishing supply of brackish water in the vermilion jug. None of them had eaten for over forty-eight hours and Philip was getting desperately weak and faint. Every word and movement, he was aware, looking at himself dispassionately from the outside, showed that he and the others were all dead tired.

There had been very little sleep this last night. At about one o'clock when Stevie and Philip began thankfully to drowse, a high-pitched drilling had started in the wall. Greg had stumbled defensively to his feet. The drill bit screeched in the brick for some minutes, stopped, and then resumed. It was obvious that no attempt was being made to disguise the operation. Philip wondered if it was designed solely to shatter them all psychologically, or whether high-powered listening and photographic devices were being installed to monitor the siege more closely. At around five o'clock the noise stopped at last. They were all wrecked. Stevie had finally run out of cigarettes, despite her efforts to eke out the supply. In desperation she began to collect up the dog-ends, laboriously peeling them open and rolling stale tobacco in bits of newspaper. They found they could not settle to sleep now, and talked on, mainly about Africa, oblivious to Greg's presence, until the new day began. Then they dozed lightly. Greg's words, delivered with great effort, like phlegm from a congested lung, broke uncompromisingly into this fitful moment of rest. 'I heard all what you said,' he repeated.

Greg's voice was blurred and truculent. He was hollow with

exhaustion and the lack of food. His stony eyes squinted out of black shadows in a face roughened by stubble and dirt. His movements -- he was struggling to his feet now -- were laboured and dull, like those of an elderly man. Occasionally, when he tried to overcome the physical stupor, his voice would crack with strain and he seemed, in the manner of the deaf, to have lost control of his words' volume.

Philip thought: this is the experience of defeat, the face of soldiers after battles lost through the ages. His historian's mind was pleased by the insight and he stored it away in case he could use it in an interview later on. Now, he kept quiet. His own innate sense of prudence told him that this was the moment when Greg would be most likely to commit irrational acts of frustrated violence. It was important not to antagonise him at this very delicate stage.

But Greg it seemed, only wanted a share in the conversation he had listened to half the night. There was a pathetic eagerness in the way in which he offered to show Stevie how to roll her own cigarettes.

'You don't smoke,' she commented, amused at his fussing over her.

'I used to. Old Holborn. I gave it up.'

'Very wise,' said Philip, encouraging.

Greg, who was concentrating on the little heap of tobacco on his knees, glanced up at him. Yesterday he might have shouted at him to keep his fucking mouth shut. Now he only said: 'I can look after myself, thank you.'

'What made you give up?' Stevie asked.

'A girl.' Greg scowled slightly as though ashamed to admit the influence of a woman in his life or perhaps at the recollection of a bad memory. 'Silly bitch,' added Greg, after a few moments. 'There.' He passed an expertly-rolled cigarette to Stevie, lit a match for her with a gallant gesture and then hurriedly slipped the gun into his hand again.

The megaphone started up in the street once more They all looked towards the window. Greg sat up sharply but he did not get to his feet. 'Same old message?' he asked, rather contemptuous.

'Same old message,' Stevie confirmed.

'The bastards don't know what to do if you don't talk to them,' he commented, proud of his strategy. He swallowed another gulp of whisky and waved the bottle at Stevie. It was still a quarter full.

'Sorry, love, it's all I've got.' She seemed rather confused by the apology. His unexpected goodwill was disconcerting. Philip imagined that he had been encouraged to join in by the candour of their earlier conversation through the night. He obviously needed the companionship. Typically, Stevie rebuffed him. 'It's against the rules, isn't it?' she commented with a mild note of challenge.

Greg reacted predictably. 'I've had enough of fucking rules.' He passed his hand over his face. 'You don't know the boredom of life underground. It's hell, I'm telling you.' He began to talk in a hoarse dry monotone as if it was the only way he could stay awake. Ninety per cent of his time was taken up with security. 'Code, decode, memorise the new code, get the addresses into your head and burn your notes, learn the next text by heart, backtrack for hours before a rendezvous. It drives you mad sometimes, I'm telling you. All the fucking rules.'

'Like not drinking on an operation,' she repeated. Philip was fearful at the risks she was taking, but dared not say anything.

'People like me,' Greg countered, 'we have to hang on to all we've got. The people who made the rules didn't know what an operation was actually like. Wankers,' he said forcibly. 'I'll tell you there was this time when the guys in my unit started a punch-up about where to go for breakfast.' He laughed bitterly. 'I'd like to see some of the guys in that set-up stand up to all this,' he waved his gun at the squalor. As far as he was concerned it was each man for himself. It wasn't his fault. Society had a lot to answer for. He was doing his best, for Christ's sake. His heart was in the right place; and at least he was doing something about it, unlike some of the armchair radicals he could think of. Here, he looked pointedly across at his prisoners.

Philip was not discouraged by the hostility of that stare. In fact he took heart at the incoherence of these thoughts, and, in the hope of tiring Greg further, he asked him what it was he was doing.

'Things that would scare the shit out of you, Mr. Taylor.' He laughed scornfully. 'Bomb factories is what. Gun-running for the big boys is what. Smuggling explosives out of Europe is what.' He wagged the toy-like weapon at his hostages. He wanted Philip to understand, he said, that he was against the system to the bitter end. He knew only too well how it fucked people up. There was nothing left to do but tear it down, throw it away and start again.

Demos, committees, pressure groups, newspapers and all that shit was one thing, but what was needed was action.

'Don't you think that peace, this long peace we've had since the war, is, as it were, rotting people's will to act?' Philip replied. The phrases sounded odd in his head, but Greg understood perfectly.

'Right,' he said. He was going to make real war against his enemies. Who were his enemies? he asked rhetorically. His enemies were the people who propped up the system: the big companies who rip off the poor, who make money out of dud products, who avoid tax, the politicians who fool people with classy propaganda and buy their votes with inflation and the fear of unemployment.

'Tax lawyers, corporate advertisers, business consultants, investment brokers, city journalists, government economists, head hunters, multinational executives, jet-set salesmen,' Stevie chipped in, running through a list of number one enemies.

Those were the enemies, Greg went on without humour, bunched up in his absurd brown business suit, his jacket draped over his shoulders for warmth, and that's where the action was, though it frightened most people to think of actually doing something about it on the street. Even the famous Daniel Taylor wouldn't take that ultimate step when it came down to it. He could never quite declare war on the system. In the end he was too much part of it to give it the two fingers.

'And that's why you didn't trust him?' Philip almost managed to sound as if he approved of Greg's suspicion.

'Too bloody right, mate, I mean that's why we're here now. Thanks to your brother.'

Stevie interrupted angrily. 'That's a lie – and you know it.'

Philip thought: this is mad, mad north-north-west.

'Shut your face.' The coarse slur with which Greg was pronouncing his words gave away how close he was to collapse. Stevie seemed to notice this and did not challenge him further. Greg himself acknowledged the element of fantasy in his accusations by moving into a more thoughtful key. 'When I came here before,' he went on, 'all your brother was doing was going on about how fucking guilty he felt and how journalism was no good any more. But what was he doing about it? That's what I want to know. I mean anyone can get pissed on their own with a bottle of Jamieson's.' With unconscious irony, he paused to suck briefly at the bottle and then, his fury tamed, slowly turned his head to study Philip like a warder. 'Your brother –' he demanded, 'how well did you know him?'

'Until this Christmas I hadn't seen him for nearly seven years.'

'When?' Greg pounced on his remark. 'Where did you see him?' He gripped the gun again, back in the role he knew best.

Philip got some satisfaction out of his answer. 'In the hospital,' he said. 'He was dead.' He tried to put the memory out of his mind.

'Oh.' Greg relaxed his scrutiny. He sounded disappointed. After a minute or two he began to talk again.

'Don't think I've always been like this, Mr. Taylor,' he said. 'I mean I've always been rejected, but there was a time before when I wanted to make money and screw my neighbour like everyone else. I've been screwed since I was a kid. It's always been one fuck-up after another.'

Almost without a pause he launched into the story of his childhood on Merseyside. It was wartime. His father had been part of the protected labour force but there had never been any money and very little to eat either. 'We lived in this tiny flat. It was five to a bath once a week and jam on alternate Sundays.' He talked about the death of his father in an industrial accident when he was six, and how his mother ran off with a married man shortly afterwards. 'I don't have any memory of my old lady at all,' he said, staring forlornly in front of him. As orphans the family (three boys, two girls) was split up and he never saw his brothers or sisters again. 'I think about them sometimes and wonder what they're all doing, if they're still alive.' His mother had been an only child and his father's brother was killed in the Italian campaign, so there was no one to take an interest in him. He was a miserable, unruly child, he reckoned. No ordinary family would have him for long. In the end they put him in a home. When he was let out as an adolescent he was found work on the railways, as a dining car attendant, but he turned to crime 'for money and kicks'. He was sent to Borstal, three times. 'That's where I learnt that my sort are just scum to be buggered about from pillar to post,' he said.

Philip thought of his own childhood and schooling, all the certainties and securities. He had thought often enough that he was unwanted, but Greg's experiences made his resentment trivial and insignificant by comparison.

After Borstal, he said, the only place he could go was the Army.

271

But after his first spell east of Suez all he wanted to do was get out. He shook his head. 'The poor buggers that have to go to Northern Ireland,' he said quietly. When he finally managed to get out of the forces he set up in business as a haulier with a friend, on borrowed money. They started in boom years, over-expanded and, when the next recession came, went bust. By the time he was thirty-five he was flat broke and with a pile of debts hanging over him. 'All I wanted to do was get the hell out of the country before one of my mates came and gave me a bloody nose.' He nodded at Stevie, as though to remind her of a story she had heard before. 'That's when I met the drunken Scotsman in the pub,' he said.

Philip cocked his head with curiosity. It was enough of an invitation.

'I was out of work, skint and on the run really. I was lying low down south with a girl I knew. I met this Scotsman in a pub in Surrey. I was pissed and he was pissed. I knew he was a Scotsman. He was wearing this bloody kilt. He was down for a wedding, he said, and his girlfriend looked like she was going to a posh do, so I suppose he wasn't bullshitting me. Everyone in the pub was laughing at him in his Scottish poofter's outfit. And so was he. He seemed like a good guy. We got talking. I said, "What's your line?" He said: "I'm a soldier. A major." So of course I wanted to know what regiment. He laughed a lot and the girl looked a bit unhappy. He said, "I fight for myself. I'm a soldier of fortune." Very grand, he sounded. A mercenary. "We're off to Africa to fight the Communists in a fortnight." Then his girlfriend, who was obviously not very keen about the idea, said he didn't know what he was talking about and that of course he wasn't going. He wasn't fit, she said. He did look a bit past it, I must say. He had this pot-belly. But he told her to shut up. He said, "Tell you what, soldier, if you want to make a heap of your own, come along with us." He said the money was good, as much as five hundred quid a week. Five hundred nicker a week, I ask you. That was a lot of dough in those days. I was on my own, no responsibilities, people I wanted to get away from and this debt to forget about. Money was what I wanted. In spades. It sounded like the answer to the fucking prayer I tell you. After my experiences with the trucking business all I wanted was to get rich again without any overheads. So I said, yes, I'd come. Just like that. He gave me this 'phone number and the next thing I knew I'm flying out Air Zaire with a bunch of lads to Kinshasa. Funnily enough the Scotsman wasn't on the plane. He wasn't in Africa either. I suppose his girlfriend talked him out of it. Lucky fellow.'

Greg paused to wipe the film of sweat off his forehead and to take another mouthful of whisky. His face was at last getting coloured with drink and his expression was temporarily animated by the excitement of these old memories. In a few days' time when he had his beard again he would be, Philip considered, quite the veteran.

'It was a fucking disaster. You know that. There were soldiers out there who were only boys, raw recruits who had no experience of the jungle. They should never have been allowed there. It was shocking to see them. Some of them were like me. They wanted the money. Others wanted adventure. There was one young guy I talked to on the plane. "This country is so boring," he said. He got all the kicks he wanted out in Angola. Some of them had no idea why they were there. There were the usual mad guys out there as well. You always get the madmen with a war. Some had been in Vietnam. They were the worst. They never slept. They had seen everything. Nothing was too bad for them. The gun was the only law. There were executions, and massacres. We killed more of our own men than the enemy. It was a kind of hell. We screwed ourselves . . .' He began to shake uncontrollably as the bad memories came back again.

Stevie said: 'Greg. Stop. You don't have to talk about it.'

He looked at her rather wild, but grateful. 'You're right. I don't.'

Stevie turned to Philip. 'His best friend was machine-gunned there in cold blood for cowardice,' she explained softly.

Philip took in the grubby haggard face with the fluttering eyelids and hanging stare and realised that he couldn't have looked very different all those years ago in Africa. 'It sounds as though he was lucky to survive.'

Greg half heard him. 'Lucky to be alive?' he repeated. His yellow teeth showed in a brief smile. He looked at them, proud and cunning. 'Too bloody right,' he said. 'Lucky in other ways too.' He was about to go on, but the drilling in the wall started again. The noise was much louder than before and closer at hand. Philip looked at the plaster and noticed that the chimney-breast seemed to be bulging above the fireplace. Greg had apparently not spotted this; he was waiting, swaying slightly, with his gun at the ready in the middle of the room.

Then, as abruptly as it had started, the noise stopped and the house fell quiet again. Philip found that quite suddenly he had a pain in his right side, an intermittent stabbing where he had always assumed his appendix to be. A new set of apprehensions, that he would die in agony beyond the reach of medical care, now monopolised his thoughts. For some moments he was not aware that Greg was talking again, ancient mariner-like, about his time in Africa.

'. . . no idealism' he was saying. 'In Spain of course, in Malaysia, even in Vietnam I've heard that there were always soldiers who believed they were fighting for a cause. Not in Angola. They talked about killing Communists but they didn't mean it. It was just a money war and a killing war, a war for the capitalists. Perhaps in some office in the Pentagon there were guys who thought they were making the world safe for democracy and all that bullshit, but if that was so they were backing the wrong horse. And the longer I was out there seeing the ordinary people of Africa, the more I realised I was on the wrong side. I'd reached the limit. All I'd wanted to do was make money at someone else's expense – and you can't go further than killing people for money. Something snapped. I just couldn't go on. I could see the people, the blacks, who suffer and die to keep the West rich. I was in this pointless war just to keep a few gold and copper mines in the hands of the capitalists. I was sickened by the whole thing. Suddenly, I saw what it was. I realised I'd always been on the wrong side. As a kid, in Borstal, in the fucking army, even when I was stoney broke and on the run in England. I'd always felt like an outsider. Now I knew why. That was my place. Outside. Fighting the system. That was what I learnt in Africa. It changed my life.' he said, waving the whisky unsteadily in the air.

'I'll drink to that,' Philip murmured.

'What's that?' Greg challenged him hoarsely.

'Nothing,' he covered up. 'How did you get into all this?' he asked disingenuously.

Greg said that would be telling, wouldn't it, but after a bit of prodding from Stevie he explained, quite amiably, how he had escaped from the Angolan débâcle, 'one of the few to make it back alive', on a French charter flight to Paris. 'So there I was, in gay Paree, skint.' At least, he went on, he knew what he thought was right now. It was just a question of waiting for the right opportunity. So he flitted from job to job for a while, finding his feet, working mainly on building sites as a labourer in and around the city. 'Plenty of work in those days,' he commented. There were, he continued, quite a number of the members of what he liked to call 'terror international' living in Paris then. He became assimilated gradually. 'Got in with this French bint, didn't I?' he said with pride, looking at Stevie. This was the girl who didn't approve of cigarettes. She, it turned out, was an on-off member of a dour little commune living in a basement in Asnières. One thing led to another and soon Greg was helping to distribute cyclostyled copies of the commune's newspaper round the city. 'Trucking again,' he said with a bitter laugh. Finally, when they found out about his military background and impeccable working-class origins, they recruited him to help ferry guns and explosives round Europe. 'I've been on the fucking road for the last two years. It feels like more. Holland. Deutschland. La Belle France. England.' He paused to draw on his whisky. 'And here I am now,' he added grimly. 'Holed up here – at the end of the road.'

'Don't give up,' said Stevie, but the tone of her words suggested the opposite, Philip thought.

Greg paused to draw on his whisky again. 'At least I've had some action in this fucking country. The people I work for spend all their time telling you to get your hair cut, wear the right suit and keep up with the rent. Housekeeping. I've had enough of that. But this is the real thing, isn't it. I tell you,' he went on, gesturing with the pistol in a flash of candour, 'this thing makes you feel like a million dollars. I can do anything. I'm the greatest. All I have to do is crook my little finger. I'm Jesus Christ Superstar. I'm Muhammad Ali. One day I'll crook my little finger – just for the hell of it. Then I'll be Number One.' He stood proudly in the middle of the room, a slightly ridiculous, gun-waving saloon-room hero. 'After all the hanging around it's a relief I can tell you.' He levelled the gun menacingly at Philip who started backwards across the carpet and clumsily planted his left hand in a pile of excrement. He recoiled with a shudder and Greg began to laugh coarsely. 'Shit, eh?' A temporary warmth came into his expressionless features and the hard lines of his mouth and jaw crumpled with cruel enjoyment.

Philip wiped his finger inadequately on the carpet and fought down another surge of nausea.

Outside, the megaphone started to stutter and whine once more.

5

Philip thought he heard bells, chiming and chiming in the distance. He wanted Stevie's corroboration and searched for her round the room. His eyes were playing tricks with him. Greg was there, propped against the doorway, draining the last of the whisky, but Stevie had vanished. He gazed wildly round again; for some reason the sound of her name was jammed in his head and he couldn't speak. Then something moved in the dim light and he realised that she had been crouching on the floor with her back to him, perfectly camouflaged, very still with concentration, rolling another cigarette in the way Greg had shown her.

'Do you hear the bells?' he asked with a slight croak.

'It's Sunday,' she said, as though that was a significant explanation. He did not dare tell her about the fear in his head that he was imagining things. He had learnt that she hated admissions of weakness.

He smiled his thanks at her and she smiled affectionately back, like a wife, he thought. Her boyish fringe was lifeless and flat after these days without a mirror or a bath, and anyway she had always been relatively careless about her appearance. She never wore make-up and her face was as he remembered it from the first time, though shadowed with lack of sleep. Her expression, he decided, had the memorable intensity and poise of the great artists' models, women who knew they were immortal. She had this confidence, arrogance really, that said, I matter, I am myself. There were the insecurities as well, but these, he knew, were to do with her dramatic sense of her own personality and her suspicion that it was being threatened or diminished by factors beyond her control. It was ridiculous even to think of her as a wife, of course. She would never marry him, or anyone else either. He had grasped, he thought, that she could never give any part of herself away on a permanent basis. She could show affection, make love, burrow deeply into a man's heart for a while, but in the end the sacrifices of a long-standing relationship would be too much and like a bird, like a spring bird, she would be off again, a free spirit. Perhaps she was not pregnant after all, and even if she was carrying his child it would be as a statement about herself and her sex, a rite of passage that she wanted to undergo for its own sake and for her own. Philip knew that finally he – and any child – were irrelevant. Even now in her smile, fading across her expression like a patch of sunshine on a wild day, she set a distance between the two of them, as though to say, I'm me, do not trespass.

The bells were still chiming and in a perverse way Philip wished that they were ringing in his mind after all. In that way the whole experience of the siege could become a fantasy.

Greg had been pacing up and down the room and for some reason he was chuckling to himself, though without much benevolence. He stood over them both, menacing them with his laughter. Philip glanced up at him, scared. Greg was sweating hard, his lips were thin and grey, tinged with drink, and his eyes were wet with laughing and sweat. He was obviously drunk and his face glistened in the steely twilight like a boxer's. He watched them sitting together on the floor and then tilted towards Stevie, grinning and leering with his wide wet mouth. 'What shall we call the baby, darling?' he said with a burp, then laughed as before and staggered back against the door-post.

The megaphone started again. Come out, said the voice, you're surrounded. The atmosphere in the room sobered. The endless repetition of the message was driving them all mad; perhaps the forces outside realised this because, on this day, for the first time, they had begun to vary their approach. The man behind the loud-hailer (Philip was by now quite used to his phoney nouveau-riche accent) had adopted the tactic of addressing Greg personally, as though they were old friends. You can't stay there forever, Greg. We've been pretty close to each other for a long time, Greg. This is the closest we've ever been. We're going to have to meet pretty soon now. Why don't you come out now so that we can talk it over. You can't stay there forever, Greg.

Philip dared not concentrate on the disembodied phrases of temptation. Greg seemed to be wavering. Stevie was watching.

The words cracked in the street, and the menace that seemed to be closing in on them all reinforced what Greg had told them in the early morning. For the first time Philip believed that Greg's boastful words about international terror were true. This sparked off another train of anxiety. He repeated his survival formula in his head. It can only get worse, he thought.

'All I want is that car,' said Greg. 'Never mind the plane. I want that car.'

Philip was astonished and frightened at Stevie's response. She looked at Greg with scorn, repeating his words slowly. 'Never mind the plane. All I want is that car.' She laughed sarcastically. 'Oh, well done, Greg.' He seemed disconcerted. 'You've stuck it out here in this rat-hole for nearly three days and you say you'll settle for a car. That's marvellous.' She paused for a fraction before turning on him savagely. 'And where is the promise of safe conduct, where is the waiting plane, the right to land in Libya or Cuba or wherever?' Even Greg quailed. 'And what happens when the car' – she lingered derisively on the word – 'runs into the roadblock they've set up for us, or when the car runs out of petrol because its tank is empty, or when the car . . .?'

Greg seemed defeated but he managed to cut her off. 'We still have him.' He gestured limply at Philip.

Stevie was not impressed. 'You're boxing yourself in, Greg. They're cramming you into a corner with sweet words. Words are cheap. You're being tempted for nothing. Once they've got you out of here they've got you. Period. Full stop. Here – ' she took in the upstairs floor with her hand, 'here you have space. You can manoeuvre here. You've got that stuff downstairs you can use if necessary, don't give up now. You're winning. Whatever they say.'

As he listened to her, Philip's panic died down: she was not as crazy and provocative as she appeared. Greg must be near collapse. They all knew that. The only strength left in him would be the desperate strength found in an emergency. In a few hours even that would be burnt out. Then they could overpower him without trouble. Out there, now, anything could happen. It was safer inside, here, in the room they knew so well. The main thing was to keep him away from any tension. Under stress, Greg might go berserk. Philip knew that in his place he would have cracked long ago.

He looked at his watch. It was nearly one o'clock. Greg seemed to have forgotten about the next deadline. With luck, they would be out soon. He didn't think he would feel like teaching to-morrow, but he felt sure the Principal would understand, so long as he was back by Wednesday, say. It was odd how his teaching duties had slipped his mind, he who was normally so conscientious. He could always squeeze two lectures into one at a pinch. On the other hand, if he got a good offer from a Sunday newspaper, perhaps he could give up teaching and go free-lance. With Stevie. He could write a book about his experiences. It would be nice to work at home. Here. There would be more time for gardening; occasionally he would take the high-speed train to Scarborough or Plymouth to give a lecture about Hostages and Terrorism.

'What was the worst thing about your captivity, Mr. Taylor?'

'Oh – knowing when I came out that I'd made a mess of my trousers.'

'And the thing you regret most?'

'I wish I'd kept that poinsettia properly looked after. You see it died. There was nothing I could do.'

The bells were still ringing in the distance. He wondered if it was a wedding. Hardly on a Sunday. Of course he would never marry Stevie. That was not her thing. Still, it was nice to have the affair. Did she mean it about the baby? There was no telling in these circumstances. At least she hadn't cracked like before. In that sense she was right; it had been good training.

In fact, she was still arguing with Greg, taunting him like a matador. In contrast to the crisp, ingratiating phrases of the voice behind the megaphone, Greg's speech had become dreary and unfocussed as though his mind was wandering as well. 'You're only boxed in,' he was saying, 'if that's where your head is.'

'So you won't settle for the car?' she challenged, teasing and playing on his pride.

Philip could see that even now – after all that had happened – Greg wanted to appear strong before her and to do the right thing in her eyes. 'Not if it's a cop-out.'

'Of course it's a cop-out. If we stay here and hold on we have a chance – all of us.' She looked knowingly at Philip, and his conviction that she was buying time was reinforced. He felt an extraordinary sense of relief. She was unequivocally on his side again.

But Greg spotted Stevie's glance, probably in a daze and by accident. It seemed to trigger a moment of red fury in his mind. 'What do you mean "all of us"?' he demanded. 'I don't give a shit about this fucker, do I?' The jealousy he harboured towards Philip and the piled-up frustrations of the last three days pushed him into uncontrolled violence. His strength was frightening; he seemed blind with rage. He was shoving them both like dummies across the floor, beating Philip on the head with the butt of the gun.

'Go on.' His voice cracked. 'Get up against that wall. Both of you. Get your fucking hands in the air.'

Philip gasped, half-winded and bruised, as Greg rammed the flat of his hand against his spine. 'And don't move, okay. I'm not bluffing, for Christ's sake. And don't let that screwy dyke kid you any other way.' Philip pressed himself against the cold wall, not daring to look at Stevie. He was wryly aware that his clumsy accident was leaving the ghostly imprint of his left hand on the recently-papered surface.

The force of Greg's blow had set little rivers of plaster running in the wall. A spray of dust settled from the ceiling, and though Philip tried to smother it with a cough, a sneeze ballooned irrepressibly inside his head. Greg hit him viciously again as though only violence was keeping him awake. 'Keep quiet, bastard.' Snot dripped from his nose and his ears were ringing from the last blow. He clung grimly to his survival formula. It can only get worse, he repeated to himself, it can only get worse.

There were other voices in his head. He no longer knew if they were real or not. Someone was saying, You can't stay there for ever, Greg. We're going to have to meet pretty soon now. You can't stay there for ever you know. The bells were still chiming. And then, for the first time that day, he thought he heard voices from the television. He twisted his head painfully and saw that this indeed was the case. Greg was pumping the buttons with his thumb. The television roared and tinkled as he jumped from channel to channel. The signature tune for the lunchtime news started and Philip decided that Greg was trying to get information about what was going on outside. Perhaps he had not forgotten the next deadline after all.

But Greg, sounding oddly muffled and out of breath, was shouting to Stevie, who had come away from the wall (presumably under instructions), something about turning up the volume and wanting to show those bastards that he wouldn't give up. The volume bellowed and Philip heard the beginning of the headlines.

His attention was distracted by artificial light from the street flooding into the room. For a moment he thought, this is it, they're coming in. We're saved. Paradoxically he was frightened.

'Mr. Taylor, what did you feel when the rescue began?'

'It was funny, all I wanted to happen was to be left alone. I didn't want the police to come bursting in. I'd got used to the room. I liked it.'

But it was only Greg tearing the curtains aside in a panic, and ordinary daylight, not arc lights, blinding and wincing in their eyes, streaming through the window, a sudden spring. Philip found himself wanting to turn his head to see exactly what was happening, but he didn't dare move. The window went up with a shriek – he recognised that – and the January wind flew boisterously into the stale airless room, setting paper rustling and tossing cigarette ash on to the carpet. For no reason he thought, there's a lot of cleaning up to do here. He was glad that the smell was at last being blown away.

And then he was being grabbed from behind by his belt and pushed brutally through the window, stabbed with shock and stiffness as his body was crammed through the gap leading on to the narrow windswept balcony overlooking the street. He wanted to tell Greg to be careful and not push him too near the edge. Stevie was right. They needed to get the ironwork put back. With his bare feet, cold on the concrete, there were splashed droppings to watch out for (birds, he thought), but his mind was maddened by fear and by the activity below. For no reason he saw his mother's pale English face and heard her voice again, ". . . A deep, deep green and rocky valley, very narrow, and filled with trees; but through the wood hundreds of feet below him, he could see a clear stream glance . . ."

The lights (there were lights after all) bathed everything – even on a bright day, the sky like glass – with the kind of glow he associated with the film world. Indeed there was a curious air of unreality about the scene, the empty street below, the blank faces of the houses opposite, and the vast silence of the Sunday city in the distance broken only by the mutter and crackle of short-wave radios and the buffeting of the high wind in his ear. More unreal still was Greg's stockinged face, smooth and expressionless like a sci-fi villain. It was not a face he felt he could say anything to, nothing serious anyway.

He expected to hear Greg start ranting on again, as he had inside, about the car and the plane, but Greg was saying nothing, or nothing that he could hear. Philip stood there. He saw the sphinxes crouched below him. When he realised what was happening, he opened his mouth to say, Stevie, but the sound was choked. Greg was gripping him by the belt of his jeans. He wanted to say, Don't do it, you're crushing my balls, but the thought was lost in the confusion of noise and lights below. A woman screamed, No, and the word exploded in his head. On the screen in the room beyond the window, Stevie, crouched in front of the television set, crying like a riot victim, saw the grey figure fall, deadweight, dead even before it smashed its thin white neck in the city street below.